PENGUIN BOOKS

THE COLLABORATOR

...aheed was born and brought up in Srinagar, Kashmir. He moved to Delhi when ...eighteen to study English Literature at the University of Delhi and worked as a ...st and editor in the city for four years. He came to London in 2001 to join the ...rdu Service. *The Collaborator* was shortlisted for the Desmond Elliott Prize and ...*dian* First Book Award. It is his first novel.

The Collaborator

MIRZA WAHEED

PENGUIN BOOKS

PENGUIN BOOKS

Published by the Penguin Group
Penguin Books Ltd, 80 Strand, London WC2R ORL, England
Penguin Group (USA) Inc., 375 Hudson Street, New York, New York 10014, USA
Penguin Group (Canada), 90 Eglinton Avenue East, Suite 700, Toronto, Ontario, Canada M4P 2Y3
(a division of Pearson Penguin Canada Inc.)
Penguin Ireland, 25 St Stephen's Green, Dublin 2, Ireland (a division of Penguin Books Ltd)
Penguin Group (Australia), 250 Camberwell Road,
Camberwell, Victoria 3124, Australia (a division of Pearson Australia Group Pty Ltd)
Penguin Books India Pvt Ltd, 11 Community Centre, Panchsheel Park,
New Delhi – 110 017, India
Penguin Group (NZ), 67 Apollo Drive, Rosedale, Auckland 0632, New Zealand
(a division of Pearson New Zealand Ltd)
Penguin Books (South Africa) (Pty) Ltd, 24 Sturdee Avenue, Rosebank, Johannesburg 2196, South Africa

Penguin Books Ltd, Registered Offices: 80 Strand, London WC2R ORL, England

www.penguin.com

First published by Viking 2011
Published in Penguin Books 2012
1

The permissions on page 308 constitute an extension of this copyright page

Typeset by Jouve (UK), Milton Keynes
Printed in England by Clays Ltd, St Ives plc

ISBN: 978-0-141-04858-1

www.greenpenguin.co.uk

For the people of Kashmir

To Jaji, Papa, Shayan
and
Mehvish

And like a prince inspecting his domain
He travels to a graveyard's empty plain
Where lie, with plaid sunshine overhead,
From old and modern times, the storied dead.

Charles Baudelaire (trans. James McGowan),
'A Fantastical Engraving', *Flowers of Evil*

I won't tell your father you have died, Rizwan,
but where has your shadow fallen, like cloth
on the tomb of which saint, or the body
of which unburied boy in the mountains,
bullet-torn, like you, his blood sheer rubies
on Himalayan snow?

Agha Shahid Ali, 'I See Kashmir
from New Delhi at Midnight',
The Country Without a Post Office

Contents

Author's Note

The Collaborator is a work of fiction. Names, characters, places and incidents either are the product of the author's imagination or are used entirely fictitiously.

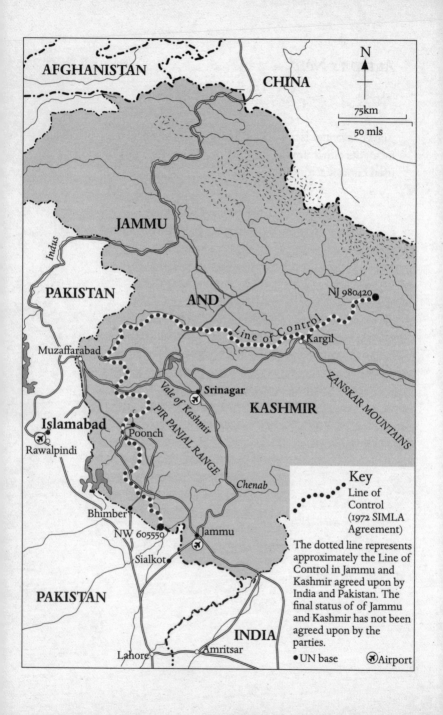

PART I

Now and Then . . .

The Valley of Yellow Flowers

Captain Kadian takes a large swig from his glass tumbler, closes his eyes for a moment, smacks his lips, and says, 'The job's not that hard, you see, you just go down once a week or fifteen days, and the money, the money is not bad at all.' He runs his fingers around the rim of the glass and raises an eyebrow towards me.

'But, but sir, won't it be easier for your men, er, since they know the area very well, and also exactly who fell where . . . ?'

'No, no, no, we don't want any uniforms down there – it's no-man's-land, you see. Anything seen walking in a uniform will be fucking dead in less than a minute. And they must know every one of us by face by now. But you, they know you're local, and with so many of you playing fucking tourist guides across the border, they won't really bother.'

'But sir, I'm sure you can . . .'

'As I said, we just need ID cards and weapons, as many as possible,' he raises his voice just enough to tell me who's boss.

The naked, dust-sleeved bulb hanging above us lights up; outside, crickets announce the evening. He leans back in his tall worn-out velvety red chair.

'So we don't want anything to do with the . . . bodies . . . then?'

'Look, they are just dead meat and that's how I prefer them. They keep sneaking in and we keep shooting their guts out of them at first sight. That's it.'

Another swig, longer, louder. Stench in the breath.

'Some of them fucking still manage to escape, probably too many, eh – that's how you have these jerks playing ball in Srinagar and elsewhere – but when they do fall to those machine guns out there, they just drop off the ridge like dolls, like cardboard fucking soldiers! One after the other, ping, ping . . . I see it all through these.'

He gently taps his massive green binoculars that are lying on the oversized carved walnut desk.

I guess they know I've been there before. Although, it seems such a long, long time ago. Back when we were children, when we were growing up – when we were all here. We used to swim in the shallow green brook that ambles its way across the meadow, and play cricket on the makeshift pitch next to it. It's a small valley, you know, surrounded by mossy docile-looking hills and a long ridge that connects the two opposite hillsides. Behind the hills are the over-reaching mountains, rows and rows of them, that turn scores of shades during the day and become a sad, disquieting dark at night. These undulating rows of peaks, some shining, some white, some brown, like layers of piled-up fabrics, are to the west and hide in their folds the secret tracks into Azad Kashmir, into Pakistan. The pass into the mainland here, into Indian Kashmir, is somewhere near the tapering end of the ridge that runs from the Pakistani side to where the Indian check-posts start: *this* is where most of the action takes place.

Valleys are beautiful.

No one bothered us then, probably no one even noticed. It was like our own private patch; during summer vacations we would play cricket and fool around all day in this secluded playground of ours. You could see army pickets on either side of the valley even then, far off, like outline sketches on a school drawing, but that was all you could see. Anyhow, it's not like the Army wants to send me down only because they know I have been there before; they'd do it anyway.

'Baba was saying they will give me . . . ?' I try to keep the conversation going, not really knowing what to make of this weird proposition from the Captain, and someone inside me badly wants to get to the bright side of a situation that is looking frightfully ominous.

'Five hundred per trip and a small bonus for every ID and weapon you bring back. As I said, the money's good, bloody good.' Fingers flick, again.

The Captain is young, handsome, north Indian. A Punjabi perhaps, or Jat probably. He is fit, wheatish complexion, clean-shaven, short hair with a side parting. Left. His nose and chin shine. His eyes burn. It must be all the drink. He is probably fourteen or fifteen years older than me. I have never asked his first name, it just says Kadian on his uniform tag. He's always nicely turned out – shiny brown belt, shiny steel buckle – and never loses sight of his beast-like binoculars. The office is a large, minimally decorated wood cabin with a big rusted iron bukhari in the middle that often doubles up as a cooker. There is a long window at the back but it's always covered with thick curtains, military blankets perhaps, so you can't see what's behind the office. There is another door inside, in the far left corner, which probably goes to the bathroom and the store, the two small high windows of which I always see from the outside when I go up the two steps to the veranda. The peon – a bent old man who seems to apply half a bottle of cheap hair oil to his sparse scalp every morning – uses the bukhari to heat up food and make endless cups of tea for himself and the Captain's few visitors. I usually go to meet him in the evening, often a day or two after an encounter, skirmish, battle, whatever they choose to call it. He's always drinking.

And he likes to launch into small speeches about his job and the 'operation', especially when I ask something. 'I see it miniature style, toy size, through these . . . They don't supply them any more, pure German technology, not the plastic Swadeshi shit that every young paramilitary jerk hangs around his neck these days. Anyhow, they are just shadows that drop off my nightly horizon, and the more the merrier, the more, the . . . mm . . . Tell me something, have you ever played a computer game? Well, this is not even half the fun. I don't even get to pull the trigger myself any more. But what to do . . . it's my job,' he mutters as an afterthought and pours himself some more whisky. It stinks. Why does every army man have to drink?

'How many, you ask, right? Okay . . . Let's see, if you have a group of twenty or more crossing over, it's usually preceded by shelling from positions beyond their pickets you see across the valley. Bloody Paki morons, as if we didn't *see* them do it, we would

5

think it's the fucking chinks. Anyhow, it's obviously cover for your boys to make their run, but our strategy is to wait and let them at least get to the middle of the ruts around the ridge, while we are returning the shelling, and just when they begin to think they are about to make it, the automatics begin to roar. But even then, on an average we only manage to knock down less than half of the group, because, you see, it's very difficult terrain out there, a lot of mounds and ruts, and of course trees, to provide cover. And the bastards will use nothing less than brand-new LMGs to return fire. Sisterfucking rookie show-offs!

'Think of this as employment generation, Kadian style, ha ha.' He tries to joke when I ask a hesitant, barely audible, 'Why me?' conveniently avoiding the fact that I am the only young civilian left in the area to do any kind of job for the Army – or for anyone, for that matter. When everyone fled for their safety – this was when they started shelling us day and night after the Governor's bizarre visit during the crackdown – Baba refused to budge from his seat as headman; he said he needed to look after the village while everyone was away and that he didn't want to sell off his livestock. And he believed people would surely be back at some point. No one believed *him*, though. I sometimes think he saw a big opportunity in being the sole cattle owner in the area with all the pastures as his exclusive domain. At other times, I think he just wanted to hold on to the fantasy of a still-functioning village. Poor man, my father. Should have known better. He has had to sell every single living thing on four legs we ever owned to the Army at dirt-cheap rates. And most Indians are vegetarians, huh.

When I go down the first time after all these months, years, it is with a sense of both pressing nostalgia and fear. The valley looks like a large green sheet hung tenderly from the surrounding foothills, with a singing, humming is more like it, rivulet in the middle. It's still the same – a calm, largely uninhabited, solitary place nestled amidst the rings of our hills and mountains.

In my childhood, it was very easy to ignore the Pakistani and Indian check-posts on either side; you forgot about them the moment you stepped on new, untouched, fresh-from-dried-dew grass and ran downhill for a few minutes before making generous boot marks – I liked long 8s and floral designs – all over the place. They were far-off, distant, almost unreal . . . And by the time we took off our clothes to splash about in the low and languid stream we had assumed full ownership of the place and didn't care who was or wasn't peering at us from some ugly check-post out there on the mountainside. After swimming in the chilly water, we would lie down on the thick carpet of grass for ages, looking at the really, really blue sky and conjuring up odd names for clouds that hung low over our valley before drifting to another one across the mountains. I spent a long time down there, perhaps all my childhood. I don't have a lot of other memories from those early days. Ma and Baba probably thought it best to let me spend all my time there, not venture out, stay safe inside the valley. So that I wouldn't clamour to move to the city when I grew up and be lost for ever. In the years of my growing up, many border boys went to Sopore or Srinagar or other towns to study, and many refused to come back. Some of them ended up as bus conductors or worked as waiters in rickety restaurants on the national highway. Their parents' cattle herds dwindled with each passing year and brought poverty, loneliness and ill health. I suppose my parents were scared too. In the years *after* I grew up, some of the boys either became guides and clandestinely scouted city boys across the border, into training camps in Pakistan, or became militants themselves to relieve their parents of their yoke of shepherds' lives and give them proper homes when Kashmir would gain its independence. Many disappeared like that from time to time; I guess those who went to the city were luckier. My friends, *all* my friends, went away too, and God only knows if they will ever come back. Not many do, you see, and those who do, don't live very long here. Because the army people, the protectors of the land, have decided that there is only one way of dealing with the boys: catch and kill. *Catch and kill.* I therefore ended up staying with my parents and their cattle. I stayed on in the valley, and in the end came to own it all by myself.

I look at the first few corpses and am immediately horrified at the prospects of what my first ever job entails. There are probably six of them ahead of me. Ugly grins, unbelievable, almost inhuman, postures and a grotesque intermingling of broken limbs make me dig my teeth deep, and hard, into my clenched fists. What an elaborate litter! There are bare wounds, holes dark and visceral, and limbless, armless, even headless, torsos. A low moan struggles, screeches inside. Gradually, I approach one of the more intact bodies, gingerly, eyes reduced to hairline slits, and look for a pocket or bag amidst all the dirt and the crusted blood on his clothes. I find the ID card in his back pocket and in some kind of limp involuntary motion throw it into the nylon army rucksack the Captain gave me last week. It's not easy, collecting identity cards and whatever else you can find on dead bodies. Bodies after bodies – some huddled together, others forlorn and lonesome – in various stages of decay. Wretched human remains lie on the green grass like cracked toys. Teeth, shoes. For God knows how long I just cannot remove my eyes from this landscape, heaps of them, big and small, body parts, belongings littered amidst the rubble of legs and arms . . . Macabre, horrid ghouls on either side of the brook watch me from their melancholic black-hole eye sockets. (I guess whoever ended up in the stream was fortunate to be washed away.) Carcasses with indefinable expressions on what remains of their faces – I hope I don't recognize anyone. *This is what we get?* they seem to ask. The smell, the smell, the smell! I cannot begin to describe what it is like the first time. You just stop breathing. *That is it.*

The stench is so powerful that your guts begin to pull your throat down, sort of strangle you from within, if you know what I mean.

On the first day, having touched my first ever corpse, I bathe twice in the evening, with scalding hot water and a copious amount of soap, scrubbing and scratching myself into rashes and red nail-slashes all over my chest and arms. I can't eat well, however, owing to the nausea that comes over me for the next few days.

It's not easy, picking stuff off dead people.

'There was a skirmish last night, I'm sure you heard it?'

'Yes, yes, Captain, I did, went on for hours . . .' I answer quickly, nervously, and wait for him to say more.

He doesn't, just watches me with narrowed eyes.

'You want me to check them out . . . ?'

Another evening, another drink-fuelled lecture. I'm beginning to get used to this. That's worrying.

'Well, we have this fucking TV crew coming from Delhi, there might be some foreign ladies as well, I have been told. So we will do something here in the camp, you don't worry about it. The stupid hacks want to film foreign militants – how the fuck do they know I am not lying? I can fucking make any maderchod look like an Afghan. The dead don't speak, remember, and I still have plenty of old photos and clothes. The only thing I can't do is Sudanese, or fucking Arab; for that you have to wait for the real thing, huh ha!'

Captain Kadian usually lightens up a bit, drops his high sturdy shoulders, after a few drinks. More so if I don't ask him too many questions before agreeing (sometimes I like to believe I still retain some choice) on another trip down skeleton lane. I wonder what this thing tastes like. It surely works.

But I do want to ask him if he's ever been down there. And I really wonder sometimes how many there are? Thousands. Two, three, five thousand? No, no, I'm exaggerating. But surely, there must be hundreds and hundreds of them.

'So is this where all the missing go, all the disappeared people? This is where they can all be found, then?' I find myself mustering up the courage to ask him.

'Hmm, one could say that, but remember, this is not the only pass they use to cross the border. This one seems pretty popular, but there are at least ten others as busy as ours, if not more.'

'Why not get rid of all the bodies, sir . . . ? Isn't this, you know, I mean, incriminating . . . ? For me too . . . ?'

'Naah, there's no fucking point, they will just disappear with time. Besides, we don't want to offend people by doing anything that can be seen as *desecration*, you see. Otherwise, all it will take is a couple of cans of kerosene every few weeks or so. These people need burials and that's what we give them – big, big open burials, huh ha . . .'

There are a million of you here, one Indian soldier to every six civilians, you could bury every single one of us alive in due course of time, I would say at a different time, in a different situation, to a cowering pig of this Captain, but for now I can only wish.

I'm beginning to spend more and more time amidst the rotting dead now. The other day, I thought I'd even started talking to my skeletal audience. You know, they look at you with their mid-sentence grins and teeth and you feel someone just said something. Some of them are in a very bad shape, with bits of flesh hanging loose from their faces, necks, chests, arms. Sad dismal demeaned reflections of their former selves. The necks look particularly grotesque. A few of them haven't been touched by vultures and crows at all, so their flesh just gets thinner and thinner, tighter and tauter, like high-strung leather, with each passing day. These are the ones you dread the most, for fear of recognition. What if an acquaintance suddenly turns up? '*Assalam-u-Alaikum.*' Some others seem perfectly calm, as if this were where they wanted to be all along.

'Captain, do you know how many you have down there?' Curiosity finally wins over cowardice – on this fourth, fifth, meeting with my boss after that first, and fateful, call of his at the house – and I really want to put a finger on how many our very own Changez Khan has heaped up in his pyramid down the ridge. In our pristine valley, around the cricket pitch, by the green river.

'Can't say for sure. Who fucking counts . . . ? But let's look at it this way, they started crossing over and back in 1988–89. Okay, let's say in big numbers the year after that, right . . . ? And we are now well into '93, so that means we have more than three years of debris down there. This is one of the biggest sectors and, as you know, very popular with the sneaky bastards.'

'But they don't come all year, do they?' I immediately find myself desperate to keep the numbers low.

'You think so . . . ? Huh! The numbers just decrease marginally during the winters, my dear. Those sissies on TV just read what we send them.'

*

Baba wants to know, I suspect, about how it's going between the Captain Sahib and me – what do I tell him, though, what *do* I tell my poor old stubborn father? That I am the official accountant of the dead now, that I dread every step of my walks in the valley lest I stumble upon one of them, lest I end up carrying their name, *just* the name, to the Captain some day, and say, here's another one for your books, sir – what do I say, Baba?

Ma, I avoid as much as I can, her silence helps, although how long can one 'avoid' one's mother, and how long can she not know, or how long can we – Baba, I – pretend that she doesn't know? Baba, better not talk to me about it, for Ma's sake, better not talk about it.

Months have passed since I was last in the village street, back when everyone left, leaving us all alone in this militarized wilderness. It's not that I haven't meant to spend some time there – but it just hasn't happened. I want to see everything again, to check how it looks, feels, in desertion, in abandonment – and yet I dread doing it. Even now, some weight presses on me as I step out on this late morning when the light is a clear blue and the sun is not yet glaring on my head.

There are trees here, and in their shadows the shadows of people on their daily chores. The breeze is a breathing, talking, real thing; it travels loudly, feeling its way over everything. As I walk towards the shops in the middle, I feel someone is walking behind me. I do not look back. It is always disappointing. The dust on the street has not seen any footprints for ages, apart from the sickly marks of some bird that might have descended to check whatever happened to the talkative grocer who used to throw out crumbs of stale glucose biscuits every morning. The light is all blue, liquid blue, the mountains conspiring to create a luminous corridor for me to look down, I guess.

Leaves lie in abandon here and there, some pale, some brown, some green and some crushed. The wind has created its own order over them. Rustle, murmur, rustle . . . Tiny dance-circles of dust rise and vanish. A few flowers, white, red and purple, rest in their dusty inclines on the edges. Some forest ferns, long subdued under human occupation, have sprouted well on the sides too. They look prosperous in their moist, fresh clumps.

The shutters on Noor Khan's grocery shop look firm and sturdy, the lock resolute. The railing at the front as if waiting for someone.

Sadiq Chechi's Red Cross has grown shades of khaki on it, the sun making it appear ruthless, still. The old green blanket he used as a curtain is folded to one side, a jute string tied around it over and over, as if . . . At the centre, just above the padlock, are two words written in blue: God's Gift. Chechi's parting note.

Asghar Ali's hardware store, three small heaps of clutter in front. Asghar had been emptying the shop of its reservoir of unusable bits and bobs collected from scrap dealers in Sopore. He had at last given up on making a sale of these remaining bits and wanted to restock with new nails and screws. Rust, soot, mud make the heaps look like barren mountains. A brazen growth of grass swerves on the side. As I leave, an old sticker glares from the side of the shop doors: *Inallaha ma'as-sabireen.* God is indeed with those who are patient.

I hear conversations murmuring in front of the three shops. Laughter of children too.

I turn away to go and see the corner of our evening meets. I stand where I used to stand, taking in Hussain on the left, closest to me, Ashfaq opposite me, looking up occasionally, Gul, fidgety, his arm over Mohammed who sets himself free but every now and then pulls Gul back towards him. I keep staring at the footprints, where there should have been footprints. There is a small muddy puddle in the middle of the group. I see myself. Today is the 6th of July. 1993. It is also my birthday, my nineteenth.

After two more rounds of the street and fleeting glances at Gul's house behind those stately poplars, I walk away. The whispers in the air persist. 'Let's go, let's go, let's leave . . . Leave it to Allahtaala.'

At the tipping end of the street, I see old Ramazan Choudhary's wooden slippers, his famous *khraaw*, the one he always wore under his long pyjama and pheran. They sit tidily alongside a clay wall where tiny grasses hang low. I get closer and see the old man's prints on the worn-out wood base. Round clear heel, faded stem like a licked bone, fine digits at the toes. I touch them, nudge the pair into symmetry, and leave.

No one, no one, will ever come back here.

On some days, especially when there's a lull in the *dar-andazi*, in the infiltration attempts and the ensuing mayhem, and he has let go of his heavy metal-green eyes, the Captain opens a blue journal and starts jotting down things here and there. This is also the time when I visit him during daylight hours, like the other visitors – wonder what these men come here for, they are surely not from around here. Seated behind his vast desk, on which the main piece of decoration is an orange and gold papier-mâché tray with rows of neatly lined-up bullets of many shapes and colours, and worn, tired-looking paper clips on a little bed of dust or sand – a miniature combat scene this, too, I wonder? – Captain Kadian looks like the chief accountant of a prosperous bank. Am I his runner, then? His label boy? *Can you please check the name tags whilst I balance the books?* Corpse-land etiquette! One of these days I must finally ask, insist, that he come down to visit where I work. To come and inspect his crops, his harvest of human remains. I so want him to come and see the putrid trench he's turned my valley into.

I have also gradually come to understand how this works. Fairly simple, actually. When they need to, they release a list from time to time about a fierce encounter in so-and-so sector on the border that continued for so many hours, went on till the small hours, and so on and so forth. The list of the dead is then sent to the police and the newspapers. The media are never allowed in except for delegations sent by the Centre and the Governor of Kashmir. And when they want to show off their catch, they film the bodies which have not been conveyed down into the valley, and store the footage for present or future use. *That's* what we see on TV. Sometimes, especially when the action has spilled out into the bordering villages, or when they have fake-encountered some poor boys in some far-flung area, they will drag the bodies, after their faces are mutilated, and quickly hand them over to the local police, or to scared, do-gooder villagers for mass nameless burials; that is, after they are done with camera-work etc. But when there's no such need they will just kick the corpses around and roll them over into the valley . . . *No one goes there except for carrion birds and animals, and now, me.* I guess I supply the names for the fresh, the latest lists. Ghazi Nasiruddin alias Abu Jindal alias Talha Jaanbaz alias Abu Huraira. Dreaded Lashkar commander.

It doesn't really matter to him what the names are, as long as there is a photo they can show on Doordarshan. All ID cards have Indian, *Kashmiri*, particulars – teacher, college student, carpet weaver, mechanic – detailed aliases for the boys to carry them through security checks and ID parades should they find themselves in the midst of crackdowns or combing operations in the country or the towns. At first I was surprised that they should carry any identification, but then, everyone in Kashmir has to, even the militants. You simply do not exist if you don't have an ID card on you . . . In any case, I feel they are little schoolboy trophies for Captain Kadian, a score he lives by in his murderscape!

By the way, did I mention there's a profusion of tiny yellow flowers growing among the grasses here? If you look from the top on a sunny day, you can see these shiny objects scattered across the lush meadowy patch around the river. These are erstwhile legs and arms and backbones and ribcages surrounded by sparkling swathes of yellow created by the thousands and thousands of flowers all across the valley. In places they have grown in great numbers around the fallen and the decaying. You can see bright yellow outlines of human forms enclosing darkness inside. It makes me cry, it makes me want to run away, to disappear. In some cases the outline has started to become fuzzy now, with the tiny plants encroaching into the space of the ever-shrinking human remains. I don't know the name of the flowers. Some kind of wild daisies perhaps.

Not very far from here is the other side, the Pakistani side, a place where these guys came from, after months of God knows what kind of intense training, or were indeed still headed towards, when they were walking, talking human beings. Turns out, around here the Indians kill just about everyone. Who will know and object, leave alone protest, in this remote, cut-off wilderness? You know, sometimes I wonder – because for Kashmir there is always an Indian and a Pakistani version of everything – what if they have their own pasture of dead boys on the other side of the border? Their own stash of the infiltration residue? Young men who lost their lives while learning to walk the perilous path to freedom. Treachery is a word everyone should learn.

Do I ever tire of this job? Oh, even if I did, I have picked too many ID cards and AK-47s off dead people to command any choice in the matter any more. And these people die, after all. Someone has to visit, pay respects – offer a secret fateha so that he doesn't catch me doing it – and drag them into slightly more honourable postures and take away their weapons if they are still there. I can't do much about the older ones, though – nothing much remains of them anyway – poor sketches in bone with miserable looks that have frozen in time. I think they should seriously consider hiring an assistant for me; it's not too much to ask, is it?

The other day, I was thinking how I'd come to assume that the big gashes on the relatively newer bodies were made by carrion birds – and some of these boys have entire arms missing, half-legs astride from their torsos. What if those dogs who always stare at me from near the foothills have joined in the feast as well and, for that matter, what if all the animals of the neighbourhood have taken to eating rotting human flesh, what if most of them now breakfast on decomposing men? It would get quite horrific then, wouldn't it? All the cats and all the dogs, all the wolves from the forest and all the foxes from the fields, the tigers and the hyenas, birds of both the carrion and the non-carrion denomination, all the rats and the mongoose – all of them tearing their meals off young men like me. I get a terrifying, gasping shiver every time I think of that. It must be strange, then, for all these soldiers with their binoculars and night-vision things looking at a man-eating mela day and night, at all the gnawing and pulling and the peeling and chewing and the grunting and . . . Or maybe they are used to it by now, so much so that they don't even look at these hideous heaps any more. But, really, what do the soldiers on the other side do? Offer fateha for the souls of the deceased, bless the sacrificed ones for their ultimate qurbani? *May your bones rest in peace after they are licked dry by rabid man-eating wolves.*

Captain Kadian has never been out of the camp.

'I don't need to, I have to complete three years here, and this is the third. I will just finish off in a few months and head home,' he says, tapping his journal a few times with his pen. 'I will live off my savings for a while before I can think of doing something else. I think I have done enough. My *leave* should be due soon, high time, you see.'

'But what about this, sir? What about, er . . . *me*? What is going to happen when someone discovers all this? I'm sure it's a human rights catastrophe, waiting to be noticed. What am I going to do then?' I blurt out in not-fully-registered panic.

'It will all go away, man. It always does. It always fucking does. Nothing will remain of these wretches down there. And then someone else will come in and start doing it all over again. That is the way it is. Guerrilla wars, you see, last ten, fifteen years at most. Don't worry. The worst that can happen is some motherfucker will discover a few skeletons a few years from now and report it to the press, and what can the papers say, apart from 'four skeletons discovered near the LoC', huh ha!

The few times I really wish I, too, had crossed over during the big rush – and not chickened out at the last minute – is when Captain Kadian has spoken, held forth, laughed it off, ordered me to shut up ever so subtly by tapping on his cane and binoculars, and taken another satisfying gulp of his brown liquid from the ancient glass tumbler.

They do pay well. Baba obviously knows where I get the money from; in fact, he is only the second person I know who knows about the valley. He doesn't say much, though, except for the occasional mumble about my friends. What if this and what if that? What will you do if you see one of them down there? he must think. To which, I always think, my answer would be, 'We'll see about that.'

There was this time, not too long ago, just two or three years ago, when everyone wanted to go *sarhad paar*, to cross over and become a famous freedom fighter. Hordes and hordes went in the early days, everyone wanted to return and be a commander, a masked legend in their own right, a liberator of the Kashmiri people, a hero. Busloads of city boys would be dropped off at the last bus stop in Kupwara, I got to know later – for months bus conductors in many towns were heard yelling their hearts out, 'Pindi, Pindi, anyone for Rawalpindi?' And then some of us, the local boys, the Gujjar boys, children of former nomads who had settled down as landed people only thirty, forty years ago in these remote border parts, would guide them across the treacherous mountains into Pakistan. (I became friends, sort of, with one Gujjar guide at least, big man Rahman, but all that's for later . . .) The Indian Army must be the stupidest in the world not to have noticed shoals of these fashionable city types appearing suddenly in a border area with their gelled-back hair and tight jeans. Some of them didn't even have proper boots to go on the long trek across the gorges and the ravines. And some actually wore sunglasses. Border lads like Rahman thus became natural guides across the border – they already knew every dirt track, every gorge, every crevasse and every valley in the mountains, and had a mental map of all the check-posts dotting the silly Line of Control separating this Kashmir from that Kashmir. Some of them made extra money by selling cheap rubber long-boots to the heroically inclined city slickers who probably thought Muzaffarabad was a tranquil waltz across a Mughal garden! My father stopped worrying about me soon after he had started because I didn't show much interest, not initially at least, not to him at least – or the courage required – in attaining either heroism or martyrdom so soon in my life. As my dear friends thought, I had read too many books – by which they meant a few more than the school syllabus – and that had compromised my ability to rebel, to take up arms. I didn't have balls, they must've thought, therefore I wasn't fit – and they were right perhaps – therefore I didn't cross the line, and ended up staying behind. So I haven't seen what the other side looks like or how an AK-47 feels in your hands when it rattles off 600 bullets a minute. I have held quite a few in my hands since, although I still haven't used one. One of these days I should be brave and ask Kadian to at least give me a pistol. What if those man-eaters decide to upgrade from scavenging to active hunting some day?

In one of my first trips down to the valley, I felt exhausted and fell asleep alongside one of the freshly arrived boys. He smelled of hair oil. He had probably combed his hair back before leaving on his mission. I talked to him, or maybe I didn't, for I don't know how long I slept in his company. Seventeen small flowers had grown between his legs. I counted. His watch was still ticking and the time was quarter past three. 16 April 1993. In my wakeful dream, he said he was from Sopore and his name was Rouf Ahmad Qadri.

'You do know where this is? How did you get here, brother?'

It's not my fault, is it? I told them we should not go in such a large group, small numbers are less noticeable, but who listens to the younger cadre, these commanders have a way of not changing their mind and staying on course no matter what and that's what has done me in. Staying on course.

'Don't you get tired like this?'

Well, not really, I kind of like not having to run any more. It's fine, really, don't worry about me. But yes, if there's anything you can do about the stench, I would be eternally grateful.

'Sure, I will do what I can. So how did you get here from Sopore?'

Oh, I left Sopore a long time ago. Soon after they burned it down. I spent the last six months in training camps, first somewhere in Malakand and then outside Rawalpindi. Our trip back into Kashmir was postponed three times, first because of the weather and then they were short of guides . . . Finally, our Chief Commander said we should start on our own. I carried two Kalashnikovs, twelve grenades and five hundred rounds in my ruck-sack. We walked for two days and three nights . . . But then, on the third night, there was this sudden burst of fire from the sky. They used all the machine guns together. Some of us fell to the first volley itself. They arrested three of us after we escaped the attack. There's an old man, oily-looking chap who came to visit us. He was the one who shot me.

*

I want to take one last dip, one last swim, in the stream of my child-hood, in the river that still flows in the same old fashion – lazy and considered, as if pausing now and then to reflect on the macabre change in the scenery around it. One nice plunge in its glistening green water, after all these years – I want to know if it still recognizes me. It would be nice to know again that feeling of years ago when we would jump into it all together, or one after the other, splashing its cool water into the sky and gazing at the pearls that would come down mixed with the sharp rays of a July sun. Why did they go? Where are they now? Are they, too, part of this detritus that lies scattered so indifferently on the banks of our river like disused, broken old furniture in an abandoned warehouse. This stream, my personal Hades, has seen everything but knows not what to say. It just flows, briefly contemplating things in its small, cyclical green pools at every small bend, and then moves on. That's what rivers do: move on, no matter what. If my friends are here, lying among hundreds of other boys from all over this sad paradise on earth, it may just as well be. It's perhaps only fair – they did leave it, abandon it, for a higher cause. But who would know where they all are? Does *he* know? Did he see them through his binoculars and then had them shot down like bottles on a wall? Did he briefly glimpse their faces – anxious faces full of fright, and hope too, lurking somewhere behind those scared eyes – before waving a 'wipe-off' gesture to his machine-gun man on the picket whilst adjusting his metal eyes for a better view? I must, must ask him how many he remembers? Does he remember any of them?

In the stream I stand waist-deep and follow its leisured journey as far as it stretches, as long as the meadow goes, to some unknown point where it probably trickles into some bigger river, carrying with it many childhood dreams, unfulfilled wishes and bloated corpses. Blood too. I come back to where I stand and see a silhouet-ted reflection of myself in the green below. Soon after I have plodded lazily through a few feet of ice-cold water, the river becomes a sea. I close my eyes and wade on. I realize I have company the moment I submerge my head. It's a party, all of them together, moving towards me in a choric huddle. The first face I recognize is of Hussain, our dear, dear singer, who at the age of fifteen could reproduce almost all of Mohammed Rafi's repertoire and was therefore the official entertainer in our group. He was handsome, lean, delicate. His cheekbones a flushed red, his slight nose almost always cold-blushed and his eyes sparkling with a fresh, just-remembered song. Hussain. He has blood smeared all over and his throat is slit. His wavy black hair, which he was fond of brushing away with such filmy flourish, is intact, though. The entourage swims closer and I see Mohammed, the master craftsman of home-made cricket bats and stumps who once ended up scraping off the entire skin of his palms, all red and throbbing and curling, as he tried to force an improvised rubber grip (from an old bicycle tube) over the coarse handle of his latest cricketing creation. I shuddered when the strong, big man cried with pain that day, standing right in the middle of the wicket, his cries echoing all around the valley. Mohammed, merry and full of big-boy bravado, the dog-owning frontman of our gang wars and school playground brawls was the unofficial protector of the group. He appears to have lost his eyes. And hands. Oh, Gul Khan nods his head from above the group. 'Handsome Qatli Khan,' we used to tease him, for his exemplary prowess with all the girls at school as they would sit around him waiting for their palms to be read and be told tall tales of love and longing. 'When you grow up you will be a huge asset to us, and very useful to me,' he once told a girl of thirteen who had begun, it seemed to us then, to show signs of becoming extremely well endowed. I liked Gulla for his attempts at bold wit. He was never as close to me, though, as Hussain was. Gul Khan's face is missing below the nose. His big, dark beautiful eyes are closed, as though in prayer. Ashfaq, the classic melancholic, the brooding thinker, appears last, as usual. That knowing smile is still there, his hair deliberately a mess, and his faint stubble the same length as always. He had predicted the end of the world a long time ago; we must have been fourteen then. 'All this is going to be destroyed, ruined; it will all meet a rotten end.' We took him very seriously and hugged each other affectionately before going home that evening. Ashfaq has holes all over his body. Big, dark holes. I can't hear a word of what they are saying – I just see their lips moving and Gul Khan making strange gestures with his hands. Are they talking about me? Are they making fun of me? By now they have formed a circle around me, but I just can't manage to touch any of them, and they don't make an effort at moving any closer either. I so, so want to put myself in their midst, shoulder to shoulder in the 'friend circle', like old times, like good old times, but instead, I find myself splashing out of the water.

I want to ask Captain Kadian if he's ever seen them, if he's ever come across the names Hussain, Ashfaq, Gul and Mohammed.

2 The Chosen One

Two years ago, Hussain was the first to disappear from the village. The musically possessed, the gentlest and the noblest of the group, was the first to fall.

We had met as usual in the street on a Sunday evening, and had bantered away into the night. But the next evening, he was gone. Vanished. That evening he had looked calm, relaxed, as usual, moving from one foot to the other as he always did, while he listened to Gul Khan's retelling of his latest infatuation. Gul had taken a liking to Nuzhat, Compounder Chechi's dimwit daughter, or more accurately, her swelling chest, and was trying hard to make his anecdote funny to give us the impression that he wasn't too serious about the girl. Like the rest of us that sweet October evening, Hussain listened, and laughed, but the next evening he was gone. And no one, or so I thought then, had had a clue beforehand. My last memory of Hussain is him shaking hands with me – he was always, without fail, the first to offer his hand, in fact it was his ritual, and it seemed to me that the joy you feel for the first time when, as a boy, you begin to shake hands with people and think you are a grown-up, had never really waned in him – the same eager manner of the arm and the deliberate shake and firm grip. He said 'khudayas hawale' to Ashfaq, to Mohammed, and to me at last, and then left for home with Gul. Theirs was the same route home – Hussain's house was in the field at the end of the lane where Gul lived in their large three-storey house. I never saw him again after that.

And I missed him, missed him very much in those first days.

I guess he and I shared a friendship within the friendship, although neither I, nor he, ever said so – we just understood it. It wasn't as if I talked to him a lot more than I did with the others – in fact he confided, wanted to confide, in me more than I did in him. He spoke about his father, ever deferentially and never, in any manner, in an aggrieved tone, and his inability to lift his family and himself from their relative poverty. I think that must have been the first time I felt he was a more intimate friend, for I was suddenly full of admiration, and wonder, for this person who spoke about their hardship and his father's life with such honest and innocent understanding, without the embarrassment that might have descended on any other boy of his age, myself included, now that I think about it.

Hussain often visited the house on Sundays. In autumn Ma begins to take stock of her many jars of dry fruits and assorted sweets: almonds, walnuts, dried apricots, Morton and Parle toffees, cashew nuts and dates and pistas, and for as long as I remember, I see Hussain in the house at this time. He would cup a few sweets and apricots that Ma handed to us and then would move away into the corner of our kitchen, just as Ma began her ritual of dusting the thick glass jars and checking them for worms or weevils. Hussain loved jaggery and little snacks, the roasted peas and pine nuts that Noor Khan sold in fifty-paisa sachets, and which I knew he longed for me to buy whenever I went to spend my pocket money at Noor's counter. He never asked me to; I just bought those bags once in a while so that I could share them with him. Obviously, I didn't want to buy them too often in case he got embarrassed. On one occasion at our house, around four years before he left, having furtively licked his lips after a Ravalgaon orange candy, he talked about his mother, and how it was she who encouraged him to sing in the house, against the strong wishes, initially at least, of his father. 'Mouji has a great heart, you know,' he said. 'She doesn't let Abba` scold me too much, takes it all on her, all the time, keeps talking to him, listening to him, because she thinks she is protecting me. She can't sing herself, you know . . .' he added, sighing mildly. I remember how I gently patted him, just a few brushing dabs on the shoulder, when he said that. Hussain's mother, his Mouj, demurely built, feeble, faint-faced, a mother forever crushed under the weight of a needy home, had stopped singing, so Ma said, soon after her marriage to the piously minded Khadim Hussain.

With time, then, I too began to think of him as a confidant like no other, a sharer of secrets whispered only in the safety of the village dusk. Only Hussain knew, for instance – and the others couldn't have even smelled it (I could never afford that) – my quiet and growing fondness for Ashfaq's younger sister Asma. Only he knew how I longed for Ashfaq to mention her name or to talk about anything in their household that might have included her, and of course for the rare visits in which she accompanied her older brother, trips which inevitably got fewer and fewer as she grew from the little sister of our friend into the delicate, and acutely self-conscious, prettiest-girl-of-the-village.

Hussain wanted me to be absolutely sure – now I know – about myself, about my intent with her, not only because she was our friend's sister, but also because, I believe, he didn't want my love to go unrequited. Although now I understand, it never could have reached that stage. I was too timid and in awe of Baba to make my wishes for a future with Asma known – mine was always just a secret desire to be with her, to know her and to be able to strike a *closeness* with her. Hussain knew that, understood it.

I missed him, missed him very much in those first days. Missed him much more than I'd thought I would. And even though I was not at all sure if I could go through with such an undertaking myself, I wanted to be with him. I wanted to go and join him . . . How could he do this?

As I said, I'd heard stories of how hundreds of young men – excited, idealistic teenagers; hurt, angry boys wronged by police or army action; vengeful brothers with raped sisters and mothers at home; firebrand youth leaders conjuring up paradisiacal visions of freedom and an independent Kashmir – had been leaving home everywhere and joining the Movement by walking the perilous walk across the border to receive arms and training and return as militants, as freedom fighters. At first, however, a part of me had still liked to believe these stories were exaggerated, hearsay, spiced-up rumours travelling to and from the mountains.

'All the boys from Poshpur are gone, gone, no one left in the village, it's empty now, all empty! It's all happening, dear, happening everywhere.' Noor Khan, our ragtag village grocer and inveterate gossip, retold, for the hundredth time perhaps, during one of my routine tobacco-shopping trips, the story of the sixteen boys (some said twenty, some thirty) who had apparently disappeared together a few weeks ago from the nearest village down in the big Valley, soon after all the women there had been raped in a night-long raid by Indian soldiers. People in my village had been emphasizing 'all the women' as if to suggest that if it had been only a few women it might not have been so bad. This was four weeks or so before Hussain was to do the same, and would, in turn, make me, a little later, yearn to go after him, to join him and to try, however timidly, to be like him.

Noor Khan's hands were always stained from the loose tobacco and the spices he sold. Sometimes even his short beard seemed stained with shades of turmeric, chilli powder and the regular brown of tobacco. Broad-faced, two long-relinquished upper teeth, Noor's mouth and cheeks sagged from a lifetime of exaggerated worrying over everything, from the next India–Pakistan war and shelling on the border to the Sixty-Five-Rupees-Fifty-Paisa which Ramazan Choudhary, the village oldie, allegedly owed him from ten years ago, and which every other customer of his knew about but he himself never asked for. Noor Chacha, as we often fondly addressed him, and in expectation of potential free candy favours, wore his old Karakuli cap with a subtle tilt. He would cup his salt-and-pepper bearded chin, loudly draw a deep breath through his nose, and then shoot a weighty projectile from his mouth on to the middle of the village street, on the left of which his landmark shop stood, the only shop on this side of the road. The other two shops, Compounder Sadiq Chechi's shady medical shop-cum-clinic and Asghar Ali's multipurpose tongs and sandals 'hardwear' store, stood on the other side, facing the hills. Noor's had been the first of the village and he took some kind of unsaid pioneer's pride in the fact. The street had, still has, just a few houses on either side of it, the three parsimoniously stocked stores in the centre, whilst most of the other houses, including ours, were, *are*, spread across the rolling foothills higher up, with large, loosely demarcated terraced fields spread between them. (Gujjars – even settled, landed Gujjars – retain their love of distance.) That day, I bought a fat wedge of sticky wet tobacco, in a rolled-up cone made of ancient newspapers, for Baba's insatiable hookah, and left for home, bewildered, and perhaps a little annoyed as well, at the new dimension the Poshpur story had assumed since the first time I'd read about it three months ago, in a sketchy newspaper report, and had then also listened to the Government's blanket denial that any such incident had ever taken place. A brand-new Minister for Kashmir Affairs from Delhi was also quoted as saying that no place by the name of Poshpur ever existed on the map!

Baba was busy with his elaborate beard trimming when I told him what Noor had just been saying. Baba used both a shaving blade and old brass scissors, the ones with 'King Mark' etched in Urdu at the centre joining the two eyes of the blades, to work on his beard. As he listened to me, he twirled his moustache, which was much thicker than his bristling grey beard, in a gentle upward motion, and then laid down his tools.

My father still looked imperious, a man of heavy build and manner. In those days, his eyes shone with the confidence and command of a prosperous man enjoying late-middle-age power as the long-serving headman of Nowgam. 'It's utter, utter nonsense. These hot-headed, foolish kids, they will come back crying babies' tears the moment they get even a minor scratch on their fingertips, mark my words . . .' Baba declared in his occasionally used, raised voice, while restocking his tobacco box with the fresh supply I'd just delivered. While he disapproved of the idea, to me it had seemed, initially at least, to belong to another place – it happened somewhere else, to proper Kashmiri families, down in the big Valley.

We didn't really seem the class for churning out committed freedom fighters, I had thought. While thousands of boys from all of Kashmir were increasingly being drawn into the vortex of a euphoric freedom struggle, my parents assumed their only offspring was safe because the romance didn't lend itself to Gujjar life, because we didn't have 'an issue with India', and because the valley people didn't think of us as Kashmiris anyway. 'It's good they don't trust us much, otherwise who knows some tanzeem might have already been here.

'I have seen this before, son, seen it all, nothing happens in the end, you know, nothing. In 1947 they went almost all the way down to Srinagar, but what happened then? Nothing! Nothing but *lootmaar*, rape . . . and they torched every single thing they could on the way. It's utter nonsense.'

'I don't think they would want to come here, Baba.' I wanted to end it just there, didn't want to press the issue too hard, knowing too well how difficult it was to steer him away once he went back in time, to years ago when he as a youth had seen, so he said, the savage raids of 1947 and how people, especially people from the border areas, had turned against the invading marauders, had turned informers, and, with their sticks and spades, fought against the very tribesmen from Pakistan who had come to liberate them.

'Oh, even if they did come, we will chase them away like always . . . We fought those beghairat, shameless, copper-stealing tribals with mere sticks, son, with our bare hands – these new kids, what can they do? Nothing!'

The truth is that I had actually believed, quite naïvely I must say, that not many people from among us would want to join the Movement, and that no militant group, neither the Liberation Front nor the Hizb-ul-Mujahideen, and none of the grandly named latest ones either, would want to come here, because for most people Gujjars were seen to be always on the move, shifting from place to place; and anyway, who would care about a small secluded community living in this tiny, sparse hamlet hidden in the midst of the mighty hills near the border with Pakistan. So I had thought. In the border areas, you see, it was a very confusing time – we didn't know how things could change between today and tomorrow, between morning and evening.

'These jumpy young fools, they will bring nothing but disaster . . . it's like picking small scabs off an elephant's skin. Mosquito bites on a giant's ass! You just cannot fight the might of the Indian Army with a few borrowed pieces of wood, they will crush you to pieces in no time.' Baba, continuing his agitated disapproval of the latest developments, always referred to the militants' weapons as pieces of junk wood. He never, not even for a moment, doubted the superiority of his old, licensed double-bore that came out of its rusted iron trunk for oiling once or twice a year.

But I was wrong. Hussain did leave.

Hussain the singer, my dear old singer . . . my confidant, my jigri dost, my most special friend. *'Parbaton se aaj main takra gaya . . .'* His nasal take-off of the Rafi imitator Shabbir Kumar always managing to send us into fits of tearful laughter; he would sit by the river, feet playing a strange tune in the water, and sing to the mountains, while we . . . we would just sit back and let him have his five minutes. The evening before he disappeared, he had been rather quiet – I only realized this later, *after* he'd left – had talked less than he usually did and also, I realized retrospectively, he didn't hum, something he would always do, something he even used to do whilst eating. We had spent much of the afternoon idling around the village, gone down to the valley just before sunset and sat down by the river. Gul and Mohammed resumed their long-running 'hand-power' championship – Gul, 7; Mohammed, 18 – while Hussain sat by my side near the riverbank, silently watching as Ashfaq and I skimmed stones across the water, trying to outdo each other. He rooted for me, I knew. I have gone over the minutes of that day, rewound every single moment, so many times that I'm sometimes unsure as to which clues might be real and which I might have invested with meaning over the last two years, because – apart from the absence of much talking and humming on his part – it was an ordinary day, full of our regular complacencies and time-passes. I often feel it should have been more momentous than that – or maybe it was, and I just didn't realize.

Hussain's family had never been very well off. Hussain was acutely aware of this and one of the ways he thought he might be able to help their situation was to become a teacher when he grew up, to earn a secure government salary; that way, he believed, they would be free of the worries of an unsteady income and not be perennially looked down upon as a needy family. As Baba put it, they had not been able to 'improve their chances' the way most other families in Nowgam had after Chief Minister Sheikh Abdullah's provision of free land and development funds in the seventies for small Gujjar communities which had settled down on pasturelands in the mountains after centuries of an uncertain nomadic life. While most people of my father's generation had then worked hard to assume a more sedentary life, building houses, procuring smallholdings of land while also adding to their livestock, Hussain's father, the humble Khadim Hussain, was given more to a spiritual life, and, most recently, to spending a lot of his time in the newly completed mosque he had helped build over the last year – the first concrete mosque in our parts.

His crisp greying beard covered with a hazy film of dust, the long forehead gleaming with tiny beads of sweat, Hussain's abba` had suffered weeks of toil when the mosque was being built. Before that, there had been the corrugated tin shed in front of the graveyard near the far foothill, with its weathered but resolute green flag, which had stood as the modest, infrequently attended house of God in our midst. Khadim Hussain was a good-looking man – Hussain took after him – and his high cheekbones, ruddy cheeks that had darkened with age and recent hard labour, and thick hair hanging down to his shoulders from the familiar shining bald spot, always made him stand out from the crowd. Stones, bricks and freshly sliced wet planks of wood from the deodars and pines felled just a week or so before – he had overseen it all, and closely watched the speedy rise of the house of God in the village. He himself worked hard, lifting rocks, moving slushy gravel, sand and mud in the improvised wheelbarrow fashioned so deftly by Mohammed – jute sacks from Noor Khan's shop strung on a contraption of wooden poles and old bicycle wheels – and mixing endless tubs of concrete mortar for the plinth with a shovel along with some other people from the Masjid Committee and the few hired labourers. The mosque sprang up in no time then, a jagged brick and mortar one-storey structure with slit-like rectangular windows high on its walls as if meant to prevent people from peeping in on the worshippers inside. Hussain's abba` was a pleased man after that; more than once I saw him looking approvingly at his creation. He was a gentle soul. Humble.

Hussain, who left exactly a month after the mosque was inaugurated by my father, had also been impressed at the sight of this sudden construction, complete with a brand-new sloping tin roof that shone like a keen new mirror on sunny days if you looked down from the hills. The window frames and doors oozed moisture for days after the building was complete, forming tiny bubbles of viscous sap, like beaded garlands on the wood frames. But all he ever said was, 'People take ages to build their homes, yaar, and even then some don't have proper windows . . .' and although his sighing did betray some kind of vague dissatisfaction, he didn't mention his father, not even once, when the conversation turned towards matters of the mosque.

When we were mosque-less and imam-less, people seldom prayed, some almost never did ('these *kafir Gujjars*, they don't even know their namaz' was the taunt often tossed in our direction by many a townsfolk); but now, everyone seemed to be in a rush to make up for a lifetime of lost blessings, to catch up with divinity. Very soon, and almost unheralded (at least as far as I was concerned), sincere religious devotion became a priority occupation for many in the village . . . And gradually, the distant cries of Nizam-e-Mustafa started echoing in our secluded passes as well. First it was the mosque, then loudspoken azans boomed; a chubby, always perspiring Moulvi Sahib appeared from nowhere to deliver poignant Friday sermons; then there were meetings of preaching, of *dars*; and soon, very soon, people's faces changed too. The simple Baba-like beards of the older men gave way to flowing tufts of piously combed hair hanging down to their chests. Moustaches half a century old – shaped, oiled and coloured for decades – either disappeared altogether or gave way to thin, austere alterations above the new beards.

And then, quite suddenly, graffiti, enormous letters in shining green paint declaiming reminders to divine duty, appeared on the two and a half walls of the village street.

'*Surprising! You don't have time for namaz?*'

It seemed to me that whoever was doing this during the night knew the street well, from the way these godly exhortations stared at me.

The newly appeared and appointed mullah, Moulvi Sahib, was thickset, with round, almost swollen, cheeks shaking well-groomed shrubs of hair on either side of his rotund face with each nod of the head.

'You are blessed. This village is blessed now. *Alhamdulillah!* You have chosen the true path, my brothers, the right path. Please repeat with me, Khudaya . . . !'

The small crowd, in the first ever Friday prayer in Nowgam, reverberated with a big 'K-H-U-D-A-Y-A' to the cleric's guttural exhortation.

'Show us the right path, the path to heaven!'

'Show us the right path, the path to heaven!'

'*Aameen.*'

'*Aameen!*'

The congregation, mostly elders but also a fresh line of youngsters – earnest boys who had started to annoy me because their godly zeal as they walked through the village put extra pressure on me to attend – answered devoutly to the sermon the already sweating cleric was delivering. I went to the mosque the couple of times Ma insisted, this being the second. 'You can at least do Fridays, beta. What will people say if no one *ever* sees you there? What will Baba say to them? Show your face at least,' she said.

'By building this pious house of God, with your blood and sweat, you have invited Allahtaala to reside among you. The days of *kufr* are over.' The Moulvi ran his eyes around; mine searched for Hussain.

A couple of men furtively exchanged 'you see, I told you' glances with emphatic, gleaming expressions of newfound conviction.

'Cure to the sick, protection to the travelling, *rizq* to the deprived, peace to the distressed, comfort and patience to the grieving, mercy to the sinning . . .'

'*Aameen, aam* . . .' Showket aka Shokha, Compounder Chechi's overenthusiastic ten-year-old son, interrupted the Moulvi's solemn dua, his starting prayer, with a premature amen.

'. . . And may our prayers, our faith in God, steer us away from the path of *kufr* . . .'

The crowd fell silent with a reverence I had never seen before, not even during Ramazan – when some of us actually did fast, and prayed at least twice a day. Something new, strange, powerful was going to happen sometime soon – an unnamed dread had begun to settle down inside me.

The mullah, I could never place him – was he a city dweller, was he an Allahwaala from Srinagar, was he from the neighbouring town? And was he Deobandi or Barelvi, was he hardline puritan or moderate *Aetqadi* – was he even from Kashmir? Most people in our village, in fact almost all, had only ever been nominally religious. As an erstwhile nomadic tribe who had taken to landed life only after the Partition, our elders had hardly had the time, or the room, to organize their religious life. The small tin shed at the edge of our graveyard had therefore sufficed as a mosque as it was used only by a handful, and then only occasionally. All Gujjars were traditional Barelvis, many probably without even knowing it. It suited their lifestyle. Before, and even after, Baba's elders had decided to settle down and advance from travelling caravans and seasonal dhokas up in the mountains to proper houses a little below, and live close to each other and invent this new village, this Nowgam of ours, it was a traditional brand of Islam that had fulfilled their meagre spiritual needs: celebrate the two Eids, pay homage and tie a votive thread or two at a shrine once in a while, have someone in your midst know enough verses from the Quran to preside over the dead and conduct nikah, and don't forget to circumcise your boys.

'My dear brothers, these are testing times, troubled times, indeed,' the fast-colouring Moulvi Sahib continued. 'Everywhere you see, there is death and destruction! Minor girls, *your* daughters and sisters, are raped every day by filthy Indian soldiers. Just imagine. Just imagine!'

Pause. As if he knew the exact time it took the congregation to visualize their women being raped by filthy Indian soldiers. To be honest, though, I shuddered at the thought.

'Hundreds of us fall to the bullets of the oppressor, to the guns of the kafir every day. We die in hundreds, no, thousands . . . all across the land. The cruel infidel kills us, tortures us, insults us and treats us like dirt, and then throws us into jail if we protest. You are dragged out of your houses at night by stinking drunken soldiers and then they search your houses while your women, your mothers, your ready-to-wed daughters and sisters are still in bed! Crackdown after crackdown, from dawn to dusk, for days sometimes . . . *Musalmano* . . . !' The huffing Moulvi raised his voice now, puffed his chest and, reassembling his breath and fiery orator's voice, resumed. 'Our patience is being put to the ultimate test, my dear brothers. They desecrate our religion; they urinate on our grave-yards. In Srinagar they enter hundreds of mosques every day in their grimy, ugly shoes; they massacre hundreds of our brothers in broad daylight because they protest against the murder of innocent children; they burn down entire localities because they cannot catch our brave boys; they send thousands of our young men, *your* brothers, *my* brothers, to inhuman underground jails in India . . .' His voice now reached a high pitch, the coarse crescendo of an orator on the verge of breaking down.

'Not only that, my dear brothers, not only that . . .' and here his voice broke, became a shrill, quivering howl, and all we could now hear was some kind of restrained sobbing, punctuated by brief but loud hiccupy sounds.

'Brothers, please forgive me . . . Not only that, not only . . . hnnhh! . . . But in Sopore they killed the entire family of a mujahid after raping his mother and sisters because he refused to say *Jai Hind* in front of them. They didn't even spare his old grandmother – even she, even *she* was raped.' With that he brought his hand thumping down on the improvised, staircase-shaped wooden pulpit, and then at once rose with his hands held high in the air. His arms were shaking.

The crowd fell quiet. I couldn't take my eyes off him, and felt charged and upset myself before the deafening silence got to me and smothered any potential spurt of emotion.

'There is a reason for all this.' He was standing in front of the pulpit now and the voice had changed to that of someone who has just been persuaded to stop crying. 'I ask you, my brothers, *why* are we being punished like this?'

An all-heads-down silence followed.

'Aye Parwardigaar, mercy! Allahtaala is punishing us for our sins. And if that is indeed the case, my brothers, *what shall we do then*?'

No one seemed to be sure if they were supposed to answer that, or if it was just a part of the sermon. Certainly, no one knew how to change Allah's mind.

'And if that is true, my dear brothers, if Allahtaala is indeed unhappy with us, with our ways, what shall we do then, what shall we do?'

The gathering breathed through yet another faintly tense pause during which I briefly glanced at Hussain, his humble father, as well as Baba, all of whom, having arrived earlier than me, were in the first row. Their eyes were downcast, although I suspected Hussain's had been roving around the gathering before he saw me look over.

'I will tell you, *I* will tell you what we shall do. We shall seek forgiveness; we shall ask for mercy, do *tobah* for all our sins and pray as He wishes; we shall thank Him for everything; and we shall never leave the fabric of our faith, no matter what, not for anything! Those who pray five times a day and forsake the ways of the kafir – all this *naach-gana* on TV and this dirty cinema thing that they arrange sometimes – will never come in harm's way, and will escape the high fires of Jahannum, the deep burning pyres of hell!'

I noticed a tinge of exhaustion in the cleric's voice and was relieved at this first sign of an end to the sermon, but a part of me also fought coils of guilt that groaned from somewhere inside. He signalled something to a front-row worshipper, who promptly produced a copy of the holy Quran from nowhere and handed it to the now pomegranate-faced, profusely sweaty Moulvi Sahib.

Touching it to his eyes and gently kissing the red and gold Rexine cover of the holy book, he began, I guessed, the epilogue to his speech. 'I swear upon the sacred Quran that I will pray, day and night, night and day, to make this a pious village. I will pray for everyone, for every single soul. Almighty Allah, let us forsake everything that the kafirs have taught us, let everyone be a true Muslim, a momin, and come back to the House of God. Aye Parwardigaar, bless us all with Your grace and let us all feel Your presence in our hearts, and let us all feel Your hand guiding us through these testing, bleak times.'

Silence. Silence.

'Shall I see you in this mosque every day, then? Shall we all pray together from now onwards? Shall we spend our mornings and afternoons and evenings in worshipping our Khaliq, our Mabood, the creator of this universe and everything it contains, the all-powerful, the all-seeing, the one and only, all-almighty Allah? Answer me, my dear brothers, answer me!'

'*Zuroor. Zuroor!*' The crowd roared back in a booming, determined voice.

'Indeed.'

'*Alhamdulillah!*'

I was the last to shake hands with the Moulvi Sahib that day, my first and only Friday prayer, because almost everyone seemed in a rush to be touched by the grace of this new visitor in our parts. I didn't see Hussain leave on either of the two occasions I went to the mosque and assumed he had had to accompany his father home – I'd wanted to ask him more about this imam. No one knew much about him, and yet many people had cried in the very first Jumma Khutba he had delivered with such filmy drama. Perhaps I was being unfair about these men, many of whom had taken to settled sedentary life only a few years ago and were charmed by the trappings of organized communal living, of which spiritual collectiveness seemed a vital strand. Perhaps I was wrong then. Perhaps I am wrong now.

Around the same time, as the congregations grew at the mosque and our otherwise listless street began to acquire something of a buzz, newspapers from Srinagar came to be full of historic protest marches, long processions, demonstrations by oceans of people, bellicose cries for freedom (half a million marched to Chrar Sharif, braving unprecedented rain and hail), big roadside massacres as if they were our destiny (blood-streaked roads and piles of de-peopled shoes in front-page photos), decrees from this group or that one (dire warnings to those who indulge in un-Islamic activities) and condemnations of the gaasib, the brutal oppressor Hindustan ('for raping our daughters and beheading our young men and slaying our children') – all this apart from the usual death toll reports and major encounters along the Line of Control in our neighbourhood. It was strange, very strange at first, reading stuff about what had happened so close to you – so near at hand that we often heard it – coming all the way from Srinagar more than a hundred kilometres away. What the newspapers said was entirely different from the evening Doordarshan news that Baba and I watched on our wood-encased, shuttered Weston TV, so I always waited for the papers, which sometimes took all day to get to us, or just tuned in, with Baba again, to the crackling BBC news on his leather-bound Philips Jai Jawan transistor.

The urgency of the radio broadcasts, which others also listened to keenly, like my father, lent a sense of excitement, however second-hand, to the street. Small corner huddles, of elders crouched around a newspaper, was something I was seeing in the street for the first time in my life. It was as if people waited for 'it', not that anyone knew exactly what, to reach the village. We were, after all, the remotest village from Srinagar, and other towns, where it was all happening.

In the black and white, smudgy pages of the Daily Aftab and Srinagar Times and a new paper ominously called The Daily Toll, I saw roadfuls of azadi-crying people on the streets; I saw columns and columns of masked militants – our heroes, our boys – marching openly with their weapons (and I did try, more than a few times, to imagine myself as one of them); I saw women and children and the elderly cheering the future martyrs on; I saw cinemas burned, wine shops splintered colourfully on the city streets, jeans making way for Khan dresses, video cassettes seized and broken spectacularly in town centres, and grandiose statements declaring independence by militant commanders covered in their Palestinian headscarves. But I also saw white shrouded bodies, neatly, piously, sadly, lined up for

Namaz-e-Jinazah like rows and rows of porcelain dolls; I saw martyrs' graveyards multiplying like eager new housing colonies; and I saw grieving men and women in hospitals and the blank, sad faces of fresh orphans. I also saw intensely worded, longwinded statements from Nawaz Sharif and Benazir Bhutto, and someone called Hamid Gul Dupandalal, promising untiring and eternal moral support to the hapless Kashmiris. Along with statements and unanimous resolutions and moral support and guns and ammunition from Pakistan also came poignant calls for Islam (*as if we'd had anything else*), for Nizam-e-Mustafa.

And, just as we'd never had a mosque before that, some of us felt we had to do a lot in a very short time. Catch up with the rest of the world, make quick ground, be a part of the momentous times, do something. Make up for lost blessings. Do something.

Khadim Hussain, even though he himself was a first-row worshipper and leading light of the Masjid Committee, couldn't entirely succeed in persuading his son to follow a five-a-day routine along with him. Hussain preferred to run away and spend time with us instead. For a brief while, though – for three weeks, I think – he was drafted as a boy-muezzin, his sonorous *Allah-o-Akbar* waking up even the most hard-boned, steadfast non-worshippers in the village, but he quickly gave it up, and, meeting us soon after he'd stopped, he told us that he had been getting scared in the mosque, waiting all by himself as he did in the small hours before bleary-eyed people started trickling in, wearing the sullen, ghostly faces of the early morning.

'If you don't want to pray, don't. If you don't want to come out of your warm, er, comfortable beds, don't!' He was already colouring with excitement. 'But don't leave me alone in that frigid chamber with the Moulvi Sahib. It gets eerie sometimes,' his protesting voice so different, so childlike.

'Ha, ha, ha . . . Hussain, I know you, I know you well, yaara, all these days you have just been looking for an excuse to avoid getting up early, isn't it?' I replied, circling my arm around his shoulders.

'If you want, I can stop singing as well.' He suddenly stiffened and broke away from me. He had always been a bit touchy.

I shut up quickly when I met the unduly intense gaze of three other pairs of eyes.

And then he left.

Hussain.

Did you leave to prove some point? Are you now a martyr to some secret dream of yours? Did you lose yourself to deny us the promise you held? Weeks, months ago, did you sound a veiled warning when you sang, with complete filmy melodrama, that sad old song while we laughed our everyday laughs?

> *Tum mujhe yun bhula na paoge*
> *Haan Tum mujhe yun bhula na paoge*
> *Jab kabhi bhi suno ge geet mere*
> *Sang sang tum bhi gun gunaoge*
>
> You won't be able to get over me thus
> Whenever you hear my song
> You will find yourself singing along

I guess I'd always liked him the most. I'd liked him for his gentle ways, for his voice, for his manner with people, for the way he always combed back his wet hair with his silver-coated pocket comb as soon as we'd finished our daily swims in the river, for the way he always adopted a serious tone when I talked to him about Asma, and for his simple, unworldly views on life.

'I don't ever, ever want to leave Nowgam; I want to stay here all my life. Mouj says this place needs a school of its own; I think I will open a big school here when I'm older, where *I* will teach everything. There will also be music and singing. Do you know how many songs Mouj knows? I'll teach all the students so that they can sing her songs after the Morning Prayer,' he had said that day, long after closing his sad song, while we basked in the sleepy afternoon sun by the stream.

'And who shall think about getting a job and helping his family?' Ashfaq responded in his usual deadpan manner, not even bothering to look up. 'People here want to earn a living when they grow up, *son*, not become useless sentimental singers.'

'Why don't you help my father yourself, then, since you think I don't give much thought to it?' Hussain retorted, while also turning to give me a barely noticeable, pleading look. I sensed a faint trembling beneath his severe tone.

Why did you leave?

Ma was worried, worried sick, when he disappeared. In her flushed face and tightly pursed lips she betrayed her anger.

He had gained considerable fame in the area owing to his Azaan days and his general reputation as a mini singing star. He was thought to be the gifted one, the charmer, the bright future of his household, the big hope of our small nondescript hamlet, and the would-be claim to fame for a generation that had spent half its life adding to their livestock and the remaining half settling down as zamindar Gujjars, the landed nomads. More than half the girls at school had, not so secretly, spun elaborate stories of how they would bring Hussain's wedding party to their doorstep one day. Hussain, our local celebrity. Our centrepiece. His poor and pious father's son. His mother's last stand. My friend among friends, my soulmate. By leaving, by disappearing like that, he hurt a lot of people. He shocked us all. He hurt my mother. She had fed him so many lunches and toffees and precious dried apricots from Ladakh that I sometimes wondered whether I should have been jealous of him.

And maybe I *was* jealous of him, of all of them. Of their talents. I couldn't do anything special, except for playing cricket and reading books, whereas they, they could sing, read palms, talk philosophy, carve beautiful things with their hands, write poetry, run like wild deer, talk to girls, everything.

'I can't believe he has fled; what will his mother do now? Poor ill-starred woman,' Ma said, forcefully shaking a quilt which yielded clouds of dust that hung over her head in the sunlight seeping through to the balcony. Ma's red face, sweaty forehead and chin, and her thick arms, her sleeves rolled up as always, shone in the soft light. Her hennaed hair became translucent. I found the stick she was looking for to hit the quilt with and handed it to her hesitantly. She was angry. 'Such a gentle boy, such a handsome boy, curse on those who misled him. Curse on this cross-border drama.' She started thrashing the old quilt. Whack.

'You know him, Maa . . .' I spoke slowly so as not to betray any signs of my own distress. 'He will be back soon. It must be one of those moods he gets into, you know.' I knew I didn't sound convincing.

She gave the antique, a-thousand-and-one-sleep-nights-old, red and blue striped quilt a big wham. The dust spread with it half-remembered smells of sleep, wintry nights and my childhood.

'You must be readying yourself too, then, haan? You think we don't know anything, hero . . . !' She said with renewed anger. 'With your best friend disappearing like this, you must also be waiting for an opportunity to slip out, haan? But remember, remember, I'm your mother, I know everything.'

Another blow. The mountains responded in kind.

'But Ma . . .'

'If you go, you will never, *ever* see my face again!'

Another loud, forceful strike.

'But Ma, I'm not going anywhere, it's not my fault if he –' I protested weakly, suddenly finding myself guilty somehow, for no reason . . . for Hussain, for not being altogether sure if I had not already contemplated following Hussain myself.

But I still tried to press on. 'I haven't done anything, Ma. If someone chooses to go, you know, what can I do? I don't want to join him. He didn't tell me!'

'Look, beta, nothing will come out of all this – this gun-shun business – it's just not going to work, they beat up people very badly, they kill . . . And what else does the Army do, kill, kill . . .' Ma knew exactly when to switch from elderly anger to parental concern. She rolled down the sleeves of her shirt. Her strong arms were aglow, and almost bulging from the violence of her quilt-whacking.

'I know, Ma. I'm not going anywhere. Trust me.' I lied.

The truth is, Ma suspected me of harbouring a secret plan to flee after Hussain, and then the others, left. Nothing would allay her fears – and now I know my attempts at absolute discretion didn't go unnoticed, after all – until I joined college and spent the next year and a half either going to the street, to Noor Khan's shop, walking from home to the Government Degree College and back the few times I did go to attend classes, or reading the few books from the office-sized college library for the umpteenth time. While they had left to become brave cohorts of the fight for freedom, I ended up staying back to face the blame for their act and for 'my betrayal in having known everything all along'. For weeks, the whole village hissed with suspicion every time I passed. No one for a moment thought that I was the one betrayed here. I'm not even sure if it was accidental that they followed each other – I think it was all well planned and kept secret from me till the last minute, till the very last moment. And that's how I ended up not going in the end.

I did try, though.

One evening we were chatting away in the street – Gul Khan doling out fresh gossip about Compounder Chechi's daughter and how she still didn't wear anything under her loose pheran, revealing her pear-shaped breasts (Gul's phrase), one bigger than the other (Gul's view), every time she leaned forward – and the next evening he was gone. Baba, looking glum and confused, had brought the news home from the evening prayer gathering in the mosque. Hussain was missing and all his woollens – whatever he had – were gone too. That's how his father had started to believe the unthinkable, Baba said.

No farewells, no goodbyes. He didn't even do a final song. On a sad Monday evening, with the sweet musk of late autumn seeping into everything, just my father saying that Hussain's father was saying . . . I guess that's why I didn't believe it at first, like so many in the village. Like Mohammed, like Gul and Ashfaq must have – or so I thought then.

His father's long-boots are missing too.

He had been buying biscuits, walnuts and almonds every other day, obviously for the long trek, isn't it?

Didn't he appear rather suspicious in the last few days?

No, no, he looked lost, that faraway look in his eyes, uff Khudaya!

This was waiting to happen. He is just the first one. How long could we remain unaffected . . . ?

All of them must have known. They must have egged the poor boy on.

No, no . . .

Poor boy.

Poor man.

Poor mother.

3   *The Kitchen Garden*

It's morning. My body aches. Last night, I was feverish. One of my many fever nights. One of these days I should go to a bank in town and deposit all this money. I look out of the window and see ragged clouds struggling against the breeze. I want to go down for my tea and breakfast but don't want to climb down the stairs. Sometimes I find the house too big for me. My room is on the first floor, directly above the kitchen. I must be the only one with a proper bed in the area; everyone else used to sleep on the floor. Baba got it for me after I'd been whining about not being able to read lying down on the floor. Ma and Baba's room has a balcony, the only balcony of the house, but it's partly occupied with hay, dried vegetables that Ma's hung from a red plastic string, and loose sacks of sawdust, firewood and overdried pine cones for our winter fuel. In the morning the house smells of grass, water and salt tea. Ma makes a full samovar because all of us drink a lot of it. The hundred-rupee notes smell of Kadian, his pungent office, and sometimes of the peon as well. Baba says it's not safe keeping cash in the house, although I wonder who would dare to break into one of the highest houses in the area and risk being chased down a steep slope by an ancient 303-wielding man. And working with Kadian *has* made me some-what fearless too. I seem to be afraid of nothing. Not outside his premises at least.

I don't have much use for the money. Baba's still got enough to insist on running the house. Ma hasn't gone out in the last couple of years, apart from collecting firewood from the forest and her long afternoons in her kitchen garden at the back of the house. I can't believe it – all these months and she's perfectly at peace with this life. But then, I haven't gone far since college either. That, too, seems ages ago now. Money. I want to give it to Hussain's family, but I can't find them now, they're gone; and even if they were here I wouldn't just be able to walk up to his mother and say, 'Here's some cash, I wanted to give it to Hussain, but since he's . . . you know . . . can you please take it?' They are gone, all gone. Why did he have to leave? I would have given it all to him. But then, I wouldn't have had this money if he were still here, isn't it?

I'm not visiting Kadian today, but maybe I should go down anyway. I could check some fresh arrivals a little more closely. Attention to detail, you see. You never know what they might throw up. Sometimes they have papers on them: letters, photographs, cards, cash, poems, diaries, messages for someone's family and things like that. I should spend some more time on these things some day, look at them, read them.

Once in a while I think the peon does much more than just make tea in Kadian's cabin. Maybe he's the Captain's spy, his other eyes, his extra hands, tentacles, his undertaker of dark grisly tasks that I would never be able to do. You can do so much with the unclaimed dead, who knows what they have been doing with the bodies that are not down there? For all we know, the peon might be the post-mortem ripper here, the handler of body parts and organs – the harvester of Kadian's crops. I read somewhere kidneys sell for a good price in India; and people do donate their eyes after death, isn't it? So you know what I mean, it's not as if they need to ask for anyone's permission around here. The peon, the peon, the slimy evil peon, I just don't like the way he looks, you know, he's got this look of – how do I say? – murky mysterious deeds about him. And maybe he really does do it all for Captain Kadian, you never know.

Baba eyes me briefly, as always, and then looks the other way as I step out of the house. 'You haven't had lunch? Eat something,' he can't help shouting from the hallway when I leave.

'I'm not hungry, Baba. Will eat something later, when I come back,' I shout back and am already out of earshot. He knows I say that every time.

I don't eat lunch these days. Helps me spend time down in the valley without throwing up. I prefer to eat a big dinner in the evening instead, after I have come back. That way I also sleep a little better.

The wide, terraced footpath from our house curves right at the bottom of the plateau to meet the village street. The street is a brief dirt track, wider than the footpath. Beyond the street the track picks up again, ascending steadily over a hillock, and then falls into the small pass that goes into the valley. This path to the valley is full of aged round stones paved into the earth, with common grass holding them tight in their place like jewels crafted into some vast design. It is about half a kilometre long – eaten into in places by reckless, drifting streams flowing from the slopes above – and probably runs parallel, by some distance, to the boundary of the army camp in the woods on the left. The machine-gun pickets are scattered somewhere towards the far edge, hidden, away from the boundary, close to the ridge. The track is good enough for cattle, bullock carts and army jeeps, not that the latter use it. I'm carrying my rucksack – I am often irritated at Kadian for keeping his binoculars so close at hand all the time, and now my bag's already become a similar appendage. Not only do I hang it from my shoulder, I also always keep one of the strings in my hand. What if I drop it and never notice?

Bees hum along the way, circle briefly over my head and then go back to their flowers, which are spread over the thick bushes jutting out of the otherwise plain, deforested lower slopes of our mountains. What do I smell of? Dead people, soap, hunger, mother's silence, bad dreams, my fever, lost friends, father's looks, Kadian's whisky, tea?

The bushes on the left of the track, these scrawny strokes on the melancholy landscape, this thicket of bushes, something happened here . . . ? Oh yes, yes, Ashfaq once set fire to it. He didn't mean to, or perhaps he hadn't imagined it would actually flare up like that, but after the initial alarm, he started to enjoy himself. What would he say to what I see now? Probably some vague abstraction on life and death: 'Beauty doesn't live for ever. It dies with everything that dies.' Ashfaq was like that, you know – moody, somewhat unpredictable, crazy even. Once, not too long ago, during one of his tedious batting episodes down in the valley, he stopped in the middle of the wicket and started cursing India and Pakistan. Mohammed had been constantly bowling on Ashfaq's off stump, making life very difficult for him since he couldn't make room to execute his murderous sweeps, and, failing for the umpteenth time, and as the evening shelling on the border seemed to be getting louder, he whacked the stumps out of the ground with a furious blow of the bat and started shouting. We fell silent at once, half in amusement, half in shock, and waited for him to calm down and carry on playing . . . but the shelling became fiercer still. I noticed a tremor run through his body, and it was just then that he let out a loud shriek as if something deep within him had come unstuck. He hit the wicket three times and said, 'They are making this a *jahannum*, we are all consigned to this hell! Look, look, look how they have killed that mountain.' He pointed into the high mountains. 'Look at that forest they have just scorched, look! If only, if only they were themselves at the receiving end some day . . . They will, some day they will, huh . . .' He seemed to have exhausted himself, while we looked on in silence, and then he quickly went to collect the uprooted stumps and started digging them back into the ground again. As if nothing had happened. The shelling waned soon after the sudden outburst. This was when I first noticed that the shelling from both sides had become more intense and frequent.

When I approach the end of the path, I begin to see the crows again, more crows than I have ever seen in my life. They look like hordes of black insects, creatures plucked out from their lightless holes and thrown on to the white sheet of a sky, flying up and down, up and down – what have you found now that gives you such heady freedom?

What if they aren't real, you know, only a figment of my imagination? But then they do look real, so real. From where I stand, close to the end of the path and just about to descend into the trough they keep diving into, I could extend my hand and grab them. Now they are there, now they are not.

Captain Kadian says he likes collecting ID cards of dead people and he has no use for what he calls 'sundry objects', unless I stumble across something very valuable. As if these folks are given Rolexes as parting gifts when they leave their training camps in Azad Kashmir. But since I'm not too interested in things like watches either, I leave them for the peon. Some of the other objects I've found sit assorted in the rucksack now; some day I need to clean up the bag as well. Wonder what the old man will do with them – take them to his pyre, after he's cleaned them of grime, blood, decaying flesh, rotting time . . . ?

Most of the watches I find are *Made in China*, in fact almost all the stuff these guys carry is Chinese.

Chinese boots.

Chinese pistols.

Chinese caps.

Chinese monkey caps.

Chinese compasses, as if . . .

Chinese grenades (I wonder how TV-wallahs always manage to say that the arms and ammunition seized had Pakistan Army markings on it – they can't be that stupid).

Chinese jackets.

Chinese pens.

Chinese bullets.

Turns out beneath all the green is a crimson red.

This middle-aged man, bearded, who I find lying on top of three or four (difficult to tell) possibly younger men – he must've bullied them into this – is carrying, among other things, an audio Quran, a small portable cassette player. Even that is Chinese. Lazy, useless Saudis.

I switch it on and am startled to hear it working at once. I listen to someone's high-pitched, shrill rendition for a while, get scared, switch it off and then on again, and have already decided to give it to Ma one of these days. Strange, listening to someone from some faraway land reciting the Quran, for my ears alone, in a place where the only religious rendition I ever listened to was Hussain's mournful voice singing elegiac songs, *nowhas* and *marsias*, during

Moharram. His mother was, is, Shia. 'I don't feel good about film songs during these days, and mother's not going to be pleased if she knows. It's not good,' he would say.

It is quite scary, listening to this electronic piety, this accidental harbinger of divine bodings, bestowing Allahtaala-knows-what vows and oaths and promises on the scores of the silent dead at my feet. I feel like I am conducting some sacred ceremony over the carcasses scattered around me, some ominous weight of responsibility suddenly weighing on my shoulders as soon as I look around while the portable player plays holy verses in a half-grave tone. I don't know what the verses mean, though, for as I said, there was little emphasis on religious learning when we were young, and in any case they don't teach us Arabic translation . . . I guess they, I mean the city folks in Srinagar and elsewhere, are not entirely wrong when they taunt us for not being able to follow all the tenets of the faith.

The middle-aged man bears a resemblance to a lot of people I have seen. He looks like any schoolteacher-turned-imam-turned-militant leader. Pot-bellied (although punctured now, holes the size of potholes revealing ugly, scorched-brown entrails), and dressed in too many clothes, he could easily pass for a dreaded militant commander if Kadian wanted him to. And who knows, perhaps he already has this man on camera, probably even from the time when he was still talking, a 'peace-loving citizen' voice-over denouncing 'Pakistan for misleading him and other peace-loving people of Kashmir into waging a proxy war that now engulfs the entire population of the state, of this *Sufi*, mystic land'. Such a rude, big joke!

'. . . One day masked militants came home, threatened us, and said if I didn't join them, they would kill my family. I had no choice . . . But now I want to surrender, there's nothing to be gained by all this . . . I appeal to all my misguided brothers to do the same . . . and join the national mainstream . . .' Perhaps he's already been recorded, packed and posted, you never know with the Captain. But I should carry the ID card (fake obviously) anyway, those are my orders, even though today is my day off.

By the way, what's this long-beard, audio-Quran-carrying portly man going to be called, what's his name going to be? Let's take a guess. Something with 'ullah' or 'Islam' at the end, of course, but that's easy, let's try and be a little more specific. Saif-ul Islam, Junaid-ul-Islam, Mushtaq-ul-Islam, I-am-Islam?

Anyhow, the card – everyone, as I said, has to carry an ID here, even the militants, even the dead! – in stencilled red print says: Shuja Naqshbandi.

ID in the bag, tape in the side pocket, my day's work is done. The crows have disappeared. Not a single black shadow across the sky now. Well fed and satiated, they must have gone back to their dismal nests, asleep, intoxicated on someone's young flesh. Do they pluck with their ugly beaks at the tender tissue on Gul Khan's fair face? When I look back for a last glimpse of the day after climbing up to the beginning of the path home, I think I see those dogs circling near the periphery again.

Have they grown fatter or am I just seeing things?

Ma will be happy with the electronic Quran. It could be her very personal narrator from the holy book. *Something* I can do for her at last. When I was a boy, Baba would occasionally invite this nice old moulvi and his sidekicks from someplace near Handwara town for an evening of Quran-Khwani, of solemn recitations of Soorah-e-Yassin, over steaming, aromatic almond and saffron *kehwa* followed by at least a five-course dinner cooked by the only *waza* in Gujjar-land, the shabbily clad and prohibitively smelly cook-cum-handyman-cum-carpenter Gulla` Shah. This happened at least twice a year. I often spied the two trainee mullahs double-speed through the verses when Baba went out of the room. Ma's contentment knew no bounds, even days after the event, for the endless blessings it brought to the house. 'It keeps our home secure, beta, no one can ever, ever harm us,' she told me one autumn evening, sitting near the door to the living room, immersed in the cyclical recitations of the three men seated behind the heavy curtain made out of an old grey blanket. Men who didn't want to see her face to face.

Ma doesn't talk much now, except for the rare occasion when she's angry. In fact, she has said so very little for such a long time that I don't even remember – two years, three, for ever . . .

Instead, she spends most of the day in her kitchen garden at the back of the house. There's a majestic view of the mountains from there – a soaring, suddenly rising sheet of rich dark green throbbing with mysterious life beneath the foliage. Someone always whistles in the dark. It's a neat little patch she's cultivated here, my mother, all by herself. I like it too. In fact, that's the only time I spend with her now. She doesn't mind my being there with her while she's tending to her creations. I do precious little by way of helping but I watch. Ma reaches and bends, plucks and mends – the various inhabitants of her magic grove bowing to her every wish. Often, she emerges flushed and coloured from the work, crouching for hours as she does amidst the low hedges and rows and beds of her leafy plants and herbs. Her broad forehead shines, eyes sparkle with vigour, the few wrinkles on her face fill with sweat, a bead or two collecting gradually, and precariously, at the tip of her shining chin. Ma is beautiful. Still.

Do I see a glint of sadness in her eye when she watches me watching her? Is she wondering how I'm still here; *if* I'm really still here? I want to ask her how she feels, how she copes, what she thinks, what she sees, how she lives – but there is no point. She won't say a word beyond a few syllables. She seems so beyond worry now.

Square partitions separate the produce in Ma's garden. Green chillies, tomatoes, aubergines, cucumbers, potatoes, wild mint – she grows them all with motherly attention. The chillies are thin but gleaming green. I like looking at them, hanging as they are from their slender branches, and managing to suggest promise in their lopsided aspect on the plant. Ma picks a few every day. Miniature canals irrigate the garden; she pours a bucket at one end and the water reaches the beds in no time. It's a raw smell that wafts up when she waters the garden: dry, dug-up soft earth meeting fresh water and gently flattening under the weight of the cold liquid. Looks like the end of waiting. Friendly insects and worms float briefly, enjoying their short escapades on the running water, before clinging on to floating twigs for support. The borders of the garden are fenced, feebly, with wilted conifer shoots and stout stumps of axed fir wood. Baba worked hard on them. The cucumber plants cling dearly to the fence and stick out stunted cucumbers here and there. Mother insists on growing cucumbers, even though she knows it's a little too high for them to prosper. Nonetheless, the plants look handsome. Her tomatoes are like any other . . . and she's got too many of them. Sometimes I want to crush them and mangle them with my feet and hands; break the tiny, hairy stems into garbled trash; smash the unripe ones into raw pulp and smear the ground with it! The tomato plants, I don't know why. It's a fleeting feeling, though, and I haven't reached a point of no return yet.

Ma tills, digs, packs, repairs, irrigates, ever so silently, except for the jingle of her large gold earrings. I never noticed when she became a hermit. Just the occasional 'hmm-haan-no-yes', and that, too, only when I ask her something. 'Wouldn't it be better if you put some polythene sheets over the aubergines at night, Ma?' In her long, heavy pheran, I always fear she might trip over during her gardening hours, but it doesn't seem to bother her.

Sometimes, I see Baba watching from the window above us. I watch my mother, my father watches me – how's that for family conversation?

One of these days I may find Hussain in Kadian's farm, happily ensconced in the midst of his fellow-travellers. What would be left of the handsome face, the large forehead of good fortune, the thick head of wavy hair, the prominent mole on the left cheek, the absent-minded gaze and those tremulous hands that were always ready with a tune and played an air harmonium at the slightest hint of a song? What would be left?

Would he suddenly break into song from the depths of this lifeless desolation and enliven the deathly setting? Would he spring to life and shake off the blood and ash from his face? Would he raise his arms and enact that old sad song again, leaning against a brooding willow, eyes downcast and voice inflected with agony over a beloved's departure, while tall shadows steadily close in?

Would Ashfaq yet again fall silent after listening to him sing? Would Mohammed clap his big, loud clap and attempt to lift our master entertainer on his shoulders? Would they all be here? Together, even in dismembered death.

Would I, the left-out unworthy leader of the pack, beg them to let me in, to let me sit with them, to let me talk, to let me share my secrets . . . ? Please, please, please don't leave, don't leave me alone. Please, please let me in, let's get together like old times, just once more, just this last time, just let me listen to him sing and let me hear what you say and let me know when you get lost and let me feel where it hurts and let me see how you die.

Would you sing to me again?

4   *After Hussain*

Gul Khan was hunched on the floor, alone in his small *kouthir*, and appeared quite glum – something I had seldom seen before. His dark eyes downcast, he looked drawn even from where I was standing in the small room at the end of their hallway. From above, I could see the curls of his eyelashes. He was wearing a new, bottle-green kurta pyjama. It was the first time I had seen him after hearing news of Hussain's disappearance; I knew they would have gone home together, they always did, after our usual huddle in the street the evening before.

Gul's older brother, Farooq 'Hero' Khan, had eyed me briefly when he opened the door to their house, before showing me where Gul was. Farooq always wore neatly ironed clothes; it was rumoured he spent hours getting the creases on his shirts and trousers right, whereas Gul wore the same Khan dress or kurta-pyjama suit for days on end. The brothers were as different from each other as a big brother and a picked-on younger brother can be. Farooq spent a lot of time on his hair, turning puffs and curls and doing or undoing left, middle and right partings, as the fashion of the day, or perhaps of last year, demanded. I often thought that with his tight shirts and 'zero-degree' clean shaves, those big Khan family eyes, fashionable hair and his generally with-it looks, he could have been the sidekick of a Bollywood villain, rather than the 'Hero' – which poorer kids in the village had ironically nicknamed him, but which Farooq had taken in all seriousness and seemed to be trying to live up to. But I did not *really* dislike him. After all, he wasn't a serious bully – and we were never scared of him, just irritated sometimes.

Gul Khan's house had the air of the well-provided household that it was, untidy enough to reveal surplus income spilling out in the form of grains and flour from hoarded containers and sacks of cattle feed. A sack of flour here and a bag of lentils there; some spare canisters of P-Mark mustard oil were also lined up in the main hall-way. Bright blue plastic jars of Dalda Vanaspati ghee too. Flecks of straw clung to the top of the cooking-oil tins, overlaid by a layer of sleeping brown dust. Outside, hens and roosters cluck-clucked relentlessly in their shit-floored, wire-mesh enclosure that stood behind the house. Three or four large square tins of Verka spray-dried milk powder were also stacked up on top of each other. Everything spoke of settled domestic plenitude. Gul Khan's father, Sharafat Khan Teetwaali – Gul preferred not to utter his surname too often because he feared it was susceptible to frivolous nick-names – was a very well-off man by the standards of our village. He had long established himself as a supplier of quality mutton to *koth-daars*, big meat dealers in the towns, and occasionally, but only rarely, to the army langar-men as well, if they came down from their check-posts near the LoC. After Baba, if anyone carried weight in Nowgam, by the sheer force of his wealth it was Gul's father. Farooq Khan's errant behaviour, Ma once said, was because he had been spoiled by a family that didn't need their sons to work too hard on anything. Although she had to concede that Gul had turned out quite well. 'It's the company he keeps,' she had joked, pinching my ears fondly. She doesn't do that any more.

'Gulla, salam, how are you, brother, what's up . . . ?' I said as I finally sat down opposite him. I wanted to get to the point as soon as possible but, at the same time, I worried that I may say something wrong. There was a lot I didn't know in those days.

He didn't say anything. I waited.

'Gulla, what happened? Have you taken an oath of silence or something? I'm not putting up with any of that sort of shit today, yaara, I'm telling you . . .' I went closer and started rubbing his shoulders gently; he always warmed up to that.

'Did he say anything to you, Gulla? You did leave together that day. I mean the evening before he left, didn't you? I'm sure he must have said something, done something . . . ?'

Gul Khan wouldn't open his mouth.

After Hussain's sudden departure, I hadn't seen anyone for a full week. Every single morning, I wanted to run to Mohammed's, Ashfaq's or Gul's, but I was kept away, every time, by Ma's sad, worried face. After a week, however, I just could not live with not knowing anything any longer and ran off to Gul. And even though the thought of going after Hussain had already crossed my mind a few times, especially during the nights, I didn't plan to share the idea with Gul. I first wanted to ask him what had happened that evening, since they would have surely gone home together. Gul Khan's house was near the shops, in the small lane off the village street – theirs was one of the very few houses on it – and Hussain's modest cottage of wood and unbaked earthen bricks was further up at the end of the lane in the middle of their maize field, apparently their only source of sustenance.

'I don't know *anything*, Gulla. Please tell me something, for God's sake – what happened?'

He looked up finally and looked at me plaintively. 'I don't know either, yaar. I really don't know, I swear to God, I don't know anything,' he blurted out, eyes downcast again.

'You were the last person he met, I mean apart from his family I guess, so how come . . . ?'

'Yes, yes, we did go home together but he didn't say much. We just had some small talk about this and that, and then I reached home.'

'So a day before he leaves home, parts with his family, leaves us all, to cross into Pakistan, into Azad Kashmir, to be a gunman, a freedom fighter, he didn't say a word to you!' I heard myself shriek.

'Well, did he say anything to *you*?'

I imagined Hussain's present situation – for surely he must be in some training camp now, part of a tanzeem. But I couldn't really think beyond that – where, when and how would I go?

'Okay, okay, did he say anything to Ashfaq or Mohammed? Have you seen them?'

'Well, we do see each other in the masjid. You know that . . . If you came too, you would've also –'

'All right, all right, don't start on that right now . . . But there must have been something, for God's sake, some little thing, please remember. You know, when did he decide, how, why? Him of all people?'

The hens and the roosters picked up their conversation after a brief lull. Farooq started singing along to his two-speaker tape recorder somewhere in the house.

'I told you, I swear, I don't remember anything he said. Why don't you believe me?' He was trying hard not to raise his voice. He now unfolded one of his legs, the left, and lengthened it straight in front of me. 'And it doesn't matter now, does it? You know where he's gone, I know, everyone knows. He's gone means he's gone, and the best we can do is pray for his safety. It's very tough out there, I have heard, and with this heavy shelling and firing going on all the time, you never know what will happen, you never know.'

Gul Khan looked at me but seemed lost, as if he were addressing someone else.

I pictured Hussain running through a rain of shells and bombs. Fire and smoke from some black and white Doordarshan film filled the scene. It didn't make sense. It made me sad again. I should really be with Hussain, I thought, by his side, in it together with him.

'Why did he go, Gulla . . . ? What happened?'

'I don't know.'

Suddenly, I didn't know what to say any more.

'But the guides are supposed to be very good,' Gul Khan resumed after a long, suffocating silence.

'Farooq Bhaijan was saying that these people who live higher up in the woods, they, I mean their men, their boys, are very good, and they have been going across for a very long time, earns them good money, he said.'

What about them? I wondered.

'They cross the border like the old times. Apparently, it's no big deal for them. Until recently they didn't even know it was not allowed to cross the LoC, until all this started,' Gul added.

I sensed a small opening, finally.

'Okay, okay, Gulla, listen to me, do you know any of these people . . . ? Does Farooq know anyone? Someone who might know someone who went with Hussain, you know.'

'I don't know, yaara, how do I know?' Gul snapped, but then took a long breath, sighed and began afresh . . . 'Farooq was saying there's this man, Shaban Khatana, who lives just across the hill, he's the man whose sons have been going back and forth. If you . . . ?'

Gul didn't need to finish his sentence. I patted him on the shoulder and left.

The name Khatana had suddenly come back to me, worryingly quickly I suppose. It brought back the memory of good old Shaban Khatana, or Shaban Chacha as we called him, the eager old handyman who had helped with, in fact oversaw from start to finish, the repairs Baba had put the house through many, many years earlier; I must have been nine or ten then. Good old Shaban Chacha.

If it was indeed his sons who were cross-border guides, I could surely go and see him, find out, there was no harm in that, though the immediate thought of that brought up some guilt (I had never thought of Shaban Chacha all these years – the usual fate, I suppose, of people who work in your house, especially when it's a headman's house and you are the son), and some fresh uncertainty too. After all, I had no idea what I would say to him – not, 'Chacha, can you please ask your son to take me across the border to Pakistan? I am missing my militant friend . . .'

Anyhow, I had to make up my mind – something had come over me. While everyone seemed sort of reconciled to Hussain's going across the border, and many even admired him for being the first one from the village, I just couldn't be at peace with it. I didn't understand it, couldn't understand it. What made him 'join', how had it all come about, who was behind it? Although he could be somewhat impressionable at times, he wasn't someone to be swayed so easily. There was something else to it, there had to be. He had rarely, if ever, talked about politics, about India or the Indian Army, about JKLF or the Hizb, about Pakistan.

Perhaps I was stung more by being left out of it, by not knowing anything about it, than by his actual absence. Maybe. Maybe not. But stung I was – deeply, terribly stung. He should have told me, he should have . . . I could still go, though, go after him, meet him midway even, meet him and stay with him, join his cause, if that was possible, you never know – there was a busy cross-border fair on in those days, and if some fashionable city boys could come all the way from Srinagar, I could surely hop over a couple of mountains.

Two days later, as the evening got darker the next-door hill felt steeper than it actually was. There was a modest gathering of stars, concentrated on a small patch of the sky that seemed to look down directly on us. Gul had protested hard when I first mentioned this expedition, trying to sound as casual as I could be, 'How about meeting him, this Shaban Khatana? Perhaps he may know something? What do you say, shall we go pay him a visit? It's just a short trek; there's no harm in it.'

'No, no. What's the point? It's not safe. And what will they think at home? I don't want them to get suspicious. My brother will thrash me, man!' he had shot back.

'Oh, come on, Gulla, we'll be back in just a few hours, I promise. Come, come, otherwise I'll never, ever talk to you . . .'

We climbed and climbed now, it just didn't seem to end, but it did fend off fresh protestations from Gul. You ask very few questions when you are panting from climbing a mountain wall. With a heavy mist pressing against us, walking uphill felt more arduous than I'd imagined. From time to time, I would grab hold of an overhanging branch and pull at it to help me wade through the thick air. Gul had slipped into thoughts of the night sky perhaps.

'Are you really sure?'

'Yes, yes, we can at least try, yaara, find out what we can. Who did he go with? Did he get there safely? Don't *you* want to know?'

I thought it best to be constantly on the offensive with Gul that night, didn't want him to contemplate too much on the sudden adventure I had sort of forced him, blackmailed him, to undertake with me, and I surely didn't want him to wonder or quiz me about my own motives, didn't want him to suspect anything – of course, when I think of it now, I realize how pathetic, naïve, I was.

'Yesss . . . I do,' he said with deliberate emphasis, and immediately then I felt sorry for having made him feel guilty, 'but this might take a long time, yaar . . . and we are not even sure where we're going.'

'Please, Gulla, please, we are already halfway up, and I know where to go . . . We can't back down now?' I said, almost imploring, and that seemed to silence him again.

My feet skidded downward a little every time we hit a mossy patch but I somehow plodded on. Soon, I could see the dim lights of a dhoka a few hundred feet above. I realized, with unexpected delight, that these were the lights that I had first thought were fire-flies. My forefathers lived like this, I imagined – even my grandfather had lived in a cabin made of wood and packed clay like the one I was headed towards now. Ma's baba, the first man to set foot in these parts, the first man to build a summerhouse in this part of Kashmir, far, far away from his clansmen somewhere near Poonch in Jammu, lived like this. Gul Khan's well-to-do family with their hoard of rice and flour and spray-dried milk must have lived like this . . . But we'd long given up this life; we were, as Baba some-times liked to say, Kashmiri Gujjars now. This was the only Gujjar village, the only village in fact, in these parts. You often see smoke coming out of a Gujjar dhoka – they are either cooking something for now or baking buffalo cheese cookies for storing – but I was sur-prised that they should be cooking so late in the evening.

Shaban Khatana's place was much bigger than the ones I had seen elsewhere. It was a massive box fixed stubbornly on the hillside, with its fat logs of wood – entire deodars and pines – forced firmly into the sloping ground. Dark trees loomed large around us. We were in the heart of the jungle. I looked up and there was no sky now, only night. The stars had begun to dim. Gul still seemed lost in some lovelorn thoughts. I began to feel the exhaustion of the climb as soon as we got to the front of the house. But I had other things on my mind too . . . *What would I say to Shaban Chacha? Would he even recognize me?* Under the pale arc of Baba's Eveready torch that I'd borrowed, without permission, for the expedition, the door revealed itself as four vertically split logs joined together, with ancient map-shaped earth filling the gaps. Tiny, frail plants grew from what must have been mud pasted into the slits between the logs. By the time I touched it I was panting, completely out of breath. Gul placed one hand on my shoulder, removed my hand from the door with the other, and then knocked, three times, as if it were a courtesy call on a respectable relative. Wood, dried mud, dung, burned wood – the smells whiffed in and out while I settled my breath.

So, first things first, we apologize profusely. Both of us.

That is if they open the door at all, I heard Gul think.

Why so late in the day?

We tell the truth – our parents are sleeping, so they won't worry.

How come their dog's not woken up? By now he should have woken up the entire jungle.

'Who are you?' I almost hugged Gul in panic when the silence of our waiting was broken by this unexpected, coarse voice. Something, someone stirred and we stood back a little. The bulky door began to slide open with a pained, low screech and I expected a tall, old-fashioned Gujjar man (that's how I remembered Shaban) to emerge out of the shadows and send us packing with an angry reprimand for bothering him so late at night. He might even twist our ears – who knows? Old men think they have the right to do anything.

Instead, the coarse voice belonged to a smallish old man, more phlegm than person, with a flowing beard that betrayed specks of red and orange even in the dark blue of the forest.

'If you are . . .' he stared quizzically, '. . . come back after a week or so. My boys are not here.' He didn't seem to recognize me – but how could he, I was a little boy then? And he didn't sound too worried either, at least not as much as I'd expected him to be. He was probably either used to young visitors turning up at his door any time of the day, or, looking at our faces, he'd decided we meant no harm.

'No, no, Chacha, no . . . We are not from the city . . . Nowgam, we are from Nowgam, the village down there.' Gul had gained a little composure and seemed to want to take control of the situation.

I was surprised by his confidence. Seeing him spring to provide a quick answer to Shaban's questions, I was also briefly puzzled. He had made sure Shaban knew immediately where we were from.

Shaban Chacha had grown old now and didn't look like the towering Gujjar I remembered him as, who had often dressed in expansively flapping white pyjamas and a waistcoat with bulging pockets. He leaned against the wooden pillar that held the door by what looked like rubber patches, and stared at us. This was the first time in my life I was seeing someone, anyone, after a gap of so many years.

'So what do you want?'

'Nothing much, just . . .'

'Then?' Shaban clearly wanted to get back to whatever he had been doing before we interrupted.

'Actually, why we came up at this hour,' Gul took another pause, a deep breath and looked at me, 'and troubled you is because we want to . . . we want to talk to you.'

'What?' Shaban Khatana's tone betrayed signs of impatience.

'Chacha, we are very sorry for disturbing you at this time. You may not, er, remember me, but I, I remember you very well . . .' I said, trying hard to sound assured. 'I am the Headman of Nowgam's son. You must remember . . . ? The thing is, Chacha, I need to find out something, I mean, it's about a friend. He disappeared a few days ago and we want to know if he's all right there? You know how it is these days . . . ?' I said in quick succession and left half a question suspended in the sighing forest air. Looking around I wondered, amazed, distracted, that this was the same deep wood that I'd seen from my house all my life and wondered at the secrets that breathed in its dark swells. I was deep inside it now.

'Oh, oh-oh, ahan . . . ! Yes, yes, of course, of course, I remember Sarpanch Sahib, forgive me, beta, I didn't recognize you, I have grown old now, you see, and you're so grown-up, haan, big boy now, God bless you, God bless you . . . So how is the headman? And your mother . . . ?' Shaban asked quickly, as if to make up for lost ground, but he did sound genuinely interested in my parents' well-being. That was very good. And bad too.

'They are fine, Shaban Chacha, very fine.'

'God bless them, such good days . . . Say my salam to them, do remember, haan . . . And what were you saying?'

'Yes, er, it is about my friend, Hussain . . . ?'

'Oh, yes, yes, you were saying he has disappeared, hmm . . . ? Many boys go missing now, isn't it?' Shaban Chacha said casually, as if we were talking about a few goats that had gone astray, and started running his forefinger down his beard. 'But you have come to the wrong person, beta, I don't know too much about all this. Allahtaala knows. I'm getting old now, you see, very old, I couldn't even recognize you . . .'

'No, Chacha, I didn't mean to say you –'

'Oh, it's getting cold here, let's go inside,' he turned, as if changing his mind about something, and went in without looking back at us.

Gul was leaning against the big tree of a log that served as the door post and had started murdering the grass with his feet. He looked at me. *Now what?*

'Now what, what? We go in. He's invited us, didn't you see?'

Darkness. Smoke-filled darkness.

My torch bore a yellow-rimmed tunnel through the smoke and halted at what looked like a mud wall. Human forms began to take a diffused shape. Shifting outlines. There were two people in the room and one of them started speaking now.

'Beta, there are too many stories. Sometimes they are all mixed up.' Shaban Khatana sighed the sigh of an old man. 'I'm not sure if you can find much about this friend of yours. So many have crossed these paths and mountains that one doesn't even remember. In any case, I haven't been across in years now. My sons go sometimes.'

The room began to have walls. Walls of clay. Seated next to Shaban, very close, was a gaunt woman with sparkling eyes. Shaban's wife had her gaze fixed on Gul, who was inspecting the one-room tenement like a child, his round eyes flickering in some kind of wonder, or perhaps simply adjusting to the light.

'So they do help people go across?' I said, feeling myself drawing up courage.

'All the same, some people make it, some don't. Doesn't matter, most boys are from faraway places, from the cities, anyway . . . You two don't want to disappear too, right . . . ?'

'Hussain, my friend, he is also from Nowgam, Chacha. Good looking, tall, curly hair – he has been gone for more than a week,' I said in one breath, a feeling of dread now getting tighter and closer within me.

There was a long silence, the old man was thinking, lost, and I just couldn't decide how long a pause a decent pause was, a hiatus after which you could reawaken someone, and an old man at that, from an apparent reverie.

'I don't know much, beta, man comes at night, gives my sons money sometimes. This man, he is the real man. Someone important, I can tell. He fixes time and tells them how many.' Shaban Khatana had a shifty manner of answering your questions, I took that in, and thought to myself that I remembered that from years ago. I also sensed we had probably begun to gain the old man's trust. He no doubt remembered me.

'Is everything all right with Sarpanch Sahib, beta, hope all's well?' Shaban Chacha suddenly asked.

'We are all fine, Chacha . . . just that this friend has crossed over, I suppose, and we haven't heard anything of him since?'

'He doesn't speak much, this man, just a few words with my elder son, Rahman. He doesn't see the boys till the last day.'

'Do you know who he is, Chacha?' Gul's look says *irrelevant question.*

'He doesn't carry too many, only ten or twelve. My boys, they can go across at will, you see, any time, any season. They have their ways, they won't tell anyone.'

Silence in the smoke-filled room. Something's burning somewhere but there's no fire. No one seems to miss the presence of any kind of bright illumination in the old couple's modest dwelling. There's a sooty candle on the narrow sill of the small roshandaan at the back of the hut. It has cried copious kohl-lined tears. Enough light. Outside, silent night presides over the woods, letting loose a hiss of faint sounds from time to time. I imagine eyes, animal eyes, darting across, here and there . . .

'But we don't mess with the Army, beta, never.' Shaban Khatana resumed his monotone narrative. 'They kill just like that. So we don't bring the boys here when they come back. We leave them at a place deep inside the forest. After that they are on their own.'

Gulla, say something, please – why do I have to do all the talking?

Shaban signalled something to his wife; I looked at Gul Khan to see if we were supposed to leave. Gul's nod said *I don't know, let's stay a while*.

Wife goes to a corner of the mud house, lights a big lantern and brings back a blackened clay-painted pan and a dented, uneven aluminium plate. The brim of the pan is wrapped around with a floral patterned cloth.

'You must be hungry, here, have some,' she smiles to show us a set of orderly white teeth behind the leather face. We look at each other. The pan reveals stacks of small smoked fish, *pharre*, in a thick gravy of greens. The fish look me in the eye.

God, they looked so very like the charred men I see below in the valley now – who knows what the Captain's men use, it must be what they call a firefight later. Smoked fish.

I see Gul has already torn into one of the bigger catches from the dish while the couple are picking small nibbles with pieces of brownish roti from the beaten-up plate. 'Have some, have some, you must eat a bit before you go.' I imagine Hussain coming to this place and eating with this old couple at night. I try to chew on a chunk from the side of the fish Gul has dismembered; it tastes like soft, wet sand.

'My sons, you know them? They should be back in around ten days,' Shaban Khatana said, brushing away flecks of fish flesh from his broom-brush beard. 'I can ask them about your friend if you want to. What did you say his name was?'

'Hussain.'

'But you must remember, beta, they just meet this man at a rendezvous point in the jungle.'

The wife wrapped some fish and roti in an oily newspaper and gave it to Gul. He looked at me for a second and then accepted the gift graciously. Where do they get fish from, so high in the mountains? There's not even a trout stream down below.

'This man you were talking about, Chacha, is he from around here?'

'I don't know, son. Why do you ask, I hope you're not . . . ? He sounds local but I have never seen him before . . .' I have to wait before Shaban finishes chewing on a morsel, and I choose to ignore his question about me. 'Last time he came, he spoke with Rahman for a few minutes . . . you know him, my elder son?'

'Then?'

'Then the man left. He doesn't come back for some time after that. You see, the boys are handed over by a headcount and that is it.'

Shaban Chacha, I noticed, and tried to remember it from the past as well, had this habit of looking slightly away from your face when he spoke. And he didn't really bother to listen to what you were saying. But I needed some clue, something? I knew I had to meet his sons, secretly somehow, without him knowing it, without any chance of Baba finding out.

My head began to fill with images of this man who probably delivers the boys to the other side. I saw him as a cold, heartless man who walked into the forest night, sent his boys into the deep, and then came back to get more. I saw him as a man of great mystique. He perhaps brought Hussain here and delivered him to Khatana's son. I saw him as a courageous man who was probably risking everything he had. I saw him as an adventurer who went on secret trips, fulfilling his role in the fight for freedom, and he had now come to our parts. This, then, was his new recruiting ground; he had come and already taken. I so, so wanted to meet this man. I wanted him to take me.

'Shaban Chacha, your son, is he supposed to come any time soon, I could ask *him* about Hussain, his family is worried, you know, we are all worried . . . ?'

Gul was beginning to get a little restless. He gently waved towards Shaban's wife and she brought him a glass of water. He drank it down in loud gulps that somehow eased the tension in the air.

Shaban Khatana gave Gul the quickest of glances and then took out a small round box from somewhere inside his many layers of shirts and waistcoats. It was naswaar; he pinched out a tiny bit of the mould-coloured powder on his middle finger and deposited it expertly on the inside of his gums. Then he shut his mouth tight. It was getting late; I was sure to get a serious telling-off at home.

'Any chance this man might come again, Chacha, he might know if Hussain is safe?' I started all over again, not unaware that I was trying my luck too hard now.

Long silence, a tightly shut mouth.

'No, beta, no . . . He doesn't tell me!' Green, mouldy specks of the mehndi-like substance filled the gaps in Shaban's fence-like front teeth. His eyes had turned red. 'Beta, listen to me, the man doesn't talk to me. My son Rahman, he knows. I worry about them some-times, you know, my boys, but then I tell myself it's not such a big problem. We have always gone across the mountains; they are ours, you see, they are our land.' He appeared glum now and turned to look away. 'I had hundreds of sheep and goats once and I used to roam all over these mountains, I have seen everything, beta, every-thing. You are young, you know nothing . . . Now this cross-border thing is happening, what can I say? People are going every day and they are dying. Allahtaala knows better. It's His will.'

Shaban Khatana's words were probably the first real proof that *a lot* of people were indeed crossing over into Pakistan every week; and when he said people were dying all the time, I sensed the seeds of some grief growing somewhere inside.

Gul Khan shuffled his feet and looked anxiously at me. He wanted to leave. I knew that he was bothered by thoughts of his older brother, more than his parents. Farooq questioned him more often than his father did and tried to act the big brother whenever he found an opportunity or felt that he needed to impose his law. He even called Gul names. We, in turn, had called Farooq the *budde bad-mash* when we were younger – knowing that calling the self-conscious 'hero' an old thug was guaranteed to annoy him – and would often stop playing altogether if he looked like he wanted to join in.

Shaban Chacha looked at me fondly, or so I thought. I remembered more of his time with us, how he had been this eager, know-all handyman in the house, doing everything Baba wanted done.

'Look, beta, all this is dangerous stuff, big stuff . . . Man comes to the forest, he brings a few boys with him and my sons take them across. That's it. If you want, you can come and see Rahman some day. It is possible, but I can't promise, that he may know about your friend. What else can I say? But tell me something, who told you about me?'

'My big brother, Chacha, but don't worry, only a few people know . . .' Gul came up with a sufficiently vague answer, after a briefly tense and unsettling quiet, and I nodded in agreement anyway, not wondering, at all, how Gul knew exactly what to say to the old man to reassure him about his son's enterprise not being too public a knowledge. He stood up at once and started to leave. Getting up myself, I told Chacha that we would visit again next Friday – at this I felt pleased, I had already found the old man more than agreeable and therefore full of possibilities for my plans – when his son Rahman might be back from his latest sojourn to Azad Kashmir. I had no idea what I would say to him.

Soon, I was running after Gul in the pitch dark of the hillside. A sheet of darkness was shutting down in front of us. I could see his black form receding into the blue landscape. He was really worried, I thought to myself, and darted after him. One dark form after another.

I now knew that our friendship had suffered its first jolt, the first major blow, with Hussain's departure. I had been agonizing over whether – and how – to act on this desire to follow in Hussain's footsteps, or whether to stay home, be the obedient boy, and not aggrieve Ma and Baba. Our trips to the valley and our evening strolls and corner meetings had come to an abrupt end, but I still didn't understand that a sequence of events had begun that would change the world for ever, that would alter the course of my life. For the thought that the others would follow Hussain soon hadn't even been born then. Shaban Chacha had appeared suddenly to testify to the truth of what I only, and reluctantly, half suspected. Death itself had started knocking on our doors, but I didn't know it, didn't know it fully then. I could only smell a faint souring of the air around me; something doleful waited on the burning horizon that I had started seeing before night fell. I agonized about what had taken place, and yet, another part of me wanted to do the very thing that troubled me.

I wanted to go. I wanted to cross over into Pakistan.

5   *Still Trees*

'Captain, I wanted to ask something?' I say after many false starts and after having established his mood. I have now completed many months with the Captain, in his service.

'Hmm . . .' Kadian grunts from his journal, where he seems not really to be writing anything in particular, just moving the pen around the same spot.

I bend forward towards the table and consider his mood again. I cannot back out now. Outside, the afternoon has gradually cooled down to a pre-evening lull when nothing seems to happen. The sun doesn't move, the breeze hasn't picked up yet, the shadows look worn-out and a boring stillness pervades. The last few days have been quite exhausting and it's been tough keeping peace with Baba and then Ma. Baba knows everything but both of us seem unsure as to whether Ma knows or not, whether she *should* know or not. Ma, who's fallen silent, and won't speak her mind until something really, really provokes her. Ma, who was once full of tales and qissas, long stories about her childhood and youth and her own baba's endless adventures. She's silent now.

'I was thinking, sir . . .' I swallow but don't drop my eyes, '. . . if I could keep a small, you know . . . er, a small pistol or something from the lot I have given you –'

'You haven't given us anything, sir, *I* have asked you to collect things for us, for a price.' He likes to cut me short every so often, or this must be the way he asserts himself with everyone, but I have no way of judging that.

'Yes, yes, Captain, from the lot I have collected for you. I was just thinking, you know, it can get dangerous sometimes (and here I struggle for emphasis), especially in the dark, so if I had something with me, you know, something for self-defence, it would be good, no . . . ?' It is not the opening I had thought it would be. I find myself already preparing for disappointment. He reminds me of my child-hood and Baba's firm nods of elderly refusal if I clamoured too much for something. I could have long ago picked one myself from the corpses, but, honestly, I was scared it could infuriate him if he discovers it later. Better to ask, huh.

'So, so, so . . . You want to carry a gun, huh?' He looks up and says firmly. 'But tell me something, who the hell's going to threaten you or your family in these parts, haan, unless you really upset my men, heh, which I'm sure you have no intention of doing?'

'No, no . . . It's just that sometimes I think, you see, there's a thick jungle on both sides, right? So if –' I'm never able to tell him about the animals, about the man-eating beasts that could descend from the woods, for fear of being made fun of by him, should he think I'm *seeing* things. If only, if only he'd seen those hovering, circling dogs. If only he had seen their scarlet eyes.

'And as for them heroes crossing over all the time, I don't think they would be so stupid as to come anywhere near your house, and for what? The bastards want to get the hell out of here as soon as they have crossed in, isn't it?' He folds the large blue notebook and looks straight at me.

'Captain, I just want a small pistol or something for my own safety, that's all. Just in case. I don't want any of those big things, a pistol should be more than enough for me.'

I already feel tired from the exchange. My back teeth and gums ache sometimes from the effort I have to make to keep a straight face when I'm agitated, or angry. I can't even shout. That's not fair.

'Hmm . . . Are you really *sure* . . . ?' Kadian suddenly drops his guard and softens his voice like someone about to give spiritual advice. 'It's not easy carrying a weapon, you see . . .' Now he pauses for the longest pause I have seen him make. He looks very grave. 'You know, you become someone else. And you, you will change from someone who works for me to someone who works for me *and* carries a gun. You know what I mean? I know this thing. I know it better than anyone else does. Besides, I will have to tell the behan-chod sentry at the gates about it, because they will still fucking frisk you if they are in the mood. What would you do then?'

'They know me now, Captain . . . They don't check me any more . . .' I say, as timorously as ever, even though I want to say something entirely different, something entirely else. *You have dozens, no, hundreds of guns in that storeroom of yours, God knows how many you and your people have sold, and who knows how many that old devil of yours has kept for himself and how many more are just lying around, rusting all over this dead land, and you have to think hard about letting me have a tiny thing? A small, insignificant toy from a mountain of guns!* But instead, I just press my lips together, hard, and wait for my boss's predictable, and dreadful, lecture.

'I do trust you, raja, you wouldn't be sitting here with Kadian otherwise,' he adds with that one-sided grimace in which the corner of his mouth stretches towards his left eye and ends with a grunty 'hnnhh'. 'But sitting here with you when you are carrying a gun, I'm not too sure about that, sir. No matter what, I'm still fucking in charge of a motherfucking anti-infiltration operation here and don't want any bloody messes with saala civilians walking into my office with weapons inside their trousers.' His voice rises again, just a little, and then, with another abrupt shift of attention, he glances towards the walnut-wood cupboard on the left wall, where he keeps his liquor stash. There are quite a few in there – Old Monk rum, a green bottle that says XXX Indian-made Foreign Whisky, a neat flat bottle of Blue Riband Gin, another hefty bottle with a smeared, darkened label that says Bagpiper, and some more. The whiskies clearly stand out in his collection. I wonder at the extent of the alcohol allowance in the Indian Army, because Kadian surely has a flowing supply of *sharaab*.

'Captain, er, there are scores of guns just lying around here, still. I just need –'

He leans back in his big red chair and closes his eyes. I try to settle my breathing and wait.

'You will fucking surrender the damn thing to us any time I say, and I should never hear – never, ever – of anyone who has seen a fucking pistol poking out of your pyjamas!' he blurts out, rising forward again, and hits the desk with his palms.

'Shukriya, Captain, I will give it back as soon as I finish this.' I half suspect, or perhaps even wish, that he might pause at the mention of the 'finishing' bit, ask me what I mean by it, or himself elaborate on it, but it doesn't seem to register with him at all.

'Okay, okay, don't you hurt yourself, all right?' Another sudden change of tone, he doesn't want me to ruin his evening, or even his anticipation of it. 'I need you in good health. In working condition, you see, ha ha! I will ask him to pick out something for you from the store,' he says in a measured, solemn tone, without looking towards the peon who sits indolently on his padded plastic chair near the door. 'Or you could choose one for yourself if you want to . . .' he adds, even more relaxed now, and gets up to pick one of his evening warmers from the cupboard.

I try to imagine what he does in the after hours, after he's filled himself with his stinking spirits; where does he go, who does he meet? Does he read the newspapers, watch TV, listen to music, what *does* he do? Some day, I want to find out, probably follow him and watch him in his private hours, in his lair, when he's lowered his guard, and is his private self. *What if I kill him and run away?*

Anyhow, now that I have his permission, I'm thinking I would prefer to choose the gun myself. One, I don't like being near the peon (although I might get an opportunity to see what's inside that stinking store of theirs). Two, I have already glimpsed a few things lying amidst the boys down there; I could easily find something small enough to hide under my belt. That way Baba and Ma will never know. A sudden wave of anticipation takes over my senses as soon as I see myself with a gun in my hands, going home with it and tucking it under my pillow at night. Wow. I know, I know, I shouldn't feel that way but somehow I do look forward to it, a bit of excitement creeps in from somewhere. Everyone carries a gun nowadays. Soldiers, militants, security men, policemen, mukhbirs, black-cat commandos, counter-insurgents, agents, bodyguards, informers, thieves, guest-militants . . . By the way, what category will I be thrown into? Badge runner of the Indian Army, official scavenger of a murderous army officer, cleaner-sweeper of the brutal Rashtriya Rakshak Rifles? (*Rakshasa* Rifles is more like it.) The armed caretaker of the unknown dead, the chowkidar of my own dead ilk, the sole witness to a machine of carnage or a shameless forager of friends' remains, a petty ID-card thief, or the grim reaper? I don't know, I don't know.

'Helloo . . . ? Are you planning on staying the night for God's sake?' Kadian has moistened his throat and startles me with his snarl from across the table where he has changed his posture and is leaning back in his stained velvet chair. A bottle and a pale glass stare at me blankly from their half-empty presences. I suddenly realize I have become used to the smell of his drink.

Kadian. Captain Kadian. Does he eat in the mess with the others or is he served separately in his quarters? What does he do after dinner? Probably drink some more till he drops off to sleep. I think that would be the best time to sneak in on him, although I may not get to see much, I suspect, but still. What if I really was to kill him?

The peon looks at me with suspicion and, I think, disapproval – he will have to take me to the store if I want to, but I suppose he doesn't want to be in a position where he *has* to do something for me. Yes, yes, I would rather go down and pick something by myself. Although, that means I would be missing my chance to check the store, to see what they have in there.

On my way out, I look at the two sentries at the gate a little longer than my usual nervous fleeting glance. As always, they are standing like gateposts, in green uniforms and identical stances. I remember I'd decided to call them Ram and Shyam at some point for this reason.

The first few times I came through this gate I was so scared I felt I might suffocate. The very sight of the two sentries would make me stop breathing, worried that any sound might provoke indiscriminate firing. I would keep my head still, eyes following the tips of my shoes in a suspended gaze. I would only let go of my breath once I reached the steps to my master's quarters. When leaving the camp, a twitching, crawling sensation wouldn't leave my neck until I was well out of their line of vision, well away from their stolid, gun-ready – both hands on the stock, on the torso of the weapon – positions.

Now one of them nods his head gently as I pass and looks back towards the dimming horizon. He looked as if he were wishing his prayers to the skies so that they might be carried to his faraway children, his wife and his old parents. What is he doing here, this godforsaken man, away from his own people, guarding a precipice of his beastly country in this alien wilderness? 'Go home, go home . . . sad soldier. Some day, you might die in these parts and no one will claim you,' I whisper to myself and speed along.

I have work to do.

Down in the valley, there are no new arrivals today. Didn't I hear something last night? The night before last? Wonder what they did with them – that is, if any were hit? Anyway, we will have to make do with what we have . . . But let's stay clear of the river today, it does something to me. Too many reflections. Too much replaying. I walk a few hundred feet through an ancient war scene, like King Ashoka who once wandered spectre-like through the killing fields of Kalinga and saw more than enough to rue his decision to wage war and then renounced it for ever. I tread very carefully through the open patches in the midst of the wreckage, you don't want to disturb anything here. Something might fall off, and there's no way to put it back. *Kadian, what, what have you landed me in?*

I get to a bunch that I have never seen up-close before. There are more than four, five, people here, cross-legged and cross-armed, heaped across each other in a semicircle but not as mangled as some others. Lucky brothers. One of them is wearing military fatigues, imitation or used ones probably bought from some second-hand Sunday market in Pakistan. He's also the one carrying quite a bit of 'arms and ammo'. From the surface, I can make out the outlines of at least six hand grenades, two each in the big pockets below and one each in the two small ones on top of his jacket. I don't need these. Where are the guns? Where are the pistols?

A shiny black thing soon screams from below the pile. Someone's still holding it, as if joined for ever to his withered, ghastly hand. New metal in the grip of old flesh. Some other metal inside his broken body.

How could I have missed it! I will now have to dislodge the pile to get to the bottom of things here. But let me try something else: if I use my foot to move the pistol-wielding hand away and the thing falls off, then I can just pick it up from there. But what if the entire thing falls, what if the whole arm comes off? While I'm wondering at the mechanics of my operation, I also see that the two guys on top are eyeing me with their brownish, fibrillated hollows – many others' eyes are gouged out – and I notice they are not all that disintegrated. I can even make out the faint outlines, the remains, of a look, of how they must have looked when they were like me – walking, talking, breathing, looking at themselves in the mirror to see what they look like, to know who they are. It's pungent here. But the fetid smell does die off at times. And sometimes I don't even notice until I see something rotten and I'm reminded of the putrid, disgusting stench it *ought* to give off. If people can get used to murder, what's a bit of foul smell.

I pick the gun with three fingers first. God, it is heavy, at least half a kilo, or even more. It says *Nicholson .9mm* on the back. In black. Black, cold metal – the world bows to it. I shall have this one. From this lot I shall have this one, then. My hand feels pulled down by the weight of the thing when I get hold of the butt at last. A sensation also travels up my arm and exits in a twitch towards the corner of my upper lip.

There are more barrels coldly rising up here and there, poking out and protruding from the crevices thrown open by some of the dead. I see grey, steely barrels coming out of dead flesh – some glistening shining metal, some smeared and dirtied. Am I hallucinating?

I have now chosen a small thing, a compact concealable weapon that could sit unnoticed, unassuming, inside my shirt. But, but, I feel temptation rising along with the mysterious muzzles of the guns lying deeper below. Should I borrow one of these big ones instead? Should I keep a mighty rifle at home, hang it from a hook on my bedroom wall? That would be quite something.

In the first, and the last, parade of militants that ever passed through our village, I had found myself marvelling at the brand-new, clean

AK-47s and LMGs that those boys from the Hizb-ul-Mujahideen carried so seriously on their shoulders. This was a year after Hussain left and just before the Army started operations here.

Heads held high, proud demeanour, weapons slung across shoulders, they had moved quickly through the street – this was sometime before the first, and the last, army operation in the village – to the awe and puzzlement of the small crowd that gathered hurriedly from nowhere, to the wordless disbelief of eyes that watched from behind silently opened shutters and rustling curtains. Some children watched in the street itself, amazed and unfazed, staring straight into the eyes of the partially masked men marching briskly but proudly through our otherwise quiet village. No one knew when the militants had arrived or assembled but they paraded in two flanks now, on either side of the road. I never understood why they'd come and chosen us for this show of strength, but here they were, marching away with a sacred zeal. The two boys at the front had large guns, with bulky semicircular things hanging under them – I later learned they were the new automatic AK-94 rifles with their 144-round bellies. They wore black kerchiefs that covered half of their faces, jeans, green army jackets with silver buttons, and new sports shoes that either said *Power* alongside a thick blue arrow or *ActiOn* with a ball inside the O. One of these two front runners also carried a green cloth banner that said *Pakistan ka matlab kya? La-ilaha Il-Allah*, and *Kashmir banega Pakistan* under a bold silver citation of the holy Kalimah. Noor Khan put his patronizing, elderly hand on my shoulder and muttered, 'What if someone was to take their hankies off, these pompous heroes from the city, what are they trying to show us?'

I patted back his arm calmly and put a finger to my lips. He obeyed, without saying anything for once. The parade ended after they had walked past the last house, which didn't take long; the gun-wielding men then soon fell out of file and stopped some distance away from where we still stood watching. They sat together on a small patch of green near the muddy track and rested their weapons against each other while some of them, almost all actually, lit their cigarettes. 'Hmm, who do you think their leader was?' I knew

Noor Khan would later narrate an elaborate story based on the day's events but this seemed too soon. 'It was not the big guy with the big gun at the front, in case some *bachche* thought so.' He turned sideways to look at the people who stood behind us. 'The man in ordinary clothes, towards the back, who was wearing a full mask, I bet he is the commander of the group,' Noor Chacha said with a triumphant swing of the head.

'You know everything, BBC Sa'eb, don't you? Huh! How do you know they are from the city? Couldn't they be from some village and couldn't they have just crossed over?' Farooq, Gul's brother, weighed in with his own knowledge of militant matters.

Soon, everyone was involved in the conversation, some owing to genuine curiosity – they had just seen a bunch of masked men walk past with heavy weaponry – and some just for fun because, in spite of the tension of the moment, Noor Khan's squabbling could always be a source of entertainment, even at a delicate moment like this.

'Aai hai, how very wise of you, why would they come *here* soon after crossing over, tell me? Or,' and now his eyes blinked, 'do you think someone you know too was . . . You know something we don't . . . ?' Noor wasn't willing to let anyone have the last word that day and even risked broaching a subject that some people still avoided in public.

Farooq fell silent immediately; the big brother was most uncomfortable at the mention of his younger brother. I felt sorry for him. Hussain and company were still mentioned in hushed tones, even if, at the time of the parade, it had been close to a year since they had left.

Generally, however, that day, after the parade ended, no one wanted to seem too dazzled by the unexpected appearance of these heavily armed boys in their midst; some wanted to demonstrate just how comfortable they were with this new reality – after all, four of our own had joined in as well, and were probably part of a similar group now. As the men marched past I had found myself wondering – from the way they walked and carried themselves – whether my friends were among them. What if? And I did see someone who was Hussain's height, but this man's walk was too straight and erect, while Hussain was always slightly hunched which, along with his gently shaking head, gave him a nodding, sing-song gait.

People didn't budge from their spectators' positions in the street until evening brought out the shadows of the mountain peaks and the hillsides, and layers of darkness began to slide and stretch over the scene. Amber glows of last cigarettes bobbed up and down in the distance, got smaller and smaller and then disappeared. They melted into the darkness of our hills. They must not have needed their flimsy masks any more, I thought. My last memory from the day is of tiny silhouettes of men and the thin arrows of gun muzzles drifting in and out of the dimming light.

The next day, a mock parade organized by some children from the houses on the street, carrying sticks and disused planks of weathered wood, with strings tied at one end for slinging on shoulders, was immediately disrupted by their fathers while the mothers, some of them at least, giggled from their window perches.

My brief moment of gun greed fades away with the aid of half-distant memories and I go back to the thing that says Nicholson .9mm on its shiny black body. It is indeed compact, neat. And yet, the cold assured touch of its butt feels like the grip of something overpowering, something I want to keep and feel safe with, something I want under my pillow when I sleep, something everyone keeps in these times and I too may need some day, for an unknown task I'm to fulfil.

It begins to get dark before I decide to leave. I slide the gun inside my shirt, forcing it, barrel-side down, under my waist. Sometimes I do not notice the passing of time until the looming shadows of the evening half-light tell me it's time to go. The dusk here does not arrive on the shoulders of golden sunsets any more, but on the heels of long, encroaching shadows of untraceable trees in the distance, gloomy parallel patterns that cascade over the undulating landscape of unevenly dispersed corpses and other things. Here I'm looking at someone's grimy ID and a daunting shadow threatens to claim the proceedings. It's time to go home.

I don't waste any time. I quickly feel my bag and leave. Ascending the gentle slope out of the valley I try not to let my eyes wander too much – who knows what might be lurking on the periphery, on the margins of my playing field. The crows are measly specks on the descending evening sky. My feet gather pace as soon as the slope begins to curve and lead to where I come from. I hear the evening sounds of crickets and the distant howling of wild dogs. Some Bakarwal scout dogs were left behind, against their raucous protests, when everyone except Baba – not just the whole of Nowgam but also the inhabitants of the scattered dhokas that dot the vast sloping swathes beyond the valley – decided to leave for good. They wanted to travel light, strange for a people who were born wanderers and itinerant farers, even though they had given up the nomadic life long ago, but then, these were, are, strange times. I guess the forsaken dogs have now been claimed by the forest, where they feed on whatever is on offer. Or who knows if they too come down when the supplies higher up are lean?

Mohammed's dog was called Rakhu. What a name! And what a swagger. Built like a horse, he had toned forelegs that glistened blue when he ran, something which he perhaps did a little too often. His eyes rolled left and right constantly on his pale-haired face. His collar was an old piece of black leather with two clumsily crafted copper stars at the front. Rakhu, the keeper-protector-sidekick of our worldly-wise friend; Rakhu, who did his master's bidding at all times, even if that meant diving endlessly into the cold water of the stream to fetch a sodden cricket ball. He would emerge victorious, a drenched, unsightly appearance notwithstanding, and drop the ball at Mohammed's feet before vigorously shaking off water from his body, and then gaze at us from the imaginary boundary of our cricket pitch where he would sit drying himself in the sun before resuming his fielding duties.

On my way home, up the slope, it's not the sounds of the forest night, the chirping and the repetitive chatter of unknown birds and insects, that make the evening feel ominous. It's the trees. The stillness of the trees. They don't rustle, their leaves don't hiss and murmur and crackle, they *just don't* make any sound. Breeze or no breeze, the small birches on these downy mountain folds just don't talk. They stand still, as if observing my every move, my every step, every thought, in total silence. I become conscious of their gaze and soon find my walk unsettled. I have never seen trees so still as these. A swift breeze blows against my face, I clasp my jacket tight, feel the strange shape of the pistol jammed into my waist, and move ahead, trying hard to get to the end of the track.

I never paid attention to them when everything was all right. Hardly even noticed these figures whose dark silhouettes, against a darker sky, now make me swallow every step of my walk home. They seem to take a long, considered look at me, to make up their mind, to judge me in some mysterious way while I'm trying hard to get away from their motionless gaze. I stop looking, but then, without knowing, I have turned to look at their forms again, deeply cast against a sad, *manhoos*, accursed horizon. It's one of those things, you know, the harder you try not to think of something, the more you *don't* want to look at something, the more you get drawn into thinking of that very thing. I suspect they will start rustling the moment I take my last step out of their line of vision. I wish I could know what they say after I have passed. *Here's the abandoned one, the left-out one, the one who must tell the story. He now goes down to check, to rummage through the pieces of those who left. He's the only one now.*

I finally reach home and go straight to my room. I have remembered something: *yes, yes*, there's a picture of us all – it should be somewhere in my books – which should have these trees in the background. Firdaus Ali, the well-oiled and fiercely combed government employee, Baba's closest friend, and the only man ever from Nowgam to get a government job and own more than a transistor radio, had taken the photo, insisting on the hillside by the path as the background. The very path I now take to go down. I want to see these trees in that picture. Were they really there? I ruffle the pile of papers on my makeshift desk (a wooden writing board balanced on top of two old trunks, Ma's 'dowry luggage') and then shake all the books upside down one by one. Nothing. I dismantle the desk and go through all the photocopied essays and handwritten notes I have stored in the trunks. No sign of the photo. My stack of old magazines – Rubaiyya Saeed looks demurely from an *India Today* cover. She was still in the captivity of those daring JKLF militants, and many media people had already declared a war in Kashmir. Dust begins to fill the otherwise lifeless room. Last chance, my old diary. Quick flip of the cover, upside down with pages opening wide, but no photograph pops out. Perhaps Ma found it and put it somewhere safe. Maybe I can ask her over dinner. No, forget it, I'm too tired. Forget it. Don't want to ask her now. Dinner too will have to wait. On the back of the photograph, I remember, Ashfaq, during his poet phase, had written something; I want to read it again. What did he say, what, what?

'You shall always remain . . .' and something else. He had these one-liners for every occasion.

I wake up when Baba calls for dinner. He will never come up, always shouting my name in his headman's voice from below. It echoes in the outside air and comes back in muffled imitations of Baba's manner. Again and again.

Ma dispenses rice from the big copper vessel and puts the vegetable stew into two separate bowls, one each for Baba and me. She will serve herself directly from the pan. She often does. Baba doesn't like it when there's no meat but he never says it. Ma sits squatted wide on the wooden platform – the old chowki that I used to slide over the floor with, my back against the wall – and eats slowly. It's her favourite place in the house – the chowki near the hearth with its smells of mustard oil, food and dried mud cakes with which she mends the chullah from time to time. Inside the hearth glow the last embers from the day's cooking. I can make out patterns on the red burned-out firewood – dimly glowing ribs, veins and square chambers of some branch that must once have sat blithely on an old tree in some glade just a few hundred feet above us. The glow from the embers makes Ma look flushed, red. Her face shines. My appetite blinds me to the details of the dinner. Mother cooks well. No one says anything.

6   *Hussain and I*

Hussain had gone missing once before, years ago, in the deep forest not very far from Shaban Khatana's home. We had gone there together but I had left him to get back in time for Baba's teatime curfew. Baba had only allowed me to go on the condition that I would be home before the evening tea. We were twelve years old. The year was 1986.

There were two main attractions to the expedition – it was my first ever trip into the mountain of sorrow, our Koh-i-Gham. We were hoping to see the famous Bakarwal shepherd Azad Range Wah-Wah who, it was rumoured, camped around in the high forests with his flocks of multicoloured sheep and goats, their coats yellow, bellies purple and legs scarlet – thus the name, Azad the flamboyant multicolour man – and drink fresh milk that he would offer anyone he met during the course of the strictly nomadic journeys he undertook across the Himalayas (it was said he never owned any property, not even a tent). The other attraction was if you managed to reach the big check-post of the Army inside the jungle, they gifted you large, fancily packed milk chocolates. This was a time when the Army was still, or had to be, civil to civilians, especially children. I had never had a milk chocolate in my life, even though I was the headman's son. We were very excited.

Hussain, I understood later, had asked only me. He had not invited Ashfaq, who had decided, early on, to be against all activities that involved too much physical exertion, claiming it was not suited to a poetic temperament. Gul and Mohammed were not much interested either, or were afraid of the consequences should anything happen inside Koh-i-Gham, perhaps because of the stories about Azad we had all heard from elders in the village – stories that he stole children, that once you fell for his charming tales you never came back from the jungle. My slight apprehensions – not that I had too many because I was instinctively suspicious of Baba's forbidding tales – had melted away at once on seeing Hussain's enthusiasm. He had been told by his mother that nothing of the sort was true and it was just an excuse that parents used to keep their children from venturing out too far, and that Azad, who was a mystic, a minstrel shepherd, was only interested in playing his flute and telling tales of his expeditions and adventures to anyone who cared to listen. 'Trust me, mother knows these things best,' Hussain said, entreating me. 'The entire jungle sings when Azad plays his flute, yaara, I really want to go, come, please . . .'

We set out the very next day, a cool breeze-filled Saturday, after having an early lunch at our house. Ma, who had participated in my deal with Baba that I would be back before dusk, packed up for us a tiffin of rice and rajmah, and a bowl of curd each. It was autumn and everything around us felt ready, ripe . . . Smoke from the many hillocks of leaves that were burned on the terraced fields to make sackfuls of fuel for winter filled the air, mingling with the bare trees of the orchards and then floating up to their fuller, denser, greener cousins on the mountain. Hussain was very happy, I could see it in his walk, in his swinging nodding head. I was pleased, too, to be going with him and him alone, excited, nervous, with only an occasional back-of-the-mind anxiety about Baba's ultimatum dampening my spirits as we began our trek through the sharp, charcoal-vapour-filled air.

Hussain forged ahead of me, reaching out his hand to haul me up every few paces, although it was not so steep yet and I didn't need any help. He hummed constantly, slapping a fir on the way, plucking a berry from here, tearing off a wiry branch from there, kicking a pine cone down, marking small signs on the winding footpath created for years by men and women bringing down bundles of firewood into the village, and talking to me now and then from up ahead.

Out of the blue, as we walked up the winding footpath, he started telling me about his mother, about his father and mother's fights (which lasted for days sometimes). We stopped near a cove of tall deodars. I sat down and opened my plastic school flask; he stopped too, watched me for a bit, and then came and sat down, putting his hand on my knee. 'Already tired, haan?' A lone woodpecker stared at us from the opposite wall of trees, jerked his head excitedly, and flew off. 'Wah, wah . . .' said Hussain. He let out a heavy, cold breath and then said, 'It's so calm here, we should come here more often, no . . . ? You can't hear a thing except for the grass and the trees.'

'You say that about every place we go to, Hussaina. Remember the river?'

'Well, I do like it very much like this, yaara, what do you know! You have no idea what it's like getting away from home. You don't know how bad I feel for Mouji; and Abba` is always very sad, never happy with anything, you know, never. I just don't know what to do.' Hussain's grip on my knee went limp; I looked at him and felt sorry about it all.

We didn't spend too long under those trees. We still had quite a bit of ground to cover before we had any chance of spotting Azad's animals and then following their lead to meet the eccentric master himself. The lore was that if you drank the milk from his goats, since it was the purest form to be found anywhere and was imbued with powers from the wild herbs and grasses that only he knew of, you could attain the pleasures of adolescence sooner than your classmates. We carried on, a bond of togetherness, of closeness – having been made the only confidant, as I thought then, of Hussain's *dukh*, his singular sadness – making me, us, feel happier.

We walked and walked. The forest was heavy with a thousand unknown events. And then we saw him. He stood among the trees, a big transistor around his neck, a thin bent stick in one hand, and a heavily stuffed bag hanging, bouncing, by his waist as if it were an animal tied to his body. The most striking thing about him was his clothes. They were a thousand shades of green – bright, striking, dark, light – he seemed to be wearing every conceivable shade there ever was: his pheran, itself a patchwork of green; his trousers, on them scraps of fabric hanging from the knees; his cummerbund, myriad strips of cloth hanging from it; and his sleeves, many, many layers of them, one over the other, with frayed bits dangling out.

For a moment I thought maybe I was just seeing things, the forest somehow conjuring up this vision, but when I looked at my friend, shook my head, and then looked at Azad again, he was still there, in all his verdant glory.

He saw us, smiled, waved gently, and sat down by the footpath. Hussain prodded me, wanting me to start talking, while I, I had had the same idea . . . I went over to where Azad Range Wah-Wah sat on the forest ground, as peacefully as a lamb, and as if it were the most natural habitat in the world (going by the dress he wore, it surely was for a man like him), and, bending low to be in his line of vision, said, '*Assalam-u-alaikum*, Azad Sae'b, how are you?' God, it took all the courage I ever had, to say those words as calmly as I did. Hussain put his hand on my shoulder; I could feel his breath on my neck.

'I am fine, the same as always, boys. What can ever happen to this free old bird!' Azad said beatifically, like an old Peer Sae'b, only, he wasn't old at all, now that I think about it.

'We came here to meet you,' Hussain said in his most sweet voice, a tinge of genuine entreaty in his tone. 'Can we sit with you for some time?'

'As you please, boys, your wish,' Azad said nonchalantly, but not in an unwelcome way.

There was, however, no sign of the goats I was dying to see; nothing colourful moved about in the trees as I gazed around again and again.

In the end, Hussain, my eager, innocent friend, couldn't resist too long and nudged the man's side, before asking him, in an almost righteous tone, 'But where are those goats of yours, brother . . . ?'

Azad looked at him with still eyes, broke into a broad smile, and said, 'My friend, what you are asking for is not with me . . . If you're lucky, you will chance upon them yourself, I cannot find them for you . . . I set them free, like I myself am, and see them only when *they* want to see me.'

For twelve-year-olds, I suppose this was the most startling thing to hear from anyone, leave alone a vagrant, curiously clothed shepherd, so we just sat there looking at him in amazement.

Hussain had wanted so much for something exciting, happy, to happen that day.

He made himself more comfortable on the virgin grass then, in imitation of the shepherd, I thought, and proceeded to hum something, his eyes closed, his face towards the sky, and was soon quite immersed in his own song. He continued to hold my hand, though, gripping it harder with each crest of the tune. I remember watching his closed eyes and the trembling of the eyelashes with every thought he sang, the forest light and its gentle shadows etching a subtle landscape on his face.

'Let's stay some more time, *please* . . . ?' He suddenly spoke in a low voice, pulling at my hand slowly.

I didn't know what to say, I understood his sadness, his loneliness. I wanted to be with him, listen to him and share his distress – and my heart did go out to him, as always – but I couldn't stay for long. I knew that. 'Haan, haan, we stay for a while, okay! But don't tell me you're going to start singing now, huh.'

In fact, he did not then sing all afternoon.

But the shepherd, standing, half leaning against the slenderest of cedars, just then began to perform a strange exercise, rubbing his hands together, whilst muttering something, and then rubbing his hands on the bark of the tree. The thousand green flags fluttering around his form in the breeze gave him a blurred look, as if he were melting into the blue sky, into the air, the forest.

I unpacked the tiffin of rice and dry rajmah and offered it to him. He smiled wryly, picked half a morsel and pushed the containers back to me. We ate the most delicious meal of our lives then, under the shadows of those cool trees, a calm low sky watching over us, the water from my flask tasting sweeter than any water I have ever had – I remember the taste to this day – and our strange companion settling down with this black flute nearby, watching us with that deeply affecting smile. The man never stopped smiling.

The sound from Azad's flute was indeed enchanting, the kind of music that makes you freeze your thoughts. I saw Hussain's eyes light up; he was probably thinking the same thing that I was – this may well be the signal for his coloured sheep and goats to come to their master. It could actually happen! I was excited again. I didn't want to miss such a scene, and be forever unable to tell the story to everyone at school, in the village, in the clan, and Hussain be the only, sole witness! But there was no sign of them, and very soon I started getting really anxious about home. How, when, was I going to be able to coax Hussain to get up and start for home with me? The afternoon was turning.

Azad's music felt like it might reign over the forest for ever. He wouldn't put the instrument down, the voice of which was getting shriller, stronger, sadder (I thought), more pressing, and higher and higher . . . I was desperately torn between staying and leaving.

At last, there was a dead calm, even the wind stopped – maybe I am exaggerating now, for I was quite young then, but it was a very peculiar hour we spent listening to that music in the jungle. Hussain's eyes were wet.

And at last I stood up, begged Hussain to get up as well, hugged him tightly when he didn't, saying sorry a hundred times, hugged him again, and then, looking back at his figure as I climbed down, I ran off home to meet my father's curfew.

That evening, there were a thousand torches alight in the forest; Baba, for all his cold disapproval of Khadim Hussain, took the situation most seriously and ordered everyone in the village to go and look for 'the boy'. There were men searching for him now, walking into the forest in all directions, slicing the jungle into diverging triangles as they progressed up in their search parties. The forest was lit up in places like houses and courtyards are on wedding days – as though a new wedding and feast were taking place inside these small mohallas, these hamlets, inside the jungle. I feared for Hussain, felt guilty for having left him there, for having failed to bring him down with me, for not having a credible explanation for Baba when he asked why I had done that. Most of all, though, I was afraid for Hussain, afraid that he would be afraid, all alone in the dense woods. I sat there by the window and waited – Baba had forbidden me to leave the house, saying he would break my legs if I even thought of climbing down from my room. I waited and waited, the lights got dimmer and dimmer, the night darker and darker, the voices quieter and quieter . . .

But he was found in the end. They had spotted him sitting alone, eyes closed in some kind of a trance, leaning against a cedar. It wasn't too late, probably only eleven or so. On being found, he had silently obeyed Sadiq Chechi's command – he was in the group which had first spotted Hussain – and walked home in front of them. On arrival at our house – he *had* to be delivered at the headman's house first – Baba spoke to him briefly but in a voice so stern that I remember feeling dry in the mouth myself. 'Son, our children do not, will not ever, dare disobey their parents and elders . . . you cannot disturb the entire village by staying out on some whim. Don't even think of doing this again!'

Hussain, wisely enough, kept his head down while being censured in Baba's court. The search party hung around for a bit, exchanging small talk on the ghosts of Koh-i-Gham. No one mentioned Azad by name.

We played cricket the next day. Hussain was annoyed with me for having left him there, for having been *discovered* like that, but I suppose he was also embarrassed at having been found by a search party comprising almost all the men from the village, in front of his father, and then brought, publicly, to be scolded by the headman himself. I, however, also felt he must have been secretly relieved that he didn't have to come back home on his own. He did not speak at all that afternoon. He stood, aloof, fielding on the leg side while Mohammed repeatedly hit Ashfaq for fours through the cover.

He had been found that first time, pulled back from the jungle with torches that burned to the very last straw, but now, he had been gone for more than a month, and no one was looking for him. He hadn't asked me to come with him this time, leaving me with a painful, delicate decision to make; to go and find him I had to go where he had gone, and I had to leave Ma and Baba for it.

The night was going to get very dark and this time I had to go into it alone.

7   *The Practice*

The pistol weighs 0.7 kg and can fire nine rounds in ten seconds. That's what Kadian says – I'm yet to try it out. He seems to approve the weapon I have picked. I'm relieved I asked him.

He is precise with his instructions. 'Never hold it too tight and don't make your arm tense, keep it firm but relaxed, otherwise you will hurt yourself. And don't take too long to aim, there is no point. Just look once, steady, lock your gaze, and pull. Not that you will need to use it any time soon,' he adds.

Then, as if suddenly remembering a point in the lecture he had prepared for me, he looks up and starts again, 'But really, where the hell are you going to use the damn thing? No really, tell me, where the . . . ? You just want to carry a gun like everyone else, huh, isn't it?'

I have now become used to KD's somewhat predictable mood swings but this is getting too intense too early in the day. What to do? Just listen.

'I think you are beginning to behave just like these jerks who come from their fucking rotten training camps thinking they are God's own fucking guerrillas. Maderchod heroes with their cheap Chinese pistols shoved in their asses.' He stops, pursing his lips as if mulling over whether to check his brewing outburst this time or let go. I pray he'll stop . . . but no . . . 'And the same bastards, when they are caught, the same fucking Rambos go down on their knees and cry, "Sir, sir, I'm innocent, I haven't done anything . . . Sir, I'm sorry, *muaaf kardo*, sir, *main garib aadmi hoon*, please forgive me, they forced me to go with them, please, sir, I'm not a mujahid, I swear, sir, sir," wee, wee, wee . . . *saala, buzdil bhosdi ke*, fucking spineless assholes, I'm filled with nothing but disgust when I see such whining sissies. Thank God for fake encounters!' Kadian tries to make a rare funny face and I see a brief glimpse of the contorted lips of this man whose humour I do not share but can't afford not to give a faint smile to. For some reason, I can't help thinking of this new group, Allah Tigers, who broke video rental shops and torched cinemas in the city and dragged frightened little girls out of school buses and checked their hands for any signs of nail polish and sent them back home to wear floor-length burqas. God's own guerrillas, indeed.

'Captain, everyone you nab, are they all like that . . . ?' I blurt out to steer him away from the subject of my newly acquired weapon. Outside, somewhere not too far from his office, dogs are engaged in a ferocious barking contest. It's annoying to hear them without knowing the cause of their tussle, and my mind veers towards the frightful circle of those panting beasts I think I've witnessed at the periphery of the valley.

Kadian weighs his response. 'Actually, many of them *are* sissies, all they know is fucking attack from behind, ambush, hit and run . . . Lob a fucking grenade and disappear, launch a rocket into someone's kitchen sink and make a run for it, those *gaandu* ISI bummers can't even teach them basic combat! They just fuck their Kashmiri asses and send them back with the usual six mangoes and a frigging plastic Kalashnikov copy.'

I shift in my seat and swallow, dreading a long tirade against all of Kashmir and 'ungrateful Kashmiris', and yes, it's already too late now.

'But yes, all of them are not like that, I agree. Some do show a bit of valour and fight. In the early days, we captured some who, holed up inside their hideouts, wouldn't eat for days at a stretch and would fight till the very last minute, till the very last bullet.' KD's breath settles down a little – it usually does after he has spewed out his abuse at the militants, Kashmir and Kashmiris, his job, Pakistan, ISI.

'Captain, I have been wondering . . . whenever there is an encounter, we hear on TV and radio that so many foreign militants were killed after a fierce battle and so on. But when your men shoot from their high pickets, or at night in the jungle during search operations, how do they know these are *foreign* militants trying to slip in?'

'Hmm . . .' He examines me with a long, considered look. I'm sure he is thinking, *It's a good question.* 'Look, my orders are to keep infiltration down, what . . . ? To stop these motherfucking bastards from sneaking in, and the best way to do that is kill anything that tries to cross into our territory, right? I don't know what the others do, but under my watch you cannot cross over without facing the fucking mortar rain that my men unleash on my command. You get my point? A lot of these fuckers still manage to sneak in, I know,' he clenches his mouth and his right fist, 'right under our noses – sometimes I even see their faces through my binoculars – but at the end of the day every single knocked-down infiltrator is a job fucking well done!'

'But how do you know they are foreign even before they are killed?' I surprise myself again.

'It doesn't matter, bhai! Don't you get it? How does it matter?' He croaks a little while trying to check his scream.

I look back at him, drawing up courage. How does it *not* matter?

He leans back and runs his hands over his face, then folds them into two tight compact fists and places them side by side in front of him, as if they were complementary parts of a machine tool. 'Look, I *want* to kill these people, all right; it's my job. Don't you get it?' He's trying hard to keep his anger in check.

Kadian now makes his strict officer's face – lips tightly pressed together and eyes staring straight at my face, not into my eyes but my face – and says, 'You see, it's not as simple as you people make it out to be. Civilians don't understand. Sometimes things just need to be done, that's it, extraordinary things, it's a requirement of the job. We may not always like what needs to be done, but it's got to be done, right?'

I don't know if I am supposed to say anything to that, so I don't.

'My conscience is clear. I just follow instructions.' He clears his throat, pours himself a surprisingly small drink, finishes it off in one go, and begins anew. 'Okay, hmmm . . . Since you insist, let me tell you a story, all right . . . ? A short story. That will make you understand, I am sure.'

*

'There was this chap once, you know, his name was Zulfiqar Ali, Zulfiqar alias Zulfi, he was a militant, a big militant, right? He had been a well-known militant in the early days but became inactive later. I was not posted here then, I was part of CI field ops, working out of Badami Bagh Cantonment, and worked closely with the G Branch . . . You know G Branch?'

I look at him blankly, *how on earth am I supposed to know any of this?*

'No . . . ? Never mind, it was the intelligence wing of the BSF and had been very successful in the early days, not only nabbing some key militants but also preventing major infiltration attempts on the LoC. When the Army took over from the Border *Fucking* Security Force after this shit had spread everywhere, we decided to carry on using these GB people for their intel, et cetera. They were fucking cunning, ruthless, but, I must say, very successful. I liked their style, fast and decisive.' He clears his throat again, with anticipation.

'Once, we were part of this massive Cordon and Search operation inside the Pir Panjal range near Verinag. It was led by the Army but all the leads had been provided by people from GB and a small group accompanied us now. Our Naga scouts had sighted a big party of mercenaries – guest fucking mujahideen, you call them, isn't it, huh! – who had been hiding somewhere inside the forest.'

He leans back in his chair, looks up at the plywood ceiling and closes his eyes. He is not as clean-shaven today as he usually is, I can tell from the faint powdery stubble under his chin. The nude lamp hanging down from the white plastic holder appears too bright. Yellow. I try to relax in my chair and spread my legs. The peon sits as he always sits, motionless in one position except for the minor tapping movement of his fingers on his thigh, as though humming along to a song only he can hear. I'm now absolutely certain I don't like him and that he's up to something. He is KD's executioner perhaps, he probably kills the injured and the maimed, puts them to rest for his boss. He seems the kind of slimy, mean person who must take delight in giving death to those who cannot fight. He must enjoy silencing the moaning and the screaming boys who are

wounded in the fighting. I'm not like him, at least – I'm just a cleaner.
I feel somewhat better, or think I ought to feel better.

'So then, during our combing operation an advance party came
under heavy automatic fire and a few ORs were killed. When we
got to the site, a gun battle was still raging, close to a drop in the
woods. There was a big gully just after the drop and on the other
side the mountain rose steeply in these wave-like formations. The
bastards had taken shelter in some caves in these formations and
were firing fucking Kalikov bursts from inside the cave system.
Now, our men had taken positions behind trees and some thickets
but, and I knew immediately, it didn't seem to be a winning position. We waited and waited, thinking we could tire them out and
then make an all-round assault. But nothing happened. The militants were, in fact, fucking tiring us out, so that they could make
their escape as it got dark. Then, guess what the G Branch in charge,
his name was Rathore, asked us to do? Well, he didn't really ask, he
just ordered all the men to run to the mouths of the three caves,
which were just a few feet apart, and use their sub-machine guns,
grenade launchers and flame throwers all in one go. And let me tell
you, dear, hell of a job it was – we were soon spewing fire in lashing
jets, launching RPGs and firing our Uzis non-stop, all at the same
time. Within the next ten minutes then – yes, that's all it took – all
those behanchod jihadis came out stumbling one after the other,
like rats. Most had been fucking blinded! We didn't have to do much
after that. My men just emptied their LMGs and soon I was myself
counting the bodies. Thirty-seven. That was some fucking operation, I loved it, loved every bit of it, and remember it to this day. We
beat the shit out of those mean motherfuckers. Anyway, what was
I saying, hmm . . . ?' He attacks his glass purposefully with his right
hand and sucks at its edges.

'You were telling me about some Zulfiqar alias Zulfi,' I mutter
while images of caves and fire and blind men still hang in Kadian's
cabin. The yellow light from the lamp throws big glowing circles over
the table. I am at a complete loss as to how the story is going to
answer my question. Sometimes I think he does this to pass time.
Sometimes I think I am here just to give this lonely man company.

'Oh, yes, Zulfiqar! That's what I'm talking about, that one . . . He had been a divisional commander of HM, and was among the first militants to surrender before the Army. It was all televised, huh ha. He was persuaded by his woman to lay down arms. Our informers, nurtured and trained by G Branch around the villages, had always had their eyes on this Zulfi chap. We knew his movements, where he went, who he met, who he married, where he got his money from, his quarrels with his old Congress-wallah father, Iftikhar Ali Karra, who didn't approve of this militancy business – we knew everything. We also knew that although he had stopped being an active militant, his sympathies hadn't changed much. The chutiya was a Pakistani at heart. One day, we just nabbed him in Handwara, and drove him to Chongoora, which is the last village before the check-posts start on the LoC in that sector, right?'

I nod quickly as though I know the exact location of all the damned ugly Indian check-posts in all of Kashmir.

'So you see, we knew Zulfiqar would die some day anyway, because, you know, the longest a guerrilla fighter can expect to live on average is around half a dozen years, right . . . ? So we shoot him dead along with three other men. Just some random guys. They were all from Handwara; we sort of waylaid them near the edges of the town and asked them to get into our vehicles. Then we drove them around sixty kilometres to the border and shot them. Do you know why? Can you tell me fucking why?'

He pauses, for effect I suppose. The bulb over my head buzzes. What am I to do with this mad man?

'No, your whining sissies, poor lying Kashmiris can't tell me! *Saala garib Kashmiri*, fucking pests, all they do is complain; you take all the aid and money from India to fuck yourselves with truckloads of rice and mutton but you still fucking complain all the time! Can you tell me why one has to do such things in the line of duty?'

I am not going to enjoy this. Kadian is already on his fourth glass and in his evil, nasty mood; this is going to be another painful, long sit-in. I nod ever so gently, attempting to make it slight enough so that I can easily transform it into a yes or no, depending on what the situation demands.

'No, I will tell you. And you go tell your fucking Kashmiri friends.' He slurps on his words a bit and my anxiety grows. 'We did it because we had to make it to the papers over the weekend.' Long pause, that stench again, it's been quite a long time. His eyes scream red at the rims. 'There was word from some quarters – and I think messages were conveyed to many units across the valley. *Show some results. Breakthrough. Success.* Behanchod! So that's what we do, we make a breakthrough. Overnight. No, no, you won't find such bodies down there. We often pass them to the police – after all, the suckers should have something to do. So we photograph the bodies quickly with a few AKs by their side and send them to those spineless Kashmir Police-wallahs – they are fucking collaborators too – who write a challan and inform the parents that their sons were crossing over from POK and were killed in an encounter with the BSF near Chongoora village. That's it. End of story.'

I look at Kadian's smirk while he rests his hands on the table; he pauses very briefly, as though to give me the quickest of opportunities to question his account. I don't, even though I am wondering about inquiries and human rights groups and fake encounters and evil. I have no anger left.

'There are always a few protests and dharnas here and there, then it's back to normal. I would be surprised if there weren't any, huh ha. We knew there would be a few questions, things such as how Zulfiqar could cross in and out of Azad Kashmir in one day, but one doesn't really need to answer anything raised in the press, or by these NGO jerks, does one? Our boys later went to the parents and offered some cash; they obviously refused at first, but that gave us a few more days. Photographs had appeared in newspapers and on TV just two days after the men were killed. The home *and* defence frigging minister was to arrive the next day. *Murti maderchod Manohar Doshi!*

'So, so, so . . . Who the fuck wants to check if the infiltrators are foreign or not before we shoot them – although I would prefer every one of them to be a fucking Pathan or Afghan or Chechen son of a bitch! You know, when we lay ambushes in the mountains, waiting on thin rations for days sometimes, do you think we do that to verify if they are foreign or Kashmiri? You can be so naïve sometimes. We don't ask their nationalities, man. We just gun them down. Fucking mow them down. Ten, fifteen, twenty, thirty, fiffty . . . sixx-tt . . . y, er . . . sometimes more. The more the better . . . Did you really think your damned valley would be full just from the machine-gun fire from the check-posts here? No sirrr, no! This camp was set up to check one of the biggest infiltration routes in all of Kashmir, you must remember – the militants had had it easy till then, come and go, come and go, all the time, like a fucking picnic. They called it the fucking "gateway of militancy"! Then I came and screwed them, I cloz-zed the gates, heh! This is ssstill just one pass, and they know we've got it covered to a great extent now, so they don't use it as much as they did in the early days, eh . . . But they still come, motherfuckers, they ssstill come . . . mother-sisster-ffuckers!'

This is the first time I'm seeing him so drunk and incoherent.

'Water, water, please!' Kadian turns to our motionless friend, who is busy with his large angular nose now. He gets up robot-like from his chair and goes to the far corner of the room where he carefully lifts the lid from the earthen surahi and pours water into a smeared steel tumbler. He comes back and puts the cloud-smudged glass in front of his Captain. I lean back, almost slithering into my chair.

Kadian drinks his water noisily, rather unusual for him, and waves the glass towards the peon, who promptly takes it and comes back quickly after a refill from the earthen pot. KD also pours himself a generous amount from the tall bottle that says Royal Challenge on its spiral-patterned gold and red label, and takes what sounds like a very satisfying swig from his tumbler. The peon hovers, spectre-like, for a while and then settles down on his perch again. I always imagine him as the sort of person who would read cheap Hindi novels at work, but he doesn't. Maybe he reads them at home, in bed.

I look at the Captain for signs of being allowed to leave. He just sits there and drinks his drink. He started so early today, it wasn't even four. Maybe this is the day when I can visit him later, spy on him and see him in his private hours – what the hell does he do when he is alone? I'm sure he must miss me, huh. After all, where will he find such a patient audience? But finally, I slip out without asking.

At night I wake up sweating. Even the blanket feels damp. It feels as if water is seeping from every part of my skin, everywhere, and it smells of fear – drenchy, sticky liquid fear. I think of KD's camp and am suddenly very scared, shit scared. What if someone shoots me dead and passes me off too as some dreaded commander; no one will ever know, I realize. I'm scared of it, there's nothing stopping him if he kills me and throws me into the dump. It is quite easily possible; after all, I'm just a local boy no one knows, and boys are all they kill. I am afraid for my life, have never felt like this before, possibly because I have never had the time, the room, to think of my own life. I don't want to die; I don't want to be killed. I want to stay alive, stay with Ma and Baba, live another day. I have never, never been this scared.

The next day, I'm looking across the stream where there are bodies I have never been close to; I don't have a relationship with them, I do not know them. I have not seen their faces or what remains of them; I have not seen their ID cards, I do not know their names. I am yet to know the extent of their decay, and if they are recent arrivals or have been lying around here for long. I'm standing away from them, my small gulf of water apart. I'd be safe from seeing what happens to them if I do it from here. I will be able to stay clear of what happens, I'm sure, and it won't really matter, isn't it? They are dead anyway. How does it matter? A dead person is a dead person. A corpse a corpse. I have all the respect for their lives and their stories, but I do not know them. It won't mean anything to them. I could stand a little further apart from the riverbank to be safely out of close vision but not too far to miss it altogether.

I take aim, slowly, steadily and tremulously, and pull the trigger exactly how Kadian said, *Just a short, assured pull, don't fight it too hard, don't yank at it.*

I see a hazy, dusty disturbance at the other end. Don't know what I have hit. I aim again, less slowly, and this time at the side of a man who appears most intact from here. This way I can see if I have really hit where I aim. Metal, flesh, click, bang, flesh. Dust again.

My palm and the back of my hand hurt – a burning throb. I look around and see a full audience of hollow eyes staring at me vacantly, as if considering a question. I briefly look towards the other side, the far side, of the valley where miniature Pakistani outposts are sketchily visible through the trees on the mountainside. I'm sure they can't see my gun from there. By now they must surely take me for some crazed local. And even if they do see me engaged in shooting practice, what can they say? I'm in no-man's-land – what happens here is off the record, means nothing to anyone. At worst, they will complain to their Indian counterpart. Kadian. Huh!

I aim again: let's try someone's head this time. No, no, that will be too cruel. It can burst open. I can't shoot someone in the head! I won't be able to. My hands will tremble. But, but . . . it's just a target. These people are gone, long dead. Some unknown skull is all you are shooting at. Come on, come on . . .

I raise my right hand and hold it firmly at the wrist with my left. Steady, steady. I aim and pull the trigger, and then close my eyes for as long as I can. Finally, I inch closer towards the riverbank and try to assess the damage the bullet has caused. Right in front of me then, perched lightly across a tangle of bodies, is the man I have shot. There is a big hole in the back of his head, with a part of the skull broken off and hanging loose, as if some animal had dug into it to pluck a mouthful. I stare and stare. A brick rises in my stomach and tries to force its way to my throat. I try not to choke. Then I sit down and hang my head down. The pistol is still clasped in my right hand and I press it hard into the earth. I find myself shivering, deeply, my teeth clattering.

A short while later, I see some tiny dark figures in the river, they look like shadows dancing their way about in the water. What are they? I have never seen them before; there were no fish in the stream.

What are these random swimming creatures, then? I close my eyes and then open them again. The shadowy creatures are still there. I feel desperate now, desperate. I look at my pistol hand and raise it from the ground. It's still warm. Standing up, I curse the infested water of my river. I still have plenty of bullets.

Bang, bang, the bullets make quick holes in the water that fill out as soon as they appear. I shoot again, one by one, and finish all the rounds in the magazine. The water appears punctured momentarily, or so I imagine, and then full again, as if I'd poked a balloon and then removed my finger. When I think everything must have settled down, passed, I gradually turn my gaze into the water and wish the slithering tadpoles are gone. I keep looking and see nothing. My wish is granted. I look again to confirm, afraid that the creatures might reappear from underneath the slimy weeds floating by the bank, but there is no movement in the water now. It's still again, the river just flowing onward.

I turn back and think of the corpses I fired at a little while ago. I do not really know what to feel – to shoot at the human form, dead or living, hasn't registered yet. I do not know what to make of the situation, *my* situation. I somehow manage to drag my feet away from the scene, and look towards the near horizon, towards the grieving red sky which overhangs the vast mountain range, the valley, the river, the corpses, Kadian, myself – *my lost friends may be around somewhere too*. Baba and Ma, the peon, the sentries at the gates of the camp, the Pakistani soldiers in their dark check-posts, the militant boys hiding somewhere in hollow tree trunks and caves, the crows that I see now and then and the dogs who lurk at the fringes – all, all reside under this very same firmament. I look at the path that ascends homeward and follow it to the point where it meets the trees, the hills and the sky.

I feel nothing in particular and decide to move on.

I want to go home, to Ma and Baba.

8   *Mohammed's Dog*

Rakhu trotted along the street and appeared to be coming towards Noor Khan's shop. The children following him probably didn't know that Mohammed had trained him well. He wasn't going to react to his small army of followers, nor hurry himself. He would just carry on indifferently or, at best, stop briefly to grunt a low menacing grunt. The children slowed down on seeing me in the shop. Noor Khan was unpacking a carton of freshly arrived Lifebuoy soap and arranging the chunky pink paper-wrapped cakes on top of each other on the shelf directly above his seat. His copper hookah stood stately in front of him. He had just smoked; a heavy smell hung like an invisible curtain at the shopfront.

It was ten days or so after I'd visited Shaban Khatana's dhoka in the mountains with Gul. I hadn't seen Gul after that, nor Mohammed nor Ashfaq. No one. I had been a bit too occupied with my best friend. One evening, I had gone up to the attic, pretending I needed to look up my old school textbooks, which were still there, packed in bulk into a jute sack amidst other sacks of charcoal and dried cow dung, to look at Baba's old long rubber boots. My own fake fur-lined Duckbacks were only ankle high and didn't seem robust enough for a long trek; should I need to set off at very short notice, I must keep myself in some kind of readiness, I thought. Hussain had been gone for almost three weeks now.

The dog walked slowly, the children slowed down too. It was some sort of game that the animal was playing with them.

Soon, Mohammed would appear behind his pet, at a distance. Mohammed enjoyed holding 'classes' in the middle of the street with children much younger than him. 'Rakhu can eat your ears one by one if I tell him to, and why shouldn't I? Give me a good reason why I shouldn't do that, hain?' He would pace back and forth in front of a row of kids, their heads bowed in pretend shame or fear.

Then, lashing out forcefully at the dusty street ground with a stick, 'If I see you troubling Rakhu again, I swear I will not stop him if he chooses to dig his teeth into your noses, I swear, I just won't stop him!'

Rakhu had come to a stop in front of the shop and stared at me. He stood in the middle of the loamy, muddy street and just stared. The children had stopped a few paces behind him. Noor Khan was done with the bathing soap. 'Yes sir, what is it that the headman wants today?'

I didn't answer him and continued to look at Rakhu's face. A short stream of greyish fluid had dried up below his left eye. It looked like a permanent, discoloured teardrop. It would soon be our time to go down into the valley, I thought, Rakhu hopping behind Mohammed who, at the front, would carry his bat and the stumps in that much-frayed old jute sack of his. Hussain and I would be in the middle together along with Gul, Ashfaq bringing up the rear, hissing occasionally, 'You two, can't you even wait two minutes for me? And you,' he would yell at Mohammed, '*bachche badshah*, what's the hurry, man? No one's going to steal our pitch!' Once we got to the valley Mohammed would walk to the pitch like a pro, inspect the area around the crease quickly, stamp on a few bumps here and there, and disperse clay over previous batting marks, as if . . .

Months earlier, Mohammed had performed his usual routine on the pitch, patting the wicket near the batsman's crease as if he were a meticulous opening batsman preparing to embark on a monumental innings. It was just before the onset of winter and our pitch was beginning to assume the heavy, unhelpful texture of winter soil. The ball didn't travel very far, unless hit in the air. Rakhu lurched expectantly near long on, close to the edge of the stream. I bowled first up, Hussain and Gul were close up on either side of the wicket, and Ashfaq faced – having masterfully taken the bat from Mohammed's hands, who was now sulking behind the stumps – appearing comfortably settled down at the crease, as if it were always meant to be that way. In a way it was; we'd long given up fighting with him over it. This was the only way to get the absent-minded, lazy man to field when it was our turn to bat. With each ball bowled, Rakhu strutted back and forth and then settled back, realizing that the ball wasn't to be fetched from anywhere far, or from the stream, but this he did only after Mohammed had bellowed out, 'Hoye, hoye, Rakhu! It's fine, yaara, wait, look, look here, it's with me, here!' He raised the much-weathered cork ball in the air and stared down at his pet.

Ashfaq liked to sweep every other ball and hit long hops over square leg. Grumbling behind the stumps, Mohammed would call him a *phatta*, incapable of playing with a straight bat, whereas the real reason for his disapproval was because he wasn't the one with the bat, and the condition of the ball annoyed him too, for it would invariably go into the stream – for Rakhu to jump and fetch it – and then would need rigorous bouncing off the ground to shed its moisture, thus delaying the game a little too often during Ashfaq's tedious innings with the bat. 'Yaara, there's much more to batting than the leg side, really, your legs just get nailed down, I'm sure your grandmother has better footwork, Mister Sweeper!' I would taunt him too, but Ashfaq, *him*, without a worry in the world, would just lean on Mohammed's sturdy home-made bat, while we shook off water from the ball, and taunt us, 'Come on, kids, come on, don't be crybabies now, start bowling again, *chalo, chalo!*'

'King of the Leg Side, Zindabaad!' Gul Khan bowls from the edge of the crease, on the off-stump, 'Here you go!' It's a quick, into-the-body, rising delivery, but Ashfaq remains motionless on his crease – his batting stance congenitally cemented towards the leg – and sees the ball whizz past in a blur. His stoicism in the wake of Gul's provocative bowling tactics sometimes brought laughter and sometimes annoyance, depending on how much batting time we'd all had.

Ashfaq's frustrating batting strategy didn't have a lot of success against Hussain's prodigious – and sometimes erratic – leg spin, however. Oh dear, he could really, really turn it, *rip* it, as radio commentators say, and since the cork ball bounced quite significantly with the turn, and had indeed hit Ashfaq in the groin a couple of times when he had tried to smother the sharp spin with those be-all and do-all sweeps, he accorded Hussain's bowling a little more respect and remained content with just blocking it until the threatening over passed.

Rakhu was like an extra player, then, who understood the dynamics of our game; a cricket-player dog, now that I think about it, he had long figured the difference between the bowling and batting ends, and had lately taken a few difficult diving catches as well. We always thought of him as a proper fielder. Mohammed liked that.

But now, Rakhu just stood watching us. Noor and me. The children hung around idly near the shops. Mohammed didn't come after his dog. Maybe he's been banned altogether from coming out of the house, I thought to myself, maybe he's just decided to wait a little longer, but, but, I realized with a start, I hadn't seen him for close to three weeks now. Something was seriously wrong; only, I refused to accept it at first. Or I was perhaps too busy contemplating how to arrange my own trip to Pakistan, now that Hussain had for some reason gone there without taking me with him, or at least taking me into his confidence.

Soon, the children had ganged up together again and stood in a loose semicircle behind Rakhu, who hung his head low; by now he was firmly parked in front of the shop. I wasn't sure what to do with him, so I just put my hand on his head and scratched it a bit. I'd seen Mohammed do this often. In return he grunted low grunts of satisfaction perhaps, nostalgia even. He bent his forelegs and looked like he wanted to sleep while I watched over him. I'd never paid him much attention before, nothing beyond what's due to a friend's pet – *Hi, hello, Rakhu.*

I must have been standing there for quite some time before Noor Khain said, 'Beta, your father must have gone to sleep waiting for whatever he sent you to buy? Tell me . . . ?'

'Just the tobacco, Noor Chacha, what else? Here . . .' I gave him the dirt-encrusted pink two-rupee note and he scooped out ugly chunks of loose sticky tobacco from his oval wooden basket and spread it on a newspaper sheet. I watched him expertly make it into a cone.

*

I sometimes think had I not been the headman's son, Mohammed would have been the leader of the group. He was the strongest and the biggest of us all and he was afraid of nothing, except perhaps of passing the graveyard in the evenings after dark. At school, it was his presence that prevented us from being picked on by the big boys or boys from the villages down in the plains, who would sometimes try to have fun at our expense – the 'shepherd boys' they called us. We were the only Gujjar boys in the Government High School, and it had been some kind of novelty for many to see 'these children of goatherds' at school with them. But Mohammed had made sure, from very early on, that he came across as a tough man, and it did do us good all through to Class X, after which all of us moved to the big boys' secondary school, where the teachers took more care to keep it civilized. Even I felt much safer when Mohammed was our frontman. Most often, the reason behind a flare-up with a rival gang would be a remark Ashfaq might have made, and we would get away unharmed only because Mohammed would stand ahead of us and ever so calmly say, *It is me you need to talk to, friends, me.*

I remember how he once cut through the barbed-wire fence of the large apple orchard near Poshpur, where we'd gone to steal fruit at the start of the first harvest. We did not go into the village; I would only go there for the first time many years later. We had arrived at the furthest boundary of the vast orchard – it was owned by one of the wealthiest apple and walnut merchants in South Kashmir, the illiterate but notoriously debauched Qasim Koun Bakhshi. He was rumoured to prey especially upon poor, husband-less Kashmiri women and, in the past, upon Bakarwal and Gujjar girls who might be walking through the orchards in the plains of the big Valley. Perhaps we took special pride in robbing this particular man of a few dozen apples every Friday during the prayer hour, with Mohammed proudly leading the charge.

It was the first week after the Class X exams were over and we'd passed many days exactly as we liked – played cricket from morning to evening, swum until my ears began to sing, talked away whole evenings until Baba sent for me, eaten unripe cherries from Gul Khan's orchard until my belly hurt, made Hussain sing till his throat gave – before embarking on one of our rare forays into the world outside Nowgam. The orchard was more than two hours' walk from our village. We had left in time to hit the orchard when most men in Poshpur would have gone for the long Friday prayer.

However, on arrival we were surprised to discover that the cunning owner had hired two guards. And one of them was the famous toughneck and gambler, Hassan Abdullah Paacha. It was strange to see such a well-known hoodlum guarding an apple orchard. But then, Qasim Koun Bakhshi was known to have both a great deal of money and a lot of influence in many quarters.

Rather than being deterred from the 'raid' – as I was – Mohammed was further emboldened. Reluctantly then, we slithered behind him into the orchard and hurriedly picked a dozen or so big green apples and forced them inside our shirts, which we had fastened tight at the waist. Mohammed smiled – his shirt bulge was the biggest. However, just as we were about to crawl under the compromised fence, Hassan Paacha spotted us from his watchman's tent and started running at us, like a bull. I grabbed hold of Hussain's arm; he had crept closer to me after I helped him cross. Gul Khan stumbled and couldn't prevent his apples from rolling out of the improvised sack he had made with his shirt. He looked heartbroken. Ashfaq whistled, trying to appear calm. Mohammed shouted now, 'Quick, yaara, quick, the pig will be upon us soon . . .' True to character, he let everyone cross before beginning to do so himself. But just then Hassan Paacha arrived on the scene, panting, scowling, and paused fifteen or twenty feet from Mohammed. I was beginning to panic and dragged Hussain away, but then turned back so as not to desert Mohammed.

The big watchman produced a short wooden club from his side and hurled it at Mohammed, who had by now almost made it beyond the fence. The club hit him with a wham in the middle of his back. We froze. Mohammed's breath stopped; he fell on his face to the ground. I signalled to the others with my arms and we made a ring around his prostrate figure. His eyes were bulging and he had turned red. Hassan Paacha glared at us from inside the fence, while Hussain slowly, deliberately, waved the club at him. His legs were trembling. Ashfaq, Gul and I held our arms together and waited for Mohammed to rise. He stood up soon and burst into the loudest laugh I'd ever heard him give. Quickly then, he took out two apples from his loot and threw them at Hassan Paacha with great force whilst shouting, 'Run, run now!' One of the apples, the last thing I saw, hit the goonda on his forehead with a sharp smack. He swore at us but did not dare to come closer as Mohammed aimed more missiles at him.

Later that evening I asked him, 'Why didn't you simply run, yaara? That man was huge!'

'It was a question of *ghairat*, brother, the honour of the whole group . . . Can't compromise on that!' he replied coolly as he sat by the river.

The next day, while he took off his shirt before our daily swim, I saw a deep purple mark on his back.

Mohammed didn't come after his dog. And now the children too started getting tired of waiting for him, for something exciting to happen. They started to walk away, with dissatisfied expressions. Noor had fallen silent too, with the tobacco cone resting on the sill of the low wooden railing that fenced off his shopfront.

Rakhu's grunts died gradually. His body shrank further into the space under the railing and was now covered in shade, only his tail and hind legs half protruding on to the street. Noor Khan looked at me knowingly, disengaged the chillum of his hookah, and started scratching at it with his thin, blackened iron pincers.

I grabbed Baba's tobacco cone and walked off towards home.

I went to Mohammed's house early morning the next day – I hadn't slept well the previous night and had felt really, really guilty, Rakhu's glum face hovering in the darkness of the ceiling. Mohammed's house, next to compounder Chechi's on the outer side of the village, away from the valley and from where all our trips out of the village began and culminated, was the oldest brick and mortar house in Nowgam. Mohammed's father, Jawad Choudhary, whose ancestors were originally from Neelum Valley in Pakistan, was the only foreign national in the village, Baba sometimes joked ... Although I wondered – some families did have quite a few near and distant relatives on the other side of the border, but you never met them of course. Among other things, the Line of Control also curtailed bonding of the blood, prevented contact between brothers and sisters, mothers and daughters, fathers and sons, as if it were a sin.

I knocked on the deep-maroon door three times and immediately felt blank, face to face with the silence of a shut door. There was wetness on the wood. Thousands of tiny rivers running in a delta of cracks in the flaked paint. My fingers smudged, ended some.

Mohammed's mother, a large woman who had always stood out with her elaborate, always-jangling earrings, opened the door just enough to let me see half her face, and then seemed to stop to take a long breath. As the darkness melted away, I saw her a little more clearly – she looked cold. For a while, we stared at each other through that little gap. I dreaded asking her the question.

'*Assalam-u-alaikum* ... Are you all well?' I said, still on the threshold, making eye contact with her through the twilight slit.

'Oh, yes, son, yes ... We are fine. Are you fine?'

'I was just passing by and thought I'd drop in ... Actually, I wanted to check something with Mohammed ... ?'

'Hmm ... Oh, you don't know? He is not here, er, he has gone to his aunt's place in Kupwara, will stay there for some time, couple of weeks or more; they are putting up a third storey to the house, so I said Mohammed would be helpful, isn't it? If you can't help your own, who will? Eh, eh ...' She coughed and looked away. Then, as she began to turn, added, 'You can still come in, so what if your friend isn't here? Come, come ...'

I saw her walk back the length of the dimly lit hallway, her earrings creating a soft refrain, and decided to step in for a while. The hallway was cold, as if it had forever been in shade. I entered the drawing room and sat by the large window with the iron bars, wishing for Mohammed to enter and sit by my side.

Mohammed's mother came in after a little while, spread the large tea mat between us, and poured me tea. Her hand trembled, the Thermos beak shook, and a jet of the pink-coloured liquid swerved and spilled on to the vinyl *dastarkhwan* with the blue Taj Mahal print on it.

The next moment she broke down.

In the gentle drip of her tears falling into the pool of tea, the conversations in my mind became an oppressive muddle. Looking at Mohammed's mournful mother (how I wish we had not given our mothers this lifelong grief), I felt my face go warm at the thought of what it all really, really meant – he too had in all probability crossed over, and I was the one left behind. Again. I could not do what he had done . . . Or perhaps it was for good, after all. At least Ma won't become this woman in front of me, incapable of conversation . . . But then, oh, that meant he too may not come back. 'An infiltrator killed on the border,' someone would plainly announce on the radio, and then I may not see him ever, ever again. Oh, what am I thinking? I should just go, join them. So what if they didn't think I was good enough? I must go.

She looked at me and sighed. A cold, resigned sigh. There was embarrassment on her face. She did not want me to see her grief. The tea in the gold-rimmed china cup had darkened, an unappealing film of abandonment clinging to the sides. There was nothing I could think of to say to her, nothing with the thought of which I could meet her eyes. The drop of her eyelids exactly like that of her son's.

I thought of my own Ma, felt terribly uneasy and dry in the mouth, and left Mohammed's house with a hurried and somewhat muffled *Salam-Alaikum*. She stood in the middle of the half-open door, the dim purple mix of light and shade veiling her face in utter sadness. I did not look back at her after going down the two weathered stone steps. We had once played Zarb-Zero here, with chalk Mohammed had stolen from Principal Jagarnath Koul's geography class.

Looking at the street, I saw a deserted path, with shadows of the trees and of the mountains over them meeting in the middle in stretching embraces. Darkness meeting darkness. Mohammed was gone.

*

I dreaded looking at their houses. Dreaded a mother's face by a window. In the week I had spent isolated inside the house, all movement proscribed by Baba's serious glares and Ma's drawn face, the universe of the village had changed.

I had to go to check Ashfaq.

And the next day, on a windy morning, I did, almost running to it, eyes almost closed, without thinking much, just to go in and check every room – our deep, melancholy friend was capable of everything – to make sure, to feel the full weight of what I knew had happened but which some small part of me still wished wasn't true. I remember my legs shivering a little as I approached his home.

I stopped in front of the creeper-draped house, aged dark green vines clinging to the crimson brick walls in one-sided affection, and saw Asma – dear sweet sad Asma – watering small white rose bushes with a copper *bushqaba* that she held tilted in her hands. This was the big bowl Ashfaq ate his meals in. I knew from the dark chinar-leaf pattern on its border.

She looked at me, opened her mouth a hesitant fraction, stopped watering the plants and came closer. I looked at her and knew. Dressed in a black salwar-kameez, she just stood there in front of me, the dupatta adrift on her shoulders and her hair turning dark and bright with each flutter in the breeze.

Three or four sparrows flew out from their nests inside the creepers. They formed a sharp chirping dart in the sky and vanished. I did not go inside Ashfaq's house.

From then onwards, I tried not to pass their houses. I did not want to see their mothers. Why did I feel guilty? It wasn't my fault. I was the one wronged here. In the street the people I passed seemed to know everything, *understand* everything, and gave me a look that I thought said, *We know you are next*.

Nowgam waited for me to leave.

9   Family Dinner

When I reach home, I find Ma picking green chillies from her garden; holding up the hem of her pheran she is gently dropping them into the fold of the cloth. They look cold to me. She's humming a tune.

I go upstairs quickly and hide the Nicholson pistol inside an old pillowcase. I don't look at it. I don't want to look at the dead people it blew up earlier in the day. Hide it, hide it, hide it. The breeze outside wraps itself around the house in a low hum. I could lie down for a while, at least until Ma comes in. Then I could talk to her. What do I say to her, though? What will she say? What about Baba? I survey the room even as my eyelids feel like they are going inside my head. The walls swivel, the handwritten chart with Ashfaq's strange scribble of 'ten best quotations' – starting with *A thing of beauty is a joy for ever . . .* and ending with *Better to rule in hell . . .* – begins to blur, the electrical adhesive tape that holds together the cracked glass of the partitioned window extends wide and blocks the whole pane, the whole sky. Through a small corner at the top, though, a tiny full moon peeps in.

> *Chalo dildar chalo*
> *Chaand ke paar chalo*
> *Hum hain tayyaar chalo!*
> *Hum nashe mein hain sambhalo hamen tum*
> *Neend aati hai jaga lo hamen tum!*
>
> Let's go then, my love, let's go
> Across, nay beyond, the moon!
> I'm ready, all ready, let's go!

Hussain is intently singing out – on high notes – to the full moon as it appears from behind the peaks and bathes the meadow and the river in silver. Silver, green, silver. We sit enthralled at his rendition of the Lata–Rafi duet, his right hand raised to the moonlit sky at Rafi and his arms folded at a more collected, subdued Lata.

Hum hain tayyaar chalo . . .

I'm ready, all ready . . .

I wake up to Baba's Philips Jai Jawan transistor croaking over a bad-frequency BBC news broadcast. A presenter introduces the day's news. Yusuf Jameel will soon rattle off a list of casualties across the valley and read out statements from the Hizb, the JKLF, the Army and the Governor. He is at least better than those puppets on Doordarshan. Noor Khan, apart from being the village gossip, earned his nickname, BBC Khan, for the way he almost always used to keep his red portable radio glued to his ear. Baba has a more organized way of listening to news – he places the transistor on the window sill, at an angle that he thinks is best suited to the BBC's radio waves, and then leans back on his two round cushions. His face turns more than a few shades of red as the world of news and current affairs unfolds in stiff Urdu. My favourite part of the hour-long chatter is the sports segment. An eager presenter makes the incessantly hissing radio throb with Pakistan's exploits on and off the field with the hyperbolic affectation of a baritone.

Dinner, after BBC news.

Ma is in the kitchen, the flat clay oven abuzz with a fresh infusion of firewood. She is seated on her chowki and stares into the blank space in front of her. I enter, almost surreptitiously – why, I do not know – and slide into the corner. Gradually, I walk up to Ma and sit beside her, like old times. She looks at me, a faint smile about to escape, and then goes back to her oven. Dinner is being heated; she always cooks in the early evening. Ma often used to ask what I wanted for dinner when I came back from a day at college, and I could ask for just about anything I liked. But now I just eat whatever comes out of the pans.

'Ma, anything I can do?' I haven't said that in ages.

No. She just nods her head.

'Okay, I will sit here with you then . . . Baba won't be coming yet, it's news time . . .' I try to humour her. She is sometimes exasperated by Baba's radio habit, which often delays our supper.

'Ma, time just flies. You know something, it'll soon be two years since I last went to college?'

'Hmm . . . time does vanish, son, just slips by. Seems like yesterday.'

She pokes the oven with her long iron tongs and gathers a few briskly burning twigs in the centre to channel the flames. Sparks curve out from beneath the two pans and soon die in the dark smoke that rises animal-like into the chimney space.

'Ma, does Baba ever talk about leaving this place, now nothing's left here any more?' I blurt out, not really thinking why I want to ask Ma that question. I hadn't thought I would. When everyone left, Baba had made his decision known ever so firmly, and neither Ma nor I could question it. But now, maybe it is time to quit, maybe that's what Ma also wants, to leave, to run away, to escape her prison of loneliness. She hasn't seen another woman for more than a year now. And I can't do this for ever either.

She looks at me, betraying no emotion, and turns back to her twin copper-plated pans. After she stirs whatever is cooking (I smell vapours of turnips and beans) and brings down the vessels from the now blazing oven, she gives a deep sigh. 'Your father doesn't want to go, so we won't go. That's how it is; we must stay,' and leans back against the wall. Her chubby round feet make a quick appearance from under the extended hem of her pheran and then recede again. In this pose, Ma looks like a chief matriarch, the headwoman of some clan seated in her leader's seat. Only, there is no clan now. I sit back too and we both stare into the blankness in front of us.

Baba, I hear him commenting on some piece of news that he doesn't approve of. 'They are all lies, *sarasar bakwas*, utter nonsense,' he will say soon, switch off his Philips and get up in a huff.

He enters and seats himself silently – I can see he's still grinding his teeth – against the wall facing the door. 'Oh, ho!' He gets up again to wash his hands and then looks expectantly towards Ma. She eyes him for the tiniest of moments and serves rice in our copper plates; mine has my name ornately carved into the brim in Urdu. I read it every time I eat. Baba got it made in the city when I was twelve or thirteen. Turnips in their own soup, no beans. The beans were clearly wishful thinking. Ma doesn't ask any more.

We eat in complete silence. Baba finishes first, Ma and I linger on like always. That is something we haven't stopped – sitting with our hands on empty plates but delaying getting up amidst idle talk. Only, we don't talk much now. Baba sits in the kitchen for a while, trying to offer company where none is missed, and then goes back to the living room to work his hookah.

'Ma, you think I should talk to him about it? After all, how long can we stay here like this?'

'I don't know,' she says abruptly.

Does she know?

Outside, the wind wails now. Soon, I will go back to my room and roll over in my bed until I tire myself into sleep. Ma's stories dried up some time ago. I miss her. Her late-night tea, her pauses – full of promise – in the middle of her tales, her sudden changes of tone. I miss everything.

Baba's hookah shudders with sudden life. I'm sure Ma doesn't want to stay either, but she doesn't want to pick a fight with him, distress him. Ma looks at me when we hear his coughing; it echoes, skids off the polished cement floor of the corridor, and enters the kitchen. I look back, assuring her with a slight nod – it's just smoking.

I dread, dread, dread going back to my room.

Ma, let me stay here, let me talk to you, and you please talk to me, please . . . Let's talk to Baba together. Let's leave, mother. I almost killed people today.

I climb the staircase reluctantly, holding each of the nine wooden balustrades and feeling the stems below their polished round heads for any prickly flakes. Sometimes, I like the thrill of a minute prick that I can withdraw from as soon as it's pierced my skin. I think of the dead people I used for target practice in the day. The room smells damp. The breeze has a touch of Rin detergent cake with it. Ma must have left washing on the balcony.

10 *Dead of the Forest Night*

I went to see Shaban Khatana twice again after that first visit with Gul Khan. I did not pass on his regards to Baba, but told him I had and conveyed Baba's fictional salam in return.

Shaban Chacha, it seemed, had taken kindly to me, but he also gave away, now that I recollect those evening sojourns into the mountain, some shades of suspicion.

No one came to his hut; I didn't see anyone else there. His wife was as courteous as ever and fed me salted Monaco biscuits with tea. His son Rahman had visited briefly, I learned in passing from the old man, but had left soon after on yet another sortie across the border.

I was, by now, beginning to imagine myself as a member of an underground outfit, a militant, a freedom fighter, with a small pistol jammed inside my waist, moving about, slinking, at night, on undercover missions, and being privy to secrets that none of these old men of the village, these moribund fuddy-duddies, could comprehend. At times, however, I felt terribly uncomfortable and guilty about these thoughts, that if I did manage to go *across* I would then be leaving Ma and Baba, that I would be breaching their lifelong trust and blind faith in me – and oh, what would poor Ma do then, all alone with Baba and his sombre regime . . . ? But I managed to fend off these pangs, for sacrifices had to be made for a big cause – one had to be brave, draw up *himmat*, and take the plunge (*not think too much, not think too much*), as Hussain had done. As the others had done.

I saw myself with a rebel beard, the kind Ashfaq Majid Wani and Hamid Sheikh and Yassin Malik sported – not too long, not too short – and I would wear a green brimmed cap, a fatigue jacket too, sunglasses even . . . but which group would I join? JKLF, I guess; they were smart, cool.

On the one hand, then, I didn't even know how Hussain's going had come about, who he had gone with, and what group he had joined, and whether he was even safe and sound wherever he was, and on the other, I wanted to be a part of the action myself, to be like him. Nothing was ever completely clear in those days: there was Hussain, and Mohammed and Ashfaq and Gul, there were Ma and Baba, there was myself, and there was this Movement, the goings of many, many boys across the border and, and, a lot of shelling across the mountains, in the jungles, all around . . .

'It is a busy time, beta, a lot of people are going over, too many I think, too many,' Shaban Chacha gurgled through a slurry sip of the tea-and-biscuit mixture on my third visit. '*Insha-Allah*, Rahmana should be back in ten to fifteen days . . . that's what he said, but Allahtaala knows better . . .' He talked in his usual somewhat woolly manner and waved his hands in the fashion of old people. 'Looks like there will be war, beta, the passes are open, hundreds of them are crossing in and out every day, there will be war, beta, there will be war,' he concluded, and fell silent again. I wanted to ask him if he worried about his sons, if he too spent sleepless nights waiting for them to return from their dangerous trips into Azad Kashmir? If they too feared for their lives? But I chose not to. I just listened to his broken-up talk, amidst sounds of shelling and gunfire somewhere not too far away. By now I was so used to the rattle-rattle that I sometimes forgot to notice, but presently, Shaban stopped every few moments and nodded towards the outside, as if to ask, 'Did you listen to that? That's what I'm talking about, *war*.'

The Pakistanis were pounding a mountain pass some distance away, the Indians were replying in kind. There would be blood, and sulphur, on the trees. Dark plumes of smoke would emerge from the green canopies. Pines, those majestic umbrella pines, would be broken, their spectacular dark green spreads turning to umbrellas of crumbling flame, smoke and ash. There would be the quick jaunts of the successful across some gorge or gully, but there would also be those caught in the big red glare of a mortar. Bodies would be dragged, bayonets would come down, eyes would be gouged, faces would be stamped on, mauled, amidst exultant cries of *Har*

Har Mahadev, I thought. They must not be among them. Hussain must not be among them.

I sometimes wished that Hussain was still on this side of the border, still waiting, and what if . . . ? If I found him, I could go with him. I had increasingly started to think I too could do it. I liked the game, the excitement of doing something secret on my own, now that they had not chosen me, now that they had probably decided I didn't make the cut. At times, I may even have forgotten about Hussain – only a few times, though – as I was now doing it for the thrill of it all. I blunted the feeling of left-behind-ness by starting a pursuit of my own. This was, then, my way of being involved. Deep down, I guess I envied Hussain his militant status. And sometimes I wondered if I had not let a movement, a revolution pass me by, by having been sceptical, initially at least, by having insisted on being different. People were talking about Azadi everywhere – why should I be the one left out of such a momentous thing? But there was still time, there was still time, I could go on my own – all I needed was to somehow meet Shaban Khatana's son and persuade him to take me along.

Through all this, Shaban's words stayed with me. War hung in the air.

News from the city was bad too, very bad. *The Daily Toll* said at least a hundred people had been killed on the Gaw Kadal Bridge in the heart of Srinagar. This would have been four days or so since I had last visited Shaban Khatana up in the mountains. The previous day, it was a Friday I remember, a celebrated Indian administrator had been drafted in as the new Governor of Kashmir. He was known to be a harsh administrator whose earlier jobs as governor had included 'cleaning up' the city, thus the nicknames cleaner, sweeper, scavenger. It perhaps owed much to the dislike Kashmiris nursed for their surname-less ruler from India. In his previous jobs, this man had bulldozed the rickety shacks of poor people in Delhi and Bombay and Calcutta, and had forcibly sterilized unwitting men in India's far-flung villages, I would learn later. I saw a photograph of him for the first time in the newspaper reports announcing his appointment and arrival in Kashmir. He had a pair of large, outstanding hairy ears and thick lips. He wore large glasses and seemed never to smile. In the black and white photographs he indeed looked strange. People had been killed, massacred, in broad daylight on the Gaw Kadal Bridge on the river Jhelum, their bullet-torn bodies either heaped up on the polished grey macadam of the bridge or thrown into the backs of CRPF trucks. 'There was a breakdown in the law and order situation and the police were forced to open fire on the out-of-control mob; as a result thirty-five people were killed,' a bald, frugal-looking middle-aged newsreader in a double-breasted suit had gravely announced on the evening TV news.

'The River of Blood', read a page-wide headline in *The Daily Sun* the next day. 'Imagine, just one day after the monster takes over the reins of power he murders scores of innocent Kashmiris, just like that. Young and old, men and children, dead, all dead, dead on a bridge; blood, washed with fire-brigade hoses, ran down copiously into the muddy waters of the river below. If this is how they want to conquer the hearts of the people, then they will surely succeed! Every heart in the valley is crying now, weeping for the slain,' declared the half-page editorial 'Thus Ponders Khizar on the Banks of Wular . . .' I mourned the dead too and imagined dark streaks of blood forming parallel lines in the cold, cloudy waters of the Jhelum. I tried hard to rationalize: maybe all of India was not evil, maybe they didn't want to kill all of us, but then again, they did seem to terminate anyone who dared to raise a voice of protest. I remembered Sadiq Chechi's matter-of-fact observation to Noor Khan: 'Noora, it's a plain and simple thing – all the soldiers they send to Kashmir are trained to be killer dogs.' Noora seemed to have agreed with this piece of wisdom with the willing ear of a veteran gossip, but had also turned grave and cast down.

Nearly a month had now passed since Hussain had left. There was talk of dead bodies in the ditches and *nallahs*, the Army had started capturing and killing hundreds of boys attempting to cross over to Azad Kashmir. They saw, they shot. They saw more, they shot more. Someone or other always brought news of bloated bodies, street funerals and seeping red shrouds. Fierce battles along the LoC, from dusk to dawn, raged on radio and TV. I wondered whether people in the city even knew what was happening along the border, in the remote areas, in the far reaches, the recesses of the valleys and the hollows of the mountain passes. On the Line of Control. Where we lived! It was strange in the beginning, reading about incidents in Srinagar and in my own neighbourhood at the same time, in the same newspapers. Sometimes, I didn't even know which was worse – unwary roadside protesters killed by the score in CRPF firing or unsung mujahids and would-be boy militants torn apart with mortar shells in the mountains and thrown into some blind gorge? But now I can tell that while Srinagar had all the roadside massacres and police firing and sensational assassinations and kidnappings, we far outweighed them in death.

Having pondered for long on the Gaw Kadal massacre, I dragged myself out, on yet another Friday evening to pay the Khatanas another visit. By now I had started alternating between a fierce, self-willed resolve to go wherever Hussain and the others were no matter what, and giving it all up at once and tucking myself in Baba's chadar on Ma's chowki in our always-warm kitchen . . . After all, thousands had left home and crossed over into Pakistan, that's what people did nowadays; and if I was so determined to find Hussain, I could just try and cross over into Azad Kashmir myself. Although I did not want Shaban Khatana to know, his son must surely have guessed the real purpose of my visits – and that was what I wanted. I dreaded acknowledging that Hussain had been lost, that he would never come back and, even if he did, it would never be the same again, he would never be back to normal life. I felt if I gave up on him, I would be assigning him too to the unknown multitudes of the missing. And in keeping my options open, there was still a chance, a hope, of finding him, meeting him. He was a bigger presence this way, and ticking him off on some list would be the end of it. The end of it all.

I set out early for the climb because I was alone and knew I would take more time manoeuvring the tedious path to Shaban's dhoka. I had wanted to go to Gul's again – but, trust me, I was really, really scared to go to their house. Farooq, who I met in the street, said Gul had gone off to his maternal home, his *matamaal*, and that he would be back in two weeks. But I heard nothing of him.

On my way up, I missed Gul's company and felt quite lonely walking through the forest. I held the same overhanging branches where I needed support and jumped over the same brooks. I made a determined face against the looming forest ahead and marched on. Occasionally, and this happened during my earlier trips as well, I did think of giving up this thing, this *zidd*, and going back home, running away to Ma and Baba and hiding in their flanks . . . But I climbed on. Without Gul it felt tougher, steeper.

When I was not far from the Khatana house, near a sort of plateau – made possible by bare, almost-smiling rock faces as if the forest had opened up its heart in welcome, in the ages past, to a beatific seer, a Peer Baba – I saw an old tree stump, and decided to rest for a while. From here, I could see all the houses of the village, including ours, scattered around the slopes. I saw the loose cluster of shimmering tin roofs, some of which had thin ropes of smoke rising from them; I saw the green valley far below with a silver ribbon snaking its way through the middle; I saw the numerous trees with their varied aspects spread across the land. I saw everything and took a deep breath. It felt cool inside. I held my entire world in the arc between my thumb and forefinger. I moved my hand closer to my eyes and narrowed down on each scene one by one – the village, the smoke, the valley, the river, the trees – it was nice to look at things like this. The day had warmed up; the early winter sun had managed to cut in through the tall trees, and there were wisps of vapour still rising from a just-thawed bough. Everything looked resolved here. I sat and took in the solitude. Except for faint forest sounds all I could hear was my own breathing. The jungle in siesta.

I must have dozed off, from the bliss of being at peace for once, when I was woken up by some human noise coming from further above. I leaned back on the stump and tilted my head. At first I thought it was my imagination. But it grew louder with every second of my suspended breathing. I swallowed and stood up at once. There were people's voices coming from above and they were getting closer. I didn't know what to do, whether to carry on unmindful of the voices or quickly find a hiding place. Maybe I could tell them I was visiting an acquaintance, and they would surely understand I meant no harm? No, no, no need to explain anything. What acquaintance! I looked up again and discerned some hazy movement through the foliage; they seemed to be coming towards me. I decided to stay still, and waited. The voices grew closer. I saw legs shuffle and lift through the tree trunks and their shadows. A shoe. A trouser leg. A blur of colour. I had now moved from the stump to behind a large tree on the side – I didn't notice when. I crept up against the reassuring, sweet-smelling cedar and craned my head out slowly, hesitantly, to see what was happening. It sounded like there were quite a few of them. They looked like they were heading past the plateau where I crouched. I sank my back into the tree and waited for them to pass. Knotty protuberances of bark dug into my spine.

Two men, in heavy clothes and Castro caps, appeared first at the front of the group. One of them was carrying a wireless set, or some kind of telephone, and had probably been using the thing until a moment ago, because it let out faint gasps of static and the man still had the receiver in his hand. Behind them were fifteen to twenty men, with huge rifles on their shoulders – some of them had rucksacks as well – walking in file. Casually. Most wore trousers and sleeveless fatigue jackets. Only a few were dressed in salwar-kameez. I was seeing militants face to face for the first time ever. A few faces looked alien, not Kashmiri. Guest mujahideen. The man with the wireless thing was one of them. Behind him were three or four boys, walking quite confidently – they must have been the source of the noise perhaps. The group was walking slowly and talking, each of them turning their head sideways to face the others when they said something. I could just about make out the first few words of their conversation as they moved closer. 'Nisar has made a big mistake, baradar. Lashkar is going to wind up soon; what will he do then?' the scraggy-looking, machine-gun-wielding boy on the left said. I marvelled at how effortlessly this *so*-young teenager was carrying such a big gun on his shoulder. I imagined myself in his place, carrying a big weapon with such ease. 'Naah, na, he was made an area commander straight away, brother, I would have done the same, they are better than the Hizb . . . much better,' replied the moustachioed older man walking behind him.

But alas! The conversation ebbed away almost as soon as I had started to hear it. The fellow walking with the wireless man looked back at the group and nodded. The group broke into mutters again – I'm sure they were from the city – and carried on. My heart flip-flopped a thousand times as they passed my hiding place. I couldn't see them now and didn't know when to look out again. What if a few less-talkative members of the company were still around? What if there were more people behind this lot? They'd grill me, even kill me, thinking I was some kind of mukhbir. But they passed soon, the wireless thing crackled a couple of times again and the two men leading the caravan exchanged a few words.

Shaban Khatana looked as if he had been waiting for me, for he showed me in the moment I reached his door. 'Sit, sit,' he said and poured me a glass of water.

I drank it in one gulp and let out a relieved gasp.

'Listen, beta,' Shaban, ignoring or failing to notice my breathlessness, at once drew closer and put his hands on my knees. 'Rahman is here,' he said in a whisper. 'I have told him about you, and your friend . . . He says are you sure that this boy is not up to something fishy? Is he all right? I said yes, yes, he is a good boy, wants to find out if his friend is all right. He says it's not a problem as long as he didn't behave suspiciously. I said no, no, far from it, he's a good boy and is the Headman of Nowgam's son and I told him about your father. He says he knows, he knows, all right then, what's the harm in talking to him? I said exactly, what's the harm . . . ? So well, you see, there it is, hmm . . .' Shaban rattled off a torrent of things he had talked to his son about and what he had said in return, but what he didn't tell me was where Rahman could be found at that precise moment because he was clearly not present in the dhoka, and that was the one thing I wanted from my difficult visits to the old man's home.

'That's great news, Shaban Chacha, er, but Rahman, is he here now, where is he . . . ?'

'Oh yes, yes, I forgot, he has gone out for a while, he will be here in a couple of hours, you have come at the right time, son, don't worry, don't worry. Just relax, have some tea, and by the time you have finished, Rahman will be here.'

Shaban beamed with the satisfaction of a man who has finally made himself useful. But I was trembling. A familiar heaviness reared its head inside. Rahman the Guide might know things that may not have crossed my mind, he may have seen things that I haven't imagined yet, he may have a story that I don't want to hear, or he may even laugh, scoff, at my idea – you can't just come here, all by yourself, when I don't even know you, and say, hey, I want to go border-cross with you!

I don't remember exactly when I finished drinking the tea Shaban's wife had served in a wide-mouthed cup, for I suddenly found myself looking at the empty bottom of the paisley-patterned, blue and white handle-less porcelain cup and kept staring at it until Shaban pulled at my shoulder. I immediately looked up towards the door where stood a good-looking, though scruffy, thinly bearded man wearing an Afghan cap and what looked like an old thick feather jacket with a grubby salwar under it. He had his father's nose, shining red. His face was jagged, all bones and skin, as if it had been left without being fully fleshed out. The pronounced cheekbones shone with hard work. The rude stubble on his chin looked greased. But his clear watery eyes gave him a genteel look in spite of the rather hard features. I liked his looks. And yes, he was very tall, looming like a poplar. Shaban's son shifted his weight as he leaned against the doorpost and looked at me, as though scrutinizing a new livestock purchase. (I guess I had done the same.) I coughed.

He entered the house; it somehow seemed to me that he did not spend a lot of time with his parents. Finally, he sat down close to where the chullah was and balanced his left arm over a tin container. His arm too was big – thick, hard. 'Beta, this is Rahman.' I nodded to him, he nodded back, although not as enthusiastically as I had. Shaban was still standing and didn't look like he was going to sit down any time soon; something in his posture told me he was anxious. What could it be? Perhaps he wanted to make sure I didn't get to speak alone with Rahman.

'So your friend has also crossed over. Hmm . . . What was his name?'

I didn't really approve of Rahman's use of the past tense for Hussain, but this was no time for being fussy about language, and I had to gain the man's trust. 'Hussain,' I said firmly.

'There are too many people who are called Hussain, bhai, what I mean to say is what Hussain, what Hussain?'

'No, no, my friend's real name is Hussain. His father's name is Khadim Hussain, but we just call him Hussain.'

'Oh, oh . . . okay, okay, when did he leave, when did he?'

'It's been around four weeks, more than that actually. No one knew he was planning to go, nobody suspected anything, I didn't know a thing, and we haven't heard anything since . . .' I said quickly.

'Look, I'm just an ordinary guide. I get paid to do this, not all the time, but still . . .' he said matter-of-factly. 'Some people come to me and say, "O, Rahmana! Five, ten, fifteen boys are going to be here on so-and-so date, we'll meet at so-and-so place, can you do it, can you?" and I say, "Yes, yes, no problem," and take the cash. Do you understand? A lot of people are crossing over these days . . . buses and trucks full of boys from the city, almost every day. It's a very, very busy time. Like a rush, brother, you see, like a rush. There aren't enough guides.' Rahman let out a surprised laugh.

Did you take Hussain across?

He probably read my eyes, and resumed. 'I don't remember meeting anyone by the name of Hussain.'

But then?

'But at the same time, I don't know everyone by name. I do meet some of these boys, but a lot of them just follow at the back, you see, and even if they do talk to me, I don't always know their names. So who knows? I may have met your friend, even talked to him – we may even have eaten together, rested together – without ever asking his name, who knows, who knows?'

Shaban looked at me sympathetically. *I told you so, I told you.*

'You see, brother, you don't really make an effort to socialize with people you are taking across the border. You don't have time to make friends, my friend, no time,' Rahman said expertly, decisively, and shrugged his vast, wall-like shoulders as if to signal the end of the conversation. It felt like something of an anti-climax to me, I wanted to keep talking to him, *somehow* convey my own interest, and to ask him how to go about it – and now that I think about it, I perhaps wanted him to do it for me, you know, make it happen somehow . . . For the moment, though, I started describing Hussain for Rahman, without being asked to, and requested him to think again, just in case he remembered something, some small detail, some kind of recognition, and what might be a way to find out if he was all fine. Rahman, however, went round and round the same crux of the story: we are just guides, we walk the passes, mostly at night, and there are people who follow at the back, end of story.

I just sat there. I didn't know what to do, I wanted him to call me out, and I looked at him with a glance that must have said as much, but Rahman went to a corner of their one-room home and sat there sipping his tea, only occasionally eyeing me from his perch. His hands were huge; cupped around the wide-mouthed porcelain cup, I noticed how big they really were, his fingers like knotty branches of a mulberry tree. The teacup seemed so small in those thick-veined hands. Shaban Chacha leaned back against a wall and closed his eyes. He wasn't a man at peace, I could tell. There was something more inside his chest.

Shaban's wife, demure as ever, remained where she'd been sitting throughout the conversation and looked at me without blinking. I was hoping I could leave just when Rahman was to go out, and catch him, try to talk to him, outside. I was disappointed, annoyed at myself for not being able to do what I wanted to do.

I can't recall how long I sat there. Shaban's wife, no one called her by any name, no one *told* me her name – it's strange, some people can get on just fine without names – she was now blowing hard at her chullah, which gushed out clouds of dark blue smoke, from wet firewood perhaps. I wondered if she had ever used a kerosene stove like our Maharaja brand brass stove that Ma always kept in such pristine condition. The dense blanket of fumes made the dhoka look smaller. A square of blue-grey sky hung low above us. Shaban's wife kept blowing at the chullah until it leapt into a hopeful golden fire. She then rose from the cave-like mouth of the oven to reveal a burning red face; two small rivers, delineated feebly by soot and ash, ran all the way down to her much-wrinkled neck. A few wayward wisps of smoke hung around her headscarf and mingled with some of her loose grey hairs. She smiled.

Shaban suddenly appeared in front of me, headless, but soon emerged in full form from the smoke screen, with a lantern, and sat down next to me. It was getting dark now. He looked at me fondly and I began to wonder how this old Gujjar, this man who lived his life in this solitary home, had decided to be kind to me. In the beginning I had thought he didn't want to be bothered and must have disliked me for having troubled him thus. But now he was looking at me like my own father did only on rare occasions. A part of it surely did have to do with the fact that he knew Baba, an important man, the *headman*, who had employed him once, been kind to him, but still . . .

Did he miss his own sons? I had possibly visited him more often than Rahman had done in the last few weeks – it perhaps made him happy. Oh, by the way, where was his other son? Shaban had mentioned him a few times but I never heard him say he had visited? Did he even exist? What was his name?

The old man wiped the glass casing of the lantern with his coarse blanket and placed it near his feet. The smoke had started gradually filtering out through the roshandan at the back. A thinnish film persisted, though, sticking close to the uneven ceiling of logs, where I also noticed – the first time since stepping inside this always-wistful forest home – God knows how many layers, eras, of smoke, of smoke turned into layers and layers of soot, as of stories told, sealed and trapped for ever.

I had to leave soon but my legs wouldn't move. I had to, had to, get hold of Rahman by myself – only he could recruit me and take me across. But this was a prospect much easier said, I began to realize, than done. I sank back and must have sighed loudly, for Shaban put his hand on my shoulder and said, 'Son, can I tell you something? This is how it is, if your friend has gone across, he has gone across, you can't do much about it now.'

He drew a little closer and took my hand in his. The old man always smelled of burned wheat flour. 'Look, he is just one of the many, many people crossing into Pakistan these days, curse on that troublesome country! We don't know, but he might still be in Muzaffarabad, waiting to be taken elsewhere. I have been there, son, have gone as far as Balakot and Malakand.' Shaban paused to look at me, probably for some kind of acknowledgement. I managed to hold a teardrop inside my left eye. 'I'm sure he is all right, he will come to see his family some day, and if he cares even half of what you do for him he will meet you too, isn't it? Don't lose heart, one must leave certain things to the Parwardigaar . . . Everything will be fine, *Insha-Allah!*'

I held his hand and breathed in a roomful of the smoke-filled air. I had to leave now, find Rahman. Baba would be back from the mosque soon and start getting worried. Ma must be busy in the kitchen. I had to get home before dinner. I shuffled a bit. 'All right, Chacha, I must go then.' A dread took over me as I said that and a pain lurked somewhere. Shaban looked at me approvingly. The wife looked up from her tray of flour. She had a small hill to knead. Her hands wore a sandy, translucent glove each. She smiled again.

'Yes, yes, you must go now, your mother must be worried.' He pressed his hands on the floor to raise himself and said, 'Give my salam to Sarpanch Sahib . . . such a good man, such a good man.'

'Please remain seated, Chacha, just give me some water.' I looked at his wife, who quickly wiped her hands with the undercloth of her kurta and stood up to fetch a glass from the lone shelf that perched austerely on the wall above the chullah. Our shelves are in the exact same position, I thought. But then, just as she turned, I heard something from the outside and looked at Shaban for confirmation but he seemed lost, so I forgot about it and took the glass from Shaban's wife, who was now standing in front of me. I was drinking, in big sips, from the sharp brim of the cold aluminium tumbler, when I heard something again – footsteps probably. It must be Rahman. I had to make for it now. I finished the water while at the same time dreading finishing it. (Procrastinations, however small, have their own comforts.) There were more sounds now. Steps – swish, shift, shuffle. Shaban raised his head, trying not to look at me, but I understood. His wife raised her eyebrows too but didn't say anything. Shaban stood up at once, suddenly animate; I tried to start for the door too but he stopped me with an abrupt wave of the hand. His wife also waved *stop, stop* with her hands.

The sounds were unmistakable people noises. *There were more people in the jungle.* This was too soon. Oh God! My heart raced, pounded. Shaban was out of the door now and had made sure he shut it behind him. I took a deep breath and leaned against the wall on the side of the door. The lantern unfurled broadening rays of a morose yellow light on the clay-painted floor of the dhoka. A disc-like part from the illuminated triangle it formed was eaten into by the red light from the chullah.

While I waited, the noises came and went intermittently. I heard nothing for a couple of minutes, then a few clomps and hollow thuds, then a fading away, and then again. It was surely yet another of Rahman's cross-border sorties – I couldn't believe I was so close to it. It meant if I was part of his entourage I could be in *Pakistan* in two days, possibly even face to face with Hussain. It meant if Mohammed and Ashfaq (and *Gul?*) had indeed left after Hussain and were still in transit, they might be right here right now, part of this very batch. It meant I was two or three days away from joining a training camp, becoming a militant myself! That's why Shaban Chacha didn't let me go out with him. The old man wanted to check everything – make sure – before I started for home. He had no doubt grown fond of me over the last few weeks, and didn't want any harm to come to the Headman's son. I knew I would not be able to stay inside for long; I had to go out but dreaded it at the same time.

I was very restless, standing by the door, when Shaban entered the hut; he went straight for the pitcher of water and drank noisily, directly, from the dark pitted aluminium ladle that always hung by its hook from the brim of the earthen pitcher. He came back, stroking his magenta-streaked beard, his eyes betraying some secret, and stood next to me in a solemn pose. 'You should go now, beta, it's very late,' he said without looking at me.

I was scratching at the floor with the tip of my old Bata leather school shoe, my back against the wall, becalmed under the weight of my own dread and hesitations. 'What happened, Chacha, er, I mean, is everything all right?'

He waited, weighed my half-hearted questions that hung fretfully in the warm air of the dhoka, and said, 'Rahman has to go, beta . . . More people, more than a dozen, arrived two days ago; they got delayed because the Army had been combing the area ahead. But they must leave immediately now . . . I had to help Rahman a bit. More people . . . You should go home now.'

Shaban then mumbled some more about 'the boys' while showing me out, about how they had been going here and there, a couple had been left behind in the dark, a few had been scared too, he said. 'They are still there.' He sounded resigned, tender. I sensed he had reconciled himself to something he wasn't telling me. I had been dying to meet Rahman separately, but I couldn't pull it off yet – didn't want Shaban to know – and felt the taste of disappointment, of defeat, acutely in my mouth. If I was like Hussain, the Hussain I didn't know, I could have simply run out of the warm hut and joined the unknown boys walking to Pakistan, probably just a few hundred feet outside, in the safe darkness of the jungle. Oh, oh, if only I could ask Shaban directly, if only I had his confidence, if only he would tell me . . .

But I didn't press him, and left – silently, in the company of too many thoughts, my arms pressing hard against my body.

11 *Birdsong*

I shudder when the shells thump for the second time – the hollow, heart-stopping crashing of artillery shells. The walls seem to shift, to vibrate. My bed suddenly feels under bombardment; it's raining bombs somewhere close in the hills. Heavy, heavy shelling is going on; gunfire, rockets and some other unknowable weapons register their sounds in between the earth-shattering booms and bangs. I hear the mended windowpane tremble – this must be something big.

They are pummelling the forest ground, burning the mossy earth, making scorching holes in the green, uprooting pines, deodars and firs, and hurling their gnarled branches and roots and burned berries and blossoms far, far away into the darkness. Sometimes, I think the LoC is like a fireworks exhibition for them, you know, where they compete to decide who has the better display, who shoots the highest, who lights the brightest, who burns the furthest. Really, sometimes I think it's just that, and the poor boys who get caught up in the fiery frenzy are just tinder.

I tiptoe to the window and see sporadic flashes on the horizon. I am not sure if they are real flashes of bombs and shells or mere reflections of them. Though we are used to all this, this is the noisiest and the most frightening exchange of fire I have heard in a long, long time. The whole jungle must be on fire, smoke and fumes and soot flying everywhere – what on earth are they doing, tearing the jungle apart, mixing limb with limb, branches and arms, grass and hair, sap and blood? Exploding the pine-needled surface, taking it to a boil. Sometimes, I do get very scared.

Why can't they just have another war instead – a proper, proper war – and get it over with. This *ikka-duka gola baari*, this damned 'sporadic shelling on the LoC', I'm sick of it. Baba is going to be all cranky in the morning, although you still can't talk to him about leaving! Ma will have spent half a sleepless night as well, but she won't say much except for the red of her swollen eyes. Really, why can't they just have a proper go and finish this damned unfinished business once and for all; what's another war after the three or four they have already had? I might at least sleep peacefully then, without waking up in the middle of the night to a massive thud on my pillow . . . And what is left to finish off anyway – the maize fields you burned a long time ago, the animals you maimed in the first few months, the people you chased away like rats? Come, come, my Pakistani brothers, come inside, come right inside and then stay, don't you dare leave this time, stay and let me sleep. And if you can't, then just let it be, really, just drop it, forget it, wind up and go. Go, go, go find another place. Go back to fucking Afghanistan.

Oh, oh, I have never heard that sound before. Some kind of a new rocket, missile, whatever. American, Chinese. What better place to test it, huh?

I now hear some noises from below; I think both of them are up. The banging will soon be joined by the sound of Baba's hookah, I can bet on it. Then some ambitious curses will issue forth, briefly punctuated by a loud swallowing of the phlegm, directed towards both the Indians and the Pakistanis. And on 'these jumpy boys running in their wet pyjamas with their silly sticks'! In the morning, he will look at me as though to say, 'Look at me, I couldn't sleep a wink,' as if it were all my fault . . . In the morning, the air will smell fetid and sulphurous; there will also be the faint whiff of burned charcoal when I exhale.

I realize this means more work. I will have to go down, probably more than once, and spend a couple of workdays there. Can't it just stop now? Whenever something like this happens, they have either scored a big hit or thwarted a major attempt – at least that's what they say. 'Militants were planning a major push into the valley ahead of the winter when the passes close . . . An army spokesperson said Pakistani positions used medium-to-heavy artillery to provide cover for the militants. In other news . . .'

In the first case there would be scores of scorched bodies strewn across the jungle and some perhaps already deposited down in some hidden gorge or valley. Some day I must, must ask him why they can't just leave them like that, spread loosely in the jungle? As I get deeper inside Kadian's game, into his story, I realize I need more answers, there are more and more questions. In the latter scenario, Kadian will send his scouts deep into the forest, close to the 'enemy territory', who will then probably drag a couple of unfortunate bodies with them as their day's work and then, and then that's it . . . Then there will be a lull. Stocks will be taken, breaths settled and paces measured, and then it will burst into hellfire again. Another night, another ear-shattering rain.

Dogs, wolves, foxes, hyenas and God knows what other creatures join the chorus all around, and soon it's a medley of competing animal sounds, all mixing up into some monstrous crescendo. I stand by the window and search for the moon that sometimes rears its pretty face through the small crevice in my broken window. No sir, it's gone today, scared away by the flashes and fires of a violent night. Tonight, it has had to run away.

Finally, the sounds begin to wane, slowly, like a tired musician's notes.

The shells are shelled now, the bombs dropped, the rockets spent – there's only the occasional, faint crack of a parting gunshot. And along with it, the slow, gradual awakening of sparrows – where do they hide when the skies rain fire? What do they make of this coarse nocturnal medley? The singing picks up, is joined by other birds' salutations to the earliest glimmer of light opening up sadly in the east, and soon, it's all over. All over. The night has ended. Dawn arrived.

I turn back from the window and prepare to go to sleep once again.

The next day I decide not to see Captain Kadian. I stay home all day and do nothing. Baba's cough is a little more persistent. The first thing Ma does in the morning is check her vegetable garden. She examines every plant and the big bed of greens and walks back into the house satisfied. Ma.

Baba disappears for a few hours, as he does now and then, and returns with a newspaper-wrapped package in his hands. I only see the blood stains on the paper when he enters the kitchen and hands it to Ma with a gentle nod of the head. I know what's for dinner. He must have walked all the way down to Poshpur to buy mutton. Ninety rupees a kilo.

At night I sleep soundly and wake up in the morning to a full–blown circus of birdsong. It's not as tired as yesterday, the morning is fresh, like a morning.

Kadian is missing. There is no one in the office. The large desk stares emptily at the open door. All the articles – the papier-mâché tray, the bullets, the paperweight, even his binoculars (made in Germany), the big rusted chimney in the middle of the room, the perspiring pitcher of water in the corner, the peon's own plastic chair – everything's there but no Kadian, and no peon sahib either. This has never happened. I look around – nothing. But then, they might just be refreshing themselves, stepped out for a while, busy in the bathroom? Or KD might be sick, *finally*, in answer to my secret prayers, anything . . . I wait a little longer in the room, am tempted to open Kadian's drawer and look at the journal he keeps writing in, but can't really summon up the guts to run the risk of being caught in the act. The office is too silent, and smells of clay and urine. I could, for once, try out a bit of whisky from his cabinet; that should be nice. How does the damned thing taste anyway? He's got other drinks too; what would *they* be like? But I just don't like the smell of it. I could get used to it perhaps. Or I could go explore their store today – get it out of my mind. Every time I see the two high single-pane windows with their grey wire-mesh grilles, I want to ask him if I can go inside.

I have never been alone in this room. Something must've happened, something . . . ? My long gaze at the drinks cabinet is broken by shouting from behind Kadian's office. There's animated conversation happening close by, but I can't see anything through the damned curtain.

Outside the office is the small veranda, brick and wood, with two steps going down to the path marked by obliquely placed bricks poking out of the ground on either side. The bricks are alternately coloured a chalky scarlet and white. I follow the gravel path to the point where it forks into two – one goes out towards the gates and the other curves back into the compound behind the office. I take this other path for the first time. This is where the voices were coming from. I move ahead, a little hesitantly, and look on either side in case someone is watching me. No one. The path leads to a small open area between Kadian's office on the right and a flat grey building on the left. Beyond this space I can see a large open field at the back. Just before the building on the left is a grey painted metal signboard that reads 'RRR 01' at the top along with some other army insignia; below that it just says 'Romeo'. Red. Another small board, pointing in the opposite direction, reads 'Kilo Force'. Thick black paint on green. A skull.

As soon as I get close to the ground the voices reappear, this time more shouting and yelling. An anxiety trickles inside, then it gushes. I swallow a bit and enter the field.

Standing in the middle of the field I see Kadian with a cricket bat in his hands; he is waiting for the ball to be delivered from the other end, which is marked by a white drum. He's turned out in blue track pants and a sparkling white shirt – and he's got proper stumps behind him. The bowler is wearing a white vest and is running towards the drum in an exaggerated fast bowler's sprint. He delivers a greenish fuzz into the air and stutters along the wicket, panting. Short pitched, the rubber ball lifts, rises and hits KD in the stomach. He lets out a yelp and leans on his bat. 'Maderchod, motherfucker, is that all you can see, my tummy, aye fucker!' I wish I hadn't come here, looks like its already turning ugly. Everything becomes silent. No one moves. But Kadian suddenly bellows out a laugh and takes his stance again. 'Come on, another one, let's see if you can get me again, fucking Malcolm Marshall's bastard child.' The fielders – fit, tan soldiers in tight T-shirts – laugh too, and the game resumes as quickly as it had stopped. Kadian whacks the fourth ball forcefully and it sails over the bowler's head, gains height, up, up and above – he's skied it – all eyes trail the trajectory, the field comes to a standstill, Kadian has thrown his bat over his shoulder and is watching like the rest of us as the ball descends amidst cries of 'sixer, sixer' and 'catch it, catch it', and it's coming down fast at the far end, shooting down, when I see the peon running in from somewhere (secretive, slimy bastard!). He quickly positions himself under the ball, raises both his hands towards the tiny dot coming down from the sky, and, and, floors it! He drops the catch at the edge of what seems like a boundary; there is uproar in the field, because not only has he dropped it, he's lying face down on the ground. Wish he was dead.

KD is running now, suppressing his guffaws and running. He gets to the peon before anyone else and helps him up on his feet. A few fielders clap but it doesn't quite pick up. The peon brushes the dust off his clothes without much ceremony, sheepishly hands the ball to his Captain and, while settling the few hairs on his head, looks in my direction. He pauses and whispers something in Kadian's ear, who turns towards me and then starts walking back to his batting crease.

After a couple of overs Kadian retires and comes over to me, 'Come, come, we are having a friendly, I haven't played in ages. Do you?'

'Yes, I did, in school. And down in the . . . nothing.'

Soon, we are walking towards a long table with a sparkling white tablecloth on it. On the far side are seated a few men in uniform – officers. There's a shamiyana wall behind them. It's green and red, vertically striped – the kind mostly used at weddings and funerals – and is held upright with strings tied to the trees in the background. Two soldiers, with their SLRs positioned barrel-side up near their feet, one each on either side, are standing motionless a few feet away from the group. Kadian walks towards the crisply dressed set and waves at me to join him. I grab a glass of water from the table and try to stride – I must look confident – towards the party.

'Come, come . . . don't be shy.'

I inch forward towards this row of excruciatingly creased khaki legs that rise from fat, shiny black boots.

'Mehrotra Sir, this is the boy,' KD says proudly.

'Oh, oh, him, he is the one? Oh, okay! Hmm, good, good work, young man, keep it up, keep it up.' Mehrotra Sir pats me on the shoulder and doesn't remove his hand after he's finished. I become conscious of my thin arms. Kadian picks up a lemony glass from a small round table placed at the end of the chairs and comes back to us. From the way they are sitting it looks as if they have been here for quite some time.

'This is Colonel Mehrotra from the DHQ; I trained under him.' Kadian beams with appropriate deference.

Mehrotra Sir nods gently and brushes aside his bushy mane of silver and black hair. 'You know, KD, we need more people like this fine young man here, committed people, you see, people with chutzpah, as they say. You know what I mean?' He looks at me expectantly, in the same manner as our always-groping Moral Science teacher, the bald and black-lipped Mr Firaq, often did in class, and presses my shoulder with his fleshy hand. He smells of Vaseline.

Kadian sips his lemon thing and draws closer. He looks a bit awkward, the conversation is perhaps not exactly going in the desired direction. 'Sir, actually, he's the only one in the whole area, lives alone now, there aren't many people around, you see . . .' He glances at me meaningfully.

'Yes, yes, me and my parents . . . That's it, sir.'

'Oh, oh-oh! That must be hard, then. All alone in this wilderness?' He looks around, but his view is almost entirely blocked by the shamiyana.

'Yes, sir,' I realize I had decided to call this man 'sir' even before KD addressed him that way, 'It was, well, kind of strange in the beginning, but we are used to it now. It's been more than a year since everyone left.'

A loud appeal shrieks out from the pitch, 'Howzzaat!' and then again, then silence. Suddenly, I'm reminded of the night before last.

'But it must be better now; things have improved here the last couple of years, isn't it? What do you think?'

Things have improved, fucking 'Sir'. People have left. People are killed. No people, no trouble, isn't it? But I do not answer.

Kadian glides in skilfully. 'Oh, indeed, sir, it's much better now, *m-u-c-h* better.'

Colonel Mehrotra finishes his drink in three precise sips and stands up. 'All right then, KD, good show, bloody good, tell the boys I said so, and let me know if there's anything else, all right?'

'Sir, sir, I will.' Kadian's erect like a rod. 'I'd hoped you would stay for dinner at the mess, but I know it's a long drive, I understand. Thanks for the visit, sir, thanks, thanks.'

I have never seen him like this. I try to stop myself from smirking.

'Oh, I forgot, don't worry about your application? We'll see what we can do, all right? Okay, then.' Mehrotra Sir walks briskly towards an armoured vehicle. A one-tonner, *taboot gaed*, the coffin car. There are two at the front and one at the rear. I imagine they earned the name for their successful role in catch-and-kill duties. These vehicles from hell are a harsh grey, with 'From Kashmir to Kanyakumari, My India is Great' written in both Urdu and Hindi, screaming out in a shining school-uniform blue. Mehrotra Sir waves gloriously from the front seat, the vehicle spews out a volcano and grunts its way ahead. Either he is the most important man in these parts or they are shit scared of the militants. Both perhaps.

I look at Kadian. He looks back, and we both start walking.

'Mehrotra Sir doesn't come too often, you know. Only on special occasions. He is not like other officers who shit themselves in the cantonment all the time or fucking pee at us from their helicopters! Very honest man, never taken anything for himself, and look at him, still active in the field, coming all the way to see us here . . .'

'Hmm . . .' is all I can manage.

There are many glasses on the round table. A jug also sits there ponderously. I smell roast meat, burned meat.

'Hmm, they have released figures for the year and it's very good news, at least for us . . .' Kadian says, in his not-so-often employed official tone.

What is he talking about?

The smell, where is it coming from?

'It's down substantially, that's what the report says, but Mehrotra Sir came to tell me personally. So nice of him, isn't it?'

'Hmm . . . Oh yes, yes, it is.'

I look around, all around. Nothing.

'It says we killed 2,837 intruders from last year until now, compared to 1,227 the year before that. That's more than a hundred per cent improvement, isn't it? Sir gave me the report. The detainee figures are down this year – guess why? Huh ha ha!'

Just as we turn away from where Colonel Mehrotra and his sidekicks were seated, away from the shamiyana wall, I see a small screen on the side, behind which is a large grill, still smoking. KD had a barbecue for Mehrotra Sir . . .

'That's really good, *sig-ni-fi-cantly* down this year, you see. Not too bad for the record, eh? It's my job, I know, but no harm if it helps the leave application. Turns out we have eliminated some fucking top shots too. Abu Jindal, General Fucking Isa, General Moosa, Umer Bhai, Shamsher Gul, behanchod, and some other self-styled mother-fucking Commanders and Generals . . . Air Fucking Marshal Noor Khan, my ass!' Kadian says to himself. I can just about hear him.

I think of all the faces from the valley below. I wonder if any of them called themselves General or Air-Vice Marshal or Admiral or Commandant. I wonder if the Captain feels angry at the ease and speed with which our mujahids adopt starred designations while it must take years of service to move up the ladder in the Army. I wonder if KD resents, loathes them even more for this 'professional' reason, huh?

'But you do this, Captain? I mean, you are the in-charge here, surely you must have had *some* idea?'

'Of course I knew it was down, but didn't have the collated figures – who fucking counts, dear? Sir called up and said he wanted to visit. That was very nice of him. The men need that sometimes. Oh, that harami hit me in the stomach, it still hurts.' Kadian suddenly appears weak, like everyone else. 'I arrange a cricket day especially for these bastards and this is how they repay me.' He pinches the side of his tummy and walks on slowly. 'Fast bowler, chutia, sucker,' he mumbles under his breath, but I suppose he is not in such a bad mood, after all. I know him. *I know you*, Kadian.

We leave the field and start walking towards the area between KD's office and the other building. Soldiers in undervests and khaki trousers rolled high up to their knees walk past, some of them with buckets of water, others with bidis dangling precariously from their lips. Most are out in their nylon bathroom slippers. At the edge of the field a volleyball game has picked up against a sun-struck sky. I look back – the net separating the two sides shines like a hazy, bottle-green dupatta suspended in mid-air.

Crows hover around the barbecue part of the ground; they go round and round in circles, round and round . . .

'Something major the other night, Captain, something very big? I am sorry I couldn't come the next day.' I finally raise the subject as we walk the path to his office.

'Oh, *that*. It was nothing much, actually. They started shelling deep inside, so our gunners decided to play ball too. You know what I mean. I don't think we got much out of it, I did send a patrol to check soon afterwards.' He walks on and approaches his den. 'I am not sure if we scored a major hit . . . But you can check if you want to, you know the routine, eh . . . ? It's been a little slow of late, you know. I guess they are planning a big push before the winter. But no worries, we're ready for them, huh ha.'

Kadian unfurls the now crumpled report on his desk and begins to read. I sit on the opposite side and fall silent. I don't want to dwell on anything, but can't help noticing the sprawling heading of the typed opening page. *Bharat Rakhshak Special Ops – CI02/92–93/07: Preliminary Statistical Report on Infiltration from POK.* As I read it again, I realize I am looking at something that I have been a part of – can you believe it? – a part, however indirectly, however reluctantly, of an official report, basically, on deaths and murders and killings!

My head spins at the first paragraph, not so much from the effort of inverted reading but because it rolls over and over through its 'howevers' and 'subsequents' and 'further tos' without making much sense. Kadian sees me trying to read the page, grabs it, looks at me intently, then relaxes his grip.

12   *The Guide*

Rahman was sitting with his back against a thick tree, an ancient cedar with a much-curved trunk as if designed to welcome weary travellers to its folds. I was both pleased and nervous on seeing him. He was smoking; a bristling smell spread around him. Something about the smoke, his posture, the tree, the moon that looked like its own reflection, gave it all a funereal air. He took a fierce drag and, looking into my eyes, said, 'What do you want, brother?' and then continued looking at me in that meaningful way, which I assumed must be the manner in which the cross-border community addressed each other to convey intent. As he spoke I realized Rahman wasn't a big man after all; he talked like an older boy – a poor old man's son probably weighed down by responsibilities before his time, grown-up but not quite having lived his boyhood in a boyish way.

When he asked me that question, I realized that I'd never voiced it aloud myself till now – I had never said it to anyone, never spelled it out, expressed it, in as many words – that I too wished to go *sarhad paar* now, that I too wished to cross the border, if not to join the hundreds who had hurled themselves into the Movement (for I didn't know how to) then surely to join the one I knew, and knew so well.

When Rahman said it, and looked at me in that way, I felt I had to make an effort to say it . . . He wrapped himself in zephyrs of blue smoke and again said, 'What do you want, brother?'

I took a deep, deep breath, swallowed once, spoke the words in my mind, twice, and said, 'I am ready to go, Rahman bhai; help me do it,' making sure I sounded and looked resolute, strong.

He looked at me, nodded, smoked and began. 'It doesn't work like that, my friend, I can't take you on my own, *aise nahin hota,*' he switched to Urdu for some reason, 'it doesn't look like you are with any group, isn't it? It doesn't work like that, brother, you can't just say, hey, take me across the border and that is it,' Rahman stated clearly, without the disdain I'd sort of prepared myself for. And then he stopped, looking at me expectantly.

'So you tell me, Rahman bhai.' I drew closer to him; the smoke smelled different. 'I . . . I will do exactly as you say, really.'

'Hmm . . . ?'

'Yes, yes – I really want to go – and only you can help me do it.'

'Hmm . . .' He looked at his ruined cigarette. 'Do one thing,' he paused and flicked his cigarette butt high into the dark. A timid glow arced by the side of the tree and then vanished at once. 'Start making some arrangements, warm clothes, I am sure you have plenty, boots, et cetera . . . Be ready, but remember, I can't guarantee anything, it's not all up to me, you know, but I will try, I will try.'

A breeze blew somewhere in the jungle, hissed, and raced to where we were.

In the silence that followed, I saw myself trekking across some cavernous mountain pass, a shadow among shadows at night, marching slowly into a different world. I saw myself, and yet, I couldn't see myself. It was dark all over. I chose to skim over the details of this vision and the rest of the trek and imagined myself on the other side . . . in the other Kashmir, in Pakistan. I imagined myself surprising Hussain – he's in a training camp, he has a thin beard, and an other-worldly look about him, he speaks slowly, seriously, all sombre and grave, befitting the gravity of his mission. He prays five times a day (will he admonish me for not having done the same, and want me to join him without further delay?), he has cut his hair short, he looks tougher, stronger, older, he is popular among his peers, boys, as he always was, and he still sings, hums and runs those white fingers over his legs ever so delicately, mimicking that old harmonium in the air. And he, he practises with his Kalashnikov with such confident ease.

'Do one thing – come again next Wednesday, remember . . . Come here, same place, same time.' Rahman is looking at me intensely, leaning his back further against the tree (I too want to get under its breathing, sheltering cover), as if preparing to go to sleep now.

'I will be here, I will be here.'

'Get your stuff with you.'

'Yes.'

'And if you have any . . . Only if you can, only if?'

'Oh yes, yes, I will.' I take a quick mental tour of the inside of my trunk and touch the ten- and twenty-rupee notes buried securely in a corner under my old books.

Rahman dozed off, his head askance – the tree seemed to have taken him over now. He was at peace.

On my way back I felt resolved – big tasks required big courage. Ma and Baba would come around gradually. Rahman didn't seem to understand, or didn't want to heed, my problems with having his father in the know; I had to somehow deal with the son without the father getting any wind of it.

Over the next four days I made all my preparations. I made strategic raids on Ma's hoard of dry fruits, of almonds and dates and dried apricots, taking just enough from each container so as not to make any of them look noticeably, alarmingly, depleted. In the attic, I unravelled bags of old clothes – Ma kept them for mendicants and the destitute – and transported some of them to my room one by one, shoving them deep inside the trunk. Baba's big boots (they smelled of old rubber and dry loam) were now safely hidden between the headrest of my bed and the wall behind it, and I had tucked two pairs of socks inside each foot as well. I chose the set of clothes I would wear on my border crossing – the three sweaters with the navy-blue round neck on top – the wool pyjamas I would wear under the jeans (I had to wear jeans), and the socks – I would wear three on top of each other (Baba's boots were big anyway) and I would carry two extra pairs, just in case. My own winter cap with the ear flaps would be just fine, and I could also carry a blanket along with the other clothes I was making a roll of, for who knows how cold it might get? Who knows? But oh, that would be too much, too much, I hesitated. I also contemplated, hard, which book to carry with me, but then I realized it was not the most important, or practical, thing for an expedition like this.

*

I was supposed to meet Rahman on Wednesday evening, and on Sunday I told Ma that my pheran needed washing. Why, I do not know. Did it matter if I wore a slightly dirty pheran on my border-cross adventure?

We were all in the kitchen; Ma looked at Baba, who was trying to dress a new roll of rags, a gasket of sorts, around the hose and stem of his hookah where they were fed into the mouth of the copper water jar at the base, and said, 'This is something you have inherited from your mother's side, beta, cleanest clothes, no matter what . . . Anything else you want me to get down from your room?'

'Hmm . . . there's nothing else, Ma. If there is, I will bring it down in the morning.'

I was calm, composed. But inside, someone was already missing Ma.

Baba couldn't fix his hookah in the end, and was visibly irritated. He would have preferred to do it all by himself in his *baithak* and not be faced with failing in front of us. He made his dismissive head-man's face and made out that it was not for him to do in the first place, and then asked me to take it to Noor Khan the next day. 'Noora can make the best hookah knot in the world, unparalleled, son, there is no match for him. Do it first thing in the morning, then, all right?'

'As soon as we have tea, Baba.' I liked saying that to him, as if I never had. Baba grunted, put his hand around the soggy, turban-like *jajeer gand*, and somehow managed to complete his after-dinner smoke.

I picked my *Collected Works* of Khalil Gibran from the shelf and pretended to read. I didn't want to look at their faces too much. Hussain loved his parents as much as I do mine.

The next day was Monday the 28th of November, 1991, said Sri Devi's supremely bright and round face on a South Indian fireworks company's calendar hanging on the first plank of the folded wood shutter on Noor Khan's shop. Sri Devi fluttered briefly in the morning breeze to reveal a more lissom and upcoming Meenakshi Sheshadri, waiting underneath with Jan-Feb-March and spring.

'Noor Chacha, Baba sent this . . . Is there anything you can do?' I said, knowing well he had often fixed it for Baba.

'Oh-ho, the Sarpanch has messed it up again. Let us see, something will have to be done. What to do?' Noor said with a pressing sense of responsibility as if he were going to repair a bridge. I looked at our grocer, at Baba's lifelong ally. What would he think of me as a militant, as a JKLF area commander, for instance, for I would surely be given a higher rank owing to my education – I could speak English.

'You know how it is with Baba.' I looked at Noor Khan and decided I was going to miss his company as much as anybody else's, perhaps even more than Baba's, for this was always an engagement full of spontaneity, without the upsetting unease of having to negotiate the path to my father through his headman's demeanour.

Noor smiled, unscrewing the lid of the jar of crisp sugar-coated cookies he often sent me off with. 'So how are *you*, then . . . ?' he said, handing me two saucer-shaped biscuits in a kind of underhand, palm-to-palm exchange, to prevent, out of habit, anyone from seeing, even though there was no one around. He was looking at me conspiratorially, quizzically; he had started looking at me this way ever since Hussain left.

I didn't want to spend too much time with Noor Chacha either. A wavering of the resolve was not something I could afford.

Until Wednesday evening, then, I behaved cautiously at home, if not too impeccably. Ma had by now absorbed, or appeared to have done so, the shock and distress all mothers in Nowgam must have felt after Hussain and the others disappeared. While there were many questions that were still unanswered, *and I knew*, there was also a gradual coming to terms of the kind that ensues when someone in your close neighbourhood dies. Inevitability, even if forced, engenders some level of acceptance. This gave me strength too. Although not much.

The last dinner with my parents was, as usual, normal – even if there was a constant, and wrenching, churning in my stomach. I'd started asking Ma for a red-beans-and-turnips stew a few days ago, and, as it turned out, she made it for Tuesday. Baba, though he fundamentally liked it, often complained it was rather too gassy.

I wanted to hug Ma, sit with her in the kitchen late into the night. I wanted to watch Baba listen to the news and issue forth his curses. I wanted to listen to any story Ma might launch into, I wanted to have our late-night tea with her, one last time, before I ventured into a different world altogether, a world without the sanctuaries that Ma and Baba offered in their constant selves. I wanted to sit on the chowki one last time and bask in the warmth of Ma's hearth. I wanted to smell Ma's presence and etch it somewhere, I wanted to look at Baba's grand face and keep it fresh with me. I wanted to wrap myself up in his chadar and soak in its smell . . . And in the end, that's all I could do – for Ma got busy with her washing soon after dinner, and Baba left me for his newly refurbished hookah. I carried my father's chadar to my room and slept. I slept for a long, long time.

So much so that I found Ma quite visibly worried when I went down around noon the next day. She hadn't sensed I was trying to see less of her. By now, there was some kind of finality to my decision; by willing it, repeatedly, I had made it real. Ma didn't ask me anything when I went out for a long walk to the street, around the large open field at the end of it, to the mosque, the graveyard behind it, just for a look, and then also down into the valley . . .

Because everything seemed to be going to plan, an outside thought did occur to me briefly: could it be possible that they knew everything and were just pretending, while they had made their plans too – to eventually prevent me from going? By letting me try it out they were just indulging a teenage fixation, letting me exhaust the option, knowing well that I would be back in the fold soon, having been unable to do what I intended. Could it be possible?

Don't think too much, man, don't think too much, I told myself and waited for the evening.

There were shadows lurking in the dark, and there was the dead of the forest night I had looked at all my life, from my snug window perch in our house far, far below these lonely recesses, marvelling at the secrets it nursed inside its pensive folds. Koh-i-Gham, *the mountain of sorrow*, I had heard Ramazan Choudhary call it sometimes, although the name didn't have much currency nowadays. In my childhood I had often sat at the window, while Ma and Baba huddled in a corner of the kitchen, and imagined life, and things, inside the jungle above us. I saw fantastic creatures and imagined strange-looking forest people; winged deer came out of its hollows and glades, and angels collected milk from gold-fleeced lambs that I would find by my bedside in the morning. I saw castles and deep palaces and forever winding corridors in the richness of the dense black. I imagined wandering into them, exploring countless secret rooms and cellars and then coming back to the warm glow of Ma's hearth. The forest had always loomed large at the back of the house, and in its mystery, it had also held promise. It filled me with a dread too, a dread which has stayed with me to this day.

I realized I had come to the jungle a little early – the spot by the tree where Rahman had sat was to be my meeting point with him. I could possibly see Shaban Chacha one last time before I left. I could surely pretend, once more, that this was just another visit.

Soon, I did. And I sat with them like I always did.

Nothing had changed.

Tea and Monaco biscuits were served. The chullah was worked to a blaze; massifs of freshly painted grey and blue smoke were amassed (they heaved and swirled), sooty streams of tears were wiped away; and Shaban Chacha, that heartbroken, wizened man, rested with a cud-like portion of naswaar between his gums and lower lip, and occasionally let out restrained gasps of satisfaction.

Shaban's wife had kneaded a thick cylindrical mound of dough – was this all she ever did? – from which she was skilfully tearing off small, lopsided balls for making rotis. She was a frail woman and appeared even smaller as she sat crouched over her hand-crafted brass tray. Was she thinking of her son, *sons*, while she prepared dinner? Was she so used to this life?

As the light inside the dhoka grew paler and assumed a distinct evening hue, I understood it was time. I had to say my goodbye.

Outside, it was dark except for the occasional puddles of moonlight that filtered through the pine treetops. My route back home was down left; Rahman's tree was towards the right, further up.

I saw Rahman seated exactly the way I'd seen him the last time – even the smoke, and the light, and the smell of the smoke was the same. He nodded. I waited. The forest air was blue and reminded me of the atmosphere that hung over the graveyard soon after countless candles have burned themselves out on Shab-e-Barat, when everyone turns up with twelve-apiece cartons of slender colourful candles to light up the graves of our dead, past and recent. Rahman flicked his cigarette and stood up at once, a small sack tied on his back, and then motioned at me, with a slow, almost sacred, wave of the hand, to follow him. Nothing whatsoever stirred in the vast forest – I almost broke. I followed him, gingerly, deliberately, taking each step as if I were going through a morass. I thought of Hussain, and Ashfaq and Gul and Mohammed, and Kashmir. I remembered Gaw Kadal. The track became steeper, and darker. Rahman was walking somewhere in front of me. A tall shadow dipped and rose. I walked and walked, with growing restlessness – and fear – as to what lay ahead. The night mist wreathed itself around my legs. I have never taken a more lonely and saddening walk in my life – even the glow-worms, the *rate kreel*, the crickets and the cicadas had receded, surrendered their feeble claim to life in the jungle. I walked and walked. For ever, it seemed. I wondered if that's what it took, walking silently, with yourself, night after night. Suddenly there was an explosion in front of me, a brusque, spiky sound and a flash in the forest cover, the silence assaulted by a single flash of Rahman's matchstick.

As we reached the meeting ground, the big rendezvous place, there soon approached a slim caravan of heads in the dark, a line of stark figures, of human outline, in the distance. I sensed it was far from the tree where I'd struck, I was more or less sure, a deal with Shaban Khatana's guide son to take me across the border to Azad Kashmir, to Pakistan. A place of which I had an obscure vision, an image, as being the country where we boys went to become militants and which supported us and welcomed us with open arms, and where they were all Muslims and were in fact sending their own sons to fight alongside us, but a place I did not really know. It was, now I understand, and still is, a *khayal*, just an idea.

These shadows, these unknown ghosts of boys, who I was perhaps to join soon, were waiting for their guide who would safely lead them, me, across the Line of Control, avoiding all check-posts and ambush routes, wading through streams and rapids, traversing ravines and treacherous gorges – they, we, would stop at nothing until we got to the other side, until we got into Pakistan. Hussain, my brother, must have travelled like this. I closed my eyes.

Rahman must be somewhere close by – his dark form had slipped out of view as soon as he had directed me, with a raised hand, to stop when the shadows had appeared – for he was yet to join the group. He must be making some last-minute arrangements, I assumed. This was the hour . . . this was the moment.

No. No . . .

Perhaps I was to meet the man Shaban had talked about, or – who knows? – to be at least shown to him (this bit of the bargain made me think it might be demeaning somehow), for Rahman had clearly said it was not up to him alone . . .

Because in his vague narration of the cross-border travel system when we'd first met, Shaban had mentioned this man who came to 'deliver' the boys to his son. He was the one who handed them over to the guide. Yes! I was alert now and decided to wait in the flanks of the endless, lengthless, dark shadows that the trees cast. The moon shone small jagged, angular patches on the forest ground in the near distance. I waited and waited. I looked around, trying hard to pierce the dark, and thought I again saw those shapes in the distance, in what seemed like a low clearing, a depression in the middle of the forest, a little ahead of where I had seen the silhouettes earlier.

And someone appeared now, slithering across the blue-black landscape. I knew it was Rahman from the way he rose, looming like a tree, towering like a poplar. I glided along a tree, and the next one, and the next, and then skidded across to a massive pine and hid by its big trunk. In the dark it felt like it breathed. The bark was cold and reassuring against my hands. I felt very small and must have had tears in my eyes. Crickets sprang to life nearby with shrill protestation.

Someone else also appeared – the man. I couldn't feel my own breath. The moon was now struggling to pierce the dark with feeble slivers of light, but the occasional ray of light that did slip through the tangle of treetops shone briefly on the man and showed me something I would relive thousands of times, every day, for the rest of my life.

Here, now, here, walking away steadily in the other direction, downhill towards the village, was Khadim Hussain. Khadim Hussain of the Masjid Committee. Hussain's father.

I had the briefest of glimpses in the cold, soft moonlight that flickered on his face and bald patch. It was him, I was sure, and I ran after him.

13   Twice Dead

You know this boy I saw in the spring? The one who told me his story in his sleep, *in my sleep*, this guy who had wanted to come back but his trip was postponed three times because of the weather and then his commanders had made him wait for months before he eventually came with a large group and was then caught in an encounter on the LoC, this boy who survived the endless rain of mortars and rockets but was eventually captured by Captain Kadian's men and later sodomized by his evil peon and then killed by the same man and then thrown in with the others – well, this boy for whose soul I prayed, he is rotting now. I miss him, I will miss him, this chap who told me his name was Rouf Qadri, and then I checked his ID card and that was his name indeed. He smelled of Dabur Amla hair oil and had combed his hair back, but now, his hair has thinned and his scalp is visible, all pallid and brown and horrid. He was wearing a watch and the time was quarter past three. It's still quarter past three.

This boy I saw towards the beginning, I'd asked him, 'How did you get here?'

And he had said, 'Well, it's not my fault, is it? I told them we should not go in such a large group. But who listens to the younger cadre? These commanders have a way of staying on course no matter what, and that's what has done me in. Staying on course.'

It is a Friday, again, and I have come down early today. I feel I have aged in these five, six months doing the Captain Sahib's dirty work. I have been fatigued, have fallen silent for long periods, gone without speaking to Ma and Baba for days on end, been hungry until it's lost on me, and have had this constant burning fever the last few days . . . so I thought I could just come here and do nothing. I was lost, looking into the middle distance, when out of nowhere Rouf attracts my eye . . .

He had carried two Kalashnikovs, six grenades and five hundred rounds of ammunition, he told me, and before that, he had spent exactly nine months in Muzaffarabad and Rawalpindi; but then when he was crossing the border, there was this burst of fire from the sky and all of them died except two other boys and him. Then a bent oily man had shot him, but before that he had tied them to a cot, one by one, interrogated them for days, and raped them, one by one, and then dumped them in the valley.

This boy, who had seventeen yellow flowers growing between his legs, had combed his hair back. He was young, his corpse fresh except for the big hole in his side that I had not noticed at first. A good-looking chap, this boy.

I see him today and think of the number of times I have been here, to Kadian's hole, to this place where I sometimes wonder how it must feel to be dead like this. This boy looked alive, almost, when I saw him the first time. I was exhausted and fell asleep by his side – and then he talked to me. He said he was from Sopore, the apple town, Kashmir ka London, and had crossed over nine months ago.

Rouf's stare is dry.

I feel bad I have not visited him more often. I should have spent more time with him, but alas, I cannot do that now. The flowers are gone too, only the slender stalks visible, flattened on the ground between his legs, like squiggly drawings of children. The yellow petals are perished. I wonder if he will still be here when the flowers grow again next spring.

He might have told me more about himself, his family, his life, his days in Sopore, in *chotta* London, his friends, his love life even – maybe, maybe he would have told me how he grew up in that rich fruit town and how he'd had such a prosperous life. He would have told me how he was driven to school in a green Ambassador by his wealthy father's driver, wearing his new red tweeds and grey wool trousers. He would have perhaps told me what life was like in his English-medium private school and the great things he did there; he would have told me about his visits outside Kashmir as well, when he went to Delhi, or even as far as Bombay, with his father – who travelled to big cities in India selling his apple-laden trucks for lakhs of rupees – and how his father took him to the cinema to see an English film and how they travelled by the train, even took a plane to Delhi, and saw all the big things in the world, the cities, the tall buildings, the big cars, the bright markets and shopping plazas of television dramas, and how it feels when a plane takes off from the airport in Srinagar.

If I had spent more time with Rouf Qadri, he would have told me how his town was won by militants one day, how they brandished their guns and virtually ran everything in the town, and how for months the Indian Army couldn't even dare to enter the place, which had come to be called *chotta Pakistan* now, until the Army moved in a whole battalion and burned down the entire town to wrest back control of it, and how things were never, never the same after that, and how everyone seethed with anger because scores of townsfolk died, burned to death inside their shops and offices because the Army wouldn't let the fire brigade into the town, and how they shouted on loudspeakers that no one could come out of their houses, shops, offices, schools, wherever they were at the time, until the Army permitted, and how for days the town burned, smouldered, smoked and turned to dunes of black charcoal and ash, and how people ate lawn grass after they had finished all the food in their houses! He would have told me how life changed irredeemably after that, after they had razed to the ground his prosperous town, and how, after they dragged out the charred limbs of kindergarten children from a school that was housed over a group of shops in the main market, and which was torched on the first day of the operation, he felt he should join the *tehreek* as well and become a militant himself. Rouf would've told me how all the boys in his class looked at their ashen town and how they then started smoking to ease the tension and the anger, and how they all started making preparations to go across, to pick up arms exactly like the militants who had roamed freely, arrogantly, in Sopore, before the Army seized it back by burning it down. He would have told me how they arranged for everything – the clothes, the long boots, the packed foods, the guides – and how momentous it had felt, starting for the border like that, all of them together, sometimes hand in hand and sometimes arms slung across shoulders, walking days and nights across the mountains, sometimes completely silent and sometimes singing songs of love and freedom and martyrdom, *'Aye Mard-e-Mujahid Jaag Zara'*, *'Ab Waqt-e-Shahadat Hai Aaya'*.

Who knows? Rouf Qadri might even have crossed through our parts, been among the flocks of boys who crossed over in the early days, even stopped near Shaban's house to go over with Rahman the guide. Poor Rahman.

Rouf might also have told me about his stay in Pakistan, in sad Azad Kashmir and in a proper Pakistani town, Rawalpindi, even described it to me and told me things about Pakistan, that goddamn country a few kilometres across the border which is never at rest and will never let anyone else rest in peace either. 'It was a strange time, brother, but exciting, being in a new country, and going to various places and training camps and being welcomed like heroes everywhere with feasts and big dawats, and picking up a gun for the first time, and shooting your first Kalashnikov bullet, it was strange, brother . . . They gave us money too, lots of money, brother, bundles of it,' he might have said.

Ah, what do I do with him now? What do I do with any of them? So many of them! There are scores of Roufs lying here, in their second deaths. Oh, Kadian, what a miserable mess you have landed me in. And now, after all this, you are planning to leave – oh, yes, his big afsar did say something about his 'application' the other day, yes, and that they would do something about it . . . What will I do then, all by myself, without Kadian up there in his piss-smelling cabin?

Small mercy, however, that there are not too many new recruits to worry about. I guess the big night of hellfire and bombs and those whistling, thumping, thudding missiles, when the very ground shook and trembled all night, did not yield many new pickings. Did you listen to that, my friend? There was this crazy burst of shelling the other night, after which Kadian played cricket with his soldiers and made barbecue lamb for his bosses, who sipped lemonade and alcohol and watched the soldiers play with a fluffy tennis ball (huh!), and the wily peon fell to the ground and everyone laughed. I wish he had died in that fall, or at least broken his dirty, bidi-stained yellow teeth, but his Captain lifted him up and gave him support and then went to his Mehrotra Sir and paraded me in front of him as if I were a prized anti-insurgent. And at the end of which, big-chip army commander, Mehrotra Shit-Scared Sir, told Kadian not to worry about his application. I wish I could have slapped that man – big-headed army man paying us a visit in his rude vehicles after all they have done here! What will I do when he leaves me here with his gifts to the valley, with you and your other twice-dead friends? I mean, it cannot go on and on and on. I must bury you some day; give you a grave of your own; grow *mazaar munje* by your side, and let you rest in peace.

When Kadian leaves, I guess I will somehow persuade Baba, beg and cry at his feet, to pack up and leave as everyone else did. I will grab Ma's hands and ask her to make Baba leave – I cannot go on like this for ever, Rouf bhai. I will tell Baba to fear no more, it has been a long time since KD met him on that fateful day all those months ago, soon after everyone had left the village. Baba, I too want to leave.

Rouf Qadri, who stares dryly from his sorrowful, sunken eye sockets, whose shrivelled arms and cobwebbed duck's-feet hands have dropped on the ground like the disassembled parts of the wooden toy soldier Baba's government-employee friend Firdaus Ali once brought for me from his annual durbar move to Jammu, and whose thinning hair and bleak forehead with its frightful brown grooves make me sad again, beseeches me to do something about this. The cycle cannot go on. It has to end, *Khudaya*, it has to end.

But will KD really leave all this and pack off, just like that, to go to his father's prim, retired army officer's farmhouse in some dusty village in dung-ridden Haryana or frigging roasting Rajasthan? How can he do that! KD, you cannot get away – I will not let you.

You know this boy, he had combed back his hair before leaving on his mission.

PART II

Then . . .

14 *The Father's Pledge*

I soon caught up with Hussain's abba` that night, and as the moon finally claimed more ground, vague outlines of the way home began to appear in the gradually stretching light. The night was chilly and the breeze nipped my face. In short bursts of speech hurled back in the dark, Khadim Hussain dealt me blow after blow. With each step of our descent, he unravelled for me what must have seemed quite ordinary to him.

Oh God.

Only a few weeks ago, the valley had reverberated with Hussain's song and Mohammed's laughter and Ashfaq's whistles; only a few nights ago the village, the street, the street corner, had warmed with our conversation . . .

My heart raced, sank, raced and sank – how had all this come about?

He dashed in front of my exasperated questions, my voice trailing a descending form marked by the random, hazy glint of his bald patch. In his sudden appearance on the scene, I understood half the story at least, although a part of me prayed that there was a redeeming twist in the tale somewhere.

'How could you let him go? Why not me?' I shouted to his back.

He walked on, briskly, stepping down the zigzag path. I waited.

'Why not me, Khadim Sahib, why didn't you take me?'

He walked on, as if he hadn't heard me.

'I just want to know, now that –?' I left it at that, making sure I wasn't too far behind him. I was afraid. The collective drone of a thousand creatures attended the night now. The skin on my arms and legs twitched and throbbed.

'Hmm, w-h-y . . . ?' finally, he repeated after me, with cool deliberation.

'Yes, why? Why didn't you tell me?'

I made sure I kept pace with his dark form. He slowed down.

'Well, I suppose, because we didn't think you'd make it. It wasn't for you, my dear, not everyone can . . .' he paused briefly, stood, and then stiffened his tone a bit, '. . . and because of your silly little ideas. That's it.' I hadn't seen him since Hussain had left. His voice cracked a little, and had a nodding, elderly tinge to it. Sadness too perhaps.

'What *ideas*?' I was panting already.

He didn't reply, chose not to reply. We sped along, down the spiralling slope, through corridors of lunging trees, his shadow making brisk appearances at the patches where the moon was filtering through.

'And your father, hmm, he has been the headman for such a long time . . . He fought against the tribals when he was young, isn't it? Don't tell me you didn't know?' He stopped briefly, as if to gauge the effect on me.

'*So?*' This was rather unexpected; it didn't make any sense. What did Baba have to do with this, with anything?

'Well, he is the man who takes grants from the government, you surely know that . . . ? He was on one of the first hit lists they took out here!'

The words came to me through a quick draught of the night breeze.

'But my son pleaded with me to promise that I would try and save your baba's life!' He sped down earnestly now, as if he had somewhere to reach, some deadline to meet. Where would he go now? Have dinner, sleep after he's done his day's work, sent away his quota of fresh boys? I marched on too, following the lead of his dipping bald spot that glistened now and then through the dark night. How, when, did it come to this, that *he* had to save my baba's life?

'Not only his – in a way, we spared your life as well, my dear. You wouldn't have coped, never. It takes guts to do all this, you know, big guts? You, with your books and – how do I say? – silly ideas, you wouldn't have been a good example, you wouldn't make a good mujahid, never!'

'But, but, who told you all this? Why did you think I didn't want to? I am one of them! They are my friends,' I said with growing unease. 'And when *did* you do all this?' I must have squeaked.

'I have seen you ever since you were a small boy, my dear. What do you mean, who told me?' His voice was measured, a reprimand lurked in his tone.

'*That* is why?' I screamed my heart out, seeking, as one does when one's crying as a child, reassurance from the intensity of my own voice. The night shrieked back.

'Hussain always talked about you, the things you talked of. He told me all about you . . .' Khadim Hussain didn't seem to be listening now, he was talking to himself, almost. 'He was fond of you, you know . . . ? I know you, son,' that must've slipped from his mouth, 'you were always, well, rather soft, always reading books, playing cricket, nothing else, just books and cricket. You didn't even join the prayers in the mosque. I never saw you. So why would they even consider you? Hussain, *my* son, yes, he has led the way. I have done my job too – I have given them the best.'

Whatever he was saying cost him great effort. The climb down-hill was getting steeper, my legs were getting ahead of me and soon I found myself waving my arms in the blue light. Deep down I must have known he was right about me. They were right about me too. I thought about the silhouettes that had gone along with Rahman. I felt the money I had got for him in my pheran pocket.

'Your own son, huh?' I lashed out. 'Do you really think he wanted to do this? Do you even know what he wanted to do? I don't think so,' I cried out. I didn't know what else to say. 'And, and, er, where is he now?' I felt a chill trickle of sweat down my back. The moon glimpsed intermittently at us. I realized I had completely forgotten about my own journey as soon as I had seen Hussain's father.

'I'm not worried about him, he will be fine – he is my son . . . And in case you still don't know, he is fighting a war, he is a freedom fighter. Even if he is martyred tomorrow, I would be a blessed man, father to a shaheed. Not a word from my mouth, sir, not a word. Except for *Ameen*. I will pray. But why am I telling you all this, what do *you* know . . . ?' He addressed the darkness around us and trotted ahead.

Suddenly, I was filled with a bitter loathing, a rising seething anger, for my best friend's father. Had I had something with me, I might have hit him in the back and ended his life, there and then. I could still push him off the side of the mountain. Send him hurtling down. No one would ever know.

In the distance, lights from the hamlet flickered like candles in a graveyard.

'But how could you send him on such a, er, dangerous, er, journey – what if he is captured?' I didn't know what else to say. 'You know what the Army does? They catch and kill, *c-a-t-c-h and k-i-l-l*. Do you have any idea what they do?' I thought of Ma and Baba, and myself, as soon as I said that. 'They behead them, Khadim Sahib, behead them,' I immediately shuddered from the thought myself, 'and throw their bodies away in some gutter!' I carried on, 'And you say you will offer prayers when they kill him? What kind of a father are you, what kind of a man . . . ?' I heard my own howl, and it made me sadder. What had become of Khadim Hussain! What had everything come to; what was I to do now?

We neared a clearing and the night suddenly let out a washed swatch of light in front of me. Khadim Hussain stopped, turned and looked at me hard. The smudgy dark patch of endless prayers hung hole-like in the middle of his forehead. I saw a different man, different from the man I'd known all my life as my best friend's father.

'You still don't understand, do you? This is exactly why we never considered you, although Ashfaq thought it didn't matter, that you would come around once they talked to you. He believed all of you should go together. The Famous Five, he used to say, I don't know why. But we refused, and we were right. How very right. For someone who doesn't even know what martyrdom means – how do I say? – there is no chance of valour.'

He flung himself forward.

'Don't run away. Please, for God's sake. You didn't include me in your grand plan, fine, but at least tell me what happened afterwards, haan? Tell me, please tell me.'

Khadim Hussain slowed down and turned towards me. He was

smiling now. A strange smile of satisfaction. He was looking at me with pitiful eyes.

I looked back intently at him. 'Who did you pack off next? Mohammed? Ashfaq? Both of them?' I started crying. Sobbing.

'Or was it Gul you took away from his maternal home next, was that the whole plan?' The night howled. I shrieked and sobbed. 'That must have been the plan all along then, *your* plan, isn't it? Tell me, tell me! Gul knew he was leaving even when he accompanied me the first time I visited Shaban Khatana, isn't it? You knew . . . everyone knew. Gulla, you too, you too . . . Oh God, I'm such an idiot. I am such a stupid, stupid fool.'

I was sobbing uncontrollably now. In the middle of the forest, I cried like a child. I guess since no one was watching I must have let go. Just the trees, their dark canopies, tall pines, their needles making slippery sounds under my feet, and a faint moon showing its face through small clearings now and then.

'Oh, oh, and the Moulvi Sahib, this is why he came here, isn't it? This is why you brought him to Nowgam?' I said through my croaking cries.

'Hmm . . .' he said; he was smoking now.

I hadn't noticed him light up. I walked on through a whiff of the invisible tobacco smoke.

'You can be so naïve, you know. They all think like this – the Government, the Security Forces, the Army, the TV people – they all like to think it's the imams, huh, that it is the moulvis, huh huh . . . And this is the problem with the likes of you, you see a bearded moulvi and think that's it, huh! Rasheed Shah was just a preacher, my dear, he knew how to lead the namaz, that is it. Your own baba arranged for his salary, and that's all the poor man wanted – he had come all the way from Varmul.'

But I wasn't listening; I had already confirmed my theory in my mind.

'So who have you sent away today, then? Gul knew, all along, isn't it? Everything. You were preparing them, then, all these days, dressing them up . . . ? Have you just delivered Mohammed and Ashfaq? They must've been readying themselves too, when I was looking for them, oh!' I felt a fresh stream of tears roll down my cheeks and cried some more.

Hussain's abba` didn't speak.

Oh God . . .

How could they, how could they all? When he broke the news of Hussain's 'disappearance' in the mosque, he must've known everything, everything. He must've known that the others were to follow him soon? He must've looked worried and sad, because he wanted everyone to be sarhad paar before anyone knew about his part in it. And he must have planned this all along, he must have put up those first posters. Oh yes, he must have brought some chiefs visiting too. And he must have identified the boys for them, rejected me, and then started planning it all. He must have chosen them, talked to them, convinced them, excited them, during all those early morning prayers . . . That was the best time. Fajr. I wish I had prayed too, woken up on those chilly mornings, shaken off my sleep, listened to Ma and gone to the mosque; but then, but then, she wouldn't have been happy with my praying in the end, would she . . . ?

'How old are you, son?' he suddenly asked.

I didn't know what to say.

'Tell me, come on. How old are you?'

'Same as your son!' That should've hurt him. 'Seventeen.' The lights had become bigger now. One of them was our house, certainly, set apart from the rest as it is, away from the small cluster in the street. I wanted to get home now. Badly, badly. My cheeks hurt from the crying, stiff and hard.

'When I was your age, son,' his voice had now settled into a resigned tone, as if he had forgiven me for my effrontery, 'I earned for the whole family. I worked long days, even nights sometimes. I struggled, worked hard, but I kept going. You know why? Because I had a purpose in life, helping my family, earning bread. And look at you, weeping like a – how do I say? – sissy, like this. Do you even realize the times we are living in? There is a war coming, soon, *jang*. This monster Hindustan has sent here, this new Governor, this zalim, this tyrant, why do think they sent him here? Young men like you are fighting. They are laying their lives down for Kashmir. In thousands. And look at you, wheezing and whining about your brave friends who have picked up the gauntlet and gone, gone to fight cruelty with bravery, avenge blood with blood, answer bullets with bullets – not cry like . . . weaklings. If we want to escape from the clutches of India, we have to fight these beastly bastards who slay our children and sully the honour of our women. Your friends, they have shown great valour. They are freedom fighters now. Don't tell me the Army does this and the Army does that! I know it much better than you, son. Why do you think your friends chose to . . . ? They rose to face a challenge; they are part of the Movement now, the first freedom fighters from among us, the very first. They will be a part of history. And look at you, whinging and crying about it all. I was right, so very right.'

We had almost reached the foothills of Shaban's mountainside now. A brook gurgled its way darkly somewhere nearby. Soon, he would be on his way home.

I had stopped crying now, only the hiccupy sighs remained.

'Have you heard from Hussain?' A small sob struggled out. 'How could you . . . ?'

'Oh, shut up! How could you, how could you!' He mimicked me and squealed like a boy. 'Of course I did. Azad Kashmir Radio, *Sada-e-Hurriyat*. Had you really bothered, you would have listened too . . . He dedicated a song to "the new village hidden in the hills" – that's how he called it – and I understood, at once.' He smiled for a moment. 'It hasn't been too long, you see – less than two months – he must be in a camp now. But you know how he is; when he sets his heart on something, he won't let go. You know how he –' Khadim Hussain looked at me, and for the first and the thinnest moment in our encounter that night I sensed a tinge of grief, even affection, in his tone. Perhaps he really did miss his son. He mumbled something more under his breath and let his legs carry him on.

I felt my interest in asking more questions begin to peter out. It seemed so futile. I had failed. I was, in reality, *not up to it*. Everything had been done, things had already happened, it was over. Maybe I shouldn't be angry with Hussain's father, I thought. Maybe times really had changed rapidly and I was the only one who hadn't understood soon enough.

That pine-smelling night two years ago, we descended slowly towards the village, each lost in his own thoughts. We must have looked like two ghosts walking in the mist. I walked and walked, without caring any more whether I was on the right path home. My chase had ended, my pursuit finished. I was vaguely aware of the person walking in front of me. He was Hussain's father. My best friend, my soulmate's father. This man built our mosque, this man prayed all alone for nights when no one was interested in worship, this man stuck to his task no matter what. This man sacrificed his own son for Kashmir. He paid the ultimate price for the struggle for freedom. This man was pious. He was perhaps already dead, I thought. Perhaps he had been long dead, from the time when he decided to give his son's name before anyone else's.

Now he was waiting for news of his martyrdom.

15 *The Street*

I came out of the house nearly two weeks after I met Hussain's abba`
in the forest, and found myself walking silently towards Noor Khan's
shop. There was nowhere else I could go. I grew a beard, what little
I had, stubbly and prickly. I told no one about the meeting. Who
would I tell? In the mirror I found myself an older boy.

Baba asked a few times why I looked pale. I didn't reply. Ma
thought I was sad because of Hussain, which was true, but that
wasn't all. She had now stopped worrying herself about me; somehow, she knew I wasn't going anywhere.

On certain mornings and evenings I heard Khadim Hussain's azan
from the mosque below. It reached my room like unreal echoes of
distant singing. Like son, like father, I thought. It was distinctly him,
though, his sharp but cracked voice wafting up into the mountains
and waking up every creature with its anguished sting. There was a
hint of pain to his voice. Perhaps he was calling out to his son.

In the street people looked at me with uncertain glances, sometimes looking at me discreetly after I had passed. Almost everyone
knew my friends had crossed over and thought I'd be gone soon too.
Nowgam had acquired a new air, a character of being *with it* now,
being a part of the Movement. There were some sad faces – indeed,
worried, drawn faces – but there were expectant faces too. Even
proud faces.

But were they really across the border now? No one knew that for
sure? Although I now knew, most certainly, that they had crossed
into Azad Kashmir, how was one to be absolutely, absolutely sure?
What if they hadn't gone to Pakistan? What if they hadn't *all* gone
to Pakistan? What if the Army had kidnapped them on the way; I'd
heard, among the millions of rumours in those days, that they
picked people for *begaar*, for forced labour, and made them work

inside camps, breaking rock faces and digging foundations, and then put them up in dark places at night only to be woken up next morning for another hard day of enslaved labour. The men sweated, frothed at the mouth, wheezed, fainted, but never stopped working for fear of being killed and passed off as some foreign militant commander – such men never came back either. Or, what if they had changed their course midway and run away – like people did in the old days, in the days before these days – to some city in India, and were now working in some fruit mandi, or were travelling to far-off places in a truck and camped in new places every week and were actually having fun? What if Hussain had run off to Bombay to become a singer? That would be fabulous too, isn't it? Like a fairy tale! Seeing him sing and wave his arms on a variety show on TV some day, I would scream my heart out and say, 'Hey, hey, he's my friend, he's *my* friend, hear him sing, hear, hear, how he sings and look, look, how he raises his hand, and look how he looks, he's my friend.'

I was being foolish. I would have known it then, guessed it, if they had been up to something like that. But then again, I didn't know what they really had been up to.

There was, in fact, no real 'what if' and 'but then': they were gone, really and truly gone, and I'd met the man who had made the travel arrangements.

I sat on the small wooden railing at the front of Noor Khan's shop and picked up a dead-looking Double Decker chocolate from an assorted stack of candy bars. The dust on the wrapper was so ancient that it had become sealed to the packet. I didn't even try to wipe it off. Noor looked thoughtful; he always did if he wanted me to talk to him.

'So what news, Noor Chacha?'

'Well, people are now waiting for *your* news, beta.' Noor teased me hesitantly, but I knew he was half fishing as well. If only he knew.

'Noor Chacha, I'm not going anywhere, so let's not plan a farewell for me yet, okay?' I tried to sound casual.

'No, beta, no, I didn't mean to say you . . . I was just saying . . . You know people, how people talk?'

'People don't know, Noor Chacha, they don't know anything.' I looked at Noor Khan meaningfully, and suddenly realized he was my only friend left in the village. Shaban was there, of course, but he was high up, beyond reach on ordinary days, huh . . . Noor looked at me with surprise as I spoke with the authority of someone who knew something that others didn't. I knew I shouldn't tell anyone. There might be things only Khadim Hussain knew about the whole Movement, the *tehreek* thing, about plans and strategies; he'd also mentioned Baba and knew militant groups and their commanders, and was surely influential. The boys' families certainly knew. And if they had chosen to stay quiet about it, what was it to me? Besides, they hadn't told me, so why should I care?

'Beta, the thing is, the situation is not good at all. I mean, it won't stay like this, and I think it's the uneasy calm before a storm, you know, the calm before a storm.' Noor's words jolted me and I looked at him afresh: this man had always been a shopkeeper, our ragtag grocer, he'd watched us grow up and knew the history of perhaps every household in Nowgam, he must have known everyone from the very beginning, from the times we were wandering Gujjars up to the time we settled down and set up this village, carved this street out, and formed a community. On his face I now saw signs of worry; he had started to fear for the village he had helped found. He was not a deeply political man, but he surely understood what was happening around him. And he did listen to a lot of BBC.

'So what do you think is going to happen?' I ventured.

'Well, people say there are crackdowns everywhere, it's some kind of an army checking system where they search homes and identify every inhabitant of the place under cordon. They take you out into the open and make you go through this identification parade. Someone behind the black glasses of an army vehicle looks at you and signals if he thinks you're a mujahid. And this is not done by ordinary soldiers, beta, they have brought in some of the most feared regiments to Kashmir. People say that the elite Makara soldiers even eat people, old people mostly . . . Many people have been caught in these crackdowns, I hear. And they don't just stop at searches; people are taken away sometimes, and women . . .' He stopped mid-sentence and started to pretend he was struggling to tune his transistor to a programme of Sufiyana music on Radio Kashmir. The thing didn't pick up the frequency clearly, so he settled for Vividh Bharti, where Kishore Kumar and Lata Mangeshkar were earnestly singing *'Dekha ek khwaab to yeh silsile hue . . .'*

'Sometimes the militants also come and visit, even stay in your houses, but I guess that's not going to be possible here, too close to the border, you see. And even if they do, what's the harm? I've heard they usually leave after food and a night's stay. And then, our own boys might turn up some day, you never know . . . ?' Noor paused, swallowed loudly and spat a projectile on to the dusty road. I resisted the impulse to see what the sample of phlegm looked like. 'And there is another thing,' he resumed while stuffing his chillum with a fresh infusion of tobacco, 'this new Governor is supposed to be very strict, I've heard he is a stern administrator . . . No wonder they dismissed the big Minister and brought this man specially from Delhi. I think he will change a few things. Tough and strict, you see.'

Two small boys with fifty-paisa coins in their palms appeared at the shop and presented them to Noor Khan in silence, in a simultaneous motion of their outstretched arms. Both wore Government School khaki shorts and powder-blue shirts whose sleeves had distinct snot marks near the cuffs. Noor Khan took out two Parle eclairs from a plastic jar – chocolate and gold wrapper – and handed them to the boys one by one. The boys turned, sighed their sighs of gratification, and left. They must have cried their hearts out for this small pleasure after school, and their mother must have scolded them for having spent their pocket money too early in the day. With their backs towards us, I could tell they were tearing at the wrappers. Then they took off in a sudden sprint.

'Ramazan Choudhary's grandchildren, his elder son's kids,' Noor remarked matter-of-factly, as if he were talking about cattle, or household pets.

Ramazan Choudhary, the oldest man I ever knew, was among the poorer citizens of Nowgam. Baba had helped him with rations and loans on a few occasions. He had two sons – one of them was married, and the other spent months roaming Srinagar as a *tabardaar*, a travelling woodcutter. I never knew the older son had two kids. He had worked as one of the few hired labourers when the mosque was being built. Baba had recommended him.

'But there is nothing to worry about, beta. There's nothing here yet, so why would there be a crackdown, isn't it?' Noor reassured himself. 'Some people worry needlessly, and I tell them even if there is one, why be afraid – we have nothing to hide. What will the Army do, haan? Just check the houses and go, isn't it?' He looked worried.

I was thinking of Hussain's father. I heard his famous azan now and then; he had never been the official muezzin of the mosque before, only on days when no one else volunteered. People thought he kept to himself more and more now because he was grief-stricken after his only son's departure. I knew better. A part of me was perhaps smug too, knowing such a big secret.

One thing was certain, though, Khadim Hussain's azan was beautiful. It echoed from the mountainside and rang enchantingly in the valley, as though many a content muezzin called out to each other from their perches on the hills. Baba said more people went to pray when his *Allah-o-Akbar* boomed from the lone loudspeaker on top of the mosque roof. Some people said he deliberately didn't do it too often because he wanted to preserve the charm of his voice. They said he didn't want to attract the evil eye and lose his touch. Excessive praise can be ruinous, it was said.

But on the evenings he was muezzin, his azan also hurt. It reminded me of everything. Of beauty. Of the past. Shaam-Namaz, at dusk, was our best time down in the valley. We would have finished with our game and huddled up near the river, chatting, whispering secrets, taking oaths of eternal friendship. Eternity was so short. This was the time Ashfaq would declare his dark dooms-day ideas, *The world is nothing beyond the moment*, and some such nonsense. This was also the time he would make his lordly *farmaish*, his song request, of Hussain, *Let's have 'Yeh duniya agar mil bhi jaye'*, *Rafi Saab! Let's have it, then*. Hussain would refuse at first but then begin, without much prelude, in the midst of our conversation. Low, slow, haunting. We would fall silent, the song sounding even sadder amidst the fading light and the long shadows of a mountain evening that would descend on us from above. His father's azan would sometimes suddenly bounce off the mountains, drift down into some hollows, ricochet off a rock face, and glide down resonantly into the valley. Hussain would stop for the tiniest of moments, sometimes touched by his father's appeal and sometimes his heart perhaps wrenched by guilt for refusing to be his father's apprentice. Ashfaq would drag hard on his stolen cigarette, and refuse to part with it, often dangling a burned-out charcoal butt of a cigarette from his lips.

'Chacha, have you seen Asma of late? Ashfaq's sister, I mean – you do know her?' Inevitably then, I moved from my philosophical friend to his younger sister. I remembered walking her home one evening from her tuition with Firdaus Ali's wife – Ashfaq had asked me to accompany her in case she got scared in the dark – and the sweet-smelling fresh naphthalene on her wool pheran as she walked by my side, but not too close. I'd, in fact, always dreamed of this as the best opportunity to be with her by myself – hoping that the evening light might also make me bolder – and couldn't believe my luck when Ashfaq, keen to use the opportunity himself for a stolen smoke with Gul, asked me to do him this favour.

'Haan, haan, of course I know her, beta, she's the one who comes to the shop now, after Ashfaq –'

'Oh, does she come often?'

'Well, let's just say as often as he used to.' Noor Khan pressed his mouth shut and sighed.

For weeks then, that's how it trudged along, until winter was beginning to thaw. February glimmered across feebly.

I often visited Noor Khan's shop and carried countless pouches of tobacco back for Baba. He smoked and smoked all day, the gurglish roar of his hookah reverberating in the house, skidding off the corridor, into the kitchen, over the stairs, sliding across the coarsely plastered walls of the hallway, and muffling its way into my room.

Everybody came to Noor's shop: children, women, old men. I spent whole afternoons, lazy afternoons, nothing afternoons, at the shop.

Good old Ramazan Choudhary, with those bright red glow-spots on his wrinkled, historic cheeks, would come for his daily bread, taking ages to walk to the shop from the corner of the road. Classic old man's step he had, hobbling on his old polished staff. He was poor and wore a torn pheran under his flowing white beard. Some people in the village said he was a holy man: 'Khuda listens to such people.' Gul's big brother, Farooq, came every other day to buy his cigarettes, Capstan Filter, two packs of ten, always; he would smile at me nervously and then leave quickly, as though some guilt of his had been caught. His appearance at the shop was always an awkward moment. I'd never really disliked him, and now we had been thrown together by the absence of so many others. He too, I felt, now wanted to be friends with me. And it did bring me some relief that he was around.

I saw Lassa Kaka arrive daintily with his wicker basket to fetch small packets of sugar and spice. Lassa Kaka had never married, lived with his ancient mother – the oldest matriarch in the whole area – in their neat little one-storey house at the lower end of the street. Even though he lived just a few paces from the shop, he never came in his house clothes. People thought he was a bit feminine. They also said he had devoted his entire life to serving his pious old mother. He was always clean-shaven. I thought of him as the kind of man who always took good care of his hair. Sometimes, Baba himself descended down from the hillside and would ask me to return home. 'There's something your mother wants you for, go, go . . .' I would try not to look embarrassed in front of Noor Khan and leave, sometimes even managing to reproduce a whistle as I walked off.

Asma came a few times; she always bought notebooks, fine-line notebooks. God, she must study all the time, I thought. I would watch her approach and count the number of steps she would take from the time she appeared on the road to the time she got to the shop-front. Asma had her brother's clear eyes; her face was a spotless, fragile white and her nose slender, and there was always a tender hesitancy to her lip. I sometimes liked to think she combined the features of Madhubala and Nargis, those heroines of old black and white films on Doordarshan, in her soft, gentle face. She would look at me briefly – I knew she was terribly, terribly sad – and then would hurry off as soon as she got what she wanted. I watched her walk away until she disappeared round the bend. My greatest excuse to see her more often had vanished.

Baba's friend Firdaus Ali's children, two sons and a girl, would come, all hand in hand, and buy toffees along with the small groceries their mother would have asked for. Firdaus Ali was away on government service – he was away most of the time, wasn't he? I guess that was because there was not much Government around here to work for.

Compounder Chechi sat behind his plywood-fronted shop, a heavy blanket hanging on the door so that no one could see what went on inside. A rippled red cross, painted laboriously by Chechi himself, hung brightly in the middle of the curtain. When I was younger, I often had trouble trying not to look at women's legs if the Compounder Sahib made me wait inside for Baba's Calpol supply while administering an injection under a partially loosened pyjama in the hope of curing some mysterious disease. Sadiq Chechi had worked as an orderly in the big hospital in Srinagar – which was called just that, 'the big hospital'– in his younger days, or so he said, and now, back in his native village, he dispensed Crocin tablets for fever and Combiflam for all kinds of aches and pains, even Calmpose and Alprax sometimes.

Occasionally, Chechi also doubled up as the village electrician, fixing clumsily wired lamps and making impossible 'connections' to achieve 'double voltage' for people who paid him twenty-odd rupees; these were electrical conundrums I never understood. He even had his own thin ladder to climb up the three rotting wooden pylons near the street, when needed – the rest of the wiring went over trees, walls and roofs – and to fix warped jungles of electric wire in people's corridors. Apart from the two tube lights in our drawing room, his shop was the only premises in the village with double tube lights, on either side of the ceiling. Tall, lean, with his short and straight, black and white hair, and dressed in that worn-out brown leather jacket I'd seen him wear ever since I could remember, Chechi would be seen lugging his ladder on rainy evenings to fix a short circuit in one house or another. He operated this second trade of his with the same precision and industry as he did his all-purpose medic's job. And it was because of this part-time work that Sadiq Chechi was sometimes called *Doctor Bijli*, Doctor Electric. And at other times, when he would appear in the doorway of your house on a rainy day – water cascading off his wet, flattened hair and down his forehead – he was also referred to as *Ruude' Bulbul*, the Rain Nightingale.

Chechi was a good man, though, who sometimes gave medicines for free to some poor old Gujjars – when and if they trusted modern medicine to cure them.

February passed. March, and spring, arrived, unsung except for the teeming buds on the trees around us. There was no news of Hussain, no word from the boys.

After some time, Noor decided to let me in, and soon I was his unofficial accountant, writing small sums of credit against the names of almost everyone who bought their groceries from him. A much-repaired, polythene-covered notebook, often symbolically locked with a cotton cord, served as his credit ledger. Sometimes I helped a bit with other things as well, mopping ancient dust and rat droppings from his wooden shop floor, an activity Noor protested about, *the son of the headman is not supposed to do such menial tasks . . .* Very soon I got to know who bought exactly what in a week or a month. I watched everyone. Initially, people tried to talk to me – being nice to the headman's son was an old game – but when they didn't meet much conversation, they got used to the idea of a second silent person sitting inside Noor's shop. I sat and watched Noor Khan dispense pulses, spices, P-Mark cooking oil, loose weevil-rich rice, Lifebuoy and OK and Hamam soap, toffees, Capstan and Four Square cigarettes, Relaxo nylon slippers and plastic shoes, Parle-G glucose biscuits . . .

I would come down on late mornings, spend the afternoon at the shop, quickly jot down the latest credits and cancel off settled monthly accounts, and from three to four every afternoon listen to film songs on his radio, on the legendary phone-in programme for 'soldier brothers', the evergreen *Fauji Bhaiyyon Ka Programme*. Rafi, that glorious sultan of song, Hussain's favourite – turns out he's a favourite with Indian soldiers as well. 'So, brothers and sisters, let's listen to what Lance Naik Makkhan Singh and Sipahi Charan Singh from Agra Cantt have requested. Yessirs, here's the song then, for Lance Naik Makkhan Singh and Sipahi Charan Singh, this memorable tune, this great tribute to our brave soldiers who shed their blood on our borders so that you and I can sleep peacefully at home. *Sunte hain . . . "Ab tumhare hawale wattan saathiyo" . . .'*

Another couple of months must have passed like this – in suspended siesta.

A lid struggled to stir somewhere, though. I sat in the shop during the day and spent the long nights reading. I read everything I could lay my hands on: yesterday's newspapers if they arrived, old books retrieved from rubbish dealers by Baba during his visits to the city, magazines from here and there. I bought candles from Noor, thick imperishable-looking candles, and burned them at night. I pored over stained, torn, mildewed pages for hours and for some time every night was transported to imaginary worlds and places and forgot my own place for a while. It was nice, reading. A sentence or a thought that I suddenly understood brought pleasure not known to me before. Some nights it made me feel special, different, and kind of privileged, from the people I knew. It was a strange time, a time that didn't change much from day to day and yet changed me from inside. Things had happened and, increasingly, I felt they couldn't be reversed; everyday life in the village had, for now, settled into a stasis. There was Noor Khan's shop and my nocturnal reading and in the middle there was my awkward time with Baba and Ma. Baba, it seemed, was upset with me for the fact that I'd been close friends with people who had left for Pakistan, but he was also relieved that I hadn't been one of them. It was a confusing time for him too perhaps – he had spent a lifetime building his village, creating a settled order, an organized life for his people, and now the boys' departure had shown the first cracks in that recently arrived order. He was the headman, after all, the Muqqaddam, the Sarpanch, but he didn't know what to do. Except for giving me admonishing looks if I stayed out too long. Ma looked on and cooked and, almost every day, without fail, talked about my college. She'd had her own dreams, of a son going to college and making something of himself in life, perhaps even landing a government job, and maybe even going to the university in the city and becoming a teacher some day. She knew the college was to 'reopen' in April after the long winter break, and it was the beginning of May now. 'You can at least go to check, beta, it's time for them to open, isn't it? At least once, for my sake . . .' she said every day.

'All right, Ma, I will go on Monday,' I replied, and then pretended to forget on Monday. I didn't know what to do at college. It was miles away in the town and, before it was taken over by the Army and converted into makeshift barracks, which eventually became its permanent state of being, it had been closed for many months. I'd enrolled the year before – we would have all gone together, had they not left for elsewhere. In fact, Mohammed had, strangely enough, decided to study the same subjects as me – BSC with English and Urdu – but I hadn't gone there after the first few visits. It had been shut for winter vacations and I'd heard that most of the teachers had now left for good, many of them Pandits who had been forced to leave Kashmir altogether, and quite a few students had left too, some for places like Delhi, Aligarh and Bangalore in India and many for training camps in Pakistan.

Spring coursed along, the mountains changed colour, and birds of the warm season began to sing their complacent song. Ma started spending more time in the garden. This was when she was still talking.

The street changed, almost overnight. Faces changed.

And soon, posters appeared everywhere. Out of nowhere.

Azadi.

Azadi.

Azadi!

Freedom.

Pakistan Zindabad.

Hindustan Murdabad.

Indian dogs, go back.

Indian dogs, go back!

Noor Khan became more and more thoughtful.

Baba sat in silence, thinking. And trimmed his beard less often.

In the evenings some people stayed on in the mosque after prayers and chanted slogans. Excitable young boys from the houses nearest to the street climbed on their rooftops at night and tirelessly beat the rusted corrugated tin sheets with sticks, creating a fearsome hullabaloo at night.

La Ilah-a-Ilallah! Superpower hai Khuda!

Jaago, Jaago, Subah ho gayi!

Indian dogs, go back!

What do we want?

Freedom.

What do we want?

Freedom!

I wanted to join their cacophonous, hypnotic chanting from our house, to respond to their roof-beating with a slamming of my own. But I feared Baba.

Hum kya chahte?

Azadi!

Go back, go back!

Indian dogs, go back!

Azadi!

What do we want?

Freedom.

Freedom, freedom!

The wave had swept all of Kashmir and finally reached our village, in some force, the forgotten last village before the border. Posters competed for space on the sparse street walls. Still, there was no sign of the Security Forces coming down anywhere near the village. They had always stayed at their check-posts at the border or in their camp deep inside Koh-i-Gham. They were always somewhere up there in the forests.

It was strange that no army vehicle had passed through our parts since the boys had left.

But in the middle of May, something new happened. Just after I'd witnessed the gradual thinning of the pink-furred roof of cherry blossoms over Gul Khan's expansive orchard, a curfew arrived.

A flag march arrived.

Commandos arrived.

Black-turbaned, menacing-looking men in fearsome outfits with big, shining rifles arrived. Their small but astounding convoy of vehicles stopped next to Chechi's dingy medical shop-cum-clinic in a forbidding cloud-shield of their own exhaust, and someone made an announcement through a megaphone perched on top of a windowless, fortress-like vehicle.

The area is declared under curfew, day and night.

No one will venture out of their houses.

Anyone violating this order will be dealt with severely.

This is a government order. Do not panic.

The alien voice made its announcements in a stern but disinterested tone. Then there was complete silence.

Later, I learned that this second curfew had arrived rather late in our village. The entire state, all of Kashmir, even the lakes and rivers and ponds and the floating gardens of the Dal Lake, had been under curfew ever since the new Governor had arrived. He liked curfews.

Those three months of curfew were the last days of our freedom. Everything changed after that. The curfew made no difference to us initially – in a way, we'd been under curfew for as long as there had been an embargo within five kilometres of the LoC, although it hadn't affected our everyday life inside the village much. As long as we stayed put and did our own small things in the street and inside our houses and orchards, no one bothered us. But it was double curfew for us now. How were they to enforce that? I had no idea. What was the difference? Curfew within a curfew, what did it mean?

It turned out that this one would be very different.

16   *The Milk Beggars*

One early summer day – the scarlet rose bush in front of the house had sprouted hundreds of bold fresh buds that looked like small red-crowned birds – a group of withered-looking women came to the village and gathered in front of Noor Khan's shop in a semicircle. Half of them were crying, and the ones who weren't were consoling the others. They wouldn't say anything – who they were, why they were crying, what they wanted. The words 'we have children' made themselves heard more than a couple of times through the din of their wet sobbing. As soon as I heard this, I rushed home to fetch Baba. On our way back I made Baba sprint downhill with me. Panting, I went inside the shop and let Baba deal with the situation, with this group of women who were still wailing in front of Noor's bewildered face.

With an urgent wave of the hand, Baba signalled something to Noor, who immediately brought out a jug of water from behind the shop – that old, much-dented unsteady tin jug of his with a million black scratches on it. Baba poured a couple of glasses of water and offered it to the women in the front. He drank some himself too. I looked at the women; they didn't seem the kind to be wandering about like this without any male company. Most of them were pale, drained. They all wore pherans made of some light fabric, no burqas, just colourful scarves tied across their heads. From their faces they all seemed unusually frail, almost anaemic. Yes, it was the faces, wan, drained of all colour, as if someone had squeezed out all the blood from them. Baba waited for them to finish drinking and then asked if they wanted to sit. The women didn't speak but nodded to suggest they were fine the way they were. I looked at one of the leaders and saw her eyes. They were hollow, sunken and dry. Scared eyes, lifeless. Noor Khan brought out more water in the jug, this time with some ancient orange squash from the shop, and in his fumbling manner also unwrapped a packet of Tiger glucose biscuits from one of his dusty shelves and offered them to the women. The woman with the sunken eyes picked a couple and started eating. Her wrist, visible briefly from beneath her sleeve, was blue with bulging, sinuous veins.

There were ten or twelve of them, all the same colour, a jaundiced pale. They must have been between the ages of twenty and thirty-five. They were certainly not from the neighbourhood. Their clothes had the distinct stamp of a relatively prosperous life. Baba put his hands on one of the younger girls' shoulders and said, 'I'm the Sarpanch of this village. Don't worry, whatever it is that's troubling you, you can tell me. I promise I will do everything to help. Tell me, what happened? You are like a daughter, really, tell me, where have you come from, what's the matter, why are you like . . . like this?'

I thought Baba was being tactless, too direct. But then I saw he had grasped the situation quickly and realized it needed immediate action.

'Assalam-u-Alaikum,' the first woman whispered. She was small, dressed in a green printed pheran embroidered with large purple flowers. Her eyes were large. She was pretty.

'Assalam-u-Alaikum,' everyone repeated after her. Their lips parted like dry parchment and then closed in despair.

'Wa-alaikum,' said Baba.

'Wa-alaikum,' repeated Noor Khan.

I just nodded, undecided whether to smile or not.

'We have come from far, far away. We have been in curfew for more than three months now, the Army is everywhere and all around, there's nothing to eat,' the first woman continued.

The second woman stopped sobbing, 'No, no, baijana, we don't need anything for ourselves, we can manage, it is our . . .' and then broke down again. She was perhaps the youngest of the lot, girlish, with a long neck, neatly crafted features, frayed hair. Small, ruined red cheeks in an otherwise pallid face.

The mournful chorus now said in unison, 'Do not turn us away empty-handed, brother, do not turn us away, we have travelled far . . .'

In spite of his best efforts, Baba looked on in bewilderment.

The third woman: 'It is for our children that we have come this far.' She had beaded tears in her eyes. A few strands of her hennaed hair flew about and shone in the sunlight. She was the loudest of the group.

'We just want milk, brother, please give us some milk.' The fourth woman. Yellow, jaundiced eyes, dry, powdery-white face, headscarf hanging loose at the back of her head; she must have looked beautiful at some point, perhaps not too long ago.

'But where have you come from?' Noor managed a half-sure question, thousands of frown lines wrinkling his forehead.

The first woman rubbed the shoulders of her sobbing companion and entreated Baba, 'I will tell you, my dear brother: we have babies, they are without milk. That's all we want.'

'There is nothing left inside us to feed our children, that is why we have come here.' The sobbing woman spoke through her tears. Threads of saliva stretched like bridges between her upper and lower lip.

'It's taken us all day to get here, we have walked through homes and orchards, climbed fences and concrete walls, and crossed rivers and streams to get here; please give us some milk, we beg you, oh gentle soul, we beg you!' said the first woman.

I remember the day like an affecting Balraj Sahni black and white film. The women stood wailing and sighing and talking to Baba, one by one and all together, sometimes indistinguishable from each other; they spoke like ghosts, in strange voices, cracked, and bearing terrible grief. I remember looking at them, their faces and their eyes and their voices, and being reminded of women, who, standing in groups like theirs now, sing wedding songs, songs of harvest, or songs welcoming the Eid. They stood, hands on each other's shoulders and formed a semicircle in front of Noor Khan's shop. It was exactly like what women do at weddings, when they get up to join each other, shoulder to shoulder, and then sway gently, backwards and forwards, singing songs of joy and celebration, one half of the standing column picking up the ballad from the other half's lines. *Wanuwun* and *Rouff*, two singing styles, this was exactly like that.

Only, these women had tears rolling down their cheeks, streaming down their withered necks and all the way to the collars and front-pieces of their long pherans, which had now darkened with moisture. I stayed rooted to where I sat, trying hard not to break into tears. Noor Khan still had the jug of water in his hand, Baba scratched at his beard – and the women continued to lean forward each time they had to speak.

'We want some milk,' the fourth woman said.

'Our babies will die. Zubieda's daughter died last night, did you hear, did you hear that?' The third woman again, the one with the hennaed hair.

'Our breasts are barren now, nothing left for our children, nothing. We have eaten all the grass in our gardens and finished all the pulses we had and cooked every grain of rice there ever was.'

'Now we have eaten our *ghairat* too, our honour.'

'There is nothing left in my bosom,' the oldest-looking woman, who had mostly kept silent till now, let out a wheezing, cracking moan and lifted her pheran up to reveal two shrivelled, wrinkled, darkened breasts over a sunken, hollow-looking stomach. Dark bite marks that looked like scabs surrounded the nipples. Baba looked away. Noor Khan and I stood still. There was a fat, gleaming candle-drop on her left breast. Pus.

'My baby will die, my baby will die.' The woman at the back shrieked and broke down. 'If you give me milk, I will give you one of my girls.'

'All we need is milk. Milk is everything.' The first woman hummed. The small, pretty one.

The mournful chorus now swayed in unison again, 'Do not turn us away empty-handed, *baayyo*, do not turn us away, we have travelled far . . .'

'It will end some day. It will. One day there will be no curfew and then there will be milk. One day the Curfew King will die and there will be milk.'

I saw my first dead body, before the population of dead bodies I deal with now, in that breezeless dry summer of last year. The fact that it was someone I knew made it more momentous, more shocking somehow.

After the brief encounter with the curfew mothers, Baba suddenly seemed older. His beard appeared tired and elderly, rather than well trimmed and prosperous. He dressed more untidily, his large bearing somewhat unkempt, and his temper was turning jittery too. As usual, he took out most of his anger on his hookah; the pouches I brought from Noor Khan got heavier and heavier. For the first time ever, he seemed uncertain, not in control of things. He was used to order – things around him moved more or less according to his wishes, not just inside his own house but outside, in the village as well. People came to him for advice, loans, judgements, and he relished every bit of it. Ever since I could remember, I'd seen Baba like that – corner seat in the living room, two round cushions squashed behind him, small trunk by the window sill, and a pregnant-looking copper hookah in front of him, always, like another character in the room. But now, things seemed to be slipping from his hands, it was beyond his grasp.

He was losing his village, his people – even I could see that. Although I'm not too sure if even I could sense it fully then, that this was the beginning of the end. The incident with Gul Khan's older brother, Farooq, was the first. What followed thereafter didn't let up until it brought the end: the cessation of life as we knew it, as Baba knew it, as his elders had imagined and created in the small village in its tiny beginnings in 1947, a year of partitions and pogroms and general ruination. The discreet border hamlet nestled in the hills was about to end its brief life as a community.

The day the curfew women had come begging, Baba had emptied

Noor Khan's shop of all its milk-powder tins and handed them to each of the women and blessed them, saying, 'Have faith in Allahtaala, He will make it easy soon, God bless you, it's just a test, it will pass, all of us face a test at some point or other in life.' And they had walked off in the same manner as they had appeared in the street, with the same young woman leading them out. Baba and I had looked at their receding forms and then gone home together. He kept nodding his head and sighing all the way home. It was a Saturday and I assume all of us spent the rest of the day, and the next, thinking about the women. *Who were they, where had they come from, why, how?* Only Noor and I discussed it at some length the next day. Noor said they must have been sent by their men, because it would have been far more dangerous for them to be searching for food, amidst the new Governor's curfew. I wondered if perhaps they didn't have husbands any more. Noor said that wasn't possible.

The army jeeps arrived on a Monday morning, screeching through mini storms of dust, and sending vagabond hens fluttering high in the air. It was two weeks after the women had come and gone. A full caravan of vehicles, with LMG-mounted windowless jeeps at the front and a menacing, dark grey tank-like truck at the rear. *We'd surely become news now.* Noor had been right: how long could it stay hidden? After all, four of our boys had left to become militants, to wage war against the mighty Indian Army, four boys, and that too from a small, nondescript village near the LoC, under the very nose of the Bharti Fauj.

I'd come to see Noor a little early that day, and had just opened the ledger and drawn a bold line under the Choudharys' previous monthly total – Rs170 in all, they were poor indeed – and started a fresh page for them, when we heard an approaching grunt and hum, and soon, too soon, we saw the green front of a customized army Gypsy hurtling on to the street.

There were eleven Gypsies in all, green and gleaming, some of them open-topped with black-cat commandos standing by the side bars with their machine guns hanging loose, toy-like, from their shoulders. The guns were smallish, metal grey, and seemed very sophisticated – I had never seen such weapons in my life, not even on TV. The men wore new dark green uniforms, overalls, and had tied their black scarves in a way that made the fabric form tight skullcaps on their heads, as the rest of the material flew about behind their backs. From a distance, from the angle we were looking from, they looked like a pack of animals – creatures different from ordinary people. At last I understood the name they had been given: *black cats*. They stopped at the mouth of the small lane leading to Gul Khan's house on the left of the street, parked their vehicles, criss-crossed on either side, and rushed in quickly – most of them – leaving only a handful behind. Dust from the street swayed upwards in short-lived clouds. We could hear the drum of hurried footsteps. The house stood there, imposing, even from behind the thick wall of willows, poplars and keekars lining their front courtyard. There was another rude flurry of steps and then I heard three or four loud quick blows. I guessed they were tearing the main door off its hinges. It first creaked mournfully, then cracked, and then fell with a sharp, painful sound. Birds flapped away.

For the next two or three minutes, Noor and I just heard screaming and shouting from the house. A low, stretched wail emerged from behind the trees. We stood nailed to a spot in front of the shop; the occupants of one of the machine-gun-mounted vehicles watched us from a distance as they closed off the lane with their backs towards it, their eyes gazing towards the shopfront and the street beyond. I felt weak. The shouting became more frantic now, as if desperate to stop something, but, at the same time, as if also aware of its own inefficacy in the face of inevitable disaster. Noor looked terrified. And soon, we saw the commandos bring someone out, with coils of rope tied around his neck and arms. His face was covered and he was stuttering forward. The wailing picked up after a brief hiatus. For the tiniest of moments, I hoped it might be Gul himself brought out of long hiding in his own house. But it was Gul's brother instead, his big brother Farooq, the bully of our childhood, the peevish inquisitor of his younger brother; even though he was covered with a sack-like tunic over his head it was unmistakably him. It happened so quickly. Almost without drama, except for the low crying coming out of the house. They hurled him into one of the Gypsies in the middle, waited for the men who had taken positions at the mouth of the street to jump into their respective jeeps, and then screeched off immediately, as quickly as they had appeared, once again sending a few hens off into laborious flight. We had no time to take it all in. Gul's mother came out with hands raised to the skies, crying. She was a short, stocky woman and, looking into the receding vehicles, gave a piercing cry beckoning them to stop. Gul's father, Sharafat Khan, stood motionless near her, gazing at the storm of dust from the departing military vehicles. Noor Khan turned to me. He looked sick.

'What can I do, Chacha?' I swallowed and somehow managed to pick myself up from the shop floor and jumped into my nylon slippers. I walked towards Farooq's stunned father and drew close to him, but not too close. I didn't know what to do. I wanted to run to Baba, to report what had just happened, to ask him if he could do something, anything, and was still trying to make up my mind and will some life into my senseless knees, when he himself appeared from the other end of the street along with Lassa Kaka.

Farooq had been taken.

No one, not even the Sarpanch himself, knew what to say, what to make of this, what to do about it, what to do about *anything*. Nowgam had become known, and we hadn't realized it until that moment. Ferocious-looking military men had arrived and taken one of us with them. A few weeks earlier, when Noor Khan had tried to convince me of some mysterious nocturnal activity in the area, I had been sceptical. He had believed there was traffic through the street at night. He had heard vehicles, he said, and seen traces of sand and red brick dust here and there in the mornings until it disappeared as the day progressed.

Later, it became known that the Army had briefly questioned Farooq's parents, before taking their older son into a separate room and shouting at him – 'You want Azadi, right? We will give you Azadi, come with us, we'll give it you!' – and then re-emerging with him bound in ropes and a black sack thrown over his head. I felt guilty for ever having made fun of him.

Farooq returned after three weeks. Tortured, he became a tourist site. Everyone came to see him. I never talked to him about his stay with the Army, but theories abounded. Some people said he was not harmed at all and he readily gave all the information about Gul and the others, and that's why he was let off so soon. Others said he was tortured day and night by Kashmiri Pandit police officers, bent on revenge after their tragic exodus from the valley, and he had no choice but to tell them everything he knew. (What *did* he know?) Some even elaborated on the methods of torture used on Farooq Khan. *He was made to pee on an electric heater while they threw ice-cold water over him; they pierced a red-hot knitting needle through his penis and then gave him electric shocks; they stuffed a bamboo cane with hot chilli powder and thrust it up his anus and then broke the cane; they made him drink their collective urine after keeping him thirsty for days; they ran a cricket roller over his feet and knees; no, they let loose their big dogs on him and that was the point when he broke, for he had always been scared of dogs . . .* At the time I had no way of confirming if he had suffered in this way – ways which had become lore in all of Kashmir. I know now, but I felt terribly, terribly sorry for Farooq. Guilty even. He looked broken, his voice had changed; he spoke like a small girl now, in a low, squeaky whimper. The man who would walk through the village with a cassette player around his neck, often singing along loudly in his rakish manner to his favourite songs from the film *Qurbani*, now spoke in an almost-inaudible low voice. I went to visit him with Noor Khan one Sunday afternoon but couldn't manage to say a single word.

'How are you doing? I hear you're going to college; very good thing you have done, really,' he said to me, smiling meekly from his mattress. There was a stink to him, or to the mattress, or to the whole room. Without our asking, or indicating in any manner that we were curious, he lifted his kurta up and showed us the area above his groin. There were small, etched black pits all over his pubic area.

I didn't know what to say. He just kept holding his kurta up and stared casually at the ceiling. I guess he had become so used to showing his bruises and injuries that he didn't wait for us to ask. *Just get it over with*, he must have thought. 'You want to see what they did behind . . . ?' he whispered, almost with anticipation.

I couldn't say yes, I couldn't say no.

Noor Khan intervened quickly and said, 'No, no, beta, it's all right, we know, we know, your father has told me everything. You don't worry, son, it will all be fine, just takes time.' *As if he knew all about third-degree interrogation methods, their after-effects and how long they took to heal.* 'Just take lots of rest – and anything you need from the shop, please send someone, all right?'

Compounder Chechi came and gave him penicillin injections. I looked at the kehwa-coloured liquid swinging inside the slender glass vial as he broke its tip against the edge of the tobacco box lying nearby. Noor Khan took out an envelope and left it by the mattress. Later, he told me it contained some money; he'd heard that Gul's father had had to spend every single penny he had to get Farooq out.

Does that happen?

Of course, anything can happen now.

For three weeks, Gul's house became a shrine. Every day somebody came to visit, to see the boy returned from army detention, to see what had happened to him, to check his torture marks, and then to sigh loudly and wish him all the best of health, while also secretly thanking God, I guessed, that it hadn't been their son. The only person who didn't visit, or the person I noticed by his complete absence, was Hussain's abba`. People from Farooq's extended clan spread as far as Rajouri near Jammu – even they came to see him, but Khadim Hussain didn't. The azans had dried up too.

While Farooq was home – and he didn't step out of the house even once after he was released – it gave an air of excitement to the streets. Yes, people talked about the horror and terror of having to go through torture, and prayed nobody would have to meet such a fate again, but something about having a young man of theirs taken and returned in a compromised state brought some kind of self-recognition as well: *We too are a part of it all.*

I never saw Farooq walk after that.

At home Baba, as I said, pondered endlessly, and smoked. Occasionally, he eyed me with some kind of an inquisition. *See what happens.*

One night, after we had eaten and Baba had left the kitchen to warm up his hookah, Ma came to sit beside me. She just sat there for a long, long time. We were both silent. Then she slowly ruffled my hair and hugged me, quickly. 'Would you like me to make some tea? I won't put too much milk in it, all right?' she said, gently touching my hair again.

'Okay, Ma. Why don't you have a cup too . . . ?'

'Yes, yes, me too . . .' She paused now, in that familiar manner of hers when she has something else on her mind. 'I was thinking, beta, that maybe you shouldn't stay up so late. I know you have to study, but you know, Baba was saying . . .' She paused again to look at me.

I decided not to betray any signs of irritation, 'What was Baba saying, Ma?'

'Oh, nothing . . . Nothing much . . . He was just, he was just saying that maybe it's not very safe having your room lit up like that all night.'

Why didn't he say so himself? *Are you now going to send me messages through Ma? What have I done, Baba?*

'He's just concerned, beta, don't get him wrong, he was just saying people could be wandering around at night; you know how it is these days, and if they see your room all bright . . . ? That's all.'

Ma grabbed the kerosene stove by its twiggy brass legs and pumped life into it with a few quick shoves of the well-greased pump. The thing soon glowed with an arc of orange and blue light. *Who the hell was going to circle our house in this wilderness at night, looking for a candlelit room?*

'No, Ma, no, I understand. You're right, it is not very safe. You don't worry, hmm, what I'll do is cover the window towards the mountain with that thick blanket Baba bought for me last year, and I'll not study until too late, all right?'

She smiled from her chowki and pumped up the kerosene stove again, this time to a buzzing cusp of azure. Her face glowed white in the stove's light. Ma looked pretty, as always, cheeks blushed red with regular work, two long braids dancing about on her back, and the sleeves of her pheran rolled up to reveal her strong, round arms.

She had started spending more and more time with me now, and checked with me every time I left the house. Farooq's state, and fate perhaps, hung heavily in the crisp frown lines on her otherwise clear forehead. She was scared. And the truth is, I was very scared too. 'You are not going anywhere else, beta, other than the shop, right?' She also hugged me more often in those days, fed me more, made me an extra *choutt* for breakfast, waited for me on the balcony at the end of the day and beamed on my return from Noor's shop, or when I'd just been hanging around the street, down in the village, alone, or sometimes hopelessly trying to chat with young kids.

Every time I left, though, she sighed a sad, suppressed sigh. Months ago, when Hussain had left, I had stayed in the house for more than a week, not even stepping out once. I had then gradually started going out again, and my parents lived with it. That's how it had worked out then, and that's how it continued after Farooq's captivity and subsequent release as a living martyr. People visited him for days, just like you visit someone who returns after the Hajj.

But that was not all.

One day, Baba returned home early from his morning prayers. He didn't always go to the mosque for his *fajr*, sometimes just making do with his prayer mat in the living room, but that day he had gone and came back soon. I woke up to what sounded like urgent, anxious conversation between him and Ma in the kitchen. They were trying to keep their voices low but the hushed anxiety of the exchange somehow drifted up the stairs. Something was wrong. Still half asleep, I went down slowly and stood in the doorway. Ma looked towards Baba. He looked back and then towards me. No one said anything for a moment or two.

'You'll catch a cold like this, come in and take that chadar, come on.'

Sleepy and confused, I obeyed silently and took the chadar over my knees as soon as I sat down near Ma. The chadar smelled of Baba.

'Beta, Farooq's gone,' Baba said at once, pressing his hands hard against his knees.

What?

Again?

Why?

Baba scratched at his beard, furiously, and bent his head down. I could not manage to speak. He had said it so abruptly that it almost felt unsaid.

'It looks like he has been taken again . . .' Baba looked up and started again, his lips trembling as he spoke. I suddenly became very sad for him, for everything, and felt my legs go limp.

'His mother was waiting outside the mosque when I got there, we couldn't even start the prayer. She just stood by the door, hands raised to the skies, and started crying. At first she wouldn't tell us what had happened. She just kept looking skyward. But soon she did. They took Farooq from his bed in a predawn raid. Sharafat went after them, screaming and crying, and hasn't returned yet,' Baba concluded, in the manner of someone knowing the end of a tale before it finishes.

Ma looked at me; Baba wiped his brow – I wasn't sure if he had tears in his eyes. 'I thought, I'll just change and get some money, in case . . .' he said, dropping his hands, and went to his room.

I just sat there, warmed up under that Baba-smelling chadar, bewildered by this second arrest of Farooq in less than a month. Had he really been up to something; maybe he did have some links after all, maybe he had done something? Although, I must say, he had always come across as someone who would more likely get up to petty mischief than take up arms as a militant. But, huh, I realized I had already been wrong so many times. Maybe Ma was right, Farooq was indeed being punished for being Gul's brother, it was all because of Gul. Was Farooq the message they wanted to send after Gul and the others' crossing over? I wondered as Baba came back. He was wearing his headman's clothes now: a grey tweed waistcoat over his salwar-kameez, the old but still respectable-looking haji skullcap, and the neatly folded green-bordered stole on his shoulder.

Ma stood up, as if to confirm what he was about to do.

'I'm going to their house to check. Not much we can do, but I must go, I must go . . . not that we can do much,' Baba absent-mindedly muttered again, 'but still, they are going through a bad time, what misery is this . . . ?' He nodded to himself.

'Baba, I'll also come with you.' I almost cried out, interrupting my contemplation of Farooq's fate.

Ma turned, suddenly, 'What will *you* do there, there's nothing you can do . . . Baba has to go. It's his duty.'

'It's my duty too, Ma,' I immediately began to plead. 'Gul was my friend, after all –'

'Yes, yes, I know, your friend! It's all his doing, this thing, you know – his brother is suffering now, his mother, his whole family, everybody, all because of them.' She cut me short and raised her voice.

A heavy pause followed after Ma's mini outburst. No one said anything.

'But Ma, that's over . . . Right now they may need some help, Baba . . . ?' I beseeched my father.

'Oh, ho . . . ! We don't have time for this, do we?' Baba thrust his hands into the pockets of his fat waistcoat and glared at us both. Silence again. 'Let's all go, okay? Farooq's mother will need some-one to be with her.' He turned to Ma now. 'Let's go then, hurry, hurry,' and with that he turned and slipped out into the corridor.

Ma quickly changed her headscarf and looked me in the eye.

I wrapped the chadar around my shoulders and started after Ma. In the morose light of a struggling dawn we were soon descending the footpath towards the village street. My mother walked, head down, behind my hurrying father. I trudged along behind my mother.

Gul's house still had the early morning look about it, greyish light of a misty morning caressing the features of the two-storey house with its poplar- and willow-fronted courtyard. As I entered after Baba and Ma, I wondered whether houses reflect the tragedy that befalls their inhabitants. Everything inside was dimly lit, as if the light of morning had just washed over things whilst passing over the house. A few people were already assembled in the kitchen, where in one corner Gul's mother sat crying hardly audible tears for her elder son (or both her sons – how could you tell?) and in the other, Noor Khan – he was everywhere – was trying to blow life into the small coals stacked up perilously in the chillum of the house hookah. I went over and sat next to him; he briefly interrupted his struggle with the diffident embers, to give me a look, as if to say it was all over.

Ma hugged Gul's mother, which made her cry a little more loudly. Soon, Ma too had tears in her eyes. Gul's kid sister, Tabasum, was still sleeping. She hadn't been woken up. I found that sad: there was a member of the family who was sleeping upstairs, and downstairs the family's destiny had changed, perhaps irrevocably, and people had already arrived to express their condolences. Soon she would wake up, as if it were just another day, come down, wash her face by the grey concrete sink in the corridor, and enter the kitchen expecting a hot cup of tea and home-made roti. But there was no tea being prepared for her today; instead, her mother's tears refused to dry up, and her father had not yet returned from chasing after the men who had taken her big brother.

Noor Khan's hookah belched suddenly and thin blue plumes of smoke twirled above us. Ma still had her arms around Gul's mother. Three more people – Ramazan Choudhary, Sadiq Chechi and Lassa Kaka – had arrived and were seated around their headman, who was keenly listening to each round of whispered advice. By late morning, the kitchen was already getting too full, so Baba got up and opened the door to their vast *baithak* – theirs was the biggest drawing room in the village – and all the visitors transferred there. Whispers ruled.

Around nine thirty Tabasum finally woke up and came straight into the kitchen, where I stood guard over her mother's despondent figure and my own mother who was consoling her. Tabasum walked straight to her mother and hugged her at once. A tight embrace. The mother started crying with fresh energy and then mother and daughter both wept for a long while. I felt a dead weight, watching these two women weeping inconsolably, for ever, as it seemed that day. Ma stood there, wordless, occasionally looking towards me. Every time she did that, I looked down. Tabasum had probably understood everything the moment she had seen people in her house. She had seen it before, after all, only a few weeks earlier. She knew the routine now.

As her cries faded into sighs, I saw someone come and gently lead her to a corner of the room; they sat there behind the open door, away from all the older women. I almost let out a gasp. It was Asma. I so wanted to be near her and help her comfort the little girl. Here were two sisters understanding each other instantly. Grief. My heart went out to Asma. But I could not invite attention by going and sitting with her, so I just walked past the two of them, brushed against Asma's sleeve – she seemed to acknowledge it – and then went to sit back down after pretending to be looking out into the corridor.

Around noon, Noor Khan peeped into the kitchen and signalled to me that I should step out. Something had happened. I jumped to my feet. In the living room everyone was standing, all sombre, as if in readiness for prayer. I looked out of the window and saw Sharafat Khan walking in. I stayed by the door and watched as Gul and Farooq's father slowly climbed up the front steps and walked into the hall. Sharafat Khan looked like he was made of dust. He had passed into some other world – there was dust all over him, his body, his arms, his hair, his lips, even his eyes. The sandy figure then stepped out of its shoes and walked right into the room. I shrank back against the wall, lest the strange dust on him might touch me. I would regret doing that later.

Baba stepped forward, took hold of his hand and led him to the far corner of the room. Baba nodded towards Lassa Kaka, who asked the gathering to settle down. Sharafat Khan sat there, in the corner, hunched and bent, folded over, and wouldn't say a word. He sat like that for a long, long time, until people, weary with waiting for him to say something, started to leave one by one; some people went off only to come back shortly afterwards to check if he had said anything. Baba, Noor Khan, Lassa Kaka and Ramazan Choudhary were the only people who did not move. I sat at the other end of the room, near the door, and watched him. A couple of times I went to see Ma – and the only girl I ever, ever loved – in their kitchen. Tabasum sat leaning against Asma's shoulder with trembling lips, her morning face smeared with long parallel lines of dried-up tears.

Three days later, Farooq's head was hurled over the fence, into the front garden of their house. It was a Thursday and I knew something was wrong the moment I saw Noor Khan come running to the house. He talked to Baba in whispers near the front steps; he didn't come in. Baba left immediately. I followed soon, against Ma's meek protestations.

They had covered Farooq by the time I reached their house. On the thick unmown grass of their garden a white chadar lay half spread over a bell-shaped mound. Baba guarded the flimsy arched entrance to the garden, made with bent unskinned willow branches, by standing in the middle of it. He had his back towards the object. Brave man, my father. On the short path from the outer door to the house, marked by the tall hedges of the garden on the right, people just stood silently, and occasionally – but only occasionally – a few heads bobbed up and some necks arched in to take a look at the chadar and the motionless object it veiled. And in doing so they made it more pronounced somehow, more delicate. That day, at least for the time I was there, no one talked in a normal voice. Everyone whispered or appeared to whisper; even Baba seemed to have lost his tongue. The women of the house were not allowed to come out into the garden. I couldn't decide if that was sympathetic or otherwise.

Noor Khan had seated himself at the end of the gravel path, at the bottom of the front steps of the house. He was squatting, and when I finally got close to him I could tell he had been crying. The moment he saw me he let out a soundless gasp and then quickly lit a cigarette. Taking a long drag, he closed his eyes briefly and said, 'Lightning has struck, beta, lightning.'

I didn't know how to react, so I just sat down and touched him gently on his knee. Just a few feet away stood Baba, under the creeper-covered willow arch, standing guard over the severed head of the family's elder son. *Why did they have to do that? Why not just kill him?* I remember tears flaming up in my eyes, at the immediacy of what had happened, and at thinking how close it was, how very close it was, just a few feet away, on the green grass under that chadar, surrounded by hedges on one side, tall poplars and willows and keekars on the front, flower beds and ancient rose bushes on the side of the house . . . It was a man until last week. And a man I knew well. I sighed for my father too, for the way he was standing guard, erect, with his hands folded behind his back, nodding to himself.

Later in the afternoon, it was Compounder Chechi who first suggested that we should start looking for Farooq's body. He said he knew what usually happened in such cases. 'Look, we must look for the body, they often dump it somewhere close by,' he declared, fiddling with his pen that he sometimes wedged behind his ear. 'It's happened quite a few times in the city – I know, I know, trust me.'

'Why?' Baba spoke only for the first or second time that day; for the rest of the time he had been mostly communicating with his hands.

'Because that's exactly the point, Sarpanch Sahib, to show you what they can *and will* do to people who get into all this. They want to send a message. They are like killer dogs, that's what they are, that's what they do. So please, please, without wasting any more time, let's go and look . . .'

I remember telling myself that Chechi's unflustered manner was owed to his profession as a medical man, and he must have indeed served in the big hospital in Srinagar.

Two days later, Ramazan Choudhary's elder son – the same man who had worked on the mosque and whose two children I had seen at Noor's shop buying eclairs and whose full name, Ishaq Jan

Choudhary, I only got to know now when we were paired together in the hunt for Farooq's body – and I were scouring the area around the dirt track that goes away from the village and tails off into the footpath to the valley, when we saw Farooq's bloated, headless body lying near a narrow stream running down from the mountain. It looked like an inclined stump, like a fallen tree.

He wore a red and black check kurta pyjama of some thick fabric. Where the head should have been, and which was now buried in the graveyard behind the mosque, stood a bluntly axed stump, jutting out over the cascading channels of the shallow brook, as if the head had been washed away by the water whilst its bearer had bent down to take a drink.

By the same evening, Farooq's grave was dug again. This time a longer trench was made, and his torso gently lowered alongside the buried head. His white shroud appeared sad, unbearable to watch, with its wrinkled accumulation at the top.

Baba oversaw the second burial too.

Noor Khan wept.

Clasping his hands tightly around the bamboo pipe of his hookah, he shuddered and cried. Like a boy. He bellowed loudly and then, snivelling, grunting and coughing in the midst of his tears, he used the much-worn sleeve of his thick and probably expensive pheran to wipe off the snot threatening to drop into the smoking chillum. I eyed him from the ledger I had been poring over since morning.

The whole village had been in a state of perennial mourning. There was the aftermath of tears on every face in the street. Some of it, I suspected, had to do with the insistent mourning that Farooq's relatives observed for more than a month. I guess people thought it rude to appear unaffected while passing the mourners' house – its façade, visible from the street, was enough of a reminder of what had happened. The image of Farooq's hacked neck came to me at night; I wanted to go and sit with Ma and Baba but felt embarrassed about appearing so unsettled. I did not know how to behave with people. Gul's extended family stayed in the village for the full forty-day mourning period. Then they left gradually. Baba had been unhappy about such a large number of mouths eating away whatever little remained in the Khan household. Noor, however, did brisk business, perhaps disinterestedly, because everyone who came smoked. They came to the shop all day, taking out weighty dirt-coated one-rupee copper coins to buy packs of Cavanders and bidi rolls. I did not comment on the increased clientele – it was sure to make Noor uncomfortable.

Khadim Hussain, whose face and words never receded from the back of my mind, had disappeared altogether from sight; people assumed he spent all his time inside the mosque, but no one I met had seen him there. Only old Ramazan Choudhary thought he had seen him a few times during the early morning prayers. Once or twice I thought I heard his azan again, that familiar echoing, surrounding melody which had now and then laid siege over our dawns and dusks in the past. I had no will to think about it further, though. *Let him be with himself*, I thought. Better not poke any more than I already had. For a short while I was content with being a keeper of secrets.

Someone else also disappeared, or just left the village. It was Baba's old friend Firdaus Ali. His wife had sent for him, and he came for a short while to collect his family. They just left. Two of his children, the elder boy and the girl, had been particularly upset during the time of Farooq's death and two funerals. On the day of the second funeral, when we lowered his torso beside his head under Baba's silent supervision, the two had somehow slipped into the assembled crowd. They had peered at the proceedings from between people's legs. Lassa Kaka, who was serving endless jugs of water to the grave-digging team, had noticed them first and we had quickly taken them home, Baba as usual communicating his instructions to me with that slight nod of the head and half a raised eyebrow. A few days later Firdaus Ali's elder son, who was five or six years old, had started playing out a beheading game at home, marking his sister's throat round and round with a ballpoint pen. The sister had refused to sleep ever since. She just lay on her mattress, hands covering her throat, and stayed awake all night. For days her mother tried to put her to sleep, sleeping close to the girl each night, but the daughter became hysterical if they tried to remove her hands from her throat. In the end Chechi had been called in, who promptly advised half a Calmpose to put the girl to sleep. Firdaus Ali agreed, but he knew this wasn't the solution – he had seen a bit of the world, he said, and drugging his daughter to sleep every night wasn't the wisest thing to do – and it pained him. So, so . . . he had no choice but to leave. Baba was expected to understand (why Firdaus Ali needed his friend's approval in the first place was beyond me), and he did, putting his hands on his friend's shoulders and hugging him, as if he were an obedient son going away on his father's duty, when he came to say his goodbye. There was an understanding between the two men that I had seldom seen Baba demonstrating with anyone else.

Life went on in the village under a spell of mournful inactivity.

No one knew what to do. Some cursed Hussain and company for having brought this on the village, some defended them: *There will always be a cost* . . . Amidst all this, Farooq's father, who always appeared with this pall of fatigue about him, spoke only once, responding sadly to Ramazan Choudhary's remarks about everything being the four boys' fault. This was on the last day of the mourning period, the fortieth, when we'd gathered over tea at Gul Khan's house. 'People can talk as much as they want, and say whatever they want, as long as it is someone else, someone else's son. I had two sons, two . . . One ate the other, you say, hai, hai . . . !' He'd increasingly started to seem disturbed, mad even.

I went about my invented routine as doggedly as ever, even though sadness crept through my very clothes.

When Noor Khan cried on that warm autumn day almost a year after Hussain had left, I saw it at first as some kind of a betrayal; I'd thought of Noor as my ally in my little game of normality. He too had been trying to go on as if nothing life-changing had occurred. But seeing him break down like that, like village women, in his own shop, smashed that illusion to pieces. He had given up.

I placed my hand on his knees and gently pushed him, to pull him out of his moment of sudden and overwhelming grief. He picked up his left sleeve again and ran it roughly over his mouth, nose, face, as if to demonstrate he wasn't ashamed of his condition. 'Noor Chacha,' I struggled, 'you can tell me if you –'

'What do I tell you, beta? You don't know, you're just a . . .' but here he stopped and half covered his face with the same sleeve. What was he going to say? *You are just a boy . . .* ? Well, yes, I was just a boy, but a boy who hadn't left him, who hadn't abandoned his parents, who hadn't brought all this on the whole village. But I said nothing and waited for him to continue. He sighed now, an old man's sigh, and tried to calm himself down. A tinge of embarrassment did now wash over his face and fresh tears rolled down, this time silently. Have you seen an old man cry? Cry big fat tears of age-old grief? I looked down into the ledger, flushed with shame, and peering down like this at Noor's account book, without seeing much on the page, I realized I hadn't cried in a very long time. A lot of people had cried over Farooq's death, even an otherwise stoic Baba had appeared moved, and Ma had wept almost as much as Farooq's own mother, if not more, but I remembered I hadn't cried at all. But now, seeing the old man burst into tears, I wanted to cry, weep for as long as it took, and then, all of a sudden, I did exactly that. Something bitter and blazing stirred under my brow; my eyes and my cheeks became warm, and soon double-visioned pearls, in their inky peripheries, appeared on the page. It felt good. I sensed Noor Khan's eyes on me but I didn't move, lest he should see my tears. Perhaps he already had, but didn't want to embarrass me. I never knew. I kept looking down at the multiplying circles of blue smudges.

I now felt a mild pat on the back of my head. I acknowledged Noor's hand with a gentle nod of my head. He brushed his fingers through my hair and grunted an 'it's all right, son' grunt. I came to my senses and slowly turned towards him. He looked back with a defeated look.

Soon afterwards, I found myself preparing Noor Khan's hookah for him. This was a first. I felt he needed it and I should do it for him. The chillum glared at me with its sudden scarlet embers. I withdrew my hands and nudged the thing towards him. He accepted it graciously and took a never-ending, although unusually silent, drag, and looked towards the sky before exhaling a grievous-looking plume of dark grey smoke that seemed to vaporize his face with it.

That night I reached home in a tender, enlightened state. For hours before passing into sleep, I thought and thought hard, and thought about my life and the lives of other people around me. Farooq's death had made people wither, slowly and silently. The initial thrill of being part of something momentous, of nervous expectancy for that great triumph – *freedom, Azadi* – had already begun to wear off. It only took one brutal blow.

I thought of Shaban Khatana, that benevolent old Gujjar in the mountains. I hadn't heard of him for quite a while – and I hadn't visited him since that meeting with Khadim Hussain. What had happened to him? Was he still up there, in his smoke-filled dhoka, waiting for his sons? Were there shoals of boys still passing through his solitary forest quarters?

19   Knife's Edge

In September we had a surprise visitor.

Any kind of visitor had become an infrequent occurrence, but when I recognized the approaching figure from our living-room window I was even more surprised. Eleven months had passed since they had left, and I had somehow managed to complete my first year in college. Mostly through absence. Summer had turned crisp. Baba had just finished his morning grapple with the hookah and was sitting in his corner seat reading yesterday's newspaper. Ma had gone to her garden, where the final blooms of *mawal*, red intoxicated coxcomb, imbued the rear fence with a fresh maroon tint, rich and new. It made our vegetable patch look like a cradle, a red velvet chadar girding it on all sides. I was still not sure whether to acknowledge Rahman Khatana in front of Baba or not, when he himself launched into an urgent introduction: 'Shaban Khatana, up in the mountains, Sarpanch Sahib, he worked for you some years ago . . . ? Yes, yes, that one, I'm his elder son.' Baba seemed to know Rahman? I never knew. Rahman looked at me quickly and he understood I wasn't entirely comfortable with his sudden appearance; Baba had not known about my trips to Shaban's place. Or so I believed.

Rahman sat down near Baba, negotiating, I thought, the first few moments of half-conversation that ensue when you meet someone your father knows. 'I'd come to take a look at the dhoka, salvage some of their belongings, you know,' Rahman said in a dry voice. He looked edgy. He was wearing a large loose pheran over his shirt, a little odd for this time of the year.

I went to the kitchen, reheated some leftover tea from the morning on the kerosene stove and poured it into the Thermos. It smelled of heat. I didn't want to bother Ma – she liked her late morning meetings with her darlings in the garden.

Baba was leaning back regally into his twin cushions when I returned. He was listening keenly to Rahman.

'I thought Sarpanch Sahib might be home, let me say my greetings. Father mentioned you often, Jenab . . .'

I had thought about Shaban Chacha often, but had never ventured to inquire after him since that last fateful meeting in the winter. Rahman looked burdened, on the brink of something.

'Sarpanch Sahib, this is what they did to me,' he started without much prelude and raised a large, blackened, festering arm from beneath his pheran, heavily bandaged around the wrist and held in place with what looked like improvised willow-wood splints. Yellow, purple and black swatches of colour criss-crossed the much-dirtied white padding. The hand looked like some animal.

He sighed noisily a couple of times and then, quite suddenly, started sobbing in a low, suppressed voice. The man who had braved frostbite and ambushes and shelling and crossfire and wildlife and terrible terrain sat before my father sobbing like a little girl with his head hung down. Baba and I stared. I wanted him to say more.

'I'd come to take a look at the dhoka and salvage some of their belongings. I just thought Sarpanch Sahib might be home,' the big man repeated through his sobs. I was sure he had come to meet me – he was just making an excuse in front of Baba, who had never been their headman, never probably known Rahman. They didn't even live near the village.

Rahman looked at me and lifted his big black hand from his lap and moved it to his side; a couple of splints creaked gently. I poured him Lipton chai from the aluminium flask, which he accepted gratefully with his functioning hand and began slurping greedily. Baba looked at me with narrowing eyes but didn't say anything. I knew what he meant: *Look, what they have done to this poor man.* I wanted to say, 'Baba, I know, I know, but these may not be Kashmiris. They don't chop off body parts. This is the work of foreigners, jihadis probably, mercenaries . . . they are the ones who cut off hands and –' But I didn't say a word. I knew he would just throw up his hands in the air, 'They are all the same, son, all the same!' and shut me up.

I looked at him and then turned towards Rahman, who was now shifting in his place, slowly nodding to himself.

'Mother is fine now. They managed to stitch back the tip of her tongue; she herself picked it up from the floor and wrapped it in a newspaper. She can't talk yet, the doctor said it will take time; but she can at least eat now, bhaijan, soft food like sticky rice and curd mixed together, also daal sometimes,' Rahman said, not without a hint of pride in his mother's bravery. I wasn't even trying to make sense of what he was saying, and of the grief he should have demonstrated while stating all this, but no, he was just . . . 'I'm thankful to Allahtaala,' he looked up immediately, as if to acknowledge the Almighty's ready audience, 'that we're still alive, Sarpanch Sahib, otherwise people die just like that these days, you know, like flies, like flies . . .'

Baba was becoming increasingly uncomfortable with the conversation, unable to make immediate sense of it, probably didn't even want to get into it, so the ever-respected and respectful headman waved Rahman shut with his hand and nodded, 'Don't worry, don't worry, what did you say your name was, Rahman? Where are you headed?'

'Yes, yes, Sarpanch Sahib, Rahman. Father had asked me to come and see you . . . ?'

Baba opened the metal trunk he kept by the window sill and brought back a loose wad of fifty-rupee notes and thrust it into Rahman's side pocket. Rahman became still for a while and then started thanking Baba profusely, with liquid eyes.

But he couldn't leave just *yet*, there was so much to be talked about. I was seeing him for the first time after that night in the forest. Someone had actually chopped off his mother's tongue! How could they . . . ? 'Rahman,' I started hesitantly, in a careful tone, determined not to make him cry again, 'when these people did this, what did they say? I mean, who were they? What did they . . . What did they want?'

Baba, grinding his teeth now, turned away and started warming up his hookah. The copper thing leaned heavily on its edge on the carpet as Baba tilted it forward to check if it was all right by blowing at it. If the *jajeer gand*, the gasket around the stem and pipe exhaled tiny jets of vapour around it, it was ready.

'Oh, bhaijan, you don't know, they can do anything, whatever they want, you don't know,' Rahman began afresh with a loud sigh. My mind wandered off to Shaban Chacha while I waited for his son to make some sense. Shaban's wife appeared too, in a smoky blur. I remembered her toothy smile and silent conversation.

'What happened, bhaijan, was,' Rahman continued, 'that they needed Father's help, they wanted him to help them find an arms dump hidden somewhere inside a mountain grove. It was an under-ground dump, near some hollow tree trunk or something, they said. Father, you see, had been a khoji in his younger days – you know what a khoji does, what a khoji . . . ?' Rahman asked hesitantly and turned towards Baba for a fraction.

'This district commander of Harkat-ul-Ansar, the one-eyed Abdullah Mullah, he was from Afghanistan, bhaijan, very old fighter, very strong, he was the one who had hidden the arms in that place but then he was killed in an encounter in some cave – they burned him alive in the cave, they were so scared of him, bhaijan, so scared . . .' Rahman paused and looked at Baba again, who was still not paying much attention to the story, or was feigning disinterest. 'So this Abdullah Mullah's men had been looking for the arms dump for months when someone must've mentioned Father, who had done khoji work in the past, but nothing too complicated: if some-one lost something, Father would just spend more time looking in all the probable places until he found the lost article, usually keys, earrings, wallets, sometimes hens and cocks even! He did this for people in the villages who would then give the khoji an inaam, a reward for the finder of their lost things. Over the years, Father had obviously developed a nose for finding lost goods, acquired a sense for sniffing things out. And that's how he came to have the nick-name Khoji Gujjar, brother, you don't know. But that was years ago, when he was younger, when he was much younger.'

I tried to imagine a young Shaban Khatana, my old friend, but couldn't really see him. I tried to imagine him as a 'lost and found' specialist, a missing items expert, walking surreptitiously in people's gardens and by roadsides and pointing triumphantly at something he had just found.

Baba must have looked at Rahman with his intense, quizzical look because he was now passionately addressing my father. 'No, no, yes . . . He did go across a few times early on – what to do, Sarpanch Sahib, what to do, if they come to you and ask you can't refuse, can you? But he didn't go often, and after he stopped we went on our own, because the few times we went with him were enough to understand all about the passes; and by the time Father stopped we'd memorized all the secret routes and tracks in the jungles.'

So Baba had known about Shaban, and perhaps he knew about Rahman too, but I couldn't be sure. He wouldn't help a total stranger with money, isn't it? And lots of money, it seemed.

'Rahman bhai, what happened after Abdullah Mullah, you were saying . . . ?'

'Oh yes, yes, someone must have told them that Father could find them the arms Abdullah Mullah had hidden before he died in the cave attack.' Rahman stopped again, this time all grave. His colour changed, and he quickly shifted his injured hand. 'They came early morning one day; it was cold outside and everything had frozen. We rarely went out, except for, you know . . . rest of the time we just sat around the chullah in the dhoka.' He looked at me momentarily. I turned my face away; he understood, and continued. 'So they came and asked Father to go with them, right there and then. But Father says to them, "Where in this cold are you going to take me, what's the rush, what's the rush?" And Father was abrupt with them, because he has seen many such men and that's why he is not scared or in awe of them, which is something they don't like, and one of them gets angry and starts yelling at us. Father tells him, "Son, there's no point in getting angry. I cannot come with you if you don't tell me where and what for – if you do that, I'll help in whatever you need, whatever." Father had now decided to be a little more cooperative, because I had been glaring at him, bhaijan, and thought that it was wise to cooperate in the circumstances.'

'Then?' Baba's first word since Rahman had started narrating the story.

'Then they told him that they knew he was a khoji and they needed him to find this arms dump in the Shiingund jungle, and they were sure he could do it because they had been told he was the best in the business. Father listened patiently and then asked them a few questions about the area under suspicion, how long the arms dump had been 'missing', how many people and what kind of people had known of its existence, if they knew how big it was and how much ammunition was hidden in the dump, and, most of all, how had it become untraceable? The fighters replied they didn't know much about the dump except that it was put together by Abdullah Mullah a long time ago, and the only two people who knew about it had been killed with him in the cave encounter. They also said many of the weapons dumps they'd known were underground wooden cellars, and in the past some had been found near hollow tree trunks. The only useful bit of information they gave, even I could tell, bhaijan, was that Abdullah had never left these mountains and it was most likely that the dump was somewhere in the vicinity of the cave complex he and his boys had been using as a hideout.'

I imagined Shaban Khatana talking in his old-worldly tone, benign and yet slightly patronizing. I imagined him fiddling with his streaked beard and his shining nose. I wondered how simple lives could hide such complexity underneath the veneer of plain appearance – Shaban Chacha had appeared a very simple man, almost retired from active participation in the life around him, disconnected even from the people whose lives changed so irrevocably once they passed through his forest quarters.

'Anyhow, bhaijan, Father requested them to come back in two or three days because he needed to prepare for the trip and thought the weather might be more kind to a man of his age by then.' Rahman almost seemed to be enjoying telling us the story. 'Father made preparations for what he said would be a tough few days in the mountains and waited, but the militants didn't turn up! Father waited in readiness for four more days. No one came. Weeks passed.

We almost forgot about it. My contacts later told me that there had been a big seizure of weapons somewhere near the forest of Shiingund. The army had called in dozens of dogs and had been combing the area for months after the cave encounter in which thirty-seven men had been martyred, and finally sniffed out the massive arms dump. They went ahead and displayed the seized arms on TV and said local people had helped in tracing them. I don't know why, bhaijan, but that's what my contacts told me. I don't know why they said that,' he sighed.

Rahman's bony cheeks, I now noticed, were dark, red and flaked – purple spots shone through his taut skin. He looked like he was in agony. Baba had rekindled his hookah now and started pulling hard at the pipe. Tufts of blue smoke gathered in the corners of the room, near the curtains and the ceiling. I was now half certain Baba knew more about Rahman's involvement with me than I had previously believed.

Taking a deep breath, Rahman the guide started again. 'A month and a half later, the same boys visited – stormed in, rather – shouting at us. They ransacked the dhoka, manhandled my mother and pushed father into a corner, and there they interrogated him for the next three to four hours, brother, asking him what he knew about the arms seizure and why he had helped the army bastards. Father pleaded with them, cried, howled and begged, but they just wouldn't listen. I also swore to them that Father didn't know anything about it and told them of the people I knew; I told them I'd met the great Ashfaq Majid and Chief Commanders Dar and Bangroo and how Operation Balakote Chief, Inquilabi, had himself crossed the border twice with me. I told them how new boys were always entrusted to my care and all I'd gone through to take so many mujahids across safely, but they were convinced that Father had betrayed them. "Gaddaar Gujjar," they said, "this is why you should never be trusted, you're all swine, all the same, you have no loyalties, kabhi India kabhi Pakistan, all for the money, hain? Bastards!" they said. Father pleaded, "I haven't stepped out of my poor dhoka for a month now, my son, I swear on Allah. I swear on my sons' lives, I have done nothing, beta, nothing!" A young tall boy then stepped forward, "That's what they all say, you filthy traitor!" and grabbed Father by his hair whilst cursing us, the entire Gujjar race, coward Kashmiris, our Indian masters, everyone. Father shrank further into the corner and bowed before them with folded hands, he had tears in his eyes, "I have done nothing, beta, nothing," he kept saying to them, "please listen to me, please spare me, please forgive me," he kept saying, he kept saying . . .'

Baba stopped pulling on his hookah now. He was getting restless, perhaps upset with how the story was unfolding. I wondered whether he was working himself up on his favourite subject. 'I have always said it, they have no religion, they are a slur on Islam, they have no principles!' He would soon launch into a tirade – partly, at least, for my benefit.

But he didn't. Thank God.

Rahman took another sip from what must have been the last few drops of cold tea in his cup. 'But, bhaijan, they didn't listen to a word Father and I said; that young beast dragged Father by his hair towards the door, pulling viciously at the thin white strands of hair at the back of his head. Father resisted, crying, desperately trying to hold on to various objects in the dhoka, a pateela, the flour tin, the central pillar with its hooks and pegs, but at each stop, at each step, bhaijan, the bastard yanked at Father's hair harder and cut him off from these last pegs of support. I watched helplessly. Two men held me with their hands digging into my arms, and a third poked his Kalashnikov nozzle into my neck from behind, here, bhaijan, here, look, it's still there . . .' Rahman turned round intently to show me his neck, where there was a large, purplish, black patch.

'I shivered, Sarpanch Sahib. Father would be dead any minute now, I thought. I had no idea what the son-of-a-bitch would do next. Why didn't he just shoot Father, who was now kicking his legs, overpowered by the brute force pulling at his hair . . . They were at the door now, Father's tormentor had one foot outside on the steps and one foot inclined against the doorpost. Father tried a last resort, I writhed in agony, can't tell you how, can't tell you . . . Father is at the door, with his legs splayed wide open and hands clutching desperately at the wood. Any moment now, any moment now. His eyes are popping out as his nails scratch at the solid deodar wood. He screams, *"Khudaya, kuni kanh chuvvna! Khudaya!* Somebody help me for God's sake, somebody help me, please! He looks at me and I see terrible fear in his eyes, bhaijan, the fear of death. I saw it, I saw it when Father looked at me – and I couldn't do anything – all crying and bawling, "I beg you, mercy, mercy, you are like my son, beta, please spare me, please, please let me go." He kept on begging them, screaming, his face red with fear, his eyes bursting with horror, brother, horror, and now blood was oozing from his nails. The doorpost had shining red marks on it. The young maniac briefly stopped pulling, and was glaring down at my father's abject form under his feet. Sarpanch Sahib, he looked like a chicken fluttering its wings under the knife's edge. I can never, never forget it!'

Rahman started sobbing loudly now, very loudly. Baba looked extremely uncomfortable – I knew there was anger seething beneath that pained look – and turned towards me: W*hat shall we do now?*

I went over to Rahman and put my hands on his shoulder, on his healthy arm. He gave in readily – the poor man had probably not felt a friendly hand for God knows how long – and leaned sideways against my knees. Rahman was a big man, looming like a tree as I remembered, and I had to make an effort to stay my ground. He raised his head and looked at me plaintively. I recalled how he had swaggered into his father's home when I first met him – what a sad mess he had become now. Eyes filling up with fat tears once more, he resumed his grief-stricken monologue. 'Bhaijan, terrible things happened, someone's curse worked on us. Someone must've surely cursed us. Terrible things.'

'Did they kill Shaban?' Baba couldn't keep patient any longer and shouted at us from his corner seat. 'Tell me, son, tell us, what happened after that?' He checked himself quickly.

'No, Sahib, they didn't kill him in the end.'

Baba took a deep breath and looked down.

'They didn't kill him, but I wish they had, I wish they had . . .' Rahman stopped and blew his nose. 'The young fighter dragged Baba's limp body back inside and hurled him down in the centre. I thought they'd let me go to him now, so I leapt forward, only to be held back by a tight squeeze on my arms and the barrel knocking hard against the back of my neck; it hurt very much. Father was still half conscious because he rolled his eyes towards Mother, who sat frozen in the corner near her chullah, shrinking back into it. She must've fainted, and I think it was a good thing in a way, bhaijan, because she didn't have to see what happened next.

'The boy took out a long large knife, a hatchet-like large knife – it was black on one side, bhaijan – and then in a swift blow of its blade sliced off a part of Father's nose. The top, the tip of it. He just cut it. Just like that. He just cut it. My father's nose. He screamed very loudly, bhaijan, but only once.

'Next, they grabbed Mother by her headscarf and chopped off a part of her ears. They didn't bleed much. Then the big brute forced her mouth open, bhaijan, and tore off the tip of her tongue! I remember the look on Mother's face – wide-open eyes, bhaijan, round and round, round and round, bulging out as if to cover all her face. Then he stopped, went back to Father, held each of his ears in his bloodied hands and sliced off his earlobes one by one. The large blade dripped with my parents' blood. I couldn't see it any more and pulled one last time, crying the loudest cry of my life, and set myself free from my captors' arms, and ran to my father, who was shivering a strange shiver in the centre, bhaijan, a strange shiver. I felt it was some kind of a dying man's shiver, when your life leaves you, when your life leaves you, you know, so I reached out with my right hand to where father was, to check if he was still alive, but the hatchet man came down on my wrist.'

Baba stopped squeezing at his hookah. He looked at me, I at him. The room felt airless. Rahman, sitting on his calves, gazed ahead with red, water-filled eyes. His black hand was hanging loose by his side, like an unsuccessful graft. We didn't know what to say.

I saw Shaban's wife, his nameless wife, smiling from her perch near the chullah, handing me water in that worn-out aluminium tumbler.

I imagined Shaban's hennaed beard, red and orange and magenta and blood red.

Rahman stopped crying now. He fiddled in his pockets and took out a polythene wrapper or envelope, folded too many times over. He then unfolded the creases casually and spread it on his hands. 'Mother's ears.'

I must've opened my mouth wide and narrowed my eyes because Rahman, sighing a few quick sighs, immediately withdrew the withered, curled-up samples in front of us.

'I don't know, bhaijan, I couldn't just leave these there when we left. Mother was unconscious, half dead when they did this, so I'm not sure how much pain she felt. But when she came to she herself quietly picked up the sliced-off piece of her tongue.

'I never lost consciousness, not even for a bit, but I didn't move from my place for fear of finding my hand gone. Then they left, kicking Father one last time in the head. I discovered only half of my hand was cut off. The hatchet had dived halfway into the clay floor of the dhoka. It stared at me. Father was hurt more and bled a lot, soaking up all the layers of torn clothing I used to cover his nose. I carried him in my arms, left him on the road near the foothills, came back for my mother, and then carried her down.'

20 *The Lull and After*

Four more months passed.

People spent time in a cowered silence.

Shaban Khatana's story receded back into memory, as if it had happened a long, long time ago. Sometimes Rahman's words entered my head at odd hours, and I felt terribly guilty. It was as if I hadn't done right by Shaban Chacha, as if by having walked into Rahman's world once, I was complicit in the gruesome wrong that had been done to them, as if there had been something that I should have done but hadn't. Rahman had left our house, I recalled, without much of a farewell – I guess years of operating in secret worlds had made him like that. He had managed to take some money from Baba, possibly to take care of his wounded parents, possibly to take care of himself as well – for his own wound too had seemed live, festering. I also wondered if Shaban and his son had somehow made Baba aware of my encounter with them, and then had colluded to make it difficult, to prevent me from going across, and now – or indeed even at the time – Baba had rewarded them for their valuable services. Many things didn't add up, though. If, for instance, Baba had known all along, then he should have surely known about Khadim Hussain, but he didn't seem to.

During those months nothing more happened; no one mentioned the Army's construction that Noor had been talking about – they were building something or had already built something – as though by not looking, by not hearing about it, we could will it out of our life. I went to college a few more times, didn't do much there except drink muddy cups of tea in the crumbling canteen. It gave me a fleeting sense of being social with people I didn't know. There was hardly anyone left there, except the auxiliary staff who hung on to a pretence of the place being functional for fear of losing their jobs.

Ma sank deeper into her silence and spent more and more time in the garden, which wasn't as dense then as it is now. Baba didn't go out too much either; he sat lazily in the living room and listened to his radio and talked to the few people who still came to visit – to talk about their domestic feuds or the small matters of the village.

Winter came.

First slowly and then suddenly. It snowed and became sad. December passed without incident, and as winter set in I gave up all hope of Hussain and the others coming back this year. The passes had probably closed now and there wouldn't be much traffic until late spring. A suspended quiet settled over everything – there wasn't going to be any excitement for the next few months, I thought. And that was the kind of mood that hung over the village too. Over the valley, over the pine-encrusted mountains and their clouded peaks, over the street, over everything. A mist, a waiting hung in the air.

Until one frigid morning in late January . . .

After a night's sweaty sleep under three layers of quilts and blankets, I was woken by a shrill and – how should I say? – *urgent* azan in Khadim Hussain's voice. I had woken up to his earnest calls to prayer before, but rarely in recent months. And anyway, this time it sounded different. Something was wrong; as soon as I opened my eyes to complete wakefulness and began to listen properly to the azan, I noticed there was something strange about it. But what was it? The notes were the same – yes, it did sound a bit insistent – but it was the same full-blown voice, tethered at the closing words. The high-ascending cries in the middle were the same, the tails of the long words dipping as always, the beginnings of the subsequent words deeply wrought, from the depths of his stomach, as usual – but what was *this*?

Khadim Hussain was belting out an *ulti* azan; it was in the reverse order, back to front! I'd never heard such a thing before. Had he lost his mind? Like Gul Khan's mother, who had seemed to suffer much more than Hussain's pious father, maybe he had finally lost it. Here

he was, rendering Allah's summons to prayer to the devoted in the
wrong order.

> *La illaha illalah*
> *Allah-o-Akbar Allah-o-Akbar*
> *Hayyi Allal Falah*
> *Hayyi Allal Falah*
> *Hayyi Allal Salah*
>
> *Hayyi Allal Salah*
>
> *Ash-Haddu Anna' Mohammad-ur-Rasool-ullah*
> *Ash-Haddu Anna' Mohammad-ur-Rasool-ullah*
>
> *Ash-Haddu Anna' La illaha ill-allah*
> *Ash-Haddu Anna' La illaha ill-allah . . .*

What must the villagers think of it? What would Baba decide to do
about it? Surely, this wasn't allowed? This could *not* be allowed?
Khadim Hussain continued going back to the beginning, with the
same melody, but there was also an unfamiliar urgency to his rendition; it was a little too brisk. What was wrong with him?

> *Allah-o-Akbar Allah-o-Akbar*
> *Allah-o-Akbar Allah-o-Akbar*

He couldn't go wrong with that at least.

There was a satisfying conclusiveness towards the end. Then
silence. I waited, still in my bed, for Baba to leave and head to the
mosque; but nothing happened.

Soon, I assumed there would be an early morning meeting in the
mosque itself, to discuss the mental state of Khadim Hussain. 'Let's
go, we'll take you home, don't worry, don't worry, it'll all be fine,
you must be tired, that's all,' Baba or someone else would say.

And when he did finally reach his finale, his ultimate *Allah-o-
Akbar*, and finish his inverse azan, I dreaded the moment at the exact
end, lest it be the tipping point of something. It could be the harbinger of something new.

I imagined everyone in the village feeling like me, waiting with early morning breath for some meaning, some explanation of the strange azan, to arrive with the first wash of the morning light. Nothing transpired for a full five minutes, when suddenly, like exploding midnight thunder, everything was cracked open, torn and ripped apart.

The hissing morning air, the feeble light of dawn, the birth of a mountain day, the quilt-and-blanket-covered cocoon of safety of my bed, the still present sense of self-willed, nervous detachment – and the largely unsaid, unvoiced fear for the worst – were all broken. Everything exploded in a single, crashing-loud gunshot that came from somewhere close by, very close, from the street, from the village.

Then a few more sounds, grenades probably, and then the crackling ratatat of SLRs – oh my God, it was some kind of an encounter, militants had come visiting, they were inside the village! What on earth was happening? My heart jumped a few miles. This was no shelling stuff across the Line, this was no indulgent exchange of fire between unseen pickets or check-posts where anonymous artillery men load shells in rehearsed, perhaps bored, motions and then go back to their Kishore Kumar or cheap Hindi novels. This was on our very own doorstep: gunshots, shot bursts, metallic whams of grenades or mortar shells. And it had followed soon after Khadim Hussain's call.

Then another one, and another . . . then there was a loud burst of gunfire. I jumped up on my bed and found myself standing, nearly touching the ceiling, the pregnant moist-looking cobwebs by the side of the thick deodar shaft that went through the centre of the ceiling. There was another pause. Then a brief exchange of fire again. The sounds were different now – AK-47s rather than SLRs or LMGs. I heard Baba shuffle and pace and grunt downstairs. Was there an encounter under way? *Inside the village?* This was no shelling across the mountains, this was no exchange of 'medium-to-heavy artillery fire between forward posts', this was a gun battle proceeding right under us. The whole village must be up now, Noor Khan cursing in his bed, reaching angrily for his mouldy earthen hookah.

I pictured everyone I could think of and came back to where I was, on my bed, in my room, in my house, with Ma and Baba downstairs, and found myself afraid, like never before. Afraid sick. It occurred to me I should have been worried much earlier. What will happen to Ma and Baba if it's something really, really serious, something big – after all, encounters between militants and the Security Forces were taking place everywhere and some lasted hours, into the night even . . .

I was still grappling with these thoughts when it suddenly struck me. What if . . . what if it was them? What if they had finally come visiting, and had ended up in a gunfight with the Army, or with the BSF (who still did some business around the border – both Noor Khan and Sadiq Chechi believed Farooq's beheading was a result of the ongoing rivalry between the Army and the Border Security Force), or whoever controlled these parts now. What if it was them? What if they had come to see their master, their guru, and were trapped now, here, here at home? Oh my God, Hussain on the trigger side of a big gun, behind some wall, or bush, or tree, or even a makeshift bunker, with Ashfaq and Gul and Mohammed by his side – *who is the leader of the pack now?* – firing these bursts from their automatic rifles at some unnamed soldier from some unknown place in India.

There was a pause now. I listened intently, trying to pick up any conversation from the combatants that the morning breeze might carry here. The whole village must be waiting, waiting for it to continue, to lead to something else, or to finish, culminating in something. I shuddered at the thought of my friends caught in an encounter with ferocious soldiers who would soon shower a rain of bullets on them and waste no time in . . .

Maybe I could rush out and do something – help them escape, perhaps, save them. Save Hussain. Oh my God! I could climb down from the window, slip out of the house, go through the orchards to get to our graveyard, then cross it at the far end to get to the back side of the mosque; that way I could see what was happening. And if Hussain really was there?

But this last pause seemed to last for ever. I waited and waited.

The encounter, or whatever it was, hadn't lasted too long. It was perhaps a minor incident after all, something that a newsreader would call a skirmish, a *jhadap*, a brief encounter . . .

I heard Baba's steps on the staircase – it always lets out a short groan when he climbs up – and soon he was standing in the doorway. I immediately knew the purpose of his visit: *You're not going anywhere, stay in the house with Ma*. You see, I couldn't have gone even if I had managed to raise myself from bed.

Baba climbed back downstairs. The sound of his steps got thinner. Silence prevailed again. The morning felt heavy. It was going to be a very long day. Sitting on my bed, hands pressed hard against the coarse and yet homely face of the blanket, I tried to concentrate. But I couldn't.

Just a few minutes after Baba had left, loudspeakers suddenly boomed from the mosque. Those cursed heralds of much grief in our times. In the early days after the mosque was built, the only sound they emitted was the sacred melody of the azan – the Moulvi Sahib, Khadim Hussain, even Hussain for those first few weeks – but later they would bring only bad news. This would be the first time they were used for this purpose. Someone not local – someone not from among us – was making an announcement. In rather unpolished Hindi, Urdu, Hindustani, whatever, the voice declared, in an offhandish tone, that there was to be a Cordon and Search operation in the area. A Crackdown.

'Ladies and gentlemen, attention, attention . . . Due to security arrangements there will be a search operation in this area. All the men must assemble in the open field at the end of the street outside your village.' The voice stopped for a moment, as if waiting for a response. 'Anyone found hiding in their houses will be dealt with strictly. This is an army order. Do not panic. Please assemble in the field in ten minutes. We will start the search after that. Cooperate with the Army. Do not panic.' The voice coughed a small cough and fell silent.

That was it: *We were in a crackdown.*

I felt helpless at once, being ordered to leave home early in the morning by an alien voice on the two mosque loudspeakers.

Ma appeared at the kitchen door, grey-faced and brooding, as I climbed down the stairs. She drew closer into the hallway, still holding on to the dull curtain of the kitchen doorway with both her hands, as I descended the last steps. She muttered something under her breath – I suspected it was *Ayatul Kursi*, one of the few duas she knows – and hugged me quickly. Then she went back in, 'Just wait for a minute, beta,' and returned with an apple and yesterday's roti, and presented them to me with a pursed-lips look: *That's all we have at this hour* . . . I took the two things from her and forced them in beside the book – Thomas Harris's *I'm Ok, You're Ok* – I had already shoved into the pocket of my pheran. She then drew me closer, hugged me, and kissed me on my forehead. I remember the smell of her dry morning breath and the feel of her parched warm lips. She drew in a heavy breath, patted me on my shoulder twice, and then I left. She muttered a short prayer again as I went out.

The day was struggling to start. I saw grey, uncertain shadows in front of me, and more when I turned round to look behind. Soon, we all merged into a sad queue of half-awake figures marching into the field, not knowing what was in store for us. The world was all grey. As soon as I reached the street, I recognized Ramazan Choudhary's two sons walking in front of me – where had the younger one, the axe-wielding woodcutter, emerged from? They slowed down and let me overtake them, as if walking behind the headman's son was going to shield them from danger. I let them do it. More sunken, sullen shadows emerged from behind trees and old decaying clay walls, from the foothills and from the two short lanes branching off from the main street. I walked past Noor Khan's shop, anxiously expecting him to jump out and take me to the open field, holding my hand and seating me beside him. But no one emerged from the dust-smeared wooden shutters of the shop. I kept looking. I turned back once again, towards Gul's looming house, not realizing that no one except his half-mad father was left there. The field appeared like a graveyard from a distance. Scattered in the middle were half-slouched figures, as if they were fallen gravestones. Grey, grey, grey . . . The light dim, the morning still straining to make sense of what was to come.

I recognized Baba's thick figure in the centre of the field and couldn't help smiling a faint smile at my father's enduring sense of self-importance even in times of complete uncertainty. No one yet knew what exactly happened during a crackdown. This was our first, although some people had been caught up in such 'operations' whilst visiting relatives in other villages or towns down in the big Valley. But my father, my dear Baba, was incapable of making himself invisible, of receding to the sides, even at a time like this.

The snappy soldiers at the edge of the field gravely waved me in, as if in grudging approval of my choice of seating arrangement, as I headed over to where my father was standing. Everyone seated around me was silent, even their breathing rationed. There were massive trucks parked at the back. More than half a dozen green and white Gypsies completed an arc at the front of the field. Further at the back, towards the end of a maize field rising into the mountainside, soldiers were clearing a space with big machetes and sickles. The axed stems lay at their feet like slain enemies. There was some sort of armoured vehicle beside the trucks. It had an upright semicircular disc on top, behind which sat a soldier in a green helmet and holding a machine gun – long muzzle, stout tripod – pointing towards where we sat. My neck twitched. A chill ran down my throat. I surveyed the field keenly, but in vain, for any signs of the morning's battle. I remember having felt rather disappointed. I looked at Baba and he nodded back: *Be patient.*

For once, he couldn't say I didn't listen to him.

Soon, at the far end of the assembled throng, beside the cluster of vehicles, some activity became visible: a movement of men, of legs and bodies, and a left-and-right dashing of heads. There appeared to be a progression of the scene now, a forward movement, a shifting towards us, to where we were, closer, closer, and quite suddenly then, it was upon us. In full and complete detail, sight and sound: *There were soldiers carrying something on their shoulders.* Something they held with their hands; they were moving ahead with it, urgently but carefully. I turned towards Baba for confirmation of what I was seeing, to check against that most concrete of my life's experiences, my father, if what was unfolding was in fact for real. Baba's look confirmed it. The soldiers moved closer and closer towards us, and now it became clear that what they were carrying was a human form. The senior army men surrounding the inner circle of bearers were looking at it as though to reiterate their ownership of it. *Take him, take him . . . take him*, they were saying. In decided anger. And they *were* taking him. A man. A body. A dead body. A red body. With blood on it, lots of blood, trailing blood. But his head was turned, turned at a horrific angle. I couldn't see. Who was it? It was someone I knew, the obscured look seemed to say.

The soldiers stopped now. They came to a gradual halt where we could see the full form of the man, but not his face, *not who he was*. They laid him down carefully and relaxed their stiff bodies. Then all of them at least once looked at the body they had just deposited in our midst. Was this the result of the skirmish in the morning, then? Who was this man? Was it some big militant, a famous commander, who had been encountered in our village? Was it him, Hussain's father the musical muezzin, who lay before us like this? Or was it Hussain himself? Was it Gul Khan? Mohammed? *Ashfaq?* My wise friend, where are you?

But how was I to find out? I looked at the faces around me, wishing they knew and had told me too, somehow, who it was. But they looked equally perplexed. I leaned this way and that, attempting to avoid notice from the soldiers standing around us, but still could not see the man's face.

We would not find out all day. We were not allowed to move from our positions on the field. While I struggled to put a name to the dead body sleeping with us, the soldiers with the impressive machetes finished clearing a big patch from the maize field. Shaved. But what for? We sat there, half dead with anxiety, and waited a century for the day to end.

Finally, after the deathly silences and endless yawns and grief-bearing whispers, the day did end. The mist that had seemed distant in the morning closed in on us now. We went home in a tormenting confusion, after a brief megaphone announcement that we were to go straight to our homes and *under no circumstances be seen anywhere else*. We were also told, *ordered*, that we had to assemble in the field *at the same time sharp tomorrow* since the Army was still conducting searches in and around the village. They said they wanted to make it *totally safe and secure for us*. What there was to cordon and what to search, I never understood. Ramazan Choudhary mumbled something about missing even the evening prayers, and the prayers the next day, but shut up immediately when an extraordinarily tall soldier approached holding, gently waving, a baton in the air.

On the second day, we were almost waylaid by the dead body. They made us walk in front of it. They wanted us to see him now, all too clearly, his face, his now dried-up blood, his lonely, deathly presence. I suspected Baba knew something already, as he appeared calmer than he should have. When he walked past the dead body, he did not gasp like the others did, he didn't flinch like most people did, he didn't stop for that extra fraction of a moment. He had already been shocked.

We walked past the body, one by one, trying our best not to appear nervous. All of us knew that sometimes the Army whisked you off for the flimsiest of excuses, sometimes just because you couldn't speak quickly enough when a soldier placed his hand on your chest and asked you why your heart beat so fast. It was torment, walking towards where the body lay, and knowing that the man in front of you already knew who it was but you couldn't find it out from him: you had to see it for yourself. All those before you knew, but they just hung their heads if you looked at them: you had to look at it for yourself. Finally, I reached the spot, stopped for the tiniest of moments, and looked down at the perforated body – *Khadim Hussain's body* – and tried to take it all in, to remember, to give due respect to the moment. Then it was someone else's turn, for the soldiers kept nudging us on.

'Move it, sisterfucker! Bastard, you want to end up like him, hain? Chalo, move on, motherfucker!'

I heard the soldier at my back but didn't quite have the courage to turn and see who my tormentor was. I took a brief look at

Khadim Hussain's face, his fair face, his son's face, and the shiny nose and the burn-like prayer mark on his forehead, through all the scars and stains and mutilations. His mouth was sort of slightly open, as if he were thirsty, and his lips cracked. His long nose was squashed, deformed, into a twisted blob of flesh. His bald head rested on a brick. His neck was twisted at a frightening angle – it might break like this, I wanted to say to them. He had messy holes in his body and there was a lot of grime over him. I may have added some details over the last few months, for it was a very short look we were allowed to take, but he did appear to smile a bit as well, a faint smile. Suddenly, I remembered our conversation, and his scorn for me, in the jungle, months before.

I reached where Baba was sitting and remembered the azans. The perfect demonstrations of sacred rendition and Quranic inflection, all the accented qira'at, and, above all, the beauty of his voice that resounded all around the village and echoed from the forests. It boomed around the field now. And then I remembered his last azan, the one he had ended on a backward note.

Who had he been signalling to?

There must have been militants in the village, most probably in the mosque, or somewhere close by, who he knew, or were indeed our own boys, you never know, his own son even, who he wanted to warn. His warning had been successful, he had alerted them well. And if there was any sign remaining of the gun battle that had raged so fiercely, it was only him. The warned had fled.

On the third morning of the crackdown, on India's Republic Day, we heard a rumbling in the skies. It seemed to come from the south, the plains of the big Valley. The sound had a vague familiarity about it. I sat in the same corner of the field as the day before; my buttocks had made a comfortable niche in the leaden winter earth and I sank back into it. Khadim Hussain's body was gone now. Even the blood spots on the ground had disappeared. The same soldiers, who had carried him and laid him like an exhibit in our midst, now stood close guard around us, hunched beneath their long duffel coats, unwieldy bamboo lathis, and standard-issue plastic brown SLRs.

The roar grew louder, slowly, and with it a mix of unease and excitement, especially among the assembled children, also spread in the crowd. All the women and children sat ahead of Baba, away from the army vehicles. The older men, who sat in a huddle to Baba's left, looked teary-eyed at the skies. The soldiers guarding the section where the children and women had been rounded up cracked their sticks against the round stones that littered the ground, or a tree trunk – clank, clank – and the few kids who had craned their necks towards the southern horizon, where the roar seemed to come from, shrank back and shut their mouths again. The nearest sentry grinned with a satisfied look.

Late January is still the time of winter proper in Kashmir, it's *chilla-e-kalan* at its potent end, and the mornings hang heavy and frigid with chill and fog. People find it difficult to smile. Sometimes the fog doesn't clear all day; it just breathes over everything like a vast, overbearing organism. Sometimes the sun may make a very small, coin-like appearance through a crevice in the blankets of fog, but mostly it doesn't show its face all day. It's the time of winter when little girls seek out much-fought-after dry patches and play hopscotch, singing.

Shiin galle'
Wande' chhalle'
Beyyi' yii Bahaar

This was another such day. Frigid. Things were still visible where we stood – mostly soldiers and their trucks, and khaki-covered, iron-grilled green and white jeeps at the back – but beyond that, there was a greying circle. Between the misty periphery and us was the ring of soldiers in their pale green anoraks. I recognized a few faces from the first day, the ones who'd carried Khadim Hussain's body. Small curls of bidi smoke rose above the wet helmets bobbing up and down all around.

The air boomed again, and people's eyes moved up into the skies. I felt the book in the large side pocket of my pheran and decided to wait, once again, before taking it out. Why should I care if they think I'm showing off? Let them think what they will. I could surely read to pass the time, I reasoned. But I couldn't muster up the courage to take the book out of my pocket.

The roar drew closer now; it rumbled suddenly and into the sky came two birds, flying towards us. Helicopters?

The Army must be doing something major; it was the 26th of January after all, I thought, and exchanged this knowledge silently with Baba. He looked back, nodding gently.

The birds grew in size as the skies rattled.

The sentries came closer to where we stood, and joined the many gazes that were held skyward.

The helicopters were coming towards the village. They were probably on some surveillance trip and would head back after a round or two. The crowd sat glued to the sight and perhaps even forgot the discomfort and humiliation of the last two days. Noor Khan, Sadiq Chechi, Lassa Kaka, Ramazan Choudhary, Baba – all the village elders – and a few others huddled together and whispered conjectures about what could be behind the arrival of these flying machines in our parts. They seemed to be headed towards where we sat. This was the third day of the crackdown and, all of us prayed, the last. Khadim Hussain had already become a memory. I was scared.

Baba looked extremely worried – it must have been quite be-fuddling for him too, to see a pair of imposing machines descend on us.

The children squeaked, and a few babies started moaning while their mothers held their small bodies against their chests to muffle the crying, not sure how the soldiers would react. The sentries them-selves, in their long coats and heavy harsh boots, lumbered aimlessly about with their SLRs and AK-47 rifles, transparent magazines hang-ing flimsily below, and looked quite perplexed. As the head of the village, Baba had earlier meekly protested against the women hav-ing to come out but an oldish-looking subedar with a fierce handlebar moustache had taken him aside and spoken to him with a certain glare in his eyes. He had been instructed, first thing in the morning, that every inhabitant of Nowgam had to come out now since they wanted to do some kind of count.

The helicopters were green, a sombre serious-looking military green, with long expansive blades describing a massive arc in the sky. I could now smell something new in the air, a faint smell that reminded me of the dry whiff our kerosene stove at home gives as its flame goes out. At the western end of the periphery enclosing us stood the young army officer in charge of the operation. He wore a crisp uniform. He had neat hair and black leather gloves, but no jacket. Shiny brown belt, shiny steel buckle. His breath made small shapes of fluffy air that vanished quickly around his head. He was talking to two junior officers. They nodded in quick, precise for-ward movements and held their arms behind their backs. A large truck, with murderous iron hooks and a brooding pale tarpaulin sheet tied all over it, appeared from nowhere and stood behind them. I could see eyes at the back.

The wind picked up, abruptly. Women pulled at their long ker-chiefs and looked up. Many eyes blinked in bewilderment at the whirr, whirr, whirring metal objects that were now only a few hun-dred feet away. Eyes blinked, mouths fell. The helicopters were descending fast towards the clearing made so efficiently on the first day; crisp stumps of maize dotted that part of the field revealing fresh, perforated earth in the gaps between them. The few standing stalks of the tall grass at the back of the clearing stirred, bent low, as the arc of the blades whoosh-whooshed closer. A gust of chilly wind blew over me. The pilots wore round helmets and oversized headphones. The pilot in the flying machine on the left wore black goggles. These machines were astonishing. Another gust, this time quicker, sharper, slapped me in the face. I clasped at my pheran, tight, and looked at the truck. The tarpaulin was pulled back. Eyes became heads, then helmets and duffel coats and then boots. The tarpaulin was folded on to the roof now, and from the iron hooks dangled loose ends of thick rope – soldiers, more soldiers, poured out like rats from the massive truck. For a moment I imagined that the truck was joined to another at the back, then another and another and another, and the soldiers would never stop coming. One of the junior officers stood facing the file of soldiers and seemed to be saying something whilst gesturing with his slender cane. A blast of prickly wind swept over us. Baba cowered beneath it. I wanted to go and hold his hand. Whirr-whirr-whirr . . . The choppers now hovered around the same spot for a while, just a few metres above the clearing, while some of the soldiers from the truck formed a wall on either side of it; big wicker chairs had appeared from somewhere, also a strip of red matting leading to an outsized metal desk. The crowd hummed into a million whispers, the babies picked up from where they had left off. Wind, wind and more wind. The soldiers close to us paced anxiously, their eyes unsettled, darting glances here and there.

I bowed my head down and felt my knees against my cheeks. My ears thudded, fluttered, with the whirring arc of the helicopter blades. Everything was being sliced into atoms, into dust. That's all there was in that moment – a constant hammering drone against my temples. I thought of Ma and Baba. I briefly glimpsed Hussain and Ashfaq and Mohammed and poor Gul. Wind. In the small blind cocoon between my knees, their faces passed before my eyes. I sank deeper and deeper into my legs until my face and neck ached. Headache pulsated through my temples. Whirr-whirr-whirr . . .

Then silence. At last.

I relaxed my hands and tried to open my eyes. The creases on my cheeks from my knees eased, I could almost hear it. I could hear the murmuring crowd. Something had happened, the cold air hung like a curse.

The helicopters had come to a standstill on the cleared ground. Just a few metres away from us, the green machines looked wet and menacingly beautiful.

The low rotor blades arched on top, slightly bent, like the out-sized wings of a giant fly. Someone hissed something in my ear. I looked again. And saw the Governor of Kashmir walking towards us. The King of Curfew himself.

A few senior army officers, lots of silver change on their clothes, walked with him on either side. Some officials in blue overcoats followed behind. Most had prominent bellies. The young officer waited, all attention, near the metal desk. The sky had turned flaming red at the edges of the southern horizon. '*Qayamatuk rang*, the colour of doom,' someone said in a corner-of-the-mouth voice.

Now the other chopper stirred too, wobbled like a dragonfly, and out came a posse of men and women, some of whom held big cameras – I hadn't noticed there were media people who'd come visiting, *brought* to visit us by the Governor. But an even bigger surprise had been kept for the last: the Minister of Sport, the man who had been replaced by the Governor as the ruler of Kashmir, walked at the back, his black Karakuli towering above everyone else. The burly politico walked like an awkward giant, his whopping cherubic cheeks shaking like meat hung from a butcher's hook.

They all walked silently, and sat respectfully in the big wicker chairs, hands placed in their laps like children at a prize-giving ceremony.

In the back row sat all the journalists, while the Governor and the Minister sat in the front with the army officers.

There was a chubby man – moustached, thick black hair that glimmered in the icy, misty light – who sat at the far-right end with a small book resting on his groin; he nodded now and then from the back at something that the Governor said.

Then there was this short woman with cropped hair, wrapped around in a large shawl from underneath which the parrot-green sleeves and hem of a cardigan made flickering little appearances. It was the kind of cardigan only people of the plains would wear – new, crisp, cheap. She had the air of an all-understanding, all-knowing jumpy teenager about her.

There was another lady at the far end – older, with crisply delineated eye-bags, chadar nominally covering her head.

Why were they here? Wouldn't it be bad publicity for the Army, showing us in this way to the world, herded together on a frozen sheet of mud, three days of misery seeping into our very bones? I wondered as my bottom hurt. And where had they taken Khadim Hussain's red body? Did the Governor know?

After all the officials had sat down, the Governor started towards us with an eager step. He was wearing a tweed blazer with black and grey checks, and dark grey pants. How could the bastard not freeze! A sarkari-style, striped red tie appeared pasted on to a white shirt; a few long strands of grey hair had freed themselves from his sprawling scalp and floated in the cold breeze. The low mist hung all around now; all I could see was the people around me, the identical-looking soldiers surrounding us, the VIP conclave on the other side of the rope, the two perspiring green machines behind them, and the trucks and armoured vehicles on the right-hand side. Everything was wrapped by the dreary January mist. It seemed that the world had been reduced to the cloud-engulfed enclosure in which we were held captive.

Baba and his band of elders were still huddled together. The previous day, one of the junior officers had told Baba that it was all right if all the older men wanted to sit together to talk among themselves – but *no one else*, he'd warned him gently. They seemed to be on the brink of some decision. Baba looked up decisively, as if to venture a question, to raise an objection . . . But then, just then, the Governor of Kashmir, the former leader of the demolition gangs and their bulldozers (who ran over the one-room tenements and lavatories of the poorest of poor squatters in India's capital because their haphazard slum-clusters had no storm-water drains), the clinical undertaker of forced, compulsory vasectomies (how many impecunious villagers had he seized and then let his surgeons loose on their genitals?), the very man I'd heard and read so much about, this man who had a fixation about curfews, started his approach now, and halted everything before my poor father could even form the first few words of what he wanted to say. *What might he have said?*

The Governor looked more hideous than he had seemed in newspaper photos. His lips were tightly pursed and looked like two fat worms in a tight embrace. His hair flew upwards in three flagrant wisps, leaving a shining plateau in the middle. The forehead, gleaming above those window-sized glasses, looked like a featureless inverted face. A swathe of weathered flesh.

This man sent by the Centre to 'fix the Kashmir problem' now stood near the metal desk, and shook hands with the smartly dressed young officer and his two assistants. The men parted to reveal a large microphone perched solitarily on the desk; a contraption connected to it through wires and a steel tube beep-beeped with amber and green lights. A loudspeaker sat birdlike on top of a forlorn pole at the edge of the field. The Governor was going to make a speech! The captive audience, half shivering, half shocked, sat bewildered but speechless in the cold mist – and the diversely armed onlookers strolled about in their massive black boots, some quickly dragging on their bidis with their backs towards the Governor's grand dais. The visiting dignitaries, with their immaculate clothes and serious, important expressions, sat tidily on the left on the chairs that must have come all the way from some district headquarters.

'Curse on your ugly eyes, *hayya shaitaana*, oh devil, who cannot see us in our state,' Lassa Kaka's saintly old mother cried and spat on the ground.

No one said anything else; people stopped breathing for a while.

The microphone boomed into life.

'*Dosto . . .*'

The echo reverberated briefly and died.

'Friends, brothers and sisters . . .'

'Screeeeeeech.'

The mini PA system had caught cold from the icy weather soon after excreting the Governor's first words.

I just couldn't take my eyes off him; off anything, in fact – the scene in front of me, the soldiers listening with wan attention, the small posse of bureaucrats sitting self-importantly on their government-issue seats, and the smart young officer looking enormously pleased with having arranged a successful show.

The microphone somehow stopped its blood-curdling howl, and the Governor started all over again.

'My dear brothers and sisters . . . You must be surprised – and why shouldn't you be? – at this unexpected visit. I know, no one has ever come here, never . . . but that is exactly why we have come . . .' he paused and looked left and right, '. . . I have come to talk to you, the common people . . . They all come for votes – once in five years, ten years, I don't know – and now even the elections don't happen, but, my dear friends, I don't need votes, you see. I don't need your votes.'

The cordoned-off, searched and combed gathering of men, women, children and babies listened in rapt attention, so it seemed, or were so astonished by the occasion, so benumbed by the incredible appearance of the ruler of Kashmir and his VIP visitors in their midst, that all they could do was stare blankly. The fog drew closer.

'Brothers and sisters . . .' the speech wasn't taking off very well, '. . . the area you live in is not like any other area. It's not just another village; it's very, very special and we're trying to make it totally safe and secure for you. There are forces that are trying to turn it into a war zone, a trouble spot, the "gateway of militancy" they call it. This is a dangerous area, but for my administration it is a topmost priority. We know what's been happening here . . . And I will personally make sure, I promise, that you're rid of this menace, of the disruptive anti-national forces operating in your area, *bahut jald*, very soon!'

Thin, long wisps of his hair were now flying in all directions.

'I see that your women are also here, out in the open, and I can understand if you are not happy with that,' he looked down at Baba and the group around him, 'but believe me, it's not something we desire, something one of the most civilized armed forces in the world would like to do. *Haalaat hi kuchh aise hain*, the situation is such that it has become a necessity, our hand is forced . . . But who is responsible for that?' He raised his voice with deliberation. 'Who?'

A scared silence hovered.

'External forces, my dears, forces who do not want peace here, who want to destabilize this country. Their agents and pawns accuse our brave and selfless soldiers of bad things, unheard-of, dirty things, when they ask you to come out of your houses but leave your womenfolk behind. And that is why, my dear brothers and sisters, that is why we have now decided to ask everyone, even newborn babies, to come out, so that no one can ever accuse our men of anything. That is also why, my dears, we are under this curfew. Personally, I'm not in favour of curfews, but for the restoration of peace, for the rule of law to prevail, we were forced to introduce the curfew, to keep people restricted to their homes. I'm not very happy about it, but it's a compulsion – and why is that, my dear countrymen, why?' He paused briefly, as though expecting a collective answer. 'Because . . . we have to foil the designs of these external elements!'

I ground my teeth. Why couldn't he just say Pakistan, if that's what he meant? What was this stupid 'external forces' thing? The cold had now overwhelmed my body.

'*Dosto*, these forces have just one objective, one motive – to break Kashmir from India, to chop off what everyone now knows and sees as an integral part of India. They want to sever the crown on Bharat Mata's head! They spread propaganda, accusing our innocent soldiers of rape and plunder and murder, while they themselves are soaked in blood, carrying the Quran in one hand and a dagger in the other. Does the Quran teach that . . . ? We are fully aware of their evil designs, my dears, and with your help, *Insha-Allah*, we will defeat them as we've always done.'

I looked around quickly to see the reaction to our surname-less ruler's exhortations and saw more than a few yawning faces, a few babies stuck to their mothers who were probably hurting at their chests by now, and some old men and women who had sunk their heads between their folded knees and would look up occasionally if they thought they were being addressed directly.

'But if they think they can train a few misguided boys and give them arms and money, and wrest control of Kashmir, they are mistaken, my dear countrymen, they are living in a fool's paradise. They are living a failed dream – how many countries can be carved from India? Two, three, four? I – we – have to stop this! And we will. We will teach them a bloody lesson; I've chosen the best of our men to defend you, to protect this border, to stop all this, with all our might. You will see.' He looked at the bunch of soldiers and the young officer standing a few feet away from the dais. Fiddling with his glasses, he then looked around at his captive audience once again.

'My dear brothers and sisters, let me tell you something . . . The bond between Kashmir and Mother India is based not just on your king Maharaja Hari Singh's Instrument of Accession and the articles and clauses of India's great constitution; it is held together by far more tenacious and lasting forces that neither the convulsions, tribulations and tremors of history, nor the anarchy and cynicism of contemporary politics, can break up!' He brought down a hand on the rostrum, but it was too low and couldn't reproduce the desired orator's thump. But, but, that wasn't the only problem. The Governor was now making his speech in English!

Disoriented glances were exchanged, ears were bent over tilting shoulders. It must have been a slip, an administrative tic of his . . . But no, he seemed intent on making the rest of his speech in a language that none of these former goatherds and buffalo-milk sellers could understand. What's more, the ruler of Kashmir was speaking at length about the articles of the Indian Constitution to a crowd of Gujjars, illiterate cattle owners, annoyed, anguished mothers and their squeaking babies, tired, dazed old men and fathers, and young boys – people who had been under curfew for months now, who had been rounded up, after having seen their benign muezzin's punctured body, for the last three days in perhaps the longest crackdown in the history of crackdowns in Kashmir.

'It is a bond of soul and spirit that has survived for millennia and found demonstration in shared emotional and intellectual output, art and literature, metaphysics and world view, clothing and, hmm ...

and food! Every lush meadow and idyllic vale that you saunter into in Kashmir, every sparkling-white peak that you gaze at, every brook that murmurs its comforting hymn, every magical lake, pond and pool, every Mughal garden, every refreshing rice and saffron field that you behold here and there, and every little settlement, town and city that you visit after crossing the Banihal tunnel that we built to bring you progress, has some symbol which is a testament to this forceful and steadfast connection,' he continued passionately in what now began to sound to me like a well-rehearsed rhythm.

For God knows how long, then, the Governor ranted and railed in never-ending English sentences – was he showing off? – before an aching, yawning, scratching, moaning, farting crowd. He went on and on about the rightful place of Kashmir in the 'sacred vision of India'. He spewed out a barrage of fist-pumped questions, as well as squirts of spit, and then, in a saliva-spraying frenzy, talked of Kalhana and Vincent Smith and Sankaracharya's Hill and King Lalitaditya and Badshah and Avanti Verman and Sankara and Swami Vivekananda, and Amarnath and Kalidasa and Sheikh Nooruddin Noorani and Sister Nivedita and Sardar Patel, and Lala Ded and the image of Shiva and the Rishi Order and British manipulations and Veer Savarkar, and the laughter of Shiva and Subramania Bharati and South Block and Mohammed Iqbal and North Block and Abul Kalam Azad and Shastri Bhavan and Shah-e-Hamadan, and the two-nation theory and the Crown of Mother India and proxy war and the valley of Kishenganga and Emile Zola and the three-nation theory and Sheikh Abdullah and the temple of the Sun God at Martanda and Nehru and General Douglas MacArthur and the history of failure and 'too late' and 'too late', and Article 370, and *Namaste Saradadevi, Kasmira Mandala Vasini* and Kashmir's ineradicable place in the Indian vision!

Settling his extra-large glasses back over his extra-large ears, he concluded, 'The response to such issues and questions, my dear brothers and sisters, is very simple: *Kashmir*, for innumberable eras, has been an important ingredient of the holy Indian vision – a placid, yet sacrosanct and solid and concrete piece, an intrinsic and indivisible part.'

Weeks later, I asked the elderly principal of our college the meaning of the last line in the Governor's abstruse rant. Professor (Retd.) Jagarnath Koul, that charming and benign old man, said it meant: 'I salute the Goddess of Sarada who resides in Kashmir.'

The fourteen army officers and eleven journalists cheered and clapped as the Governor finished. His hair was like a leafless tree now, his lips wet with slimy spit. His thick tongue ran over them a few times. It was big, like a fat rat. He gazed around one last time, looked me in the eye, and went back, panting, to the row of chairs, where everyone stood up – the officers saluted and shook his hand again – and then sat down together. I was reminded of a debating contest that Ashfaq and I had won in Sixth Grade. We were given fifteen rupees and ten rupees as first and second prizes, in coloured envelopes with our names typed on them.

A woman broke down and started crying, sobbing incoherently, trying to say something to the woman sitting next to her. Her neighbour was trying to console her, but the crying woman could not stop. I just caught the word *ghairat*, honour. It was Ramazan Choudhary's daughter-in-law. Gradually, her sobs settled down into a rhythm as she hid her head between her hands and buried herself in her pheran, only the top of her floral kerchief visible. Low, muffled cries spread mournfully around her folded form. I wanted to get up and find out what had happened, but Baba clasped my arm and glared at me. *No, not a good idea.* I sat back down, protesting in my mind that I had intended nothing too heroic and, as I did, two pairs of boots came close to where we were sitting, a rifle butt whizzed past, and a cane swung loosely in the air too. Baba was right.

The Governor of Kashmir stood up now, at once; so did the officers and the journalists. The Minister of Sport waited, nodding curiously at the crowd. I shifted my weight, my buttocks ached from the cold earth. Something more was about to happen; in addition to the fatigue and pain, I was getting bored now. I prayed, achingly – you know, one of those from-the-bottom-of-my-heart moments – for a rain of bullets. I wished Hussain and the others, *oh, long-parted friends*, had planned a massive attack on the VVIP gathering,

I prayed they'd had it planned all along, and now was the time perhaps, a hail of rockets and grenades and a rain of bullets from somewhere behind the trees, from the heart of the grey mist around us, burning, scorching, thundering projectiles from the dense trees beyond the field – one long burst of fire and that would be it! The Governor, this monster, would be gone, blown into pieces, the Minister gone too, his burly gluttonous mass torn apart, the fawning journalists dead too, the prim and proper, crisp officers too, burned, blown up, the soldiers laughing at us with their menacing boots and large guns and long sticks, they too would be dead, exploded into dirt, blown into dust. Helicopters, their impenetrable green sheen cracked and curled into twisted metal, like in films, smoke and flames engulfing the expensive machinery and turning everything into charred scrap. I really wished, for the first time with such intensity, that I'd gone across too – I wouldn't be here now, trapped like this. I would be a part of them, relieving our people of this misery. I imagined the scene and derived pleasure from it – all these men with their grins and smiles, their condescending words and lofty speeches, dead, dead, dead!

We'd walk free then, Baba and I, hand in hand perhaps, we'd walk free and go home.

A growing restlessness sighed from the crowd – shifting buttocks, aching and cramping legs, downcast mothers with no milk left in their breasts, angry babies, and moaning old men and women leaning against each other. A prickly murmur arose us and I had to abandon the last glimpses of my daydream. No deadly militant attack seemed imminent. I was very much here.

The VIP gang had now gathered behind the desk, Governor and Minister in the middle, and the sleeveless-jacket-wearing photographers were clicking pictures. Click, click, click; flash, flash, flash. The Minister's fat, baby cheeks and enormous sack-like eye-bags glowed momentarily in the flashlight, the Governor's face stayed as grim as ever (the bastard never smiled), the senior army officers looked into the cameras with straight, matter-of-fact faces, showing their shining Vicco Vajradanti tooth-powder teeth only for the briefest of moments. The photographers took turns for the vantage shots and then lined themselves up with the dignitaries one by one.

The shorthaired woman was whispering something, smiling, to a big soldier with a thick, black-barrelled mortar gun on his back. Very soon, she and the Minister of Sport were posing for a photo with the mortar man, who had placed his sturdy weapon in front of him. The girl handled it first and then held it to her chest for the photograph.

There was, obviously, no applause during the photo session, just the squeaking of a few babies who'd perhaps wet themselves and the mumbling of their mothers who, somehow unmindful of the animated spectacle in front of them, were struggling with the rags tied between their children's legs. The smell of baby piss spread in the moist air.

The VIP group broke into huddles of twos and threes now. The Governor listened intently to something the most senior-looking officer, with the sparkling grey moustache, was saying. He pointed towards the smart young officer a couple of times. Two other army officers nodded rhythmically.

The Minister of Sport was talking to the journalists and smiling, the shorthaired one beaming in return, the dupatta-clad one suppressing some kind of matronly disapproval.

On the other side, a queue of soldiers was relaying piles of small brown bundles and stacking them up on the metal desk that had served as the podium for the Governor's speech. Soon, a tower of bundles was sitting on the desk. The soldiers filed out of line and stood guard with their rifles touching the ground. The Governor sat cross-legged, smoking a large curved pipe.

The Minister stopped talking to the younger journalist – I think I saw his hand on her shoulder – and approached the gathering, accompanied by the imposing young officer.

Everyone stopped talking. An air of expectancy, anxiety too, hung over the proceedings. The mist had closed in, or so it seemed to me, and formed a tight wrap around our life.

The officer called out Baba's name.

Silence. Even the babies stopped their crying.

Hiss. Heads turned with gradual, cracking sounds.

Baba looked up, turned towards me, trying painfully not to be seen looking at his son for some tacit guidance, then stood up slowly like a broken man, hesitated, finding himself the lone man standing in the midst of the crowd, and stepped forward. He stood like a pupil summoned before the headmaster. His legs trembled as he stood there in front of the desk, his trousers flapping – no, vibrating – from the trembling. My poor Baba, who had grown weak now, his legs shivering from the cold, his heart from fear, his hands from shame perhaps. The crowd looked at their sarpanch, their leader, their headman. I looked at my father too – when had he grown old like this?

A pale sun hesitantly showed its face through the grey sky and briefly changed the colour of the scene.

The young officer picked up two bundles and waited for a cue.

'Jinab, Sarpanch Sahib, a very small present, it's nothing; our honourable Governor Sahib said he couldn't visit the brave residents of Nowgam empty-handed, and it is the 26th of January, after all . . .' The Minister spoke loudly and turned, smiling, towards the army bosses on his left. 'So we brought these small things . . .' the officer now extended his packets to the Minister, '. . . it's nothing, really, here, let's start with the Sarpanch himself. Here, the first one for you, take it, take it.' Baba stretched out a limp, lifeless hand – I knew his hands would have been cold, very cold – and placed it under the packet. He must have looked at the two men in front of him, for I saw the officer smile a grinning smile, more like a one-sided grimace in which the corner of his mouth twitched briefly and stretched towards his left eye. The Minister nodded his head as if in approval of a well-behaved ward. I swallowed, almost choked, at the thought of looking at Baba's face when he turned round.

Baba turned, with the brown packets stretched on his hands, weighing him down as if he were carrying cloth for a fresh shroud. His head drooped low, but not before I saw the colour of his face, a wan grey, the same as the misty clouds all around us. It was the colour of shame. Deathly shame. Baba walked towards his people, towards his wife and son, head down, and quickly sank back on to the vacant ground.

We then collected our brown bundles one by one. All the men and the women with their babies and all the boys too; we went like school children and collected the packets made for us by the Indian Army, presents brought for us by the Governor. A little something for everyone in return for three days of the crackdown. Photos were clicked, notes taken. The Minister of Sport sweated and breathed like a buffalo, in spite of the cold. The Governor fingered the free-standing hairs on his bald head and pasted them back with his spit. The shorthaired woman clapped loudly and giggled as each bundle found its recipient. Baba shivered until the end of the evening. Ma consoled the woman who had been crying earlier and who was still hiding her head inside her pheran. Lassa Kaka's holy old angry mother went and spat at the metal desk. Luckily no soldier saw her, or so I thought.

The Minister and the shorthaired one were the first to leave; they sat together at the back of the second helicopter. For a moment I thought he was trying to make her sit in his lap, while she struggled coyly. The soldiers paced about quickly, the chairs soon disappearing into the back of the truck with the killer hooks. The two junior officers shouted orders here and there. Ten or twelve sentries joined to form a wall in front of the periphery that enclosed us. The mist from one side merged with the mist from the other side. All I could see now was cloud.

I shuffled across towards Baba and then both of us waited for Ma. Noor Khan lit up two cigarettes from his crumpled Cavanders pack and gave one to Baba. I so wanted to try one. The trucks roared into life first, the screaming headlights bathing the field in a phosphorescent light. I saw yellow faces. The helicopters had started churning their blades. The desk remained where it was. Two armoured vehicles emerged from behind the trucks and came to where the soldiers were guarding us. A swarm of army boots was stamping away and jumping into the waiting trucks. The smartly dressed officer was sitting in front of the first armoured vehicle and leaned out to call for Baba. Baba went forward and listened to the officer. 'All good, bloody good, huh ha ha . . .' he said, stretching out a hand to pat my father on the back. The officer's driver then revved up the engine, his monstrous vehicle spewing out hot pungent smoke. The momentary warmth in the air felt strangely reassuring.

The trucks roared their engines but didn't move immediately. The smell of exhaust rose all around. The helicopters, dark now with red lights and small reflections peering out from their insides, whirred into windy life, the Governor's machine lifting up first and then the Minister's.

The soldiers in the back of the trucks watched as the machines shot into the sky, became ghostly birds, then flew off. I kept watching them for a long time in the twilight, focused on the receding red lights, until Baba, in a low and subdued voice, said, 'Let's go now, beta, everyone's leaving.' The army trucks too were turning now and their lights lit up the place in revolving semicircles.

Ma had managed to move the crying woman and they were walking in front of us when I suddenly turned to look at the place where they had been sitting and found the ground dark. Wet dark. Piss smell. I looked around and saw similar wet patches spread evenly across the turf: small maps of urine eating into the ground. The vehicles turned and grunted themselves out of the ground. I followed Baba and looked at his legs; they were still quivering.

Ma did not walk with us.

22   *Kafila*

'We must leave.'

Compounder Chechi clasped his palm tight on the fat roll of rags around the pipe of our hookah and resumed, 'There is *no other* way.' He started drawing vehemently at the pipe, and blew out jets of brisk smoke from his nostrils.

Baba looked worried but seemed determined to keep everyone calm.

It was the week after the Governor's visit. Since then people had mostly spent their time resting their bruised, fatigued legs and worrying endlessly about the future. People sighed all the time. Half a dozen old men were still in bed, nursing their aching bones, when Sadiq Chechi had made his declaration that everyone should just leave. Although I think most people had started thinking about leaving even before the big meeting at our house.

I was content with serving the tea; this way I could hear what everyone said without having to eavesdrop from behind the curtain. Ma stayed in the kitchen, sitting as usual on her chowki. After Farooq's death, she had assumed a sad, quietly disapproving stance. And after the crackdown, she had become even quieter. It hurt me, deeply, to think of the humiliation she must have suffered. Her sole interest in life now was making sure I returned home early whenever I left the house. She had also put on weight. Her arms bulged more than ever, so much so that she had difficulty rolling up her sleeves in the manner she always used to. Her face, plump and red, perspired often. She had stopped applying henna on her hair, or it had just stopped working, and long streams of white ran out from the corners of her headscarf and spiralled down her neck and shoulders. She still looked beautiful, though. I preferred her staying put in the kitchen. And today, for some reason, I was sure she wouldn't try to listen in on the discussion under way in Baba's durbar, as she had sometimes done in the past.

'It is not a decision we should make in haste.' Baba desperately tried to assume his headman's demeanour. 'We have spent all our lives building this village, these houses, these fields, the shops, the mosque, everything . . . You will never be able to build them again, we will be back on the road, what will we do then . . . ?'

'What will I do with the house if my family is no more, Sarpanch Sahib, if *I am* no more?' Chechi cut Baba short, looked around for endorsement of his views, and went back huffing to the pipe.

'All I'm saying is, we should consider other options, look at what we can do to stay safe, that's all . . .' Baba tried to raise his voice, succeeding only in conveying an aching protest instead.

A dragging silence followed. The air in the room sagged with the weight of a life-changing decision.

I saw my Baba grow old in those few hours in the midst of his people. He tried to beg and plead, argue and protest, even command . . . but everyone seemed to have already made up their mind. In a way it must not have been such a hard decision for the older men to make – they had settled down as pucca dwellers only in their own lifetimes, they knew the way of the road well. They were now on their way to becoming wanderers again, after just forty years or so as settled nomads. In 1947, many people of my father and mother's tribe had crossed the mountain passes into Kashmir after their flight from their usual seasonal camps near Jammu and Rajouri, where they had become easy prey for marauding rioters of that wellspring of all bloodshed in our parts, the Partition.

'This is your home! Where will you go?' The hookah had moved to Baba now and he attacked it with the ferocity of a man possessed.

The samovar hissed. Steamy vapour slithered upwards, curling its way out of the peacock nozzle of the ornate copper kettle. It kept me busy and safely involved among the sad murmurs in the room. I looked at my father and saw a hunched man, looking tremulously at his old friends and their sons.

The gathering stayed silent for a while. I lifted the samovar with the now soggy towel tied to its brass handle and poured a second cup for anyone who didn't say no. All the heads of families had gathered at our house on the first Friday after the back-breaking crackdown. After the prayers, I'd seen them walk solemnly towards our house, some in twos and threes exchanging brief talk now and then, and understood that the time had come. I knew many had already decided to leave – they were too scared for their lives, for their children, their women, their cattle, their honour. The day after the Cordon and Search operation, I had tried to reason with Baba that many people, like his close friend Firdaus Ali, had decided to leave even before the operation. Even old Ramazan Chacha had somehow made his intent known. After Farooq, many had stopped their children from going out altogether, although I was the only 'eligible' grown-up boy left to be taken by the Army or to go across to the other side on my own. Some cattle had disappeared too. A few people said they had met militants outside in the jungle – although that wasn't what had really scared them – while some others had been forced to work, to do *begaar*, by the Army, clearing land for new check-posts and hidden bunkers inside the forest. 'Baba, they cannot stay any more. They are scared. I think that's what the Army wants – the area cleared of people so that they can have a free hand . . .' I had meekly ventured my opinion.

Baba had looked at me with the unaccepting but defeated look of a man who knows that what is being said is right and there is no getting away from it, but still persists in some kind of last-minute stubbornness borne out of hubris more than anything else. Perhaps he had chosen to ignore the steady increase in the nightly shelling. The hollow crashes of the shells at night certainly kept the rest of us awake – I could, by now, guess the number of people deprived of their sleep by merely looking at their faces or by the way they walked the next day. I'd practised well on my parents. The village was a bleary-eyed village – red-eyed children and watery-eyed old women would pass me on the road. No one said much. Everyone knew how everyone else felt. But soon, the dam was bound to burst. People had finally decided to *do* something about it.

In the end, it did not take too much talking; the arguments were just repeated a few times. It was a question of whether you were with the group led by Chechi, which was sizeable and voluble, or the half-dozen men Baba seemed to be counting on – Noor Khan, Lassa Kaka, Asghar Ali and a few silent others.

I poured Chechi a fourth or fifth cup while he railed on. 'If we don't live, what use is the village and the houses? Don't you agree, brothers . . . ? That's fairly straight, isn't it!'

Baba sighed deeply, and that's when I realized he had given up, and said, 'All I'm saying is, are the people living in all the other villages leaving, just like that? They must be suffering too, everyone is, in this miserable time, but does that mean everyone will just leave?'

I knew, at once, that Baba had made a tactical mistake.

Chechi leapt up with the gleeful flourish of a triumphant but undeserving victor and addressed his newly acquired cohorts after a scornful sideways glance at Baba. 'Perhaps Sarpanch Sahib doesn't know, people have *already* left. Those who can are indeed leaving, sir! Those of us who move around a bit and see other places know people are no doubt departing. Bag and baggage, sir, disappearing overnight to save their children's lives. Everywhere . . . and why shouldn't they? Why should they see their sons' throats slit like . . .' Here he paused for effect, shot a half-disguised look at Gul's drawn-looking father and threw his final salvo. 'Just because someone doesn't seem to care for his young son, it doesn't mean we should all throw our children into the fire!'

Baba's face went red.

I regretted having served Chechi all those cups of salt tea. The scheming quack! You want to leave, leave man . . . Why attack my father, why launch an agitation about it? I remember thinking this at the time, although in retrospect I think he was probably right. He may even have saved many lives.

Baba's voice sounded weakened now. 'So what do you want to do, then? Where will you go, er . . .' and here his voice broke, '. . . and when . . . ?' He looked plaintively at the gathering as a despairing king might look at his subjects from his deathbed.

I peered into the funnel of the samovar and saw that the column of red embers had crumbled down to a pyramid of sad, grey ash.

Thin membranes of clotted pinkish tea had settled down and painted the inside of the kettle in long gashes. A few flecks of ash travelled up and died on my face.

'We could cross the border, I am sure they will welcome us . . .' Chechi answered coldly, forcing a fresh silence on the assembly.

'Huh, you will be nothing but refugees there – in a refugee camp or something. Paraded in front of politicians and newspaper-wallahs. Humiliating!' Baba answered quickly enough, and seemingly without thinking.

Chechi broke in again. 'At least we won't be beheaded, Sarpanch! And the crackdown wasn't humiliating at all, isn't it, huh!'

The silence after each of Chechi and Baba's jousts was now broken by a new voice. Ramazan Choudhary spoke deferentially, tenderly, but decisively. 'I'm sure there are still safe ways into Azad Kashmir, I've relatives in Chakoti, er, Lassa has cousins in Muzaffarabad . . . Muqaddam Sahib, think about me, at this age I cannot stand up to these callous badtameez soldiers, these murderers! They don't even consider old age. Our haughty rulers, they descend on us from the skies and hold our babies to ransom, and then part, insulting us further with these blankets . . .' He pointed to the still unopened 'gifts' from the crackdown lying by Baba's chest near the window sill. His voice began to melt now. 'My daughters, they won't even raise their heads any more. I haven't seen their faces since the crackdown. How can I stay here?' The oldest man in Nowgam now tried to regain his composure, and concluded, 'If we must leave, we must leave soon. I'm ready to go by this coming Friday.' He looked around for approval and people nodded, grunted and shifted in their seats, some with their heads bowed.

'But you could be killed on the way, Kaka!' Baba protested, meekly.

'Oh-ho, and how safe are we here? Even *your* son is in danger, sir, I know . . . Have you even heard of Papa Two? No one comes back from there, Sarpanch Sahib, no one!' Compounder Chechi added with that air of always seeming to know more than everyone else in the village. 'Do you know Operation Tiger? No . . . I know . . . It is swallowing dozens of young boys every day, Mr Headman! Look, brothers, the point is, we must leave – we will decide where after everyone has agreed . . .'

'I am not going anywhere! I never said I would.' Baba's raised voice echoed like a teacher's classroom reprimand. What he said didn't come as a surprise to me, but there were a few gasps from the cross-legged throng.

The headman tried to collect himself. 'I will look after the village, I mean, your houses and your land when you are . . .' He struggled again – was he containing his tears? – as he approached those last words.

I kept my head down, only occasionally glancing at the speakers.

Finally, they reached an awkward peace, where no final words were said or any definitive conclusions declared. Baba sat down in his corner seat and lay back on the cushions as if he didn't want anyone to have a clear view of his face. In that position I saw his big chin, his untrimmed beard from below, his jaw – his defeated face. His was a grand defeat, the tribal chief outwitted not by an adversary but by fate herself. He stretched out his left leg and cupped his right knee, and looked as if he were contemplating every word that was being said.

The meeting soon split into small murmuring groups of threes and fours, some talking about *this Friday*, some *next*, some saying *no*, some protesting *why not before that . . . ? What's wrong with waiting a few more days? No, no we can't wait any more, let's leave tomorrow. Yes, yes, tomorrow. Naah, na, we must at least gather what we can to take with us . . . What is a few more days? But, but, where exactly do we go?*

For me the village, as I knew it, as Ma and Baba knew it, as Hussain knew it, as my childhood knew it, ended in that moment. I looked at the familiar faces in some kind of half-conscious daze, as if they were walking past me one by one and then disappearing into the background.

I exchanged a few glances with Noor Khan, who seemed to say it didn't matter to him: *In spite of everything I am staying*. That single acknowledgement, that one confirmation, brought with it the solidity of the thick tree you hide behind while playing hide-and-seek and it suddenly gets dark in the woods. Noor carved out the crisp debris of burned tobacco left behind in the chillum after the intense smoking of the afternoon and busied himself preparing a fresh one; he cleaned the tip of the hookah pipe with the now steaming moist towel I'd been using to haul the heavy samovar around the room.

Baba was silent, only occasionally muttering sedate 'Wa-Alaikums' and 'God bless yous' to his departing subjects. People started dispersing one by one, each shaking hands with my father, who was trying hard to conceal his anger. I don't think he was frightened. *None of us – Baba, Noor, me – could have possibly registered the full import of what was transpiring.* In fact, Baba has never really revealed the full scale of the grief he must have felt that day. He's like that, you know, used to making decisions and pronouncements, passing judgements, issuing instructions; he doesn't like to express his feelings as normal people do. I'd seen him like that all my life – unwavering, consistent, never revealing what he truly felt. An assured, not unhappy, stoicism marked all his dealings in life, even his relationship with his wife, which, since I'm talking about him now, has always appeared rather functional to me. I had never seen them deal in emotions, not even of the muted, restrained kind . . . But on the other hand, I hadn't seen them fight much either – not even argue, really. One of them has their way when they want something and the other acquiesces easily. Ma knows that he won't give up or reduce his hookah habit, so she doesn't protest much, apart from the cold disapproving looks she sends his way from her kitchen seat from time to time. Baba too has seldom prevented her from doing what she wants. When Ma decided to expand her small vegetable patch, against the weather, into a full-fledged kitchen garden, he cut the wood for the fence, axed neat little poles and spikes for it, dug pits for the beams at the four corners, and put up the thigh-high enclosure around it. I guess that's been a blessing. Hussain's parents had rows and rows, mostly over money, for there was precious little that Khadim Hussain brought home. I should be thankful for the absence of discord in the family rather than complain about the absence of too much love between my parents, isn't it?

'The samovar must be cold by now, should I put in some more coals?' Ma called in from behind the curtain, probably thinking there were still people inside. Did she really not realize what had just happened?

'Oh no, Ma, no. I don't think we need more tea.' I looked at Baba and Noor, and stood up with the now perspiring copper kettle. As I left the living room, I poked the curtain with the curving beak of the samovar, lifting it aside, and saw Ma standing in the kitchen door. She nodded and went back into the kitchen. I followed with dragging heavy steps.

'Has your father decided anything, then?'

At first I didn't know what to tell her. I wasn't completely sure myself about much of what they had talked about. I sat down near her and held her hand.

She swallowed. I heard it.

'Ma, I think a lot of people are going to leave. Soon.'

She pressed my hand, not too tight, just a gentle squeeze.

'Compounder Chechi says everyone should leave; he thinks no one is safe here any more.'

She looked at my face, straight.

'Most people agree with him, Ma, and, and –'

She put her other hand on my shoulder and pressed it gently. I felt burning tears welling up somewhere in the back of my head. *Ma, we are going to be left alone.* An ache shot through my temples from the effort to stop myself from crying.

'Hmm . . .' She sighed and raised her eyebrows slowly.

I took a few deep breaths, trying not to make too much noise. I had to be an adult now. 'Ma, I think since many of them have already made their decision, they will probably leave sooner rather than later. It makes sense, isn't it?'

'Hmm, yes, yes, if they are leaving anyway, they might as well leave soon. But what did the Muqaddam Sahib say to all that?' There was already a kind of helplessness to her tone. 'Are we also . . . ?'

Was she choking?

I suppose she already knew the answer to that but carried on with the conversation nonetheless, so as not to let anything weigh too heavily on me, on herself, on the bond between mother and son, as we sat together like two scared children on her good old chowki. I couldn't remember having crawled on to it. Ma's right hand was still in mine, her other hand firmly dug into my shoulder. My heart was flapping feverishly against my chest. Ma was breathing heavily from the attempt I suppose she too was making to suppress her emotions. She was feeling as heavy-hearted, as suffocated, as I was. She looked into her silent clay oven; I was looking away too, out of the window, out into the garden, up to the tall thick mountains behind it, further and further and further . . .

Later in the evening, Baba came in and asked if dinner was ready. Ma said it was and got up to get the plates from the shelves above the oven. They dripped condensation. I ate silently from my copper plate and stared at my name. Ma and Baba, I have a vague recollection, exchanged brief, strained words over dinner. When? Where? Why not us?

Chechi did indeed manage to organize the 'move' the Friday after the meeting. Everyone, well, everyone just left. I had only recently discovered that our quirky medicine man had put the whole village on Alprax and Calmpose – turns out that after Farooq's beheading he had been liberally handing out tranquillizers to the sleepless, anxious people in the village, which was just about everyone. I'd found out about the pills only after Noor Khan once blessed him out loud to himself, 'God bless Sadiq for the araam pill, I hardly notice how the night passes now.' Chechi had now taken control of the whole village.

They left in a small caravan, in a kafila that reminded me of movies I'd seen, of black and white scenes of Partition, and of the tales Ma used to recount of her own journey from the plains to the mountains, and her father's adventures on such journeys. I watched the entourage as it first gathered in the street after much hollering and arguing, and then started to move . . . slowly, awkwardly.

The caravan throbbed with things – everything – both animate and otherwise. Mules, dogs, sacks of flour and rice, hens, goats, crying blabbering children (they must have thought it was going to be one big picnic), fathers, mothers, old matrons leaning on ancient turbanned-with-rags walking sticks, heavily bearded emaciated grandfathers, young women with towers of utensils balanced on their heads, buffaloes, a few cows, a couple of old wobbly Hero bicycles whose stainless-steel bells glistened in the early morning sun and produced a continuous ringing at the hands of the small boys seated on the handlebars, and, above all, the motley group of caravan leaders that Chechi had put together – Ramazan Choudhary's elder son, Ishaq Jan, Asghar Ali, an ashen-looking Sharafat Khan and Compounder Chechi himself. All jerked and bobbed and shifted and moved away.

They marched in one buzzing, breathing, sinuous line, and were trying to hurry on, lest someone stop them. I watched the group thin out as it proceeded gradually, assuming a serpentine shape. The mules nodded their heads, as if in disagreement, or in exertion owing to the absurd loads on their backs. The hens scattered every now and then, the older children gleefully chasing them back into line again. The buffaloes snorted and sneezed and tried to pull at whatever foliage they could grab on the edges of the dirt track. The old men, and you must trust me, stopped every minute or so, bent on their curved staffs, and then slowly swivelled round to take a last look at the village. The old women – all of them somehow managing the same impoverished look – muttered prayers.

Asma walked quietly with the big girls, a new green and red scarf tied over her head. It had almond patterns on it. She bowed her head the moment she saw me. I couldn't get a proper last look at her face.

Gul Khan's mother appeared in the crowd. She looked fragile and thin. Half of her former stout self. *Hai, Gulla.* Hussain's mother, frailer than ever, followed her. She showed no emotion on her face – dead and dry. And Mohammed's old mother walked behind her, in a straight line, in case she strayed from her comrades in suffering. I had not realized, until then, that they had formed this mothers-of-disappeared-sons band. They walked on after each other, as if on cue, not swerving from the line, not outpacing anyone, in a unified motion.

For a moment it looked as if the whole village were moving. It felt as if things had just lifted, unhinged from their mooring places, and acquired a will of their own. A dust was sweeping away the village. Oh, the look of it when they got to the centre of the street, near the three shops, the nerve centre of Baba's village, the look of it all. It was like a mourning procession, an elegy dressed in rags of many colours running a lap through the village. I moved along too, on the edges of it all, for one last glimpse of Asma's face. No one talked to me. No one even looked at me: *Did they not see me?* With each metre of their progress away from the village, I grew old. What did I know of the ways of the world? There was a full-scale armed movement under way somewhere, everywhere, and things like this must be happening everywhere. There were people dying everywhere, getting massacred in every town and village, there were people being picked up and thrown into dark jails in unknown parts, there were dungeons in the city where hundreds of young men were kept in heavy chains and from where many never emerged alive, there were thousands who had disappeared, leaving behind women with photographs and perennial waiting, there were multitudes of dead bodies on the roads, in hospital beds, in fresh martyrs' graveyards and scattered casually on the snow of mindless borders. So what was a little village exodus in comparison to all that? I crept along for as long as I could. Still, Asma looked down.

Then I saw Noor Khan. He was walking at the back of the parade. For a moment my heart perished. How could he? How could you, Noor Chacha? What will Baba do, what will I . . . ?

Noor detached himself from the group at the back as soon as he saw me and started towards where I stood, waving his hand in a *no-no, don't-get-me-wrong* motion. I stopped and waited for him. My breath was settling down now, until Noor came close and leapt forward to put his hands on my shoulders.

'No, no. . . beta, no. Don't you think anything silly. I'm not going away, no way am I leaving you and your father. How can you think that!'

I inclined my head and must have looked disbelieving.

'I'm just, let's just say making up the closing flanks of this parade.' He pointed a limp finger towards the back end of the anxious throng. 'To see them home, to make sure.'

But why?

'Your father asked me to. He is concerned, worried, but said he couldn't go himself, so . . .' Noor pressed me closer to him now. 'Don't worry, I will be back soon. Promise. I will. I swear on Allah.'

I swallowed and looked at my old friend tearfully. Baba knew my only friend now was Noor, so why? Why couldn't he just go himself if delivering the fleeing flock to some faraway place, away from here, was suddenly so important to him?

'Hmm . . . But where are you going, I mean where are *they* going?'

'Beta, where will they go? I guess only as far as Udhampur, or Jammu at most, where else? That's how it used to be in the old days – we did this all the time, although I had stronger legs then.' Noor Khan tried to smile.

I tried to look at him meaningfully, not knowing what to say. This was wrong, everything was wrong. The situation was almost laughable – people from my village were fleeing to escape the wrath of the Indian Security Forces and were doing that by running away to India itself, for what was Jammu, or any part of the plains beyond the mountains of Kashmir, but India? *India!*

Noor looked back as if in agreement. I guess he didn't know what to say either. He hovered around for a short while, gave me a tight hug, and then dragged his legs to join the 'closing flanks' of the gradually shifting caravan.

In a way, I was eager for it to move more quickly now, for the caravan to disappear. In another way, though, I dreaded the moment when I would have to let go. They would be gone; he would be gone; she would be gone.

Noor looked at me one last time; it was a guilty look. All of them wore that look.

Baba did not come out, not even once, to see his Nowgam take flight. Ma had met up with the women the day before and a few in the morning as well. At the time of the start of the journey, though, she too chose to stay indoors – perhaps in solidarity with her husband, or perhaps she had her own anguish to deal with.

Near the far end of the dirt track, in the opposite direction of our valley, towards the widening but unknown horizon, I had to say my final farewell to the waning, receding figures. Silently, with a laboured wave. I could still hear some inchoate sounds wafting up from the departing kafila: a mixture of old people's muffled moaning, children's squeaking, the braying of cattle and the panting of beasts, and the restrained sobbing of young girls.

A long, curving wisp of dust, a few centimetres off the ground . . . was all that was left.

Soon the sounds died too. The sun rose to the middle of the sky and made everything too bright. When I turned to take one last, last look, there was nothing. I stayed still for an age, looking nowhere in particular.

In the end, without knowing how I got there, I found myself at home. Ma was still sitting as I'd left her in the morning. The kitchen smelled of burned tea. The corridor of Baba's hookah.

I went straight to my room and sat near the window, looking out into the vast, dark jungle at the back. It was impervious. Nothing had changed in it, all these years. I looked at its dense wrinkles all day, until it got darker and darker.

That was all it took to end Nowgam, then. Baba's dream of fifty years.

That night, after a wordless dinner, Baba had dimmed the light in the living room while listening to the evening news. I couldn't see his face clearly when he said, 'Your friends did this.'

23 *The Officer Visits*

'Sarpanch Sahib, so . . . how are you doing, hope everything's fine? Quite a show we put up the other day, isn't it? Good, bloody good!'

Captain Kadian entered the house unannounced, in the manner of someone used to people making way for him, although it was just poor Baba and me standing by the veranda, waiting for him to ascend the front steps to the house. I glanced around quickly, left and right, back and front, trying to see if there were soldiers with him who'd taken positions around the house. He was, after all, someone important. He had been in charge of the whole operation during the crackdown and the Governor's strange visit.

After the exodus, after everyone left, Baba had mostly kept to himself.

I had written many love letters to Asma that I knew I would never be able to send. I also copied some verses from Khalil Gibran and Keats.

Ma withdrew, aged, and fell silent. One day she just kept looking at me, wiped away a few tears, and then went into her garden.

I ate a lot in those days. I guess I wanted to survive.

This was only the second time I had seen Captain Kadian and I wasn't sure whether he knew what had happened in the village. Although, it was impossible that they didn't know. There was a new camp they had set up to check infiltration not too far from the village. Noor had been right. Good old Noor Chacha, why did you have to go? Baba said he was sure Noor would come back soon. I wasn't.

This was the first and only time Kadian would visit the house. Baba seemed to tremble to his very bone. I saw all the fears he had hidden, or not acknowledged, in the last few months collect in his eyes now. He had seen Farooq's head and then his headless torso and had perhaps understood why. He had seen Khadim Hussain's broken corpse and had perhaps known more about it than all of us. He had seen his village become lifeless in a day. In the presence of the Indian Army officer from the crackdown, then, he quivered now.

While we sat there with Kadian, in the living room, Ma hovered behind the curtain. I could see the faintest of shadows behind the grey blanket. I don't know how much she heard but I was sure she picked up the vital parts. She heard when Kadian laughed and said, 'The headman is very well off, then, bloody well off,' and Baba nodded as if some theft of his had been caught. Ma must have heard when he addressed me – this was the first time he talked directly to me – and said, 'So, young man, what do you do, then? Hmm . . . Play with toys, eh? I hope not, huh ha ha! You know what happens . . . ?' She must have heard when Baba said his pathetic little *Yessirs*, and *Jee, sir* and *Jee, sir!* She must have felt the shame her proud husband felt in his obsequiousness. She hovered around in the corridor, perhaps to stay in tune with what was happening in her house, perhaps to stay close to the action in the faint hope that she might be in a position to intervene. I could see her figure behind the curtain as I listened to the smartly dressed young officer from the Governor's crackdown. I wondered whether this was the man who had shot Khadim Hussain? What if he had been the one to chop off Farooq's head? I saw him running a long knife over Farooq's throat.

Ma signalled tea – the Thermos nozzle poking through the curtain – and I went out to get it. When I looked at her, she was struggling to get rid of the unwelcoming look on her face. *What to do, Ma?*

As I came back, I heard Baba say something about college. My heart fluttered a thousand times. Was I the subject of the conversation? Why? I put the Thermos down and went back to get the teacups. As I sat down a little later to pour tea, they stopped talking at once and the Captain seemed to be smiling. I felt a deepening chill in my chest. Then he looked halfway towards Baba and said, 'I was telling your father that we may have some work for you. You know what I mean? I know your college is shut most of the time, I understand . . .' He raised his left hand to forestall an anticipated interjection on my part, although I had no such intention. 'So rather than sitting at home idle all day, why not do some work, you know, gain some experience . . .' he said approvingly, as if I had already seen his point, as if I were on his side. He turned towards Baba again. I looked at Baba and saw the same weak, defeated man I'd seen during the Minister of Sport's 'prize-giving' ceremony. His pride was broken, gone. His shoulders stooped like the very supplicants he was used to ruling over. I swallowed. 'Yes, yes . . .' Baba seemed to swallow too, '. . . Captain Sahib was saying you could visit the camp some day, they have a lot of activities there.' He gathered himself quickly. I looked at the two men, not fully understanding if this was a serious idea or idle talk just to keep the conversation going? This was, after all, a first meeting. My gaze, all of a sudden, became locked on to Kadian's holster. He was wearing a dark brown uniform, of some thick woollen fabric. It was fresh and crisply ironed. His gun shone with its black back from the glossy brown leather holster. It looked imposing on this man's hip. In films they always look smaller.

The Captain held his cup elegantly, the handle delicately pressed between his fingers, and took gentle sips of Ma's tea. There was no slurp, slurp – no grabbing at the cup. I couldn't tell whether he liked the tea or not.

'So what do you think? When should we expect your company, then, my dear?'

I honestly didn't know what to say. What *work*? Were they really serious? Since when did they start employing civilians in high-security camps – we hadn't even known where and when and how the camp had come into being? I must have looked blank when the Captain continued. 'Oh, don't worry about Sarpanch Sahib, he won't refuse, will he . . . ? After all, there's no one left here except us, huh ha.'

Without much waiting about, after an awkward silence had run its course, he then proceeded to give me directions to the camp. Before that moment, even at the time, you could almost believe it didn't exist, as if it were just a product of hearsay, as that rumoured thing Noor Khan had been going on about. It was, Kadian said, at the far end of the ridge. If I went from the village street towards 'the hidden valley' and took this small diversion near the highest point of the dirt track and then kept going left towards the wood rising at end of the ridge, I would see the first signs of the camp. I sort of half listened as he gave detailed directions. He then stood up, pulled at his army jacket and said, 'I will be on my way, then. See you Monday afternoon, all right? Ya, ya, just drop in, just drop in.'

I knew, and my father knew too, in that very first moment, in that very first meeting with the Captain, that we had to do *exactly* what we were told. We just knew. Ma had fortunately – or unfortunately, I don't know – already taken the kettle and the cups from me and was busy cleaning up in the kitchen when Kadian was saying his goodbyes. She did not see him leave. Perhaps she hadn't heard the last part of our brief conversation.

Baba scratched at his beard.

He smiled an embarrassed smile, in that difficult manner of fathers who have been belittled in front of their sons. Long ago, when a mad vagrant beggar had inadvertently slapped Baba, while he was trying to intervene in a scuffle in the street, Baba had smiled in the same way. Hesitant, pained. I wanted to console him for the way he felt; I wanted to give him a hug and make him feel strong again – I'm a grown-up man now, don't worry, Baba, don't worry – I wanted to make him feel like the man he was used to being, but I didn't, I couldn't.

PART III

Now . . .

24   *Choices*

I don't want to do this any more. I never, never wanted to. Baba, I am tired, I am exhausted. If we run away there would be nothing to fear. I don't want to count the number of unburied boys remaining to be searched, don't want to pick guns off dead people and hand them over to that evil man, don't even want to see this rucksack and its contents any more. You know, there's small stuff that I still haven't given to KD and his peon, it's somehow stayed at the bottom of my bag: fountain pens with glittering gold caps marked *Made in China®* in thin chiselled letters; clunky, big plastic electronic watches, Casio or Sharp; letters, usually starting and ending with age-old Urdu couplets – *tum salamat raho hazar baras / har baras ke hon din pachaas hazar*; a couple of music cassettes, Hassan Sofi, Kailash Mehra, Raj Begum and Shamima Dev songs from that old black and white film *Habba` Khatoon*; a few hand-stitched amulets, now sodden, green or black jacketed, because I couldn't bring myself to throw them away lest I disrespect some sacred verse. There's a compass as well, in its smooth aluminium case, and a couple of pocket combs too.

And I don't want to stink any more; sometimes I think I have a permanent headache from the smell . . . It's almost like a second skin. Sometimes I can't get rid of it for days. At night I go home smelling of rot, death, and I just can't wash it off. Even after the hot bath and the scrubbing and the scratching it is always there, a dense, greasy thick stench that soaks deep into my skin, into my hair, into the creases of my palms, into everything.

But here I am, in my valley, and here are these poor fellows, lost for ever, murdered, beyond grief, beyond redemption, beyond brutality. Here I still am, unable to decide what to do now. Do I run away, flee with Ma and Baba, cross into Pakistan finally, or try to bury these poor boys – one by one, part by part, limb by limb, smile by smile, grin by grin – offer my fateha, and then leave? I have got to do something about it.

Slowly and steadily, I realize, I seem to have become used to everything, as if it were normal, as if it were all inevitable, as if it were my destiny; and if it goes on like this I won't even be able to tell whether I am mad or sane. What if I am already crazy?

Kadian is on a different planet – homebound thrill, I suppose. The other day he mentioned his father's farm – I was so bloody right – and said he wouldn't mind spending some time looking after it since 'Papa' is getting old now. There is a spark in his talk and a spring in the little walk I have seen him taking to the store to fetch brand-new, cardboard-boxed bottles of whisky – the store must be some kind of a vast army reservoir, with endless supplies of everything. Not much has altered on the drinking front, though – he pulls out a half-finished bottle and pours himself glass after glass and drinks and drinks and then reeks and reeks of it. He seems to finish off his bottles more quickly now, another sign that he is actually getting ready to leave. He has even been a little less aggressive of late, you know, a little less belligerent in his lectures and speeches, but only a little. At times, I can't believe he is really going to leave – how can he? It's his place, he created it.

I'm sitting in front of him, as usual, and waiting for him to say something. *Did he invent this job, spin this elaborate ruse, just to have company in his lonely cabin? I sometimes wonder.*

'Don't get impatient, bhai, you will be out, I will be out, we will fucking all be out, huh ha!' He plonks his old tumbler on the table and wipes his mouth with his handkerchief in two measured swipes.

'When do you think I can . . . ?' I leave my question half finished as he starts to wave his hand at me. Don't want him to launch into a fresh barrage of expletives. Maderchod this and behanchod that. Motherfucking this and sisterfucking that!

'You will know in due course of time. And look, when I leave is my business – you will know when you need to know, all right?' Change of tone, brief glimpse towards the peon, and then he stares back at me with that familiar smirk: *Who do you think you're talking to?*

'Go home, man, there's nothing more for you to do here today, is there?' he says as I take things out from the bag and put them noiselessly on his table. I don't want to be a hoarder. Along with Shabbir, Gulzar and a few other chaps' IDs, I also leave the roll of currency notes I'd picked from Shabbir's trouser pocket. I don't want this money, Indian *or* Pakistani. Since there haven't been any major encounters here in recent months, I haven't had any guns to bring along, otherwise, in the early days, I used to leave them by the door for the peon, who would have taken them into that dark storeroom, or wherever else, by the time I left.

'You can keep the cash if you want to.' He's calmed down a bit. He has had a haircut recently; I can see the skin on his head through the closely cropped hair near his temples. There's an animal sheen to it.

'No, Captain, no, I don't want to be carrying Pakistani currency on me, although I wouldn't mind a small souvenir . . .' I try a small shrug. Humour.

'Oh, these fuckers, these stupid naïve fuckers, what on earth do they think they'd do with fucking Pakistani rupees here?'

'No, no, it's not much, just a few notes . . . I think they just wanted to show them around.'

'Ya, ya, fucking maderchod Pakistanis . . . All of them! Saala, even your shitty rice in your sisterfucking ration-ghats comes from India, you can't even make a fucking two-bit bathroom slipper here, and all you fucking want to do is carry Allah's own currency to show around. What kind of idiots do these guys recruit now? Already short of good people, huh . . . Fucking idiots!' He unravels the roll of cash and hangs Jinnah from the tip of his index finger and thumb, as if holding something brittle or dirty. 'Islamic Republic of Fucking Jihadistan, my ass!'

He stops talking and leans back in his big chair, eyes closed as if in meditation. I hate it when he starts abusing Kashmir, Kashmiris or Pakistan – it's difficult to maintain a straight face when he does that.

I look around and notice that the peon's left sometime during our conversation. He still gives me the creeps. The door to the store is open and I try to look in. I must go in some day. The cold, urine smell is coming out of there. *What have they dumped in that dark room?* I hope not what I fear, what I dread in the darkest of my dreams. Clay, urine, wetness.

I get up unobtrusively and take my silent leave of the Captain. Even with his eyes closed I think he's watching me.

'I'm leaving in two weeks,' he says abruptly from his seat, slurring slightly, as I'm about to reach for the door. 'Yes, my dear . . .' this is the first time he has addressed me this way after that first meeting in our house many, many months ago, '. . . yes, you'll be out soon, my dear, very soon, don't you worry. I'll be out, you'll be out, we'll all be out, maderchod, we'll all be out.'

I only have two and a half weeks left.

25 The Peon's Story

Sixteen days to go exactly. I have to know the Captain's timetable during the day.

We are walking around the camp, close to the boundary I think. It feels like he's giving me a guided tour of the place, well, a nominal one. I'm certain he won't get anywhere near the places he doesn't want me to see, although he does point out, in a limp, disinterested gesture, his own quarters – a pretty, tourist-style bungalow, red bricks and wood structure with a painted roof and a chimney. There are three more bungalows here, identical, lined up one after the other in a compact little zigzag. The vegetation in the camp – at least, in this part of it – is trim and neat. There are pine coves, like the ones we used to draw in our watercolour exercises at school, in the corners, and triads of rose bushes with mute pink November roses on them. Behind these patches of domesticated prettiness – I am sure they have a retinue of army gardeners doing all this – are three tiers, in irregular order of height, of fierce concertina wire fencing, electrified: I can tell from the small clown-like red skulls hanging in the middle of the iron-wire wall, which have *Danger* written on their foreheads and its Hindi equivalent *Khatra* beneath their flimsy mouths. Honestly, they look like twisted little children's skulls – a whole ensemble of scarlet-red heads bobbing all around us as though in a cackle, as though in some secret children's sport. Why have so many of them, I wonder? I begin to understand why we never got much view of what was going on here. Behind the barbed-wire rings is the densest of tree covers I have ever seen, and it's only towards what must be the ridge – and where I cannot go – that it is somewhat open. A phrase begins to form somewhere in the back of my head, remembered from the sombre new NCERT history textbooks we were asked to buy in high school – 'concentration camp' – and I begin to imagine this as a hidden killing factory of sorts, the mother of all interrogation and torture centres, a ghastly death chamber for all those who dissent and protest and raise arms. I feel small. I feel hurt.

'So what is wrong with him, sir . . . isn't he, you know, kind of strange . . . ? Sometimes I'm so wary of him, Captain, just can't get too close, you know . . .' I start at once, fretful that my strenuously drawn-up courage might desert me. The Captain is walking in front of me, an unlit cigarette suspended from his fingers. But he doesn't answer me immediately, as if he isn't even listening. I have no choice but to follow. As I walk behind, another question strikes me then, with renewed force, with fresh anxiety – what *am* I doing here? When did I morph into this person? The hideous reality of my situation, the lonely horror of my fevered nights, comes over my senses as I see the Captain's form in front of me with the same upright, commandeering aspect I had first noticed during the Governor's crackdown many, many months ago. He keeps going, throwing smoke from his freshly lit cigarette my way, until we are back to his dark cabin. *This must end.*

'Oh-ho, don't worry about him, he is no harm to you, trust me,' Kadian says finally, sitting down, and busying himself with his journal.

Yet another sitting in front of this man. A stiff tense back, an anxious stomach. Breathing in silence is worse than listening to his belligerent talk.

'But what does he do, sir – I mean, er, apart from sitting here all day?' Instinctively, I turn towards the peon's empty chair. This must only be the third or fourth time I have not seen him in the room.

'Hmm . . .' Kadian gives me a curious look. 'We have never talked about him, isn't it? He's quite a story, you see. You call him the Peon, ha ha, isn't it?'

'No, Captain, I was just curious. I have been coming here for eight, nine months now and all I have seen him do is sit in that chair or make tea.'

He puts his bright-green Pilot Tecpoint pen down and sort of purrs. 'Let's just say he was not always like this, my dear. He is a subedar by rank, you know. Was a very reputed field operative once . . . A bloody good, professional army man. When they first created the CI formations here, he was in the first battalion we raised. They say the bugger had a great ear for sniffing people out. He could dig militants out from all kinds of hiding holes, from underground cells, from fake ceilings, granaries, fucking water tanks, cubicles concealed under kitchens, once even from the bottom of a fucking houseboat on the fucking Dal Lake! His was the frontline unit that came to be known as the Sarp-Vinash Romeo Force.' Kadian stops for effect and I let out a half-genuine, half-deliberate gasp: *So this man worked for the Romeo Force . . . ?* As if I 'fucking' care.

'Yes,' KD reads my mind, 'in fact, he technically still does.'

I turn towards the chair, then towards the door. 'He still does . . . ? Sorry, but I mean, he's always here, dozing off . . . ?'

'Huh ha ha!' He laughs his signature laugh, twice, and looks at me as if I were an alien struggling to comprehend the world of men.

What?

'You can be so *naïve* sometimes, man . . . You shouldn't be here, you shouldn't be here, heh.' Kadian suspends his gaze in mid-flight and slowly nods a few times, as if weighing his own statement. *Do you really want to know what he does?*

I hang my head down in age-old indecision. Even though my relationship with him, on the face of it, may border on the cordial now, even friendly if I want to call it that, I still can't take too many liberties with him. The room closes in on me with a familiar anxiety. I am filled with images of the peon in various disguises.

Kadian settles his breath, loudly. 'You see, my dear – I have never told you this, have I? – from time to time we have these inquiries and cases against our men for violations of fucking human rights, et cetera. Bloody fucking civilians – really, they just don't get it sometimes. You know, a lot of the times, it's just some procedural error, some silly, logistical, technical mistake, some simple human fucking error, in short. These things happen during operations, we have to meet our objectives and we go about it purely as a business; it's a task, a fucking job. But people don't get it, they just don't get it . . .' KD sighs in the manner of a teacher accustomed to not always being fully understood. As his departure draws closer, he's been getting a little, as I said, reflective. He likes to hold forth, as always, but in a more parental way, with humanity almost, sometimes looking at me as if I were a hopeful, promising pupil. They must have people like me in mind when they say in India that we must join the 'national mainstream'. As if it were a placid river in my neighbourhood.

'Anyway, what was I saying –?'

'Oh, sir, you were telling me something you have *never* told me.'

'Yes, yes, this dedicated man, this committed soldier, whom you in your naïvety think is my peon, this man too was the subject, no, a fucking victim, of some inquiry commission shit some behan-chod, bleeding-heart lefty human rights fucker from Delhi engineered. Bastard, if he were to endure even half a day in this dark jungle, he would forget even his fucking grandmother's rights!'

'All Dasrath Singh fucking did was arrest two cowards hiding in a secret cell under someone's kitchen in Civil Lines, Srinagar. He had been watching the house for a long time before making the swoop. Now, this was a family we were dealing with, but Dasrathji was angry . . .' Kadian gesticulates with growing passion, '. . . and I would say, naturally so, justifiably so, angry at these people for harbouring militants, isn't it? I had just joined the Research and Analysis CI Cell at Badami Bagh Cantt – you know where that is . . . ? Anyway, at the time of the raid, one of the women of the house resisted Dasrath's attempts, in some kind of a frantic state, to uncover this secret door to the cabin – it was under one of the kitchen counters. In the melee, he must have pushed her. They fucking accused him of attempt to double-murder – the woman fell to one side and hit an LPG cylinder; only then did the poor bugger see she was pregnant. I am sure had he fucking known, he would have acted in restraint. I am absolutely certain of that.

'I read his file and reports at BB. I read all his history. At first no one really bothered; such small incidents happen all the time, really.

And who the fuck knows what is a perfect way to deal with frigging proxy soldiers sleeping under kitchen sinks, when you never know which one amongst your *in-no-cent*, garib Kashmiris might take out a fucking rocket launcher from his ass and blow you into smithereens? Really, how does one fucking know! Anyway, you won't understand.

'Things carried on, no one fucking cared until this woman gave birth. Everything was normal, she lived, the baby lived, but . . . the girl was born with fractured limbs – now who would've fucking thought? – probably her left arm and leg. They were kind of folded when she was born, so the report said. I don't know how that could've happened, a frigging medical mystery, huh.

'That is how it all started. Some overeager rights-champion bastard visited the woman at the hospital, who said she had been repeatedly kicked in the belly – although Dasrath later told me that he had only kicked her once – and then invited entire teams of these motherfucking NGO pests and lawyers from Srinagar, even from behanchod Delhi and Calcutta! They also managed to raise the question in the Lok fucking Sabha of the Parliament. They even gave it a name, the "Fractured Foetus Case", as if, huh . . . You see, that's what the media here does – it exaggerates, distorts, sensationalizes – negative stuff, always fucking focusing on the negative stuff.

'And these thankless NGO bastards, they take all the fucking grant and aid from the Government and just because they can call themselves non-government they think all they should do is screw their own Government from behind!' Kadian clenches his fist in an 'I rest my case' gesture, pumps it twice in the air, and glares at me.

I don't know what to say, sir. Your efficient 'bloody good' professional soldier maimed a foetus, what do you expect me to say?

'But nothing really happened in the end, even after all that, huh, I mean nothing really drastic. Some big chips at 55 Corps came down, sodding military lawyers, et cetera, and decided that his unit should lie low for a while, at least in some parts of the town, and he was put in a desk job when this camp was set up . . . That's how I got to meet him and he has been, let's just say, very useful ever since. Fucking useful. He's an old hand at this shit and hasn't lost his touch at all. *Interrogator extraordinaire*, I should know, eh? Some of the tough nuts we nab here, I make sure he meets them, if you know what I mean, eh?

'Hmm . . .' *Would Hussain qualify as a tough nut, then?*

What hmm? His tilted head seems to ask.

There is a long pause.

'What I was wondering, Captain . . . Is he going to stay here when you, er, leave . . . ? I mean, like this?' I try and recover my poise.

'Well, it's up to him, really. They offered him early fucking retirement some time ago. He refused, didn't want to go back. He has no family, you see. But I guess we have to go our separate ways at some point, I'm not married to him, huh ha.' He pours himself a drink, slowly, gingerly, from a McDowell's bottle, and starts peering at it. 'By the way, I did tell you I'm leaving soon, in fifteen days, didn't I? Three years, man, three full fucking years in Kashmir.' He fiddles with his glass.

I won't let you go, Captain, I won't.

Finally, having shoved his journal and some other paperwork into one of his many drawers, he gets up and smiles, unusually nicely, at me. 'Tell me something, you must get bored with this sometimes, isn't it? Why not come on a field trip with me, you know . . . ? I haven't seen any real action myself in a while . . . And you know what, I might go on one last trip soon. Mehrotra Sir called, you know – you should just come along, really.'

I have more than a fair idea of what a field trip might be like. *No, sir, no, I don't want any of your 'action'.*

'It will be fun, what do you say, haan?' He carries on matter-of-factly, as if I were always a part of his team, as if I were a long-serving counter-insurgent, a loyal servant of the Indian Army . . .

'Do come, my dear, do come. It will give you a break from all this, you know, and you don't really have to do much, just watch, huh ha.'

He goes back to his favourite pastime whilst I struggle. I don't want to go.

'Okay? See you next week, then. One fucking last tango, huh ha.'

I go home with a dread racking through my mind. What does he want to do with me now?

Baba is praying in the living room, by the almost private light of the gasoline lamp. Watching him, I stand still in the door. The mildly worn-out, green velvet of the Ja-e-Namaz looks so sympathetic that I too want to run and prostrate myself on the prayer mat and cry and be with my father and never, ever leave. In the phosphorescent glow of the silken Fargo gas mantle I see my father is an old man now. In *sajda* now, in complete surrender before Khuda Saab, I see my father is a *weak* old man now, his proud bearing reduced to bony haunches visible under his loose kurta. Baba.

26 Cat's Eyes

There are twelve jeeps behind the one-tonner APC leading the convoy. Kadian's dark green Gypsy is the first. It has big steel-rimmed headlights, and a black iron grille covers all the windows. My heart won't stop pounding. Some day, it will just pop out or implode. That would be it then. I wish.

The vehicle I am sitting in smells of camphor. I don't like it. There's a small idol, pink-robed, gold-laced and red-faced, on the dashboard. A wiry black twirl, balanced on a tiny steel metal plate – it looks like bird shit – is spewing out a thin spiral of acrid brown smoke. Outside, it's windy. Trees, misty mountains, sleeping villages, vast denuded brown rice fields and an indifferent sky pass in a watercolour blur in the light of the winter dawn. We are going at what they must call breakneck speed. Bumps. I can't even think of removing my hand from the handlebar in the corner of the roof. The driver, a starchily dressed soldier wearing his khaki-green cap in an immaculate tilt over his left temple, hasn't said a single word to me. He seems cold, hostile. Our Gypsy is behind Kadian's and we maintain a steady distance from it, following him in faithful imitation, turn for turn, grunt for grunt, screech for screech. We are, after all, behind the 'Commanding Officer' himself. Wonder what the unfortunate locality, which in all probability is going to be under siege soon, is called? God, how did I ever get into this!

The last time I visited, Kadian had a fresh scampering of papers on the desk. The envelope, torn open neatly, had the three-lions Government of India mark on it, chiselled red on polished light brown. It looked weighty. My hand stirred in temptation a couple of times but I didn't really dare browse through the pile of tall sheets. I've been very angry of late – he can't leave just like that! It's not right, it's not fair. He can't just say, 'Okay, my posting is over, so bye-bye,' and be completely free of what he has done here, as if it were just another job. *I kill you and maim you and rape you and burn you and leave your bullet-torn bodies, naked and unburied, in the dirt and snow, so my job's done and I will go home now.*

He talked about his strange desire again – that I should accompany him on some kind of 'last mission'. I couldn't believe it. How could he even begin to think that I would want to? I may not be a very brave man but I'm not going to be a traitor, and that's what I'll be like – a *gaddaar*, a turncoat – if I join him in some kind of an operation. What if someone sees me? Part of an army Cordon and Search team! They'll surely think I am some kind of mukhbir, an informer – a cat. I didn't want to go, no way.

But look at me now, look at me, here I am, travelling with Kadian and his black-bandana'd men in their frightening fortresses. These fearful grey coffin cars.

He said his colleagues down at the district headquarters had asked him to lend some men. That he owed it to Mehrotra Sir. I was surprised at his casual demeanour. They might pick up a few people, hurt someone, even kill some – that is what they do here – and he was talking about it as if it were one last game of cricket.

'What the hell,' he said, 'what's one last operation before *chutti*, before I leave this shit! And you, all you need to do is just sit inside, my dear, that's it. It's routine stuff, but you'll at least get some experience, get to know things . . .'

I don't want the experience, sir: people nabbed, beaten up, taken away, never to come back. In the event, I never really had much of a choice.

It soon approaches: a large settlement in the midst of expansive sheets of erstwhile paddy fields lined by lean poplars and willow trees, weeping, on the fringes, a hazy green line somehow connecting everything to the far horizon. The one-tonner seems to have already curved towards the village. I find myself praying, feverishly. God save them! Our vehicle begins to calm down too. There is the smell of dew, grass, in the air. Everything looks fresh, wet. The area is at the edge of these low hills that I reckon stretch all the way here from the mountains in our parts. The highest of the scantily treed hills has a small, domed hut on top. A shrine perhaps. I pray again, to the small minaret silhouetted against the washed sky this time. A long-lost couplet rears its head from God knows where: *Tang aa chuke hain kashmakash-e-zindagi se hum* . . . Some film song, some deeply melancholic lyricist desperately trying to fit his poetry on to a film tune.

There are muddy puddles in the lane going into the big village. A few ducks – ugly, mud-smeared fat bellies – stutter away from the edges of a drain-sized stream running parallel to the lane at the sight of the massive metal machines, and as we wobble and jerk forward I see a few grainy splashes paint the windscreen of our Maruti Gypsy in knife-like diagonal strokes. Something dreadful is going to happen to these people. As the vehicle comes to a stop behind KD's caged carriage, I understand there's no escape from it now: nothing unexpected has happened to interrupt the 'mission' that I don't want to be a part of, and nothing can change now, now that we are here in this big mohalla, as it seems, where he said some 'hard-core' militants had been hiding. I don't know, man. What *is* hard core?

And already, then, they are having some kind of a standing conclave at the front of the now still convoy; I can see curves of thin smoke rising from the small gathering of military men. I wait and think about the residents of this place and what they might be doing at this exact minute – sleeping, dreaming, turning, coughing, rubbing hands, going through a cold and cumbersome ablution for the morning prayers, or perhaps leaning against closed shutters, trying to figure out what that noise was. I don't like it, I don't like it.

Soon, that familiar sinister announcement bawls from a loudspeaker somewhere – oh, a voice, a loudspeaker, a mosque, *yes, yes,* I know all of that. All of that. I curse my kismet. I think of Baba – is he responsible for getting me into all this? What about Hussain and co? What about Mr Kadian? I spend the next few minutes – while we are humming our way again, this time into a sketchily fenced field behind the village, under the hills – in some kind of an unceasing moan. Resignation, I have gradually come to understand, is a hollowing state.

I just sit there, in the back seat of that acrylic- and camphor-smelling vehicle and watch the gradually extending morning through the mud-stabbed window. As I look around, I gather that the ground is the Eid prayer ground, the *Eidgah*, of this area, for there is a small pulpit at the far end, in the centre of a low white wall at the back. It has a small arch on top, with a big glaring *Allah-o-Akbar* written on it in sparkling green paint. The same people who must pray here together, shoulder to shoulder, twice a year on Eid or when there's a big funeral, are now being rounded up like cattle in the same place, some still rubbing their eyes, some in their crumpled nightclothes and some still finding it hard to close their wide-open mouths, glaring in disbelief and suppressed anger, as they must be, at this conquering arc of shining army vehicles and the swarming fauj of bidi-smoking soldiers around them. Our Gypsy is towards the left flank of the menacing curve now, I think it is second from last at this end. There are people still trickling in, the reluctance of their legs evident in the strained expressions on their faces, goaded silently towards their seating area by a deliberate swish of those dreadful bamboo batons. There's danger in every movement, every stir of the wind. A part of me is relieved that I'm inside the vehicle and not outside. I remember Baba's trembling legs. He never really recovered his poise after that. But I feel ashamed too.

When it looks like all the people the Army wanted out have gathered in the ground, a short interval, some kind of strained stasis, occurs by itself. Someone perhaps wanted to finish a cigarette or come back after a pee. From the left flank of the arc, in front of which the assembled crowd sits squatting, or with their heads in their knees, I have a clear view towards the right, where ten other vehicles are parked like ours, each a couple of feet behind the preceding one and then, starting from the middle, a couple of feet ahead of the previous one. I gaze at people, at the whole setting, the trees, the hill, the sky, and stop at the brightly painted green pulpit to check something that had struck me as familiar earlier and – yes, *my God*, yes – there it is, painted dimly beneath the *Allah-o-Akbar*: 'Eid Mubarak, Mohalla Committee, Poshpur' . . . and I feel a leaden weight, a sinking feeling, of guilt, of shame, descend on me at once, for long ago – Oh, Poshpur! – when Noor Khan had told me about the nearest big village, Poshpur, whose women had been raped by Indian soldiers and from where a lot of boys had left together for Pakistan to become militants, I had taken it with a pinch of salt, thought of it as yet another Noor Khan exaggeration, but now, looking at these men – *there is not a single boy here* – I believe everything at once, know it was true then, know it is true now, and in so doing feel guilty again, and am filled with a rage both past and current! You have no idea what people look like when their women – *all their women* – have been raped. I realize I can't see a single raised eyebrow now; all of them are looking into the ground. (*Oh, my God! Is it possible that those women, those curfew-hounded mothers, were from here?*) These men are either looking down – a kind of defiance, this, I think, a profound defiance of the multitude of soldiers surrounding them in this exercise to *look at* their faces – or talking to each other in reserved gestures. Someone has come out with a red transistor and a few people are seated, loosely huddled, around it too.

At once now, the scene stirs. Soldiers are hauling up men from their seats on the ground and lining them up to walk. (My buttocks itch, from a not so distant memory.) Someone is already walking now and the soldiers are yelling at him; then, after a few paces, he stands erect, walks tall, approaches the first vehicle, pauses, looks into the front seat, stalls, and then moves again when the officer standing by the driver's window nods him on. Another man walks behind, while the first man moves to the second dark Gypsy, and he too pauses briefly, looking straight into the vehicle, and then moves on. The third man does the same and the fourth and the fifth and the sixth, until I too begin to see men walk in front of me and then they stop, and I look at them – they at me – and then they walk on . . . I, of course, say nothing, nod nothing, neither to the man on my right, nor to anyone in any direction. And thus it goes on and on, so on and so on, until something else happens. At the fourth or the fifth vehicle there is a commotion, and crying too, and now the soldiers drag a man out of the ID parade, shouting the most obscene expletives I have ever heard on his mother and daughter. An informer inside the vehicle has *ID'd* someone and they have grabbed him by the scruff of his neck and hauled him away while the man protests in vain. In a breaking, despairing voice. I shudder. I too feel like I am an informer. Oh, Kadian.

The sun is beating down, screaming now – even though it's the very core of winter. Men come and go, men come and go. Soldiers goad and shout. Rifle butts and batons do a blurred dance over the men's heads and shoulders. An oppressive light rules all around. I sit and watch. Everything's planned, rehearsed. There's a method to everything, relentless, and there is no let-up. I watch and wait. Until . . . until a blinding bolt of recognition makes its intent approach through the light from the far right. I first see him, still some distance away, from the corner of the driver's windscreen, and then, after a few pauses, he moves into the front screen, into the bright white light, then he stops, straight-faced, and freezes me in the millionth of a second. He's in my face now. Everything seizes.

And then, Ashfaq walks away. As quickly as he had appeared, like an apparition. I don't know what to do, what to think, what to make of it all.

When I come out of my glaring eyes-wide-open shock, he's gone. I look around furtively, suddenly thinking a thousand things about this whole exercise, and try not to appear too animated, too – how do I say? – excited. He's not in the crowd in front of me. There's no one familiar there. He's not anywhere! And I can't tell whether he has just gone back to wherever he appeared from, or if they have grabbed him too, and taken him away. For a moment, I feel a sinking helplessness and think of going and seeking out Kadian to ask for help, to beg him, to plead with him . . . My mind hears hollow crashes. Again and again. But I think the better of it: what if that was the whole plan? What if that is what KD wanted me to do? I try to calm my nerves, look around discreetly once again, rub my eyes, and shake my head, but can't find a single face I recognize.

By late afternoon the ordeal for the squatting, frowning crowd is over, for now at least. The sun is on a melting descent, shifting from yellow to blushing red as it makes its approach to meet the distant wall of mountains at the back. I keep looking at the empty field, wondering how many of the men I saw a while ago won't return home today. How many mothers, daughters, sisters, wives, fiancées, are going to wail into the night and, clinging to the feeble hopes of their prayers, faint into sleep at some ungodly hour? The willows and the poplars cast surging shadows, which begin to gnaw at the tyres of the vehicles – I wish they could just eat up, swallow everything. Where the men were seated I can see inclined patches of grass here and there as if a picnicking family had just left for home; a few broken walnut shells also appear scattered, and there is a lone slipper on the side too.

There's a knock on my window, a scrawny soldier is asking me to pull it down, waving his hands overeagerly. I obey silently. 'Sa'ab has sent this,' he says with the kind of mildly condescending disdain reserved, I suspect, for informers, and hands me a large old-fashioned aluminium tiffin box and turns round briskly to go back. Kadian has sent me food. There's tightly packed rice, a solid blob of yellow daal stains it on one side, and a lonely piece of meat sits like a tree stub growing out of snow. Two shrivelled green chillies lie on top of the combination meal.

I eat the cold caked rice, swallow, and hold back half-throttled tears.

'Did you guys get anything from the crackdown the other day? Any *big guns*?' I try a casual tone, and let a shade of sarcasm slip out as well.

It's the third day after Kadian's 'one last piece of action', during which I hardly saw him. Only eleven days are left now. I have had enough, much more than enough. I'm beginning to know what it must feel like to be totally on the edge; also less and less sure if I really saw Ashfaq the other day. It could have just been a –

'Those people looked utterly miserable, you know, I watched them all day. I know how they must've felt, waiting for their turn to stand up in front of the vehicles, knowing it could be their last moment of freedom, their last breath of life even!'

'Oh, come on, you . . . Don't start that with me again? I told you, it's fucking nothing, part of the game here, man, fucking everyday stuff. We catch a few, kill a few, release a few – it cannot be perfect.' He stands up at once, starts pacing back and forth in his work space, and then stops and leans on the table in the manner of an earnest teacher.

I have been through this so many times.

'This is an insurgency, my dear, and I didn't create it, it's your fucking movement for Azadi, your frigging freedom struggle, isn't it?' he says, sneering at the desk. 'If there was no problem here, no impediments to the restoration of normalcy, if you didn't take this anti-India shit so far, none of this would happen, no one would be arrested, interrogated, or fucking *tortured*, as you say. You think I like this? You think we kill them for sport, isn't it? You think we do this just like that, for no reason, huh!'

Why do I invite this?

'Okay, tell me something, you remember the firing in your village? Of course you do. You know, there were militants hiding in your mosque, for more than a month, they could have been your friends, they could have been some other people – even we didn't know for a change – but someone from amongst you, definitely the man killed that morning, alerted them, helped them escape . . . Why else do you think we had a crackdown after that, *hain*? It's hard, but it is all incidental, my dear, *in-ci-dental*, can't be helped, part of the job.'

I go back in time and see Khadim Hussain's body in front of me – I can't even walk properly but I do see that hint of a smile on his face, his son's smile – he had died for something then, he had helped save some boys, our own boys perhaps.

'We have to do it, my dear, we must physically remove all impediments to our task, it is totally legit, lawful, and if they then call it repression, oppression, occupation, whatever shit, they've got it all wrong, totally wrong.

'I too have a family to go back to, you see . . . Daddyjee needs his son exactly like your father wants you. I am just doing my job here, that's all. You say thousands have died, but I didn't do that. They fucking *chose* to die, they got themselves killed for Azadi . . . Don't you fucking look at me like that, mister!' He suddenly catches me eyeing him and probably suspects how much I loathe him. 'I gave you a job, kept you busy, otherwise you would have been fucked a hundred times over by some stinking Afghan jihadi with a penchant for Kashmiri boys. But what am I saying? You are not even proper Kashmiri! Forget it, man, this is war, and these things are elements of the business here. I'm the fucking Commanding Officer and they have given me a responsibility, to cleanse this place of anti-fucking-national elements, and that's what I'm doing, and if I were not fucking exhausted I would probably do it as long as it takes – you get my point? Mister human rights violations champion, my ass!'

His eyes turn a strange, berserk red. I swallow.

'And *you* didn't pick anyone the other day. No "innocent" mother-fucking guerrilla sidekick lost his balls because of you. They would have been picked up anyway, my dear, there could have been a real mukhbir in that shitty Gypsy and we might have even nabbed a few more than we actually did. So, please, get a grip. This is what happens here, this is what we do, this is our fucking work. There's trouble here, infiltrators come from across the border to fuck your place up, to screw the peace in fucking Paradise on Earth, and I try to stop them. *That is it.* And, and I get paid to do that. The Govern-ment of the Democratic Fucking Republic of India spends billions of rupees to keep this place intact, I'm just a small, teeny-weeny, meeny cog in that machine. Even if I agreed with you for a minute, even if I believed you, what can I do? Nothing . . . naa-thing! You still don't understand, do you?

'India, my dear, is a sisterfucking giant, a colossus with countless arms and limbs and tongues and claws and hands and mouths and fucking everything else . . . Even if you have these small ulcers fes-tering in various places and crevices, they don't matter to it; it uses one of its many hands or claws to scratch at the sore, soothing the irritation, and then waits until the ulcer dies on its own, or just plucks it off and throws it away. It's a huge fucking jinn, small tics and scabs and cuts don't harm it much, it just carries on, sometimes waving a hand and blowing, crushing to pieces, whatever it is that's bothering it. And you know what, you know what? I *am* that blow, and there are hundreds like me.'

If I kill him, it will put everything to rest, for good. I must. Only then will I be free. Only then.

At night I take a long look at my pistol – a hard, considered look. I don't take it out of the pillow, though, just watch it lying there like an animal. Then I touch it, feel it, caress its trigger, turn it slowly. It hisses. From its deep, black bearing.

I have to do it very carefully – with extreme caution – don't want to be caught trying to do it, no way, that would be the end of it, end of it all. All these soldiers, resentful angry soldiers, all around me, if I am caught with it in the camp they will tear me to pieces, mutilate me beyond recognition, my face, my face . . . They will tear me to shreds, shoot at me from all sides, then stamp on me, hit me, kick me in my ribs, in my face, mangle my body and throw it down into my valley, into the ditch with the others. Poor Ma and Baba, what will become of them? Oh, they will kill my father and mother too, even rape Ma! I must be extremely cautious, then, rather die than get caught. Oh, all this Army, all around me, thousands of them and just me with a puny pistol! If I am caught with it, I know I am dead.

At the thought of my own death, I have tears – sudden, hot tears – in my eyes. I feel sad for Ma and Baba, sad for how sad they will be without me.

27 The Storeroom

Eight days left. Time is running out.

It's four o'clock in the afternoon, Ma and Baba are yet to come out of their afternoon naps – Ma near her chowki in the kitchen, Baba on his twin cushions in the living room. They are getting old now. I must wait for them to rise, and have our tea together, although Ma, in the absence of much conversation, sometimes just drifts with her cup into the kitchen garden.

On my way to the camp a couple of hours later, the birches and the firs, and the cedars and pines behind them, sing short tunes one after the other in the evening breeze; the bushes Ashfaq set fire to a long time ago have swayed backwards in a sustained, leaning gaze, a resigned welcome to the wind. There are no bees. The black dots swinging in the sky above the valley must be the crows; their permanence makes their existence seem uncertain sometimes.

The sentries, on their worn-out stools, smile their customary limited smiles – too much, I guess, would amount to lowering their guard – and nod me in. *Go home, go home . . . sad soldier. Some day, you might die in these parts and no one will claim you.* I remember the first time I saw them and the next time and the time after that. I remember the itchy fear of a bullet not leaving the skin on my neck until I was well out of their line of vision. I walk past the sunburned Romeo, Kilo, Sahayak, Cobra, Vinash and RRR signs, and run my glance over the red and white zigzag brick pattern lining the gravelled path to KD's premises. I will soon complete nine months – or is it more? – in the Captain's employment. *Too much, too much.* Baba can't think I can do this for ever – and it can't go on for ever! Corpses will be discovered one day, one day.

I stop near Kadian's office. Time is running out fast.

In the distance, visible like a TV scene, through the gap between the office and the flat building next to it, are soldiers in their under-vests playing something. I pause to look closely at their activity, some of them are in the centre of the field – no, they are not play-ing, they are digging, sort of, marking something with shovels and spades and rods. The cricket season must be over and they are mark-ing a badminton court perhaps, or another volleyball pitch. Soldiers play a lot of sports. I'm filled with nostalgia on seeing these forms: darkened, shining bodies, busy at creating something from scratch. We did it once too: first, we marked the area with sawdust and then Mohammed suggested, since it would soon disappear in the wind, we should make it more durable by digging thin lines into the ground and then filling them with the yellow chaff. It took us ages, finishing the badminton court like that, so much so that by the time we ended I had almost lost the will to play, but nonetheless, I loved everything about that day – marking, digging, measuring, arguing lengths and widths on soft-baked earth.

Oh, but I cannot look too long; it is one thing being out in the camp with Kadian around and completely another being here on my own, staring down at his soldiers like this.

I drag my feet away from the scene, turn right towards his office and climb the three steps on to the veranda. In a week or so it will be my last ever trip to this dark room.

Kadian nods me in briefly when I enter the room. I have timed my visit when he's already had a few. Have an important task to fulfil today, I am prepared, I am ready. After the usual awkward start – sitting in front of him, as I said, still unnerves me, still makes me swallow – I just ask casually, not too loudly, not too deliberately, if I could take a look around in his office in case I find something useful for the house, some used stuff perhaps . . . 'I was just wondering, Captain, if I could look around, maybe find some things for home, you know, things you may not need any more, winter is upon us, you see . . . ?' As I said, it's something I have been rehearsing for quite a while, and it shouldn't seem unusual to him as I have been his 'boy' long enough now and he shouldn't have a problem, should he, if all I am interested in is used second-hand stuff? He trusts me,

I'm reasonably sure of that, if not out of any kind of friendship but surely out of a firm belief that I can bring him no harm; he knows I am weak. He always knew.

And that is how it more or less works out; he looks at me for a while, nodding, trying to work out if I am up to something, but I also understand he is doing that because he knows I expect him to be like that. He thinks I am naïve. 'Oh, sure, sure, go, go take a look, my dear, just don't touch the guns, huh ha. Not that you can, but still . . . And you've had your fucking weapon,' he says, not very different in tone and manner from that of Baba's when, in my childhood, he would allow me, after I'd sworn to be back well before the evening tea, to go out to the valley with my friends.

I wait for Kadian to go into his intense late-evening drinking phase, when he starts to suck at the edges of his tumbler.

Inside the store are stacks and piles and heaps of things. The walls are unpainted, dampish concrete. Sandy, grainy from the look of it. It's like I'd always imagined it: shady corners, cool, with the combined smells of the material lying around masked now and then by the stench from the other end of the room, which is where the bathroom must be. There are numerous cartons here – the shapes of which I gradually make out as I adjust to the pregnant, dim light characteristic of storerooms – crisp, musk- and cardboard-smelling cartons of many sizes and shapes. Supplies. Liquor, lots of it, XXX and Old Monk Rum, Royal Challenge and McDowell's whisky – I'm sure it must be for the entire camp, KD can't be drinking all this by himself. So this is how they keep them going, huh.

Guns, not too many, are lined up tidily on the shelves, many of them reclined against the wall and held shut behind metal bars locked at one end by round, silver padlocks. But these are mostly old-fashioned, standard-issue SLRs, all polished and shining but silent in their orderly angular reposes. They somehow remind me of Hindu–Muslim riots on TV.

Then there are a few trunks here, heavy-looking metal trunks that I've always associated with the Army – war films on Doordarshan perhaps – padlocked. They must contain ammunition, or personal belongings, whatever. At the end of the right wall – unpainted plaster with minute holes here and there as if made by incessant rain – is the door to the bathroom; the stench tells me. Most of the containers are metal, and green, a cold, official green. Separating the vegetable cooking-oil canisters from the kerosene ones – again, bulky army-issue jerrycans – are bales of folded plastic sheets, waterproof tarpaulins and tents perhaps. The kerosene canisters are the kind every household aspires to own, and some actually do, buying second-hand from the market or procuring a new one through some complicated connection from the Army Canteen, the kind Firdaus Ali once brought all the way from Jammu. I was fascinated by the locking contraption of its cap when we went visiting once, years ago, after he had returned from his long stay in the winter capital. I could try one now, I'm tempted – but no, it'd make a noise. They have been in use – the green paint is cracked and flaked on the handle and the cap and its locking mechanism. Too many kerosene cans here . . . Everyone hoards.

Then, here towards the end of the canister rows are large bags, synthetic-fabric bags with monstrous metal zippers running across their bellies, like long gashes stitched together by a clumsy surgeon. Tents, sleeping bags, waterproof covers . . . ? Ma would sure like a tarpaulin cover to keep her winter fuel hoard all dry and crisp. But I don't spend too long on deciphering what they might actually contain, a part of me is scared of opening anything here.

Turns out, nothing extraordinarily exciting has leapt out of the store so far, except that I don't see any of the weapons I've brought up from the valley, snatched from the bony grasps of dead men – where are those guns? I did bring them some Kalashnikovs and pistols – all right, not too many, although at first even two had seemed an overwhelming haul – where are those?

I've got to the far door now: the smell, the smell, I'm absolutely sure, comes from here. I push the cold iron handle gently and it swerves, moves, readily, and then the door lets out a minute-long hiss, as if passing wind, and opens gradually –

It's not a bathroom.

But it is a room nonetheless, a dirty, smelly, creepy room – with things lying in the half-dark corners trying to assume a shape, a face. My legs lose their sense of life. Coming to gradual peace with the dark, I begin to see things – that's all I have been doing ever since this started – as they begin to assume names. The muscles around my mouth start to twitch and quiver by themselves; I feel on the verge of crying.

I begin to see things: clothes, shoes, all kinds of clothes.

Clothes, dirty clothes, jeans, kurtas, sweaters, shirts, even underwear – VIP Boxer, Rupa briefs and banians – and shoes – Action and North Star and Warrior and Kamachi. I see torn shirts, ripped trousers, smeared sweaters, and a few pherans and jackets as well. It all looks like a messy mound of things left behind, as though after a crude burglary. Strewn articles rescued from a ruinous fire. There is a sad sense of abandon to these clothes lying on the wicked-smelling floor. Oh, my God! What have they been up to in here? What is this? The evil, twisted, killer bastards, how can they do this! My legs are completely limp now. I lean against the wall, gasping, lips struggling to break free and howl, and slump down to the floor, which is cold and smelly, but I hardly have any will left to change my position. Sitting on the grimy floor of their storeroom, I quickly, hastily go over everything again, trying hard to see connections, links and patterns, questions and answers, things I have seen and not seen, things I have known and not known, but it's all a big fuzzy swirling blur.

Resting a short while, I suddenly remember the naked bodies I saw at some point, not too many but there were indeed a few. Yes, yes, down there in the valley, there are these naked bodies, half skeletons. I'd assumed when I saw them that these unfortunate few must have lost their clothes in the process of being dragged down (no one would steal *dead* men's clothes), or those feral dogs might have done this to them . . . I did not think then, not even for a minute, that it could be because –

Oh, oh my God!

You know, under the clothes you don't see what has happened to the bodies, worms may have eaten them, the crows may have poked through small holes here and there, but you don't see it. But naked bodies, splayed across each other, as in those old paintings in our history textbooks, reveal everything in bare detail, in their absolute, core nakedness: white ghostly bodies, bones nudging into each other, elbows and knees, white kneecaps, red and blue and purple buttocks, sometimes with big chunks missing from them, sunken rib cages, portions of dinosaur-like spines visible under the skin, shameful somehow – they make you look away.

28   *The Captain's Bedstead*

Evening.

In the corner, some kind of decorated alcove, there's a long low table, Formica. On it is a large cassette player, one of those chunky fat things with a sun-shaped speaker on the left side and a big cassette door on the right marked by a prominent 'Play' arrow. I can see the red record button even from here. Low, continuous, crickety voices attend the night. The air smells of pine, such a relief. Captain Kadian has finished his long day and is walking about in his quarters. This is the first time I've managed to come this far on my own. The three other cottages here, at the edge of the camp, towards the far end of the densely wooded trough that encloses it, have no light inside them. Wonder who lives in them. I waited for ever for him to leave. He was almost blabbering to himself, must've been missing me.

Apart from other objects, there is a small, portable temple on the other side of the long table. Four red-panelled pillars stand guard under the shining aluminium dome. A miniature triangular orange flag completes the ensemble. Shrivelled, stained marigolds hang loose by the neck of the idol. I can't fully recognize the deity, though – they have so many. In all probability it must be Bhagwan Krishna; it's a good-looking god, pleasant, benign, not intimidating. In spite of being blue. I can tell, even from outside the room, that he's seen some neglect of late, but the fact that it is there, in KD's bedroom, is quite a surprise, although, I tell myself, it could easily be a leftover from the previous occupant – if there ever was one, that is. The room itself is large, extraordinarily big bed, photos on the side table – there is a sari-clad woman and a fat-cheeked baby – small TV in front of the bed, another table, smaller, with a few bottles on it, a few clothes hanging indolently by the hooks on the door, and on the same wall as the TV a calendar with a long car on it: June 1993. Five months behind. Exercise dumb-bells, shining a metallic blue in the white light of the room, sit stoically next to what must be the door to the bathroom or the kitchen. I'm sticking close to the window and looking into the room through the generous slit between the curtain and the edge of the window – if it were only slightly wider, I could see it all in one take.

The door opens and he re-emerges in his nightclothes, a formal, government-style sky-blue striped shirt and pyjamas, bordered with piping of a darker blue on the sleeves and the buttons.

He stops near the table with its range of articles and the temple. Is he going to pray now? A night-time prayer perhaps, to wash away the sins of the day? I never thought he was the devotional kind. He fidgets with something on the table, I can't see, his back is towards me. Am I soon to hear him recite some mantra or hymn? What will he pray for – his safety, his family back home, his unit, normalcy, peace (huh)? Or offer his gratitude for being granted leave from Kashmir?

This is my chance, no one will know, no one will ever know. I should just keep my hand firm and aim at his back, and he'll drop dead in a moment. *Yes, I must shoot him, right here, right now – and then run away. No one will ever know. I could slip away in the spreading darkness and beg Baba to leave, to leave to-very-night. I could shoot him in the middle of his back, probably aim at his spine – there's no way he can survive that! Or perhaps blow his head apart – that will be the end of it, in one single moment! The end of this man. This man, who has sinned, and done horrible, horrible wrong. This man who calls it his job, who wants to leave after finishing his 'Kashmir stint'. This man, who may have killed hundreds, thousands of us, this man who makes people disappear, this man who cannot do anything but kill, I must kill him. This man, my boss, Captain Kadian* . . . I just need to stay calm, use both my hands to keep the pillow in place, his back is still towards me, if I just pull the trigger now – that will be it, *that will be it. The end*. I will be freed. Baba will be freed, Ma will be freed. My palm sweats, I take it off the butt and rub it against my hip. I am trembling. I grab my right hand with the left and clasp it tight, press on it hard to hurt it back into a steady manner. Kadian is looking for something on the messy tabletop,

I'm sure he is still drunk, and I won't be surprised if he is still drinking. I lean back a little and slide the barrel into the slit between the edge of the window and the dusty contours of the folded curtain inside. Waves of sweet, rich forest scents sweep across, I close my eyes. The smell of the past. Of childhood. Of that soporific siesta hour, years ago, with Hussain and Azad Range Wah-Wah and his flute by the cedar cove in the jungle. I settle my nerves and one last time think about shooting him in the back – *it's all right, it's all right, this is the only way*. The gun is cold, heavy, powerful. I take a deep, deep breath . . .

Suddenly, too suddenly, a familiar voice booms in the room. I'm caught completely unawares and become absolutely still, holding my breath tight. The voice echoes painfully in the room, and Kadian sits down, leaning, with his elbows on the bed, the grandest bed I have ever seen, so big that it looks like an elevated room in itself. The bed sheet is a Kashmiri chain-stitch piece, maroon, with large chinar leaves embroidered in white on the margins. I recognize the singing voice but take time to speak the name.

He is playing Mohammed Rafi. *'Din dhal jaaye, raat na jaaye . . .'*

I'm thrown, weakened, stalled by it. How can he listen to this? The familiar, smooth voice of Hussain's idol fills the room and Kadian reclines further on his bed, taking in that melancholy song of angst and lost love. For a moment, I'm transported into another world, a world far, far away, a world far, far behind me, and I am filled with overwhelming pity.

My grip on the pistol has loosened now. Heart attacks must feel something like this. The perspiration on my hands cools. It's getting chilly. I have nothing left to do.

29 *Graves They Will Find*

For three days, I have been making graves.

Not graves in the strictest sense but messy heaps of earth covering shallow scratchy ditches. It is so, so hard, even though I do look forward – well, almost – to the process towards the end, when I have a dune ready and I get to carve a headstone. Not a real tombstone, but a small hill of dirt that I know will weather down gradually, but which *will* stand for something for now.

Five graves I have made in all, this being the fifth, on a raised patch of ground just a little away from the main field, at the far end of what was once our cricket pitch – my very own martyrs' graveyard. I hear they have plenty in the city now.

When I'd first tried to make a tomb for one of these boys, my hands just wouldn't stop trembling. I would make half a grave a day, and bury the first available man by next evening. Then I thought it was fine, I wouldn't be able to do it – and I haven't been able to.

Anyhow, these look like sad, mournful dunes of mud basically, like faceless sleeping ghosts. Mounds that speak of abandon through every wart on the heaped earth. On this third day, today, I go to our real graveyard, by poor Khadim Hussain's locked, abandoned new mosque, uproot a few irises, and come back to deposit them at the feet of each mound. They may or may not flower – and I wonder if I will still be here, *if Baba and Ma will be here*, when they do. I really don't want to die. Five pretend graves in three days – I will never be able to finish this, but someone will at least discover them some day and tell others about what he has seen . . .

The sad thing is, it actually doesn't matter what I do, or don't do; Kadian doesn't give a damn. He doesn't even believe in mass graves, let alone individual ones . . . But then what can I do, brothers? You must understand, I don't have many options.

I cannot help a last stratagem towards the end, though. I make sure I put these boys' IDs, photo IDs, wrapped over and over in polythene, on top of their bodies. I may not be here, but someone may discover them some day – there will at least be some record, some evidence, of what they have done here.

As I begin to leave, I suddenly wonder if I have company somewhere else in the world, far, far from here, in some foreign parts where they speak a different tongue and where they look different and have different stories from us, but where people are killed like this nonetheless. I survey my own dead – sad sores on the face of my old valley – think about myself, and feel tender about it all. Is there anyone else out there who does the things I do and feels the things I feel?

The end is near.

On my way up, I see the crows after a long time and remember how even they have changed now. Fat old crows, they have turned into these ugly hideous things – their youthful black turned to a fading grey, their feathers waning, shedding, to reveal dreadful bristled bodies. At first, it had just seemed a play of the evening sunlight, the oblique rays filtering through their wings and rendering them pale. But soon, I realized that my evasive aerial companions were, in fact, losing their blackness. They were turning ashen, cloudy versions of their former stark selves, and a little later, discoloured feathers began to drop from the sky, like forgotten snowflakes. They just look like large flying insects now, their skeletal wings flapping hard to keep them afloat, their mean malevolent heads darting here and there. The scavenging dark bastards! Their evening concords are dull affairs now – no swivelling dances against an iridescent setting sun – a hazy, sickly imitation of their erstwhile confidence.

I'm scared of it all. A sighing weight makes me feel lonely, sad.

Three days left.

Captain Kadian takes a large swig from his dirty glass tumbler and says, 'The job's not that hard, then . . . ?' It's probably his fare-well drink with me. *Does he know?*

He grasps and ungrasps his glass, rotating it in half-circles with each tightening of the grip. 'I know, I know, you may not be enjoy-ing it exactly, hnnh . . . but what the hell, who the fuck enjoys a job, eh, especially in this fucking mess? The money is good, though, isn't it?' He seems content with speaking to himself. 'And everyone is pleased, sir, frigging pleased . . .' He takes another satisfying gulp and looks me in the eye. The dust-flecked lamp hanging from the ceiling throws pale, sickly light on his flushed face. Objects on his table make stout shadows on the sombre wood surface.

'Yes, Captain, I understand.'

I have failed. I was full of questions, anger, when I started out from home. Baba doesn't even look out from the window any more to ask if I have eaten. Ma performs her long-suffering, silent-pat-on-the-back 'God bless you' ritual and then waits for me to come back. It keeps her busy. The garden has withered. No, not her negligence, not much flourishes in the winter months anyway – except for the many-veined leaves of frigid *wande haakh*, of sad stunted winter greens.

I focus hard . . .

'Why this mess, Captain? You know, I still don't understand,' I blurt out and wait a moment or two. We have talked about this before, but he either rails on about how Pakistan does this and how Pakistan screws that, or just jokes about it all. (Pakistan, I have real-ized, is his favourite excuse.) I start again, in a more mature tone, 'I mean, why all these bodies here, Captain, while they could just, you know, stay where they are shot in the first place, or even be handed to their –? Why have them brought in here – wouldn't it be a huge problem if someone discovers them? It's pretty messy down there, quite horrific; and although I'm used to it now, it's so, so miserable! Do you even know the smell –?' I check myself.

'Hmm.' KD grunts in the manner of a sulking bull and gently raises one of his eyebrows.

I swallow, not without fearing what my remarks might provoke.

'Good question, hmm, good question . . .' He gazes into his glass. 'And the answer to that, my dear, is simple, very simple. I don't want bodies turning up everywhere, from rivers and fields and gullies and ditches, naah, I don't want that in my area. Nope. Not under my watch, sir. I would rather have them in one place, like this, and I know no one will ever fucking get there. It's shut on three sides, you see, walled in almost, a closed arena so to speak, no one can ever get there without walking past us, so, my dear, we are fine. A body or two turning up in the jungle sometimes, or someone stumbling upon an old skeleton in the bushes is not a problem, but at the rate we have been going you would have had a dead man under every fucking tree, so, no sir, that dump down there is fine, *just* fine.'

'Captain, sorry, but there is one other thing . . . ?' Have I got too friendly with him?

'Ya, ya, go on . . .' *Did he say motherfucker as well?*

'You know, I can see the Pakistani check-posts on the other side, and I am sure they can see us too. Isn't that a problem, the Pakistanis knowing what you have, er, I mean, what *we* have down here? Why have such a large mass in front of them, in front of anyone, for that matter?'

'Because that is exactly *why*,' Kadian says triumphantly, and looks at me as if I am some kindergarten dud, a gnome struggling to comprehend the world of big men. (He often gives me that look.) He breaks into a meaningful smile, smacks his lips with relish after a longish sip, and continues, 'That is why, my dear, that is why. Since you insist, hnnh, let me tell you, that is *exactly-fucking-why*. It's very simple – it's a slap in the Pakistanis' fucking faces, don't you get it? I *want* them to see it.'

I just stare at the glass tumbler without looking at my bizarre boss. Pale stars dance and grow. Does the bulb make a buzzing sound?

'Oh, come on, you! It's fucking simple, it's like a game – I show them what happens to the boys they send across ever so readily. It's my way of telling them, look, here are the wretched remains of your proxy soldiers, here are the rosy Kashmiri boys you trained, here lie the dreams your motherfucking ISI weaves – and it is not as if I do this on my own, it must have approval right from the top fucking brass in Delhi. It's our bloody answer to their fucking devious ways: *Look, look, you back-stabbing bastards, here's your fucking jihad in a hideous heap, look at it and squirm*. And they can't fucking do anything about it, you see, not a fucking fig! Because *what* will they say?'

He pours himself generously from this tantalizingly green Vat 69 bottle. In the harsh silence of his office, the noise the liquid makes is crystal. Why couldn't I kill him? Why?

'Besides, as I have told you before, I don't do mass graves, my dear, I don't believe in them. You see, by burying them somewhere secretly you're inviting scandal, you are inviting discovery, you're asking for an 'uncovering', you're making news . . . But by leaving them like this, I have already made them acceptable, you see, it's all open, kind of common, maybe a bit ugly, but normal. There is no sensational disclosure happening here. No one's going to be doing any digging, or any – how do they say? – *exhuming* here . . . Mass graves, my dear, are passé.' He loosens the top button of his shirt. His uniform has changed to the rich, dark texture of the winter version. It is a deeper, and furrier, khaki, and although he wears some kind of thick vest underneath, making him stockier than he is, it still looks polished on him. Smart. I am amazed how he manages to look so neat, so compact, all the time, irrespective of the season. His hair is roughly the same length as the first time I saw him. My mind wanders into the storeroom where soiled clothes of God knows which boys lie in a pile as if mauled by wild dogs. They couldn't possibly belong to my friends, could they?

'And guess why they can't do anything about it – because what will they do? What *can* they do? Call some fat old bastards from the fucking UN or some other activist assholes and show them, look what the Indians have done; they have killed all the boys we sent across, huh! Is that what they will motherfucking say?' He carries on impassioned, but also measured in some way, as though bent on expounding on a well-put-together theory. 'No, my dear, no. On the contrary, they just look at it every day, look at the boys they fucked with, and then send more in the hope they will sneak across, and that's what it fucking maderchod is – they send more and more, we kill more and more, and these sad heroes keep springing up from all the frigging villages and towns of Kashmir, all the fucking way from Srinagar and Anantnag and Sopore and Baramulla, seeking Azadi. Then they get assigned as fucking Supreme Commander and Chief Commander and Area Commander and whatnot by their maderchod ISI masters and cross over; some end up dropping off like toys from the mountains, some get mauled in the ambushes and some just fucking die insisting on fighting till the end, and that's what we give them – a long, long night of serious fucking fighting in the jungle and then we just drag their punctured bodies to the edge and fucking roll them down! Sometimes the men take photos with them, but sometimes we don't have the time to fucking frisk and check all of them, especially when they land directly into your sad valley, and that's fucking when I think of you!

'And by the way, yes, we didn't want a hundred per cent exodus from your village, we wanted it to remain, at least on paper. You see, there's a ration supply still listed and active in the Food Fucking Corporation of India, and development-shevelopment funds in the behanchod DC's office, and the damned last village before the LoC still exists, doesn't it? And your father is still the frigging headman, isn't he? Eh, sorry . . . Any more questions?' He concludes with the eager triumph of a school debater.

No, nothing, my evil sir. What can I say?

I don't exactly remember now how many times I have met Kadian, after that first ever meeting months ago in our house when he proposed the 'job' for the first time and we felt we had to do whatever he asked us to. Baba was scared, transformed overnight into a weak-kneed old man. I was scared. Ma was scared. We were all, all alone. But now I really don't know what is worse – ending up like Farooq or this!

*

At night, I cry in my bed.

This is the first time I've cried in a long, long time. I guess the first time since that night two years ago when I bumped into Hussain's abba` in the forest. That is, if I don't count the tears that dropped by themselves on to Noor Khan's ledger in autumn last year. At first, it feels nice, you know, a smothering heaviness lifts – and you know of its existence in its lifting – and the after-sighs feel tender and sympathetic, but very soon it makes you feel like a weakling again. It's more like a knowing – as though someone is telling me I'm being a sissy, a chicken. I turn on my side and pull the blanket all over my head, completely dark. Once inside my favourite hiding place I think of Ma and Baba – what will happen to them? I think of the house, Baba's cherished life's work, his house and his place in it. I think of Ma and her aubergines, her tomatoes and chillies, and her silent suffering. I think of our life before all this, I think of the village, the precipitous clusters of cedars lining the western mountains, beyond which, I always romantically thought in my childhood, lies Pakistan, where Hussain, Gulla and Mohammed might still be. Alive. I think of Hussain and remember I should never have deserted him in the forest years ago, in our childhood. I think of Ashfaq, who's perhaps, perhaps here somewhere, perhaps not. Perhaps alive, perhaps dead. Perhaps in some high-walled jail in Delhi or Rajasthan. There is no way I can know now. Or maybe I will some day. I think of our valley, and the green stream in it, by the banks of which I once sat with Asma. That was the only time. I had tried touching her fingers, pretending to be scratching at them absent-mindedly, playfully, and somehow I did manage a fine chalky, powdery scratch on the back of her supple winter-blushed hand. I will never see her again.

I think of Noor, and of Gul Khan's deranged father, I think of the village, the musky street, the dirt and the dust and the smell of it, the cherry trees and their spring flourish, I think of how grand Gul's house was, is, although locked and cobweb-ridden now. I think of the mosque too; it did grow on me, after all – nice gatherings they'd have there sometimes. I think of Shaban Khatana and his big son with the scary, blackened gangrenous hand, and Shaban's leather-faced, wordless wife. I think of all the corpses I can remember and recognize – and at that, a nausea begins to churn somewhere inside – I think of all the shelling across the border . . . Why, why? Why would you want to pulverize land, the earth, the ground! I think of Kadian – who's still breathing and alive – and the first time I met him and the second time and the third time and the fourth . . .

I turn on my side – it's pitch dark outside, nothing breathes – and think of the valley, and of myself, not without a fresh rash of pity. In my room, on my bed, under my blanket, thinking about myself and everything else and . . . Oh, oh! I wish I had gone across too then, wish I had stayed close to Gul Khan. It wouldn't have been my business now, none of this would've happened. And whatever happened, we would've been in it all together. I wouldn't have been trapped here with this hideous man. And I wouldn't have known, I wouldn't have known . . . Even now, even now, if I could just sneak across . . . Oh, Rahmana, take me, take me too, please.

I get out of bed silently and climb up to the attic. Making sure I walk as gently as possible. I quickly locate the bundle of warm clothes I'd put together more than a year ago when I'd hoped Rahman the guide would take me across the border to Pakistan – blue round-neck sweater, two more, socks, three pairs, old wool pheran, Baba's long winter boots and the big red scarf. I had eventually hidden all these behind the jute sacks containing my old school books. Everything smells crisp. Of straw and sawdust. I carry the rolled-up bundle downstairs, put it behind my headrest, and crawl into bed again.

The night has laboured halfway somehow, I guess from the feel of it, the dark, thick smell of it. It will take ages until dawn, but I must be patient. My decision is made. The plan is made. I trace the path to the camp, the curving, ascending and then descending path to Kadian's office, and make myself resolute. I must act absolutely normal: past the sentries, faint smiles, and then on to the brick-lined pathway, enter as I always do, noiselessly, deferentially. I must seat myself as I always do, and listen to everything he says, let him talk and talk and drink and drink and see him get completely drunk, for the last, last time ever.

I cannot dither again.

The day I have been waiting for arrives late with a cloud-bothered sun. It's a Friday. Kadian is leaving for home tomorrow.

A troupe of sadhus led by two high priests, who probably arrived yesterday, come out in the afternoon and immediately get to work in the field behind the office; many soldiers also join in. The two sentries from the gate, my Ram and Shyam, do some kind of last-minute digging. They want to put up a shamiyana, a marquee perhaps. It's all dusty and hazy out there; the sun seems to have won, finally, stalled its half-arc over the sky and is beating down on the sweating godmen. Their half-naked torsos shingle amidst the digging and shoving motions. I see that the preparation for the ritual KD was talking about sometime back is in full swing.

Once inside, I stay on in his office for a long, long time in an anxious siesta, until I think it's time to take a quick look down below.

So I go, quickly and intently, and get there in no time. I want to take one last look over everything before it's gone. One last swim too? No, no, I don't think I can. I look at everything, every single scene. A sweeping, silent gaze to take it all in.

Having stared at my dead friends, scattered thus around me, for a while, having beheld my valley from its centre for a long while, I ascend now, feverishly looking, for every half-step of the climb, at everything on my two sides – even the ancient, half-charred stumps of the bush Ashfaq burned a long time ago. Quite a burning that, my friend. My walk back takes a while; time passes so minutely that it aches, but eventually, after much reflection, after going over everything a hundred times, I am back.

Garish musical devotion booms all around. There's the redoubled echo from the mountains, reminiscent of the sonorous echoes of our daily azan in the past.

This goes on all afternoon – there's an intense frenzy in the air,

long-working soldiers unburdening their homesicknesses and dis-
eases and smells and annual-leave tensions and guerrilla-warfare
trauma in the throes of melodramatic Bollywood paeans to Sher-
awali Mata, the lion-mother-goddess resident not far from our parts,
somewhere in the low hills near Jammu. Most of them are seated in
concentric circles around the firewood pyramid, while a few are
standing too. A harmonium squeaks, the mini PA system – is that
the same loudspeaker the Governor of Kashmir used long ago? –
snarls with a shrill-voiced sadhu singing bhajan king Chanchal's
concrete-piercing devotional song, 'Chalo bulawa aaya hai, Mata ne
bulaya hai' – the mother beckons you, and the mother . . . – and then
settles down into a range of other bhajans sung to film tunes I recognize through the din but can't exactly put my finger on. As the
singing of hymns grows, I summon courage, gather my wits, collect my nerves. I must be brave.

I light the fire. There's a buzz in my ear. It's early evening.

Out there, in the distance, dark forms circle in a steady motion –
those dogs, those hyenas, those eyes, again – and I lower my eyes.

Flesh, bones, hair, clothes, leather, rot, blood, combs, photographs, letters. Boys from the city, boys from the villages, boys from
towns, boys from saffron fields, boys from the mountains, boys
from the plains; rich boys, poor boys, only-child boys, and boys with
sisters at home; weak boys, strong boys, big boys, small boys, singer
boys, thinker boys, lonesome boys, naked boys, scared boys, martyr
boys, brave boys, guerrilla boys, commander boys, soyeth wannabe
sidekick boys, orphan boys, unknown boys and famous boys, boys –
they all burn in the big fire I've cooked up, the fire I watch now, my
fire, my only act, my only decision in years, my fire. The flames leap
up and burn everything inside them, they leap out from limbs and
groins and heads and backs and chests and faces and hands, and
everything burns; the feet burn too, those lonely dismembered feet
in their boots, they burn too and look like cinders hurled out of a
big fire; everything burns, the piss-smelling yellow flowers, their
stalks and petals burn too, everything. Shreds of camouflage jackets
and boots and handkerchiefs and currency notes with Jinnah and a

tall mosque on them, and wallets with small pictures of girls and children in them, and ballpoint pens, and plastic glasses and money; the flames grow and grow and burn everything that there ever was; half-faces, torn smiles and part-grins and frozen anguish and remnants of surprise and glimpses of fright and split expressions of grief and pursed lips of resignation and despondent embraces with oblivion, and those dark, dark eyes of eternal sleep! I burn all that ever was there, and look at the rising tongues, the snakes, the coils that engulf all that I've beheld and touched in the last few months.

And the flames burn the smell into a new smell, more stink, more stink – a scorching, groaning, writhing stink. I am burning death itself, that must be the smell. In some places, where the fire is showing signs of dissipating, I pour more kerosene oil from the canisters. There is still plenty left in them, enough to burn the whole place down all over again if I wanted to, huh! I throw splashes of the liquid over some crackling half-corpses and the flames leap up once more, high, high and screaming, as if reaching out to some place in the sky. At one point I see a reflection of myself in the undulating yellow sheet created by the flames and I duck down. My stubble has grown. The sweat twitches.

I hear the distant drone emanating from the puja in the camp; they must be worshipping Agni in the camp above, I think, the priests chanting long hymns placating their god of fire, asking for deliverance for all, the soldiers swaying their earnest heads to the incantations, their eyes closed, and floating along the pungent waves of spiritual upliftment and the general mood of divine auspices. Kadian will be returning to his wife in the morning.

Kadian, this is the place, this place that you have turned into a ghostly graveyard, it glowed with the warmth of my friends around the *alaaw* of our childhood. Right here, by the serene river, near the cricket pitch of which only the faintest of outlines survives now. Perhaps only I can see it, where I now stand surrounded by men departed long ago and recent: fathers, brothers, husbands, lovers, sons, cousins, and uncles and friends and mates, all dispersed rubbish-like in your playground, strewn on the banks of the river with the things they carried with them. Sad, dismal, demeaned reflections of their former selves. Look at them, look at their faces, mouths ajar, screaming out hollowed lives. Look at the splintered human furniture you've amassed here, and made me its munshi, its journal keeper. Look at that hollow throat, that empty nude stomach, those broken feet, look, look at that exhausted expression on Shabbir Sheikh's rag-like face. Look, look at Rouf Qadri's toy-like ribcage; look at Gulzar Mir's lean and lanky headless body. And look at what they brought with them, what's still left scattered here and there, Kadian, look! Here, look at that torn prayer mat with Mecca and Medina in its two corners, look at the dried blood- and dirt-smeared green velvet of it. And here, a mauled water flask, green and ugly in its military camouflage. And this, by the side of the same man, what is this strange-looking sandal, this pointy thing that is also green? A Peshawari slipper, I suppose, all the way from Pakistan, the deluded love of which inspired some sad man to carry it across the firing line. What a waste, what a waste!

I stand near the river and see the scene twice over, first the burning pyres I have created along the centre of the valley and then the reflection of it all in the water. The river too is burning, the fire has taken over the water here, swept over the cool surface of the stream and covered it, taken it over, burned it! My face throbs warm, my armpits begin to drip, my stubble feels prickly, I scratch at it and collect a few beads from my chin and run my hand over my throat. I have water with me, in Baba's old Thermos flask. Oh, Baba, Baba.

I pick the loaves of dried grass I'd spread here and there and break them into small swatches. It's time to make sure. I spread the sheaves of grass over the burning circles and watch them instantly consumed in the restless flames. I spread the tinder trash, twisted tendrils and bent strands everywhere. I want everything burned to ash. I don't want to see a single foot, hand, arm, finger, toe, buttock, ear, nose that is half-burned or not burned. I don't want to see that at all. To hell with this all, I think, to hell with them all, to hell with the Indians, to hell with the killer dogs they send here in their millions to prey on us, to hell with all this swarming Army here, to hell with the Pakistanis, to hell with the Line of Control, to hell with Kadian and his Mehrotra Sir, to hell with India, to hell with Pakistan, to hell with jihad, and to hell with, to burning, smouldering hell with everything! It must all end. It must all, all end. I let loose shards of the crisp chaff as I move over the burning mounds. I feel satisfied for having thought of that in advance.

It is my final *alaaw* – our *alaaw*, our bonfire – then, I say to myself. One of my favourite evening pastimes of childhood: astride the cricket pitch, here, here, we collected twigs, leaves, crisp papery leaves, dried grass, thorns that got stuck in the webs of my fingers, a bit of this and a bit of that, autumn dust from hollowed tendrils, slender branches long broken and crushed, hundredth parts of brittle, delicately shaped veinous leaves, a bit of this and a bit of that, and made a pyramid, thick and busy and tall and dense, promising warmth and glow and golden flames we so loved and welcomed in the twilight of the valley's evening. Our private evening sport.

One blue September evening, Ashfaq, insisting as usual on being the man with the matches, lit the newspaper wick protruding from the top of the mesh-mash pyramid with such deliberate finesse that we all fell dead silent for a minute. He did it with such intense concentration, as if performing a sacred rite. Then I watched, all of us watched – huddled around that immense knot of grey leathery twigs of common pine – the slowly rising and leaping orange flames. Crack, crackle, crack, crackle, their faces soon glowed red from the heat and the colour of the fire. Gul Khan smoked and choked on the filterless Capstan cigarette he had stolen from his brother. We laughed: *Drop it, hero! You will get TB. Drop it!* Hussain looked very calm, immaculate, so very content as he seemed to be with his time, with his glowing-warm company of friends, with me, standing next to him, a hand on his shoulder. I watched as the fire grew and dozens of red-blushing beads began to be born. Standing up that day, I saw the scene repeated in the river and stored it for ever in my mind. The gentlest of ripples animated the picture, wave-like, and then settled down to a sparkling stillness again.

My own fire is a great success, then, all leaping and bristling with the new fodder I have spread. And I still have some kerosene left, I remind myself. Nothing shall remain here.

I know, I know, *I know*, they should have all had a burial, but that would have been a logistical nightmare . . . And it's not as if I didn't try. This was the only solution, then, the last resort. (I am aware that these bodies, these remains of our 'disappeared' boys, might serve as evidence one day . . . for someone to make a shocking discovery . . . for someone to write a front-page story . . . for someone to order a judicial inquiry. But then, who actually cares or does anything in the end? No one is ever punished here. It will only ever be a story.) He had himself mentioned *a jerrycan of kerosene every few weeks and that's it*. Graves for all would have been impossible and leaving them like this would have meant doing nothing about it. I'm sorry, brothers, I know you deserve better, surely last rites according to our religion, but what can a lone man do? I'm sorry I have had to do this, but there wasn't much choice. I know you deserve better, but then who doesn't? Even I deserve better, perhaps even Kadian does. No, *not him, not him*.

I turn away from the river; faint echoes of voices emerge from it, and I decide to move away. Although I'm still tempted, and a part of me really does want to stay – *they might perhaps come back into the river and meet with me, like before, and talk to me, and let me listen to him sing* – I do not, because I'm scared of it as well.

I sit down at the far end, near the slope that rises homeward, and look at the rising flames – there's still plenty of fodder left.

I sit for a long, long time, watching the self-absorbed dance of the flames, struggling to find a name for the stench that I have created with my kerosene hoard.

And what are my Pakistani brothers thinking, if they can make out what is happening here from their faraway pickets? What are they seeing from their murky machine-gun holes? They must recognize me now, surely. What would they be doing, then – thinking of a big Namaz-e-Janaza of their own, a solemn funeral prayer, eternal moral support for Kashmiri freedom fighters? Really, what would they be thinking now, having screwed it up once again, having fucked us up, used us in their venal sport yet again, what would they be thinking now? Are they looking at these sad flames and wondering if any of the boys they groomed so well in their camps are now burning in that valley across the ridge on the Indian side? They would perhaps pray for the thus departed and seek martyrdom and an eternal resting place in Jannat for them. Would they be aggrieved on seeing the martyrs they nurtured not even receive a dignified burial, not even a small prayer; no green coffins, no fateha for the *shuhdaa'* either? Would they now arrange a big gathering of their own, in their own camp, and get some revered moulana to say the last rites for those who perished across the border? My Pakistani brothers, what would you do now, having seen this funeral pyre that burns our boys, my brothers, in these acrid flames? Would you still pray for their souls to rest in peace? Offer fateha for the souls of the deceased, bless the sacrificed ones for their ultimate sacrifice: *May your bones rest in peace, after they are licked dry by rabid, man-eating wolves?*

But then, what do I care now? How does it matter now?

I must pay my respects to these lost ones, though; I should at least pray for these poor boys, I should offer my own fateha to these sad tattered souls whose stories I shall tell one day. I should pay my respects to these hundreds of unknown dead, to these unsung, unrecorded martyrs, to these disappeared sons . . . I am so, so sorry for the cremation.

I stand up at once then, and gently, piously, raise my hands in front of me, spread sideways and joined together in the middle, side to side, little finger to little finger, forming a large, arching cusp. My hands tremble a little. The nails itch. The tears dried up in the heat. The eyes burn.

> *Bismillāhi r-rahmāni r-rahīm*
> *Al Hamdu lillāhi rabbi l-'ālamīn*
>
> In the name of God, the Most Gracious, the Most Merciful.
> Praise be to God, the Lord of the Universe,
> The Most Gracious, the Most Merciful,

King of the Day of Judgement.
You alone we worship, and You alone we ask for help.
Guide us to the straight way;
The way of those whom You have blessed,
Not of those who have deserved anger,
Nor of those who stray.
Aameen.

The fires burn brilliantly now. It is time I left.

Afterword

More than 70,000 people have been killed in Kashmir since 1989; around 8,000 people have disappeared; at least 25,000 children have been orphaned; and over 4,000 people are in Indian prisons. Thousands of women have been widowed in the conflict, including 2,000 'half-widows' whose husbands remain missing.

Source: Jammu and Kashmir Coalition of Civil Society.
The Government of India disputes these figures.

Acknowledgements

I owe gratitude and more to:

Mohammed Hanif, greatest of friends, unofficial mentor and one of the sharpest critics the book has benefited from.

Mary Mount, my supremely brilliant editor, without whom the book might never have happened.

Martyn Bedford, for high appreciation first and then telling me how it is done.

David Godwin, for perhaps the most important lunch of my life.

Musadiq Sanwal, who believed in the novel when it was just a raw draft.

Basharat Peer, friend, fellow traveller, champion and the most patient of readers.

Sam Miller, whose support and meticulous feedback arrived when I needed it the most.

Shân Morley Jones, for her sharp editorial eye and making sure I did everything right in the end.

Badri Raina, bard and tutor, who showed me 'this is that' during those brilliant years at Kirori Mal College, Delhi.

Sumana for enriching our life in London, and for putting up with my moods during a critical phase in the writing of this book.

Dennis Charlton, whose big vote of confidence and those 'epic' words early on spurred me on.

John Murray, for ruthless honesty, and for that first reading at Arvon.

Sajjad Haider, who took me on when I hadn't even earned it.

Riyaz Masroor, for providing answers to important as well as trivial questions at all times.

A big one for the bravest of the Mirzas, my grandfather Mirza Ghulam Mohammed, who melted down his fingers during a lifetime of papier-mâché art so that his children could go to school.

My sisters, Nighat, Tabasum and Nazima; my brothers, Shuja and Reyaz; and my uncles, Fida Hussain, Nisar Ali and Mohammed Jaffer, for a life full of love and care. And for supporting me in all my unwise ventures.

Mehvish, my wife – the book, and life, might not have been possible if she hadn't arrived on the scene.

Opening lines of the song 'tum mujhe yun bhula na paoge . . .' quoted in chapter 2 are from the 1970 Hindi film Pagla Kahin Ka. The lyrics are by Hasrat Jaipuri.

Opening lines of the song 'chalo dildar chalo . . .' quoted in chapter 9 are from the 1972 film Pakeezah. The lyrics are by Kaif Bhopali.

Opening lines of the song 'tang aa chuke hain . . .' quoted in chapter 26 are from the 1957 film Pyaasa. Lyrics are from a ghazal by Sahir Ludhianvi.

Opening lines of the song 'din dhal jaaye, raat na jaaye . . .' quoted in chapter 28 are from the 1965 film Guide. Lyrics are by Shailendra.

All lyrics are used with permission from Saregama PLC / Saregama India Ltd.

Grateful acknowledgement is also made for permission to quote from the following: Charles Baudelaire, 'A Fantastical Engraving' from Flowers of Evil, translated by James McGowan, OUP Inc., New York, (1993, reissued 1998); and Agha Shahid Ali, 'I See Kashmir from New Delhi at Midnight' from The Country Without a Post Office, WW Norton and Company Inc., New York (1998).